"IT'S NOT YOU I WORRY ABOUT, ELLERY," HE SAID.

"What do you worry about?" Her voice wavered. Broke.

"Starting something I can't stop—can't control." He grazed her side with his hand, the pressure of his touch catching her breath in her throat.

The bugles blew. Retreat. Retreat. But by then, she'd stopped listening.

She took the final step that brought them together. Reached up to skim a hand over the planes of his torso. Caressed with gentle fingers the line of his latest scar. This time, he didn't stop her. "I've had a lifetime of looking after myself. I've gotten quite good at it."

Out of character, the corner of his mouth quirked in a little-boy smile as he stripped her with his molten-honey gaze. "Until I came along, anyway."

Had she come here wanting this? Knowing what would happen? Her mind screamed at her to get out. Run while she had the chance.

"Conor. Please," she whispered, not knowing whether it was a plea for him to stop or continue.

Lost in You

ALIX RICKLOFF

ZEBRA BOOKS
Kensington Publishing Corp.
www.kensingtonbooks.com

ZEBRA BOOKS are published by

Kensington Publishing Corp.
850 Third Avenue
New York, NY 10022

All Kensington titles, imprints, and distributed lines are available at special quantity discounts for bulk purchases for sales promotion, premiums, fund-raising, educational, or institutional use.

Special book excerpts or customized printings can also be created to fit specific needs. For details, write or phone the office of the Kensington Special Sales Manager: Attn. Special Sales Department. Kensington Publishing Corp., 850 Third Avenue, New York, NY 10022. Phone: 1-800-221-2647.

Zebra and the Z logo Reg. U.S. Pat. & TM Off.

ISBN-13: 978-1-4201-0452-3
ISBN-10: 1-4201-0452-7

First Printing: August 2008
10 9 8 7 6 5 4 3 2 1

Printed in the United States of America

For Maggie & Maureen,
who were always there with advice and laughs
when I needed them most.

For John,
who urged me to dream bigger,
and to get my stories out of the drawer
and onto an editor's desk.
Or else!

And my apologies to the Cornish language,
which I've butchered mercilessly,
but whose beauty seemed made for magic.

Chapter One

Carnebwen, Cornwall
Spring 1815

"I wonder what it's like to face creditors without worrying where the money's to come from," Ellery pondered to no one in particular as she gnawed on the end of her pen. She sighed and stretched. It had been a month since Cousin Molly had died and even though the two had never got on well, at least she'd been company.

She smelled rain in the damp wind twisting the curtains at the open window. The promise of another spring downpour and the quiet of the empty cottage made her long for Spain and the laughter and camaraderie of her father and his friends as they talked late into the night outside their billet. Then she remembered those same friends scattered dead among the hills and heights around Vittoria and her father's belly ripped open as if a huge claw had scythed him from chest to thigh, his staring eyes almost angry in his bloodless face. She shuddered. No, she was better off here. She may not quite know how to pay for everything, but there would be food and drink and heat and clothing. A roof over her head that didn't leak. A home that didn't move upon the whim of England's army. All things she'd never counted on before. This was security. This was what she had always wanted.

The rain came, soft at first and then louder and harder, drumming on the roof, rattling in the gutter. So loud, she almost missed the sound of movement outside her window. She went still, listening to hear it again, but the yard was quiet. Nothing stirred but the wind and the rain and the distant wash of the ocean.

As she relaxed back into her seat, laughing off her fancies, a howling cry split the air. It seemed to come from down in the village. It was followed by an answering call farther away, and soon the hills around Carnebwen echoed with the eerie baying of hounds giving chase.

She remembered her father's campfire stories of the faery court's Wild Hunt sweeping across the lands searching for villains to capture or kill. Her blood ran cold, and her heart pounded as she crossed to the parlor window to push aside the curtains. She dismissed the notion almost as soon as she thought it. Magic and all things *fey* were no more. Only the most superstitious still clung to their old beliefs. The howling calls of the hounds faded back into the night, leaving the empty silence even more palpable.

She'd always been embarrassed by her father's obsession with the *fey* realm, and refused to believe in his nonsense. More than likely this was Lord Pearne's gamekeeper in pursuit of a poacher. Her heart went out to the offender, whoever he was. She only hoped the gamekeeper was there to call off his dogs before they tore the poor man to bits.

The clock struck ten, and Ellery realized she'd been woolgathering when she should have been working her accounts. A strong cup of coffee would perk her up for the long task ahead. Throwing her shawl across her shoulders, she followed the passage from the parlor to the small kitchen at the back of the cottage. The candle's guttering flame threw wicked shadows over the walls, and she paused, thinking she'd heard another noise—this time in the kitchen yard.

A cold wind sliced the air, snuffing out her candle and throwing the room into darkness. The latch jiggled on the back door, there was the sound of hoarse, raspy breathing, and a low growling moan prickled the hair at her neck. Her mouth went dry, and a lump formed in her throat. The moan came again, but this time it ended in a curse she hadn't heard since she'd left the Peninsula.

So far the lock held. Then she felt a slide like silk across her skin as the lock clicked, turned, and the door swung open. She froze, unable to scream or run. A figure loomed in the doorway, one hand braced against the frame, the other hanging heavy at his side. The smell of battle clung to him, the combined scents of sweat and blood and fear and rage all too familiar to someone who'd grown up with them.

He took two limping steps across the threshold, and Ellery's breath caught in her throat. This couldn't be Lord Pearne's harried poacher. This man seemed to suck the very air from the room as he entered, and even draggle-tailed and soaked with rain, his presence commanded respect. He watched her, and she knew the shadows that kept his features obscured did nothing to hide her from his hot golden stare.

"You're Ellery Reskeen." Not a question, but a statement of fact.

She swallowed and nodded.

His gaze flicked around the dark kitchen before returning to her, and he gave a long shaky breath. "I've come for the reliquary."

Before Ellery could answer, he took another step into the kitchen and pitched forward onto the flagstones to lie, still as death, at her feet.

* * *

Conor came awake to darkness and the sound of rain. Pain knifed through him, the physical agony of blade and claw almost bearable compared to the poisonous mage energy coursing through his body. He shifted, hissing as sizzling heat lanced across his shoulders and down his arms, but he couldn't wait for the worst to pass. Even as rapidly as his body renewed itself, there wasn't time. The *Keun Marow* could be back any moment. He'd done his best to lay a blind trail for them to follow, but in his condition, it hadn't been his best effort. If they caught even a hint of his blood, no amount of wizardry would keep them from tracking him—or the Reskeen woman.

Clenching his teeth, he ignored the effects of his battle with the *fey* hunters and sat up. He lay on the kitchen floor in front of a warm stove, cocooned within a nest of blankets. But this was his hostess's only accommodation. He remained dressed in his damp and bloody clothes, not even his boots removed. So much for Cornish hospitality. Dropping his hand to his scabbard brought him up short. His blade was gone.

He caught her scent just before he heard her voice.

"Who are you?"

He spun around, biting back an oath as his knitting skin tore and bled fresh.

She sat in a chair at the far side of the room, gripping a pistol aimed unerringly at his heart. Her hands shook, and Conor prayed she wasn't as jumpy as she was accurate.

He brought up his hands in surrender. "Do you always greet guests with a loaded weapon?"

She eyed him over the top of the barrel. "Guests? No. Intruders? Yes. And you haven't answered my question. Who are you?"

Despite the situation, Conor found himself impressed with the girl's bravery. She might be frightened, but she wasn't backing down. That was good. She'd need that courage before long. Sooner if the *Keun Marow* returned. "My name's Conor Bligh. I've been searching for you, Miss Reskeen, for almost two years. You're a hard woman to track," his lips curled, "even for one of my kind."

He sensed her surprise. She lowered the pistol, just slightly, but enough that should it go off it would hit the brick hearth to his right, and not the center of his chest. "And what is one of your kind? A poacher? I warn you Lord Pearne is relentless when it comes to catching anyone hunting illegally—"

"Do I look like a poacher?" He leveled his gaze upon her and felt her tension increase. The beast in him smelled it on her skin, sensed it in her rapid, shallow breathing. "What have you done with my sword?"

"I hid it. You'll get it back if you answer my questions."

Conor felt as if his insides had been pulled apart and jammed back together. Arguing with this girl wasn't helping. His temper flared. "Well, unhide it. I'll need it."

She didn't seem to notice the dangerous light in his eyes. "I don't trust you."

"If I wanted to hurt you," he snarled, "I wouldn't hack you apart with a heavy blade. My fingers could be around your throat before you had time to scream."

She cocked a brow. "And a statement like that is supposed to make me trust you? If you're not a poacher, why were the hounds I heard after you? You're wounded. I saw the blood."

Conor flexed his muscles while reaching out with his mind. In both instances, he felt the prickle of healing. "Not as bad as it looked. The *Keun Marow* were sloppy. Next time they'll wait to be sure of a clean kill. Asher doesn't tolerate failure twice."

The pistol steadied, and Conor knew she was close to using it. "I'll ask you one more time. Who are you? What are you? And what do want with me? If these *Keun Marow* want a clean kill, I can give it to them."

Trying to hide his growing annoyance, he began again, taking the time to explain what he could, lying when he couldn't. "I've given you my name. I'm a friend of your father's. He was holding something for me—keeping it safe.

I was injured in the same ambush that killed him. By the time I recovered, you were long gone and so was the reliquary."

Her brows drew into a puzzled frown. "You knew my father?"

Keeping his gaze locked with hers, Conor edged his way out of the blankets. "I'm sorry he died." The worst of his wounds burned at the movement, but he kept talking to distract her. "I tried finding you through his army records, but there's no mention of a daughter."

Her lips twisted in a cynical smile. "The army doesn't keep records of the bastards it leaves in its wake."

Her gaze shifted, and he froze. Calling on the power of the *leveryas*, he drew her attention back to his words and off his steady approach. A few more feet and he'd be close enough to spring. "Your father must have loved you very much." He felt the power rise within him, felt it focus on the girl.

"As much as any officer cares for the servant who darns his socks and cooks his meals."

"He left you well provided for. Made you his heir."

"Heir? You make him sound like some kind of gentleman. He stole the French loot like the lot of them did when King Joseph's army crumbled. And when he died, who was to say he didn't leave it to me? Even so, I'm not quibbling. It got me away from there." She took a quick, sharp breath, and shook her head.

Her reaction startled Conor into breaking off the link between them. How could she have felt his touch upon her mind unless—

He never finished the thought. With the connection severed, she saw his approach and understood it for what it was. She raised her pistol. "I gave you fair warning."

Conor's shout was drowned out by the gunshot. Feeling the rip of the bullet's path across his ribs, he put out a hand as he hurled himself at her.

Chapter Two

Snatching the spent pistol from her grasp, Conor dropped her to the floor, pinning her beneath him. "Do you try to kill all your visitors?" he gasped.

She struggled, all flailing hands, knees, and nails. "Let me go, you filthy bastard."

He grunted as she elbowed his side. "Not until you promise to hold off murdering me. We need to speak."

She twisted, trying to use her knees and hands to leverage him off of her, but he'd caught her wrists, and his weight held her fast.

"And then I can shoot you?" She looked up at him, hatred blazing in her blue eyes, a tumble of dark curls glowing chestnut in the fire's glow. There was no doubt; even as a spitting fury, she was a beauty.

"By then, you may not want to." His gaze flicked to her parted lips, full and very kissable. "While we're down here . . ." He smiled suggestively. It had been too long since he'd lain with a woman.

She began to struggle again. "You arrogant, self-important—"

A low sinister howl cut her off in mid-insult, followed by another and another, each one closer and more intense. The

Keun Marow were back and tracking him. She stiffened beneath him.

Holding her silent with a look, Conor whispered a cloaking spell, throwing it out as far as he could. They might trail him to the cottage, but there they would lose the scent and, if Conor was lucky, move on. Noting that he was lying wounded on top of the woman who had just shot him, he didn't count much on luck tonight.

The growling, snapping snarls of the hunters curled around the cottage. They sniffed at the windows and doors, slavering as they pressed to find Conor's lost scent. The girl shuddered, her face ashen.

"Keep quiet," he whispered.

Outside, a low keening began, growing as each hunter broke off the chase, frustrated at losing their quarry—again. The walls seemed to vibrate under the ululating crescendo of sound. Then just as suddenly, the howls faded, leaving only the echo of their presence behind.

"What are they?" she asked. Conor started to get up, but she grabbed him and wouldn't let go. "Answer me."

"They're gone. But I doubt I've fooled them for long. I could cast a cloaking spell over the whole village yet, with all the blood I've lost tonight, they'd track me eventually."

His body hummed with edgy tension, but whether it was his own restless energy or the horror in her eyes that spurred him on, Conor didn't know. He only knew that her body was taut beneath him, her face luminous in the light from the new-risen moon. Without answering, he lowered his mouth to hers, claiming it in a hungry kiss.

She fought even harder, but only for a moment, then her body relaxed and her arms came around him, holding him close.

Her mouth moving over his sent an unexpected wave of desire through him. He considered pressing his advantage. The way she was responding, it wouldn't take much to get her wanting more. A flip of a few buttons, some well-practiced moves, and he could bury himself inside her. Pound deep into her and feel, for a few moments, at least, something besides the gnawing guilt. The hurricane fury. It was tempting. Why the hell not?

But she came to her senses first. Broke his kiss. Jabbed him in the ribs with her elbow. Then rolled away as he grabbed his wounded side with a whoosh of pain.

She got to her feet, wiping her mouth with the back of her sleeve, her eyes glazed with anger and confusion. "Who the hell do you think you are? You can't just come in here, attack me and then act as if I'm supposed to be grateful you've saved me. Mayhap someone needs to save me from you." Her voice grew louder and shriller as fear wore off. "And then you molest me as if I'm some slag who'll welcome your advances." She blushed and dropped her gaze to the floor.

His gaze roamed over her body. It was just as well she'd stopped things when she did. As desirable as she was, she was definitely off-limits. No entanglements. It would only make killing her more difficult in the end.

"It was a kiss," he said. "But don't worry. It won't happen again."

Ellery hadn't moved since the man sat her down with a mug of tea and ordered her to stay put. At first she'd been too humiliated at the dismissive way he'd looked her over as if once he'd kissed her, he'd decided she wasn't worth his effort. Then belated fear had grabbed hold of her and she'd shivered, teeth chattering, until he'd shoved the tea in her hands. She hadn't even noticed him brewing it.

She stared down into the milky liquid with a wrinkle of her nose. A good, strong whiskey would have gone a lot further to calming her.

One hand on the door, he glanced back. "I need to check

the house and garden, and see if I can pick up their trail. Be the hunter and not the hunted for a change."

She ought to be glad he was leaving. After all, those horrible hounds had been chasing him, not her. If he was gone, she was safe. But then, why did she feel as if she'd never be safe again?

She clutched the mug tighter. Had it been only hours ago she'd wished for someone to share her empty nights? She had someone now. A hunted man with the power in his broad frame to snap her like a twig. A man who attacked her, kissed her, and insulted her all in the space of five minutes. She burned again with embarrassment, remembering the kiss they shared. She'd accepted it and even returned it. She closed her eyes, mortified at her easy surrender. Like mother, like daughter?

Thinking of her parents made her remember the man's explanation of his arrival. He said he knew her father from the Peninsula. But she'd lived with the army long enough to recognize that this man's skills far outstripped the common soldier's. In fact, she thought few could best him in battle. So if he wasn't a fellow soldier, then what brought him to the Peninsula and how would he have cause to know her father? A reliquary, he said. A treasure that her father kept safe for him. More than likely it was this man's own stolen loot. The French rout had made rich men out of more than one soldier that day.

"I've secured the house, but dawn's near. They won't be back tonight."

Ellery looked up to find him standing in the hall. He must have come through the front door and explored the whole cottage in the time she sat here mooning.

He watched her. In the darkness, his amber-gold eyes shone bright against the hidden planes of his face. "Are you better?"

She struggled to throw off the weight that pressed upon her from all sides, resenting his sympathy. "The tea helped. Thank you."

He reached to his scabbard, fingering the pommel of his sword. "I found this while I was looking around. I hope you trust me enough now to know I'm not planning on murdering you."

That was the point, wasn't it? What did she know? Not much. Since his arrival, she felt like a spectator in another person's story. She needed answers, and she needed them now. "Mr. . . . Mr. Bligh. What's your name again?"

He gave a hint of a smile, but his gaze remained cold. "Conor. And you're right. You do need answers. I'll tell you what I can, but some aren't mine to give and some you won't believe even if I do tell you."

Her eyes widened. "You see? It's things like that that make me feel like I've wandered into a nightmare. You pluck my thoughts from the air, you . . . you," she waved her arms at him, "you walk about perfectly normal as if you never fell at my feet or were shot. And these *Keun Marow* hunt you. Death hounds out of a faery story."

He drew up a chair and sat down across from her. "I pick up a stray thought or two. Only the most focused, the most forceful. It's a gift, like my ability to heal, my ability to fight. I was born to it as were all of my kind."

Trying to concentrate on his words, she found his nearness disturbing. She crossed her arms as if that would keep a safe distance between them. "What kind are you?"

"We're known as *Other*. Those born holding both *fey* and human traits. Witches, healers, wise men," he paused as if weighing his response, "the brotherhood of *amhas-draoi*."

"But the *fey* world isn't real. It's legends and myths. Faery tales to pass away an evening by the fire. No one believes."

His voice was firm. "It doesn't take belief to make the *fey* world real. It just is. And you wanted answers."

"And those creatures hunting you? Are they of the *fey* world as well?"

He leaned toward her, the line of his jaw hardening, his

face inches from her own. "Yes, But they aren't hunting me, Miss Reskeen. They're hunting you—and the reliquary you're holding."

She shoved her chair back from the table, glaring across at him. "I've heard enough. I don't know what you hope to gain by barging in here and trying to frighten me, but I'm not such a dupe as you imagine."

He reached out and grabbed her arm. "I need that box. It's about"—he spread his hands a little over a foot apart—"this big. Very old. Jeweled. Do you remember now?"

She closed her eyes. Tried to remember back to the days after her father's death. The confusion. The grief. And then the excitement at finally escaping the camps for a normal life here in England. "I do remember something like that. But I haven't seen it in ages. It must have been lost during the journey. Or stolen." She offered him a pointed look. "It's more than likely you stole the thing yourself."

"It was looted. Twice. Once by the French and again by the English."

"By you?"

He shrugged off her question. "After the fighting was over, it was every man for himself. Five million gold francs are hard to pass up when until then all you've had is the King's shilling."

Weary of arguing and seeing she wasn't going to get any more straight answers, she shook him off. "I'm going to bed. You can sleep down here tonight, but I expect you gone by the time I wake."

"You trust me?"

She thought about it. "If you wanted to harm me, you could have done it at least half a dozen times already. Trust you? No, not hardly. But I trust those things out there even less." She gave a dry laugh. "Besides, after the welcome I gave you, a dry place to sleep is the least I can do to make amends."

She started down the narrow hall to the stairs, but his voice drew her to a halt. "And the reliquary?"

She chose to ignore his question. "Good night, Mr. Bligh. And if I'm lucky, good-bye."

A long silence followed. Ellery waited, listening for the stinging retort or the sarcastic comment, but none came. She climbed the stairs, slowing her steps as if she hoped for some word from him and annoyed with herself for doing so. She laid a hand on her bedchamber door.

His voice rose up the stairs, deep and calming after the disturbing events of the night. "*Nos dha*, Ellery Reskeen. Sleep well."

And somehow deep in the corners of her heart, she knew that for the first time in months, she would.

Chapter Three

The man standing at the window, staring out on the dark London park, worked at his pose of indifference. What he really felt was a burning rage that curled through him like a nest of snakes. "You lost him?"

Asher Jevan was not a man who liked failure.

The reptilian creatures behind him whimpered, sniveling their apologies. "We thought his grief would weaken him," the leader of the two answered. "His sister's death was a blow." The words hissed through jagged-sharp teeth.

Asher had a moment's satisfaction at that past success, but it was gone almost immediately. Conor Bligh was a much bigger problem. The eldest of the Jevan brothers spun on his heel to stand before the pair of cringing death hounds.

Hounds in name only, the *fey* hunters could follow scent or blood if called to. What set them apart was the ability to track the mage energy any *fey* gave off, and use that energy to grow stronger. More powerful. It's what made them hated and feared by human and faery alike and why Asher relied upon them. They were perfect for his purpose.

"You had strict instructions to keep your distance," he said. "To track Bligh, but not to hinder his search. 'Tis he who shall lead us to the reliquary."

The leader of the *Keun Marow* bowed his head. "We did only as you ordered. Caught us following, he did and laid in wait for our passing. We'd no choice."

"And the pack of you couldn't subdue him?"

As if expecting a blow, the *fey* hunter hunched over, the bones of his spine pressing against the skin of his back. His nose slits widened as his breath came loud and raspy with fear. "Weren't at full strength. A scouting party broke off to follow another scent. Magic. Faint, but potent. Thought we could take him with a smaller number."

"Some peasant's get with a touch of the *Other* about him took you away from your task?"

"No, milord. The mage energy was unlike any we've scented. Wild, flowing in ways we've never seen. Magic beyond our kenning."

Wild magic? New magic? Something that even as old as he was, he'd not felt or seen before? This interested him. Not enough to break off his hunt of Conor Bligh. That held a two-fold purpose that could not be postponed.

The *amhas-draoi* would find him the reliquary, and once the casket was discovered and the three Jevan brothers re-united, Bligh would serve as a feast for his growing pack of *Keun Marow*. The power of the greatest member of the legendary brotherhood would enrich and strengthen the death hounds ten-fold. Make them an army to be reckoned with.

"Very well. Keep your watch on Bligh, but instruct your followers to track this new scent as well." He grabbed the creature by the neck, his fingers tightening around the beast's throat. Its nose slits flared as it fought to breathe. "Don't let me hear of a second failure. And don't underestimate Bligh. He may be a half-breed, but the raw magic of the *fey* in him has been tempered to a keen edge under the schooling of Scathach. The ranks of the *amhas-draoi* haven't seen his like in a thousand years. He has the power to strip you to bones if he chooses. Be grateful his foolish honor forbids it."

A flash of light, then the stench of charred flesh and the leader of the *Keun Marow* was naught more than a pile of putrid ash. Asher wrinkled his nose as he dusted off his hands. "I work under no such restraints."

He turned his gaze on the second creature cowering before him. "Bring me the reliquary and Conor Bligh. The first must be unharmed. My brothers' lives are bound to it. The *amhasdraoi* can come to me in any form as long as he still lives. His meddling at San Salas postponed our return. His death will be slow."

"And the second source of magic?" the *Keun Marow*'s new leader asked.

Asher's mouth curled in a cruel mockery of a smile. "Bring this *Other* to me in one piece. I'd like to study it."

Ellery came down in the morning, surprisingly refreshed and prepared to find the previous night had been a hallucination brought on by exhaustion and stress. Why her imagination would conjure watchers in the night and sword-wielding men, she didn't know for certain. Mayhap her father's fanciful camp tales had affected her more than she cared to admit.

The clock chimed seven as she left her room, but that was the only sound breaking the silence. She peered over the banister, but the parlor door was closed, and the dining room was empty.

"Mr. Bligh?" she called, her voice loud in the quiet cottage. "Conor?"

No answer.

So she had imagined it. She squashed a twinge of disappointment. She couldn't say she was upset to find that life was as uneventful as she expected. After all, that was how she liked it, wasn't it? Tame, with no surprises. But there had been a tingle of excitement deep in the pit of her stomach when she woke this morning. A feeling that something was coming. For good or ill was unclear, but a change that would affect everything that came after. She descended the stairs, pushing those thoughts away. It was obvious her wild dreams had simply carried over into her waking.

The kitchen was empty, but folded neatly on a chair were a bundle of blankets. A basket of eggs sat upon the table with a note. She snatched it up, reading it through and then twice more, her stomach's tingling back and growing.

> *Mr. Freethy brought them.*
> *Conor*

So it hadn't been a dream. She had found a dying man on her doorstep. Conor Bligh was real and dangerous and—she clutched the note tighter—chatting with the biggest gossip in the village. In an instant, her excitement became anger, and she crushed the paper in her fist. Perfect. If Mr. Freethy knew there was a man staying under her roof, then the entire village of Carnebwen knew it. She'd spent two years trying to outrun her scandalous past. Mr. Bligh had ruined that in twelve hours.

Crossing the floor in a rush of frustration, she noticed a wink of gold caught between the stones of the hearth. Bending down, she discovered a ring carved in the shape of a wolf's head, its tail caught between its teeth. She'd seen one similar on Conor Bligh's hand last night. But this ring was far too small. Not his then, but obviously something he dropped and would miss. But would he know he lost it here? And would he come back for it? She wrapped it tightly in a handkerchief and placed it in her reticule. She would hold on to it for now.

She ate and washed up, focusing her worry on the more immediate problem to her mind—the overdue rent. Mysterious intruders scaring her with tales out of a faery book would have to wait. A tightness knotted her stomach. Her meeting with

Mr. Porter hung above her like a cloud. She'd donned her best gown, hoping it gave her an air of respectability. Her land-lord was a stickler for propriety, but she wondered if after last night she had any reputation left to protect. She tugged on her gloves. Mr. Porter knew her. He should know she didn't enter-tain strange men in her home.

And Conor Bligh was as strange as they came.

Her cheeks grew hot remembering his kiss. After twenty-two years following the drum with her father, she knew men, how they thought and how they acted. Conor Bligh was a prime example of all the worst characteristics of the male species. The kind of man her father had always warned her about. After the heated kiss she and Conor had shared, she could understand why. It was far too easy to get lost in that swooping wild joining of lips and tongues. To be teased into thinking that heady pleasure signified something more.

The hazy blue sky and the twittering of larks in the hawthorn trees around the cottage had dispelled the last lin-gering shadows of the night before, but stepping out the front door, she was brought up short. The bushes and flowers be-neath both front windows lay crushed and scattered. And in the lane and garden hundreds of footprints had churned the drying mud into ruts. A muddy handprint dirtied one win-dowsill, as if someone had stood and peered into the cot-tage. Waves of heat and then cold washed over her, and she swallowed over and over, trying to calm herself. *Keun Marow*, Conor had called them. Hunters from the faery world sent to find her.

Suddenly, the empty lane seemed ominous and the quiet morning felt oppressive. She needed normal. She needed people and the comforting surround of the village. She hur-ried down the harbor road toward Carnebwen, thinking even the dreaded company of Mr. Porter would be welcome now.

Chapter Four

By the time Ellery left the milliner's, the day's warm weather had given way to evening's dirty gray clouds and a chill breeze. Disapproving stares and barbed comments followed her up the harbor road toward home, but she refused to feel ashamed. She'd lived her whole life in the shadow of such unjustified cruelty. At least it was her own supposed sin she was being scolded for this time and not the guilt of her parents.

A crowd of young women watched her pass, a flurry of whispers springing up in her wake. One girl, bolder than the others, spoke in a carrying voice. "Her brother, he says. I'm wishin' I had a brother or two like him."

The giggles that followed this jibe almost made Ellery whip around and answer the accusations. She was saved from doing so by the approach of a lanky, round-shouldered gentleman dressed in a fashionable coat of dark blue and a cravat tied up to his long jowls, a huge pearl nestled among the folds. "Haven't you anything better to do, Miss Yeovil, than to mock your betters?" He shook a dismissive hand at the group. "Off with the lot of you!"

He eyed the women as if they had crawled from beneath a rock, his demeanor as well as his words scattering the group like a fox among hens. Shifting his attention to Ellery, he sketched her a bow. "Your pardon for that display of incivility, Miss Reskeen."

Not sure whose incivility he was speaking to, she merely gave him a grateful smile while inwardly wishing him to the devil. "My thanks, Mr. Porter. I'm sure they meant no harm."

"Low-born trollops, and no better than they should be," he replied, adjusting his cuffs. "I heard you stopped by to see me earlier today. I was quite cast up when I found we'd missed one another, but I had ridden out early to collect the rents."

Ellery wished her savior had been anyone but Mr. Porter. Her landlord had always been friendly, but since her cousin's death, his kindliness had grown cloying, and his smile smarmier.

He made a show of flipping open an enameled snuffbox and inhaling a pinch from between his fingers. "I came to see you as soon as I heard about your . . ." He sneezed, then lowered his voice, "your problem. The talk in the village is quite salacious." His eyes gleamed, and he stepped toward her, reaching for her hand. "I refused to believe it until I spoke to you directly."

Feeling suddenly cornered on this lonely stretch of lane, Ellery backed up. "That's gallant of you, but really it's not what anyone thinks. A storm in a teacup." She tried changing the conversation. "My reason for coming to see you was the matter of my rent on the cottage. I know I've been late—"

"I understand your plight, Miss Reskeen, and I sympathize. It must be hard to be a woman on your own with no family or connections of any kind." He reached again for her hand and this time refused to let her elude him. His palms were sweaty and soft. "No one to lean on when times grow hard." He squeezed her hand, his gaze resting on the neckline of her gown. "No one to offer comfort when you need it most."

Had she not owed him three months rent, Ellery would have wrestled out of his grip and boxed his ears. Instead, she tried easing away from him without his noticing. "I think you misunderstand, Mr. Porter, but if you give me a bit more time, I'm sure I can manage to pay it."

But he would not be put off. He tightened his grip, his fingers crushing hers, his breath sour on her face.

"Miss Reskeen—Ellery, if I might be so bold. Your cousin told me of the unfortunate circumstances surrounding your birth and early years. From that moment, I only wanted to help you." He was so close she saw the nicks his razor had left on his chin and the broken veins across his nose. "I can't offer marriage—Mother would never approve of your lack of birth or breeding—but I would be pleased to ease your way if I could. Your rent would never again be an issue between us."

Ellery tore her hand away. Anger knotted her throat, and her chest burned with fury. "My cousin overstepped her place when she spoke of such private matters. I was born just as you were, Mr. Porter, from between my mother's legs, and though my childhood was harsh, I'm no man's doxy to barter myself for rent money."

He raked her with his gaze as if he already owned her, the tip of his tongue sliding across his lips. "Aren't you? They say the apple never falls far from the tree. Whatever the man staying with you offered, I can top it."

Ellery spun on her heel and began to walk on toward the cottage. She'd gone only a few yards when he caught her up and whipped her around. "We can make this difficult or we can make this easy. You owe me, Miss Reskeen."

A deep voice, cool and impersonal, brought them both up short. "And what does she owe you, sir?"

Ellery looked up to find herself under Conor Bligh's insolent gaze. Candlelight hadn't done him justice. He was one of the most beautiful men she had ever seen. Dark hair cut short and choppy as if he'd hacked at it himself without aid of a mirror. On a lesser man, the style would have seemed ridiculous. With his strong, chiseled features and warrior's body, it only made him seem harder, tougher. He leaned against a

tree, his arms folded across his chest, arrogance rising from
him like steam. In the half-light of dusk, his face fell in and
out of shadow; only the sun-gold glow of his eyes remained
steady and fixed upon her.

His lips curled in a thin, mocking smile. "One should
always pay one's debts, little sister."

How had she not seen him approach? Mr. Porter had distracted her, but surely she would have seen or heard something. The lane was narrow, the hedges on either side sparse,
yet there Conor Bligh stood as if he'd conjured himself out of
the dark trees. She swallowed. Maybe he had.

Mr. Porter dropped his arm to his side. "You must be Miss
Reskeen's—guest." He filled every syllable with venom.

Conor straightened, not so much stepping as melting out
of the shadows. Dressed in unrelieved black, Ellery thought
he might make a good pirate . . . he came closer . . . or high-
wayman . . . closer still . . . or predator. He stopped inches in
front of them, his intense gaze never wavering from her face
as if he were memorizing her stupefied expression. Then his
eyes flicked up to meet Mr. Porter's. "Not her guest, sir. Her
brother."

Mr. Porter's brows snapped together in disbelief.

Conor shot her a fierce glance, but instead of anger or resentment, Ellery only felt a coward's relief at his arrival.

"Brother?" Mr. Porter said. "You'll have to do better than
that if you expect me to believe you."

Conor shrugged. "Well, perhaps I stretch the truth slightly.
Half-brother, but family nonetheless."

Mr. Porter sniffed. "Another by-blow? Miss Reskeen's
mother was quite busy."

Ellery's face burned with shame. "You've no right to say
those things."

Conor Bligh forestalled her with a restraining hand upon
her shoulder. "I never met Ellery's mother so I wouldn't know.
Ellery and I share a father. Major Robert Galloway. I've fol-

lowed him into the army, so I rarely get back to England, but when I do I like to check in on my sister and make sure she's well." His gaze narrowed. "A shoulder to lean on, you might say, Mr. Porter."

Her landlord flushed pink, but he held his ground, staring down his long, sharp nose at them. "Your cousin was right about you, Miss Reskeen. A whore, she called you. Just like your mother. A soldier's bastard playing at being the great lady."

Ellery's fist shot out, connecting with Mr. Porter's jaw in a solid punch. He staggered and straightened, a line of blood oozing from his mouth. She started to advance on him when Conor's hand caught her up short. "That was ill-done of you, little sister. You should never lead with your left."

Mr. Porter wiped at the blood with a handkerchief, his face purple with rage. "You have until this time tomorrow, Miss Reskeen, to clear out the cottage and be gone from Carnebwen or I'll draw up charges on you and your . . . your brother."

"I've nowhere to go."

"That's not my concern," Mr. Porter replied.

Ellery rubbed the bruised knuckles of her hand. With one punch, she'd lost her first and only real home. She tried feeling remorse over her actions, but nothing could push aside the dull press of hurt and humiliation. Had Molly truly hated her so much?

"Give her three days, and she'll be gone," Conor said.

She glanced over her shoulder up at him. This morning's zinging thrill seemed a lifetime ago. She should have known it would turn out to be a warning. Life didn't hand you happiness without trouble hard on its heels.

In less than a day, Conor Bligh had turned her stable little world on its head. She needed to get away from him before his presence wreaked even more havoc. She opened her mouth to break in, but Mr. Porter spoke first.

"And why should I?"

"I'll pay you everything she owes you, but only if you give her the three days."

"I don't believe you," Mr. Porter answered, but greed narrowed his eyes.

Conor gave a casual shrug of his shoulders. "My offer stands. You'll have her rent by tonight. If not, then you can evict tomorrow. You've nothing to lose."

"Don't pay. I'll go." Ellery ground her words through gritted teeth.

Mr. Porter flicked an imaginary speck of dirt from his sleeve and smoothed a hand down his chest, fondling the jeweled pin. "I can see now why she chose you as a protector. Money always attracts her sort."

"Enough." Conor's voice cut like a blade. "You'll get what's owed, but be careful. You've felt Miss Reskeen's fist. You don't want to feel mine."

Conor's words carried a danger not lost on Mr. Porter. He glowered. "The back-rent. By tonight. Don't be too late."

Instead of challenging her landlord, Conor looked up at the few stars bright enough to be seen through the haze of clouds. Down in the village, a dog barked and was hushed with a shouted curse.

"I pray I won't be," he said.

Chapter Five

"I told you to leave," Ellery paced in front of the parlor fire, her expression thunderous.

Conor felt her anger. It shimmered in the air around her like a heat mirage. He braced himself for the argument he knew would come. He'd searched the cottage while she was gone. Any weapons had been safely disposed of. She wouldn't catch him with that trick again. He twisted his lips in a cold smile. "Did you imagine you'd driven me away? I don't frighten easily, Miss Reskeen."

She shot him a dagger-glance. "If you hadn't shown yourself to Mr. Freethy, none of this would have happened."

Conor had known only one other woman brave enough to speak to him so bluntly, and she was dead. His heart constricted with a familiar ache, but he crushed it, concentrating instead on watching the slide of Ellery's gown over every tempting curve. With her dressed in such a way, it was no wonder that miserable lecher had thought he could make advances. Her sudden stop broke him from his wandering thoughts. His attention back, he met her stony gaze. "I won't leave without the reliquary."

She crossed her arms, a wall of disbelief shutting him out. "There you go again with that blather about a reliquary. I don't have it. It's gone. Lost. Probably fenced a hundred times over by now."

"No. It's here. I know it. I can feel it."

"You're not making sense."

Conor had to be careful. The truth sounded outrageous even to his own ears. And why waste words? Would understanding the strength and brutality of the Triad and their desire to realize a new beginning for the *fey* world make her more pliant? The Triad would make the world believe, but with that belief would come a terror, greater even than anything Napoleon's armies had unleashed. If Asher alone could succeed in bringing down four *amhas-draoi*, how much more power would be unleashed with the brothers reunited?

He couldn't take the time to explain, but he also couldn't risk alienating this woman further. He needed her as much as he needed the reliquary.

"It has to be here. Your father had it at the time of the ambush. In his hands. I saw it."

She spun to face him. But instead of the fight he expected, she dropped into a chair as if she'd had the air punched out of her. Her fingers twisted together in her lap, and for the first time she seemed vulnerable and lonely. "You were there? With Father?"

Conor's hand went to his shoulder, memories of the battle in the Chapel of San Salas bringing with them a licking burn deep within tissue that had never completely healed. How could he answer her question and yet not answer it? He took a deep breath. "I was. It was in a small abandoned chapel in the hills north of Subjiana de Alava and well off the road."

"I know the spot. When the orders came to march, we couldn't find him. We searched everywhere. I went back with some of Father's men. Do you remember the blood?"

Her voice shook, her gaze turned inward on images seared into her brain. Images no innocent should witness.

"I remember." And he did. It was one of the few things he did remember from his last encounter with Asher.

"I try not to," she said, her voice, empty of emotion. "But I'll always see that chapel. Three of them lay just inside the door, another farther inside by the chancel. Multilated. Torn apart, really. Lt. Cordry and Ensign Hall tried to hold me back, but I've always been stubborn." Her eyes flickered with the warmth of memory. "Too smart for my own good, Father would tell me. He lay in front of the altar as if prepared for sacrifice. His body . . ."

Her neck muscles worked as she fought to control her voice. Her eyes shone, but no tears fell. Damn, she had courage. He stepped in, unable to let her continue. "They were no match for what happened."

She cleared her throat, wiping her eyes with the back of one hand. "You didn't say we."

"What?"

"You didn't say we were no match. You said they. But you said you were there in the chapel." Her voice strengthened, and she sat straighter in the chair. "You said you saw Father with the reliquary. So where were you?" By now she was almost shouting. "Why didn't you die with the others?"

How the hell had he walked into that one? He knew. He'd been weak, distracted by Ellery's beauty, the supple strength of her body, the flash of her crystal blue eyes, the way the expressions raced across her face, so clear he had no need to read her mind to know her thoughts.

He reined himself in, gaining time by pouring himself a glass of claret from a decanter on the buffet. She was beautiful, but that didn't make her special. A lot of women were beautiful.

The only thing that marked her as exceptional was her blood. And once he'd spilled it for the sacrifice, she'd be one more corpse. And what was unique in that?

He tossed the wine back, wishing it were whiskey.

"Why didn't you die?" she demanded.

She sounded as if she'd have been happier if he had. She wouldn't be the only one.

"Why are you alive?"

"I almost died," he spoke over her. "I came as close to it as one can and live to speak of it. But you've seen how rapidly I heal."

"You weren't in the chapel. We searched for survivors." Her voice lowered. "There were none."

"I know it sounds as if I'm an escapee from Bedlam, but trust me."

She looked down and away. "How can I trust you? I don't know anything about you."

Though her body was stiff with tension, her voice was softer. She may not believe in his world, but she seemed ready to listen. He'd use that to his advantage. Her cooperation would make his final task easier.

He took the chair next to hers, hoping to seem less intimidating. Not that she had been all that intimidated by him up to this point. "What do you wish to know?"

She lifted her head, and he read surprise in her eyes. Surprise, but also a great curiosity.

"Ask me anything you like."

She shifted in her seat, her fingers twisting her skirt as she thought. Finally, she looked up. "You say you're an *Other*. That you hold both *fey* and Mortal traits. Why? How?"

He thought for a moment how to answer. "Think of the *Other* as mortals plus. We're men and women. Just like anyone. But there's something extra. Something that marks us as *fey,* too. It can be an innate talent like sensing or even controlling local weather patterns. Or a gift for premonition. Mayhap it's as simple as the woman whose garden produces vegetables and flowers like mad when her neighbors can grow only weeds."

"But how?" She remained skeptical. It was obvious in her crossed arms, the thin line of her mouth.

He had a vision of his mother trying to explain some ancient text to him in years past. Remembered his own doubt and cynicism. Now he wished for even a tenth of her patience.

He grit his teeth. Bit back the urge to say *because I said so* and be done with it. "The stories tell us that long ago, Faery and Mortal interbred. The walls hadn't yet been created that separated them. That latent inheritance can emerge in any generation. Without warning."

She only looked half-convinced. But prepared to let further explanation slide. "You told Mr. Porter you served in the army. Was that part of the same lie as your being my half-brother?"

All right. This one was tricky, but not impossible. And he sensed her relaxing. "Yes and no."

She rolled her eyes as if to say, *here we go again*.

"I'm a soldier, but not in the British Army. I belong to the brotherhood of *amhas-draoi*. Masters trained in weapons and magic. We're charged by sacred oath to defend and protect both the *fey* and Mortal worlds. Most of the time from each other."

He felt her summing him up with a long weighing glance before she asked, "Where are you from?"

Another fairly easy question. So far, so good. "The southern coast near Penzance. My family still live there."

Her eyes widened as if the idea of him having a family shocked her. Did she think he'd sprung from the ground fully grown and sword in hand?

Apparently beginning to enjoy this game of twenty questions, she smiled. "Do you have any brothers or sisters?"

Damn her to hell. "No."

Ellery flinched at the fury concentrated in that one word. She'd touched a nerve. His jaw hardened until she thought she could hear his teeth grinding. His eyes darkened to bronze, the pupils like slits.

"No, Miss Reskeen. I have no brothers or sisters." She watched him struggle to regain his earlier composure. His hand went into his pocket, and he frowned. He fumbled, his hand searching deeper and then moving to the pocket on the other side. At last, his shoulders slumped, the heated glare of his gaze replaced with a dull resignation.

Hopelessness dimmed his eyes. For some reason, this was more frightening than his rage. She didn't want to feel anything for this man who'd spent the last day doing his best to sabotage her life.

As if he'd quashed whatever memory her question had evoked, he pushed himself out of the chair. "Any other questions?"

Ellery needed to hold tight to her anger. Sympathy sapped at this hotter emotion, leaving her confused and more determined to keep her distance. If that meant letting him search the cottage for this ridiculous box of his, so be it. Let him find it or not and be gone. "Just one," she said. "Will you help me look for the reliquary? If it's here, it's yours. But I wouldn't get your hopes up. I told you I haven't seen it since I left Spain."

He straightened, and Ellery found herself staring. She imagined herself held protected in those hard, muscled arms while the worries of the world faded to less than nothing around her. A pretty thought. But not likely. Those arms didn't gentle, they controlled. And those hands didn't caress, they crushed.

She snapped her gaze back from his chest to his face. She wouldn't make a fool of herself—again.

"I've searched the ground floor," he said. "It must be in one of the upper chambers."

Her lips thinned to a line. "You searched my home? When?"

"This afternoon. You were out."

"It's obvious this family of yours never taught you any manners. How dare you creep around my home?"

"I didn't creep, and you just said I was free to look."

"The point being that I just said it. I hadn't said it this afternoon, and unless your powers include telling the future you didn't know I'd let you."

"I haven't got time to argue. The *Keun Marow* were confused, but they'll return."

He glared at her, and Ellery's gaze flicked back to his arms. How easy it would be for him to subdue her and take what he wished without her consent. But he hadn't. He'd asked—almost politely. She thought back to the hundreds of tracks in the soft mud around the cottage and shivered. Not exactly paw prints, not exactly handprints, but something in between.

She met Conor's whiskey-gold eyes. Not exactly human, not exactly *fey*.

Something in between.

She swallowed hard. "We'll start upstairs."

"How could Molly have kept such a secret from me?" Ellery looked up at him from where she knelt upon the floor, her feet tucked under her skirts, her dark curls cobwebbed and dusty from their thorough search. "I know she always envied me the money, but I shared all I had with her."

Her expression held such bewildered sorrow Conor thought that if Cousin Molly stood alive in front of him, he might kill her all over again.

He cursed himself—not the first time—for his moment of weakness. He couldn't begin to care for Ellery. He couldn't begin to think of her in any way. She was a means to an end. Nothing else. "A family member's treachery wounds more deeply than the mightiest sword thrust." He ought to know.

She wiped the back of her hand across her eyes and sniffed.

It was the closest she came to crying. "She was all the family I had. I thought . . . but I was wrong."

"You're right to grieve, but let it be a small grief. She doesn't sound as if she was worth too many tears."

Ellery's gaze returned to her lap.

The reliquary lay there, pulled from the back of a clothespress in her cousin's bedchamber. Wrapped in cloth and placed within a larger box, they'd almost passed it by. But Conor had felt the power pulling him forward as they searched the room, sensed the reliquary's dark magic in his blood. He knew it was there.

It had taken one year, nine months, and sixteen days, but he'd found it again. The ancient silverwork was tarnished black, the jeweled lid warped and twisted as if a great energy had forced the metal open. These things Conor knew he'd find.

It had only been as Ellery pulled away the last scrap of fabric that they'd seen the recent damage and the reason her cousin had kept it hidden. Decorating the face of the casket was one great onyx, the black stone seeming to swallow the very light around it. On either side, nothing but two empty settings. One had held a ruby, the other a pearl. Both were gone. But this alone was not enough to cause such pain to shadow Ellery Reskeen's face. It was the letter folded into a corner of the outer box. A scribbled note to Mr. Porter from Molly, requesting aid in selling the last stolen jewel and keeping the money safe from the "peasant whore's whelp."

It had never made it to Mr. Porter's hand. Cousin Molly had died before she could pry the onyx from its resting place.

"Here. It's yours," she said, holding out the reliquary, her lip caught between her teeth. "I'm sorry about the damage. I'll pay you back if you give me the time. I promise."

The mage energy surrounding the box sparked like lightning in the space between them. But it was a dark energy, a subtle drag on his own powers. He murmured an incantation, strengthening his wards of protection, hoping they'd be enough to hold the pull of the reliquary at bay. More sharply than he intended, he answered, "The jewels alone are worth more than you could make in ten lifetimes."

She lifted her chin. A flash of the fighter glittered in her eye. "I said I'd pay you, and I will."

He took the reliquary, wrapping it back within its cocoon to muffle its influence. "I think your cousin should repay her own debts, don't you?"

She frowned. "She's dead."

"But Mr. Porter isn't. And if I'm not mistaken he wore a pearl of unusual size and quality in his neckcloth today. I arranged to meet him tonight. Mayhap it will take him only one lifetime to pay me back." He flashed a dangerous smile. "That is if I allow him to live it out."

A smile tugged at the corners of her mouth, her face shining with suppressed amusement. "Would you really kill him for this?"

He remembered Porter's greasy repulsiveness. The man had the personality of a snake. Conor's fingers itched to be around his throat. To tie him in knots. "For theft, dealing in stolen goods, lechery, and just for being a complete ass, I'd be more than willing to kill him."

She laughed. "That's the nicest thing anyone's ever done for me."

Chapter Six

Ellery looked around her parlor with a grimace. Had it been only twenty-four hours since she'd sat in this very spot and wished for companionship, a friend during the long, dark hours? She gave a dry laugh. Well, this was a warning to be careful what you wished for.

An open valise sat upon her sofa. Her few pitiful gowns lay in piles on various pieces of furniture in readiness for sorting. Even with Conor's help, she only had three days to be gone from here.

She glanced up. The damp had become fog. It shrouded the cottage, muffling sounds, gathering like cloud at the edges of the lighted windows. Conor had left, assuring her he'd be back as soon as he could and with his pound of flesh—or Mr. Porter's, he'd added with a wicked glow in his eyes. Would he return to tell her that her landlord had relented? With what she knew so far of Conor Bligh, it was more likely he'd come back to tell her Mr. Porter had taken an unfortunate fall off the cliffs below the village.

She tried not to give voice to the needling thought at the back of her mind that asked would he even come back at all? Now that he had his reliquary, why bother? He could take it and be gone before those horrible creatures returned. She folded a pair of stockings.

That was what she wanted. She folded a chemise.

With the reliquary gone and Conor Bligh with it, it stood to reason the unearthly hounds would follow him. She folded a gown.

Didn't it?

Looking down, she gasped with dismay. The clothes were a jumbled mess of wrinkled wool and muslin. So much for packing.

A low howl sounded from beyond the fog. Somewhere near Keigwin Tor.

Ellery's blood froze in her veins. She couldn't breathe.

The quiet catch of the door threw her to her feet. She took swift inventory of the room, snatching up a heavy candle stand, brandishing it like a spear. "Show yourself. If you dare."

Conor stepped into the parlor doorway, running a hand over hair silvered with fog. He eyed her makeshift weapon. "Crude but effective."

"You've gotten rid of all my proper weapons."

He reached out, taking the stand away from her and putting it down. "And for good reason. Had that been your pistol, I'd have another hole in my ribs." He touched his side. "I heal, but the power isn't unlimited. Enough wounds, and I'm as dead as the next man."

She appreciated Conor's attempt at humor, but it wasn't nearly enough. Too much was happening too quickly. She sank into a chair, rubbing her hands up and down her arms. "I heard them again. Now that I know what they are, I feel the difference when they're near. It's a bitter taste in my mouth, a pain in my lungs as if I can't breathe the same air."

Conor raised a brow, but didn't comment. Instead he said, "They search for the reliquary. Their master desires it beyond all things. He'd do anything to have it within his possession."

"Will they come here?"

She wanted to flee the cottage, run until she could no longer feel the relentless pursuit of the *Keun Marow*. But another part of her wanted to stay and challenge them. How dare these creatures think she was easy prey for their sport? She'd grown up with war. She knew how to fight.

Conor seemed to suffer under the same restlessness. He moved like a caged animal, stalking the corners of the room. "We're safe enough. I've strengthened my defensive wards, hiding my presence without alerting them to my magic. I also laid a false trail away from Carnebwen. That's what detained me. I needed to make it traceable without being obvious."

"Why do they want the reliquary?"

He paused at the window, closing the curtains against the night. "Asher wants it. They do his bidding."

Ellery felt as if she were drawing teeth. Every question answered only brought ten more to her mind. "And who is Asher, or is that one of those things you don't know or can't tell me?"

His expression was one of uncertainty.

"Take a chance I might believe you. It's the least you can do after having me thrown out of my house."

Her stab at amusement fell as flat as his had earlier. Instead, he approached the hearth and the dull fire lit against the damp chill. He clutched the mantel with both hands, his head bowed as he watched the flames. "Asher is one of three brothers, demons of the faery realm. Sons of the witch, Carman. They sought dominion over the *fey* once before, but were defeated and imprisoned. Now they seek to return."

Finally some answers. Not exactly ones that made sense by any normal standard, but she had left normal far behind. "And the reliquary?"

"The Triad were imprisoned within the reliquary. Bound to it for all time. It was hidden away to guard against their release."

Ellery didn't like where this was going. "But someone opened it."

Conor's eyes locked on her. Lit with an amber glow, they reminded her of a wild animal's. Deadly. Ruthless. Without pity. She looked away, unable to face him.

"Yes," he said, "someone broke the seals. Asher was set free and escaped, but I kept the other two contained and maintained hold of the reliquary." So much said in that one simple sentence. Ellery remembered the blood and the carnage in that Spanish chapel. She couldn't see how anyone had survived that battle. He continued, "I was wounded. I lost the reliquary. I couldn't follow."

She knew exactly what it had cost him to stay alive. He bore the scars of that struggle in the dark emptiness of his eyes, the loss of his humanity in return for the power of the *fey*.

"But you did follow. You followed me. The reliquary was among my father's things."

He nodded once. "It was." He left the obvious assumption hanging unspoken. "But just as I followed your trail, Asher followed mine. He knew I'd stop at nothing to get the reliquary back. And where I can travel easily in the mortal world, he cannot. He's not of this time or this place. It constrains his hunt. His power. He hopes I'll lead the *Keun Marow* to it."

Her father. Her father had brought all this about. Had he known what it was when he found the ancient casket among the treasures abandoned by the French? Or had it been simple curiosity that started such a cascading chain of disaster? The air seemed colder, the room's familiarity suddenly unreal. Her lungs worked to expand as she fought for breath. "And then what happens?"

"Either I send Asher back to his prison," Conor's head snapped up, his body tense and on the alert, "or he destroys us all."

In the silence after his words, she heard the sounds outside the cottage. In the garden. In the lane. A shuffling of bodies

and a chink of weaponry. She didn't need to hear their cry to
know the creatures were there—and waiting. The *Keun
Marow* had found him.

Conor heard the hunters almost the same instant Ellery's
thought seared his brain. His muscles tightened. His lips curled
back from his teeth as he growled low in his throat. They
wouldn't take him. He wouldn't be dinner for Asher's army. He
thought of his sister. Nor sport for his sadistic pleasure.

He thrust his hand deep in his pocket before he remembered
her ring wasn't there. Instead, his fingers curled on a stone the
size of a hen's egg. The pearl. He'd wanted to present it to
Ellery and watch her reaction. But the time for that had
passed—if it had ever been.

A low keening wail shivered the air, echoing down the high
hills, curling up from the deep coombes closer to the sea.
More took up the call as the *fey* hunters encircled Carnebwen.

An anger grew inside him, a hatred born into him with his
fey inheritance and sharpened to a loathing over years of
watching people he cared for and loved taken from him one
by one. His blood burned, his muscles thickened and warped
in preparation for a renewal of the battle on the tor. He pushed
the urge away, restraining the shift before Ellery noticed.
She'd accepted his explanations this far. He didn't want to test
her limits yet.

He swung around, pinning her with a sharp stare. "Do you
trust me?"

She froze, scared but defiant. "Do I have a choice?"

Reassured that she wasn't about to panic, he slid his sword
free, testing its balance as he sized up his options. Now that
they'd been discovered by Asher's pack, subtlety and subterfuge were no longer needed. But magic was out of the
question as well. Any spells he might wield would only

increase their strength. Make his task harder. He gripped his sword. "Stay out of the way, but follow my orders."

Smashing glass and splintering wood sounded from the kitchen as a pack of hounds stormed the back. Others hammered against the sturdier main entrance. "We'll force our way out."

"Through them?" she shouted.

His eyes flicked to a window, overlooking the west side of the cottage. "Only if we have to. Can you manage the drop?"

She followed the track of his gaze before offering him a grim smile. "I'll manage."

The hammer blows grew vicious. Howls split the air as the first *Keun Marow* crashed through the back kitchen.

Conor smashed the window as the lead hound pushed his way into the room. Then another behind him. They slid to a stop. Their gazes narrowed, their nose slits widened as they scented the power he was giving off. He hoped they choked on it.

The first creature drew a knife from his belt. "You?" he hissed. "Here?"

Conor pulled Ellery behind him. "I'm overjoyed to see you too." He whipped a dagger out, releasing it before he'd finished speaking. It sliced through the air, embedding itself in the first hound. The creature howled and crumpled dead to the floor.

The second *Keun Marow* paused as if surprised to find resistance. Then he stepped over his dead comrade just as the main door smashed back on its hinges. "We'll feed well for this night's work." His lips drew back over long yellow teeth.

Conor heard the scuffled footsteps as the pack entered the cottage, felt their presence in his mind as a nauseating stench. But he waited. The more of them bottled up inside, the longer he might have to use his power to aid his escape. He had to time it well. The magic would give him an initial edge, but he couldn't draw on it for long. They'd track it—and him. Once he was away from the cottage, it was up to his natural abilities to keep him and Ellery safe.

He held his sword at the ready. The *fey* hunter kicked aside a table as he slashed down with his weapon, aiming for Conor's head. He deflected the blow, then slipping beneath the hound's guard, Conor's sword bit deep into its side. The *Keun Marow* shrieked and fell.

Conor shouted, "Now. Go."

Ellery scrambled toward the window, as two more *Keun Marow* pressed the attack. One lunged for Ellery. Conor stepped between them, cutting down and through, feeling the satisfying crunch of muscle and bone under his blade.

The second attacker leapt for his throat. To keep the beast's claws from impaling him, Conor twisted away, but fell over a table. The hound struck him in the shoulder, the glancing blow sending a sudden pain knifing through Conor's body. Dark mage energy tore through him, the cold excruciating, the numbing pain dulling his sword arm.

Conor staggered for the window, but stumbled to a halt, seeing Ellery still perched on the ledge, watching the battle with wide frightened eyes. "Jump!" he ordered.

"I can't leave you."

"Jump, or we're both dead."

She leaned forward on the damaged sill as a hound fought to get to her. Conor lunged, but his sword arm remained clumsy. The hound whipped around, his claws unsheathed. He struck Conor a blow across the chest, before turning on Ellery, raking her arm from shoulder to wrist. She screamed, plunging off the ledge into the darkness.

Chapter Seven

Using the butt of his sword, Conor knocked the hound back before he could strike again. The *Keun Marow* tripped over Ellery's forgotten valise, Conor's blade sliding cleanly home.

He surveyed the damage. Three dead. Two mortally wounded. The pack that attacked him on the tor numbered at least twice as many. He grabbed one of the wounded hounds, fixing him with a deadly stare. "Where are the rest?"

The creature glared back, blood dripping from the corner of his mouth. "Didn't expect you here."

"Why have you come?"

The hound lolled, his eyes glazed.

Conor shook it. He'd no time. He still needed to find Ellery. "Answer me."

It raised its head. "Magic. Strange magic. Asher wants it." It said nothing more.

Conor rose, less confused, but more suspicious.

His chest on fire, his head muzzy with the hound's poisonous mage energy, he forced himself to step over the dead and dying to reach the broken-in front door.

He discovered Ellery in the crushed bushes beneath the parlor window. She lay sprawled on her side, one arm flung out as if she tried breaking her fall, the other bent oddly beneath her. The left side of her dress had been shredded by the hound's attack, revealing deep bloody gashes down one arm and across her shoulder. His heart hammered as he knelt beside her, pushing aside the dark cap of her hair. She couldn't be dead. Not yet. Not like this.

Her breath caught on a moan.

"You're alive."

She opened her eyes. "Am I?" She tried sitting up, but fell back with a string of curses that would put any soldier to blush.

He hid behind a stern expression. "Your arm looks broken."

"It feels broken."

"The wounds are deep, though the bleeding is sluggish."

"All words to warm my heart."

Conor couldn't help it. He laughed. Few faced what she had and came away with their sense of humor intact. Asher and his minions had stripped his bare long ago. "We'll see to both injuries once we're clean away."

She gave a panicked glance back at the cottage. "They're—"

"Dead, but we can't stay here any longer. It isn't safe. Can you travel?"

Ellery closed her eyes for a moment before biting her lip and nodding.

"We won't have to go far before I can see to your wounds. You'll be throwing punches again by tomorrow."

Her eyes snapped open. "Tomorrow?" She lurched forward, bit back a scream, and collapsed unconscious.

"Just as well. This will hurt," he whispered before gathering her up in his arms.

Her head rested against his shoulder, her short crop of curls brushing his sleeve. He found himself staring. His heightened eyesight picked out the freckles across her nose, the sickle-shaped scar by her temple. Not so many years ago, he might have pictured himself finding a woman like her. Loving.

Having children. Living a life rich with laughter and passion. But that felt like another lifetime. And those fantasies had been replaced by darker dreams.

Conor paused, listening. Something felt wrong. He lifted his head, testing the air for danger. Beneath the dull pound of the surf came another noise, a dissonant chord against the comfortable night sounds. A second pack hunted. A second pack approached. Conor couldn't hold them off, not with the mage energy frying his blood. He glanced once more at Ellery's sleeping face. "I'm sorry for using you. But it has to be."

Then with a phrase, he gathered the invisibility of the *fethfiada* around them both and slid into the trees.

Ellery opened her eyes, looking up into the night sky, a thin smudging of gray in the east. Tangled branches overhung her bed, and the rush of spilling water sounded to her right. She moved, and pain lanced her side. Across her shoulder. Down her arm. But beneath the sharper agony was a dull throbbing that pulsed through her entire body. Even her toes hurt.

How had she gotten here? Nothing came to mind other than fragmented flashes of trees and rain and Conor's steady breathing as he carried her. That last impression had been the strongest and the one she clung to when all she wanted to do was scream.

Conor's heat, the rhythm of his heart beneath her ear, the hard, muscled feel of his arms holding her close kept the suffering from taking over.

"You're awake." His voice sounded behind her. "I'd have worried in another hour if you hadn't moved."

She tried tilting her head to spot him, but even that slight gesture sent the spasms spiraling out of control. "Come where I can see you."

He slid into view, looking as sleek and deadly as he had last night. Mayhap more so with his jaw shadowed by whiskers, his eyes shadowed with worry. He wore only a cambric shirt tucked into his leather breeches. Ellery understood why when she realized what she lay wrapped in. Beneath his greatcoat and jacket, she had on only her thin chemise. "My clothes?" she asked.

"They were shredded by the *Keun Marow*."

She started with a sudden thought for the ring she'd stuck in her pocket that morning.

"Is this what you're concerned about?" He held up the wolf-head ring.

"I found it," she answered, no longer surprised at his ability to read her thoughts, but ashamed she hadn't given it back to him earlier.

"I took it." He rolled the ring between his fingers, making it glitter in the thin light of the setting moon. "It belonged to my sister."

"You told me you had no sisters."

"I don't—anymore." He tucked the ring away in his pocket, his tone curbing further questions.

Kneeling beside her, he pulled aside the coat. She winced at the sudden explosion of cool air across her torn skin before Conor placed one gentle hand on her shoulder and one at her waist. His fingers traced each bloodied gash, felt her arm from elbow to wrist and back again. She didn't even question whether he knew what he was doing. Of course, he did. He knew how to do everything. Or so she was finding.

Time seemed to stretch out in all directions as he explored her hurts as if he sought to memorize every mark the *Keun Marow* had made on her body.

Ellery watched his eyes as he worked. They glowed with an unnatural light, and she found if she concentrated, she could push aside the other thoughts. Thoughts triggered by his healing touch, but curving off into outrageous and highly inappropriate directions. A warmth spread through her body, a delicious heat that begged for attention. Her gaze wavered, dropped to his clenched jaw, the line of his mouth. Could he know what she was thinking?

He spoke under his breath, whispered words lost on the breeze. His shoulders tensed, his chest heaved with every breath. Her wandering eyes snapped back to his face.

She was wounded. Bleeding and broken after the attack in the cottage. How could she be imagining Conor Bligh's body wrapped around hers? It didn't make sense. She should be writhing in agony. She should be weeping. She should definitely not be wishing he would take her in his arms and crush his mouth to hers in a kiss that would shatter her like cannon shot.

He shuddered, squeezing his eyes shut. His neck muscles strained, his whole body rocked back with a jolt as his hands fell away from her.

Conor knelt, head bowed, hands at his sides. As if the whole world waited, all went quiet. He raised his head, his once bright eyes gone black and staring. "How do you feel?" His words came clipped, raspy.

Ellery frowned, but now that he'd asked, she did feel different. "Better."

She moved her head. Her arm. Nothing. She sat up. A dull ache, but no more than if she'd slept on it ill. Dried blood streaked her side, but her skin was intact, as smooth as if the *fey* hunter had never clawed her. "What have you done?"

He shook his head, slowly as if it weighed him down to do so. "Only what I had to." He paused. "You'd never have lasted."

His shirt. Black as the rest of his clothing, she'd not noticed at first. But the sky lightened with every second and now it was clear that patches of the fabric were stained and wet with blood. Across his shoulder, down his arm. Wounds that were not his by right.

She scrambled across to him, taking his head between her hands, forcing him to meet her eyes. "What have you done?

How could you take this on along with everything else? I need you, you great lummoxing brute."

A glimmer of amusement touched the black of his eyes. "Need?"

It had slipped out before she knew it. "I need you to keep me safe from those creatures," she backtracked. "You've gotten me into this mess. You've got to stay alive long enough to get me out."

He caught her wrists in his hands to free himself. But he didn't release her. He held on, their hands and gazes linked, a questing look in his eyes as if she were a stranger. "It's all right. I've told you I heal."

She slipped her hand from his, touching his bloodied sleeve. "But the wounds. They're awful. And my arm was broken—or is it your arm now?" She dropped her hand to her lap, her eyes hot with tears she wouldn't allow to fall. "It's like blindman's buff. Just when I get my bearings, I'm spun about and can't tell up from down."

He tucked a curl behind her ear. "Not blindman's buff at all, but that game we all used to play. You fall backwards without looking, not knowing whether your friend will catch you or let you drop."

"Trust."

"Exactly." She saw the toll the wounds were taking on him in the tight lines of his face, the bleak hollows of his eyes. "Most today believe like you do. That the *fey* world is a child's tale or a crone's superstition. Even the *Other* keep much of their powers hidden. But that doesn't make the magic any less."

"So I should give myself up, fall backwards and trust that you'll catch me. That you'll never let me fall."

Though only inches separated them, it felt to Ellery like a chasm had opened at her feet.

His expression went flat; he pulled his hand away. "Never trust in the tameness of a wolf."

"Shakespeare. King Lear."

His eyes widened in surprise.

She grimaced. "My mother had a book of plays," she explained. "She read it to me over and over when I was little."

"It's true, Ellery. I'll keep you safe from Asher and his hounds. Beyond that, I make no promises."

His words were meant to be cruel. To destroy the moment she knew they'd shared, even if he wouldn't admit it. She didn't understand his motives, but she would heed his warning. No promises. No future. That was the way of men. And women had two choices. Accept it, loving only for the moment, or accept it, never loving at all.

Ellery had seen what the first choice had done to her mother. She would not commit the same mistakes.

"So what happens now?" she asked. "We can't go back. And those beasts are out there. Somewhere."

Taking a shaky breath, he pulled himself up. Gingerly, he moved his arm, flexing his fingers, bending and straightening his elbow. "We'll travel toward the coast. Lands End. Keep off the roads. Stay hidden. It's only until the first of May. Beltane."

"What happens at Lands End at Beltane?"

Conor flinched as he buckled on his scabbard. "I cast Asher back into his prison and seal the reliquary."

"And that will end it? I'll be safe then?"

He said nothing, all his attention on breaking camp, erasing the signs of their stay.

"Conor? Answer me. What happens after Beltane?"

He met her gaze, his expression unreadable. "Yes, Ellery. That will end it."

Chapter Eight

"Twice in two days? You grow sloppy." Asher stood in the front room of a rundown cottage among broken furniture, smashed glass, and dead bodies. None of them Bligh's. His hunters had failed again. At least Bligh had saved him the trouble of punishing the *Keun Marow* himself.

The creature shrugged. "These not for Bligh. Not expecting trouble." His nose slits widened. He half-closed his eyes as he searched the house for scents.

"The *Other* did this?" Asher gestured at the dead hounds. "You lie. I sense Bligh's magic. He was here."

The *Keun Marow* nodded. "But not alone. He and the new *Other* we seek. Together."

This new information sent Asher into a fury. The reliquary should be his. His brothers should be free. With the renewed power of the Triad, they would seek vengeance on those *fey* who'd dared to imprison them. But alone, he was nothing.

His hands curled into fists, his nails digging into his palms until blood dripped between his fingers. He'd only needed minutes in the chapel. Minutes before the casket's seals would have been irreparable. But Bligh had gotten to the man first, halting the release. Asher had tried to take the reliquary then. He'd come close, the chapel stinking of blood and death before it was over. But he'd been weak from the escape, and the *amhas-draoi* had won—that battle.

Asher smiled, thinking of Bligh's sister. Now that had gone as planned. One more victory like that one, and Bligh would beg for death before the end.

A tentative knock on the shattered front door broke him from his thoughts. "Miss Reskeen?"

Was this the *Other* his hounds kept speaking of? The owner of the house returning to survey the damage? With a flick of his wrist, Asher extended the spell of *glamorie* over the *Keun Marow*, both the hound standing beside him as well as the dead scattered around the room. Whoever it was, he would see nothing Asher didn't want him to see. If it was the *Other* he sought, all to the good. And if not, he still might supply some answers. Who did live here? Why had Bligh come? Where had they gone?

Not put off by the broken door, the intruder entered. "Ellery? Is anyone here?"

Upon seeing Asher, the man stopped short. His eyes traveled over the room, but his mind showed him only a tall polished gentleman standing amid a tumble of discarded clothing and torn furniture.

"Who are you?" the man blustered, casting wary glances at the mess. "What have you done with Miss Reskeen?" He drew his scrawny body up in a pose of haughty belligerence, running a hand down his front, drawing attention to a large pearl pin.

Asher's lips curled in a sneer as he stepped over a broken table. "Do you mean the owner of the house? I'd hoped you could tell me. A broken door. Evidence of a scuffle. And now you, sir, skulking about outside in the dark. What have you to say for yourself?"

The man's skinny neck worked as he swallowed. "I'm the—" he squeaked before clearing his throat. "I'm the owner. Mr. Porter. Miss Reskeen rented this cottage from me."

"But no longer?"

"I evicted her for lack of payment." He warmed to his sense of ill-usage. "A deceitful baggage. By the looks of things she came to a bad end, and I'm not surprised. Her brother, he says. I know a criminal when I see one."

Asher could hardly contain his delight. It was almost too easy. "You say this woman left with a man?"

Mr. Porter nodded. "A scoundrel. He threatened me. Me, sir. A man of means in this community. Not an ounce of respect for his betters."

"Where did they go? Did they tell you?"

"I can't imagine where Miss Reskeen would go. She's no family that I know of. A dead soldier's bastard."

Asher's body went still, his mind turning Mr. Porter's information over and over. A soldier. The reliquary had been breached by one such. A man in a scarlet uniform armed with sword and musket, though they had availed him little against Bligh's attack. Could there be a connection? Was this why Bligh was here? Not because she was an *Other*, but because she held the reliquary?

Wait. The reliquary. A dead soldier's bastard. The pieces fell together, sending Asher reeling back in horror. The soldier who opened the reliquary at San Salas was dead. But this girl carried his blood. She could be used to repair the seals.

She could destroy everything.

His concentration faltered, dissolving the *glamorie*. The *Keun Marow* dead and living reappeared. And the elegant façade Asher had chosen for this world vanished, revealing his true form. He stretched, the black expanse of one wing tip coming within inches of the man's face.

Mr. Porter shrieked, backing toward the door. But Asher's *fey* hunter was there before him.

Asher licked his lips, enjoying the man's terror. "Do you always come calling on an empty house at such a late hour?"

The man fell to his knees, blubbering, his eyes round with

panic as they flashed back and forth between Asher and the gray, reptilian creature behind him. "Dear God in heaven. What are they? What are you?"

"Where is Bligh? Where is this girl? Answer me, or it feeds on your flesh."

Mr. Porter wagged his head back and forth, moaning and clutching his hands. "I don't know. I came for my treasure. My jewels. They're mine. Hidden away. I came to get them."

"Describe these jewels."

The *Keun Marow* placed a clawed hand upon Mr. Porter's shoulder. He screamed, his words spilling out of him like vomit. "A pearl like this one. A ruby. Molly gave them to me. She said there were others. It was Molly."

Asher stiffened. The reliquary *had* been here. He took a long look at the stone on the man's chest. Mr. Porter cringed as Asher tore the pin off his shirt and held it to the light. "It's no pearl." He threw it to the floor where it shattered into dust. "It's paste."

Mr. Porter sobbed. "No. It's not true. It's real, I tell you."

Asher tried to reach out, feel the presence of the reliquary. But there was no answering call.

The casket and his brothers were gone. Bligh and his sacrifice were gone. So too was his chance at prying into this girl's magic, gaining pleasure in her screams, arousal in her pain.

But he would find them before Bligh could act. And he would have his revenge. On Bligh. On the *fey*.

He walked past the cowering Mr. Porter, calling back over his shoulder. "Burn the bodies."

Once again the elegant English gentleman, he closed the door behind him.

Conor scanned the rain-laden clouds with a sinking feeling in the pit of his stomach. Or was that the nausea again? For the last few hours just putting one foot in front of the other was a victory of sorts. Sweat stung his eyes, yet he shivered with cold.

He glanced across at Ellery. In his jacket, with his great-coat dragging out behind her like a train, she looked like a child playing dress-up in her mother's things. Or maybe her father's. Anyway, there was no help for it. He couldn't very well take the only clothing she had from her. He'd make do.

It was fatigue coupled with the transference of Ellery's wounds; that was all. And it didn't help matters that his body had still been healing from his first tangle with Asher's hounds. No wonder every muscle screamed in agony, his bones grated together with each step, and his stomach was somewhere in his throat.

He stumbled, Ellery gripping him with a steadying hand.

"When were you going to admit that you're ill?"

"What are you talking about?" He winced at the pressure of her fingers around his arm. It remained sore and stiff, the break slow to knit.

She put a palm to his forehead. Her touch felt cool against his hot, achy skin. "You're feverish. And you're pale as chalk."

He pulled her hand away. "I'm fine." He eyed the clouds again. "But we need to find shelter. Rain's approaching. And the *Keun Marow* will be active once night falls."

"Mayhap we can find a posting house or tavern."

"And why'll we're at it, why don't we leave a trail of bread-crumbs for them to follow. I was thinking of a barn or a shepherd's hut. Somewhere safe."

Ellery stared at him, stubbornness evident in the jut of her jaw and the way she stood with her hand on her hip. "If you think I'm going to wander Cornwall until May first in my petticoats, you're mad."

He remained silent.

She threw open the coat, holding her arms out to the

side. "Look at me, Conor. I'm not exactly dressed for a forced march."

She had a point. Her gown and stockings were gone. Her bloody shift hung to her ankles, allowing him easy glimpses of her long, muscled legs. His jacket draped over her hands, the gaping lapels doing little to hide the shapely curves of her breasts.

She hugged the coat back around her. Her gaze softened. She took his hand, clenching it tightly. "Please, Conor. If you feel half as bad as I did before you . . . before you healed me, then you feel bloody awful. You can't keep going without some time to let yourself recover."

He should oppose it. Tell her to soldier on for a bit longer. That they couldn't afford to stop. But he didn't want to admit how nice it felt to have a woman fuss over him. For some reason, Ellery's concern didn't instantly set him on edge.

His indecision must have been clear in his eyes. Her lips curved in a shy smile. "A day in bed for you, time for me to re-supply, and we can be back on the road by this time tomorrow."

Conor found himself focusing on Ellery's lush full lips, before dropping to linger on the tempting body he knew lay hidden within his coat.

She cocked her head, waiting for his answer.

He turned away, hoping his thoughts weren't visible to her. "Conor?"

"All right. I do know of a place where we might be safe. It's to the west of here. Another few miles. But we leave tomorrow at dawn." It was the most he could compromise.

Ellery flashed him a quick smile that lit up her face. "Done."

He turned off the track to head across the fields, praying he could make it as far as Evan's place. One foot in front of the other. Eyes ahead. Every sense alive to the presence of trouble. Ignore the crushing exhaustion. The deep, pressing ache in every bone and joint. The throb of mage poison coursing through every vein. Just another mile or two. He could make it that far. He had to.

They passed the first few cottages just as the rain began. He raised his face to it, letting it ease the heat of fever and frustration.

Ellery's voice snapped him back to the present. "Up ahead. We'll find a room there."

The inn sat back from the road, light spilling through greasy mullioned windows, the steeply pitched roof black with moss and smoke and rain. As they approached, the door was thrown open and a large, ruddy-jowled man emerged, jamming a hat on his head as he muttered about the weather. Conor's eyes flicked to Ellery.

Damn. Speaking of breadcrumbs. He couldn't let her be seen like this.

He summoned the *fith-fath*, throwing the illusion of two well-dressed travelers over both of them, hoping his strength would hold.

He caught and held the man's gaze, daring him to challenge them. Praying he wouldn't. It was taking all his strength just to keep their true appearance masked. Apparently sensing something of Conor's true nature, the man crossed himself as he stepped aside. Conor's lips gave a cynical twitch. Did he really think that would do any good? Cold iron. Maybe.

The man's gaze followed them as they passed through the doors of the inn. Superstitious he might be, suspicious he most definitely was. Conor pulled Ellery close. She glanced up, but he gave a warning shake of his head.

The interior of the inn smelled of boiled meat and stale beer. Long scarred tables sat under each front window, two uncomfortable-looking wooden settles beside a great stone hearth. All stood empty. No sign of Evan.

The publican greeted them before they had shaken the rain from their heads.

"A private room if you have one," Conor said. "Overlooking the street. And water for bathing."

"And your luggage, sir?" the man asked, mistrust evident in the way he sized them up. "I heard no carriage arrive."

"We lost a wheel on the road south of Bolventor. My coachman and groom are attending to it. My wife was impatient to be in out of the weather. We walked."

"But that's five miles and across Maidenwell Heath. Rocky, it is. And wild country."

"Which is why we'd appreciate a room and not a lecture." The floor swayed, the long tables tipping and falling like boats on a river. Black specks danced at the corners of his vision. Ellery's hand encircled his upper arm, and he focused on the aching pressure to steady him.

A rush of cool air signaled the opening of the door. The man from outside had returned. Conor's hand moved to the grip of his sword. To the men, it looked only as if he dropped his hand to his empty waist. But Ellery did see. She tensed, her eyes moving from the tavern keeper to the man and back. Without warning, she went limp. Conor almost fell, trying to catch her. His arm burned, his fingers went numb but he managed to pull her in close.

Ellery's eyelids fluttered open as she wiped a trembling hand across her forehead. "I'm sorry. I'm feeling ill and so very tired." She gave the tavern keeper a wide-eyed pleading look that would have done Sarah Siddons proud.

"You have money for a room? I won't be havin' no tinkers or gypsies sourin' the place for my payin' customers."

"Give 'em a room, Kay." Conor whipped around. He'd never even sensed Evan slipping in from the kitchen. But there he stood, looking as he always did. Tall and gangly with a shock of black hair and eyes dark as pitch.

The innkeeper looked as if he wanted to refuse. He muttered something about troublemakers and brothers-in-law, but he ushered them toward a rickety set of stairs at the back of the inn. Conor had to duck as they followed him down a low-ceilinged hall, stopping at the third in a row of four doors.

"It looks out on the stable yard. But it's clean."

"And the water?" Conor asked, surveying the musty chamber.

"I'll heat it. But I ain't got no bath nor help to carry it. If'n ya want it, you'll have to come and get it. There's a pail on the table there for washing. My name's Kay if you need aught else."

The spots were back and growing larger. He shook his head to try and clear them.

"You're too kind. Thank you," Ellery said firmly. The invalid act was obviously over. She pushed the man out the door, shutting it just as Conor's control slipped and the *fith-fath* dissolved.

She blew out a large breath. "That was close."

He would have nodded, but the nausea that had plagued him all day sent him diving for the wash pail.

Afterwards, he rolled up and over onto the bed. He'd lay here. He'd rest. Just a few minutes, and he'd be better. He was sure of it.

"So much for using that pail for sponging off," was Ellery's wry comment.

Chapter Nine

Ellery leaned back against the headboard, closing her eyes. Conor lay next to her, sleeping—finally. The room had only the one bed and no chairs so it was together here or alone on the floor, and she was just too tired for worrying over conventions.

Conor had passed between raging fevers and chills that left him curled into a ball. He'd emptied his stomach long ago, but still he heaved until blood stained his lips. She'd tried offering him water, but he pushed it away or it dribbled down the corner of his mouth, untasted.

She couldn't see any injuries. So why did he sicken? Where was his ability to heal when he needed it most?

She had some nursing skill. No one could live in the tail of an army without picking up the basics. But it was just about enough to make her well aware that she was as unprepared as she could be. She didn't even have clothes, for heaven's sake. She needed help. Or at least, supplies. Something to fight the fever—and the *Keun Marow* if she had to.

Conor's sword belt hung on a peg by the door. Ellery rose, hoping her absence didn't wake him. Her fingers found the worn ridges where countless others had gripped it before her. Or was all that due to one man? She glanced back at the bed.

Could Conor alone have caused such wear? It seemed doubtful, but then just what did an *amhas-draoi* do?

She slid the blade free, catching the awkward weight of it before it clanged to the floor. It was far heavier than her father's saber, but looked more deadly. The polished edges gleamed red in the firelight.

The sword was useless to her. She could barely lift it much less wield it effectively against an enemy. A knife or a dagger would stand her far better and would be small enough to hide beneath the greatcoat. Though, beneath Conor's greatcoat, she could hide an entire armory with no one the wiser.

She returned the sword, taking a dagger instead. Now this was a weapon she understood. Her father had made certain of that. He'd had her practice hour after hour until she could throw it with a good chance of hitting her mark, and she could fight in close quarters if cornered.

"It's best to know a bit of knife play. You never know when the enemy might be on our heels." He would eye the faces of the men as if one of them might drag her away by the hair if given half a chance. "Or when a friend might fall to drink and bad judgment."

Ellery had never had to use what he'd taught her. But she sent him a quick prayer of thanks tonight as she strapped the belt around her waist.

Assessing her apparel took only seconds. Her gown was gone, her shift in tatters. What she had was a pair of worn walking boots and Conor's jacket and coat. She would need to find a milliner's shop in the morning, but tonight she needed an apothecary or a surgeon. She couldn't leave Conor. And she couldn't wander the village in what she had on. She would need to send someone. Perhaps the innkeeper. All that remained was the money to pay for it. She didn't have any, but Conor must. He couldn't conjure food or clothes, and she doubted he rode a straw besom from place to place. Men needed money. Even *Others*.

She turned out the pockets of his coat, then his jacket. Nothing. She searched his breeches, praying he didn't wake while she did it. She wasn't sure how she would explain her hands placed just so or the hot flush in her face. If past experience was anything to go by, he'd have her pinned to the bed, his lips teasing a path down her neck, nipping at the flesh behind her ear. She stood up, yanking her hands away, her stomach still quivering. Where did that thought come from? What was happening to her? She shook her head, focusing again on the immediate problem. Money. Or more to the point, the absence of it.

So perhaps Conor *did* conjure up what he needed with a spell or two and a flick of his wrist. Unfortunately, he wasn't in a position to spin a few straws into gold. And Mr. Kay wasn't running her errands without payment of some kind.

Telling herself it had nothing to do with the feel of his muscled body beneath her hands, she returned to his breeches. Passing them by the first time in her search, this time she drew out the contents of his pocket.

Two items. Both valuable.

The first, the pearl she had last seen pinned to Mr. Porter's chest. A smile tipped her mouth. So he had done it. He'd recovered one of the reliquary's stolen jewels. She could only imagine how. Mr. Porter wasn't the kind to give up his riches without a fight.

Her eyes jumped to the sword again, but she dismissed the idea. She couldn't say how, but she knew there were lines even Conor wouldn't cross.

The second object Conor had hidden away as if protecting the Crown Jewels. His sister's wolf-head ring.

The delicate gold work was exquisite, and Ellery couldn't help trying it on. It stuck at her knuckle, but she forced it, and once over, it fit comfortably. She held it up, admiring the detailing in the animal's face, its ruby eyes like twin drops of blood. She'd never seen anything like it nor worn it. Money went for necessities. You couldn't eat jewelry.

She would use the pearl for the doctor. The ring, she would put back with Conor none the wiser. She tugged at it, but if it had been difficult getting on, it was impossible to remove. Perhaps some lard or grease would loosen it. The tavern's kitchen could provide that easily enough.

"Ysbel?" Conor mumbled. His dull gaze swept the room. "Ellery?"

She closed her hand over the pearl, hiding her arm behind her back. She had hoped he'd stay asleep until she had spoken with Mr. Kay. "Feeling better? I've ordered some broth. I'm just going downstairs to see about it."

He wiped a hand down his face, grimacing as he tried to sit up. "Not going out like that, are you?"

"Unless you want to lend me your breeches and boots. It's fine. I've done it once already. Your coat hides everything."

He raised a skeptical eyebrow. "You obviously haven't seen yourself if you've come to that conclusion."

"You mustn't be that sick. You're still as nasty as ever," she snapped.

He fought to rise, but just rolling onto his side sent him groaning for the pail. Ellery winced at the retching that went on and on, long after Conor fell back exhausted into bed.

"Mage . . . mage sickness . . . never like this . . . never so much." His words faded out as he closed his eyes.

"I'm sending Mr. Kay for a doctor."

But he was already asleep. And she hadn't even thought to ask him if he had any money.

She opened her hand, staring down at the stone in her palm. She would explain once they were back on the road. He would laugh and praise her resourcefulness, and all would be forgiven.

At least that's what she told herself over and over as she sought out Mr. Kay.

Ellery assessed the situation from the bottom step. The innkeeper stood behind a counter, wiping down glasses while he watched a darts game. The man who'd interceded for them earlier sat at a corner table, an untouched pint in front of him.

Mr. Kay glanced up. Catching sight of her, he stiffened, his face falling into long lines of displeasure. But when she gestured him over, he came.

"I need you to go for the doctor." Sudden inspiration struck. "Lord Bligh is ill."

The title didn't lessen the belligerence in Mr. Kay's face. "His lordship got the money?"

"Something better." She opened her fist, showing off the pearl.

"What'll I do with something like that?"

"Sell it. Trade it. I don't know. Whatever you like, I expect."

"They'll think I stole it. They'll be questions."

"I can't help your neighbors' distrustful natures. It's all I have."

"I knew it," he answered as if she'd just confirmed his worst ideas about her. "What's that? On your finger there."

"This? A ring. It's a bit stuck. I'll need some grease."

"I'll take that for your doctor call."

She caught her hand to her chest. "You can't have it. It's not mine to give you."

"Not yours? Stole it, did you? I knew it," he repeated.

"It's been in Lord Bligh's family for generations. It's quite dear."

He grabbed her wrist, studying the ring. "A mite small, but my daughter's wanting a bit of sparkle."

She snatched her hand away. "I said it's not part of the deal."

He crossed his arms over his chest, his expression hardening. "No ring, no doctor."

Ellery thought of Conor upstairs. She thought of the battle at the cottage. The claws, the teeth, the weapons. And even if she didn't carry the scars, she remembered the pain.

She fingered the hidden dagger. Who was she fooling? It

would be like trying to fight a tiger with a table fork. Ellery made up her mind. It was the ring or her, and it wasn't as if Conor's sister was going to ask for it back.

She held out her hand to shake on it. "Very well. I'll need some—"

Mr. Kay grabbed her by the wrist and with one painful wrench tore the ring from her.

"Grease," she finished, rubbing her injured finger. "You could have given me a bit of warning. I use that hand."

Her words trailed off as a shadow fell over both of them.

Chapter Ten

Mr. Kay glanced up.

A flash beyond Ellery's right shoulder became the edge of a drawn sword, one she had last seen hanging in her room.

She wheeled around, coming nose to tattooed chest with Conor. Dark swirls of color stained his arms, his shoulders. Mage marks. According to her father, the signs of magic and power. Right now, Conor radiated both with enough force to knock her back on her heels.

"You stole it," he said, his voice sharp as his blade and just as deadly. "You stole Ysbel's ring."

"Let me explain," she started.

But he wasn't looking at her. His glittering gaze was focused on Mr. Kay.

The innkeeper backed away, shock fast becoming indignation. "I didn't. The girl gave it to me."

Conor didn't register the words, his glassy stare remaining fixed as he stepped down off the final stair.

Mr. Kay threw the ring at Conor. "Here, take the cheap, ugly thing." It pinged across the floor to be lost in the dark corners of the taproom.

Conor threw himself forward, his sword sweeping out in a wide arc.

Caught between them, Ellery dodged Conor's attack, an easy feat since he could barely stand, but made difficult by the fact that her coat was sliding down one shoulder. She grabbed for it while trying to hold him back, but pushing against his chest was like pushing against a stone wall. "Conor. Stop."

Mr. Kay called on his dart-throwing friends to help him. They stood gape-mouthed for now. Ellery prayed they remained so. At this point, she couldn't be sure who'd win such a battle. Conor sick was bad enough. Conor dead and she may as well stake herself out and wait for Asher and his pets to come and get her.

"Move aside," Conor ordered.

"No. You're sick. You're not thinking, and you're going to get us tossed out of here."

He advanced on Mr. Kay, dragging Ellery with him. "That bastard stole Ysbel's ring."

"Careful tossing that word around. I might step aside and let him have at you." The coat fell open again, giving one and all a great look at her legs, but by this point Ellery was past caring. "Stop, you great lumpen bullock."

Ellery was quick. No matter which way he turned, she was there. But beneath her hands, a change was taking place. His chest was broadening, if that was possible. His arms pulsed as if the muscles would burst through the skin. His eyes glowed yellow as suns in a face that was his and yet not, the angles hardening, the jawline lengthening. And, Good God. Fangs?

She jumped back as if his touch scalded.

"He's one of them," Mr. Kay yelled. "Knew it, I did. One of them *Others*. A monster." He plucked a knife from behind the long counter. "Boys, get him. Before he springs."

"Out of my way, Ellery," Conor growled.

"They'll kill you."

He flashed her a predatory smile. "Do you really think so? Move, or you'll end up as dead as your father."

A knot formed in her chest. Stunned, she stepped aside, the fight sucked out of her by those horrible words. But around her the chaos still swirled.

"Corner him," the voices shouted. "Hold him there. Watch that sticker of his."

"Hold!" a new voice shouted. The man at the corner table stood up, his round face grim.

Blood and smoke disappeared back into memory, her father's staring eyes vanished beneath Conor's furious glare. She held out a hand to stall the three others. "He's fevered, and no harm to you. He doesn't know what he's doing."

Conor's animal-stare moved slowly over them. She felt like a rabbit caught in the mesmerizing gaze of the wolf.

"Enough. All of you," the man in the corner said, and Ellery sensed the balance of power in the room shift in her favor.

Even Conor hesitated under the command. Although that might have been weakness. Already, the beast was fading back into the man. He wavered on his feet, and Ellery rushed to catch him. She braced herself against the stair railing, trying not to think of the transformation she'd just witnessed. What else about him didn't she know?

"Bugger off, Evan," the innkeeper said.

"I won't have you stirring up trouble," the man answered.

"Me?" Mr. Kay sounded aggrieved. "You saw what he done. Tried to murder us."

"He's sick," Ellery interrupted.

All eyes flicked to her, making her suddenly aware of the state of her dress. The open coat showed off her bare legs. Conor's jacket hung askew off one shoulder. With as much grace as she could muster, she pulled the jacket up and swung the coat closed around her legs.

Evan stepped forward, placing himself between Conor and the men. "He calls on the animal spirit to fight through him. That's powerful magic."

"He didn't mean to," Ellery said. "He suffers from mage sickness. He can barely stand, let alone fight. And he thought Mr. Kay had taken the ring. It was my fault. All of it."

"Your fault? How so?"

"I was trying to get him a doctor, but we haven't any money."

Evan studied Conor's slack features, his shaking limbs. Now that the fever madness had passed, he trembled as if palsied, even his voice gone.

"If it's truly mage sickness, no doctor can help him. Only time and his own strengths."

"Get him out of here, Evan," Mr. Kay repeated. "He's one of them. He's dangerous."

Evan shook his head, and Ellery wondered how she hadn't noticed how wise and kind his eyes were. "He'd be more dangerous if we let him loose."

"I won't stand for it," Mr. Kay warned, but Evan was already taking Ellery's place at Conor's side, helping him up the stairs.

"Come. Help me get him back to bed."

Ellery glanced back.

"Evan." Mr. Kay stood between the dart players, his face splotched with unreleased fury.

Evan never even paused or answered.

"Are you sure we can stay?" Ellery asked.

Evan dropped Conor's unresponsive body back onto the rickety bed. "Only until he's well enough to travel. Those men downstairs can be bought or threatened, but not for long. I can't guarantee your safety more than a day or so. Once an *Other* reveals himself, it's safer if he disappears."

"Other," she hesitated, "*Others* come here?"

Evan straightened from tucking the blankets around Conor. "Many. This is a place of refuge."

"Some refuge."

"My brother-in-law worries over his sister and his daughter living with such people." Evan offered her a smile. "And being dependent on my charity also grates on his disposition."

"But what can I do?"

"Rest. Sleep. He will mend, or he will die. That's the way of mage sickness."

Perfect. Mend and she had to confront the fact that her traveling companion was part wolf and may be her father's killer. Die, and she had to face the *Keun Marow* alone. Neither one a thought to make sleep come easier.

"Well?"

Conor woke to Ellery spinning in a circle, showing off a dress of sprigged muslin. Was this another dream? He'd been drowning in a swamp of hallucinations, each nightmare ending with his waking—or so he thought until the next nightmare began. So he couldn't be entirely sure. Although, he had to admit that this one was a thousand times better than any he'd had yet. "Are you real?" His voice sounded thick and croaky. He cleared his throat. "Or are you another bad dream?"

"So I'm a bad dream now, am I? That's rich."

Conor pushed himself up on the pillow, even though it made his head swim. He wanted to say he preferred the half-naked look, but doubted by the challenge in her eye that it would go over well.

What could he say? The cut was simple, the style plain, but Ellery's height and generous curves filled it to perfection. Even the color suited her dusky skin and picked up the brilliance of her blue eyes. She brushed the bed, and it took all his will to stop himself from dragging her by the skirts in beside him. Then reality hit, and he felt sick all over again.

"It's better for traveling," he answered lamely. "A lot of buttons, though."

Her expression showed exactly what she thought of his answer. "You're just grouchy because I won't let you get out of bed until you've had a day to rest."

"If you hadn't forgotten, we're being hunted."

She settled at the edge of his bed. "I haven't, but thank you for reminding me. We won't be any better off if you fall ill again on the road. At least here, we have a roof over our heads."

"You take great stock in ceilings," he commented.

"Try living without one."

Her eyes stole to the window. When they met his again, the earlier light in them was gone. Hesitation and worry clouded their depths.

"Do you remember last night?"

Oh God, what had he done? What had he said? Had he tried groping her in his sleep? Or stolen a kiss? Did he snore? By the look in her eye, it was much worse. He had a moment's panic that she'd found out the reliquary's secret, but no. She would have been long gone if she'd made that discovery. "Very little," he answered, vying for time. "I expect you're about to fill me in on the gruesome details."

She twisted her hands in her lap, shifted about on the bed. Sighed. She was vying for time too, it seemed. Finally, she spoke. "I've been thinking since you woke how to speak with you, what words to use to ask the questions."

"I hadn't considered you the timid type."

"I'm not. Straight forward and bull-headed, that's me. But that's when I'm dealing with the world I know. You're from an entirely different world where different rules apply. You tell me to trust you. You tell me I can't understand. But damn it. I want to understand. I deserve to be trusted in return."

Clanging anvils filled his head, he felt like something

scraped off a boot heel, and now Ellery was carping at him. He closed his eyes.

"Don't you get sick on me again, Conor Bligh. I want to—"

The force of her thought pushed through the pain. "A *Heller*," he spoke over her, not allowing her to finish. "That's what you wanted to know, isn't it? I'm what they call a *Heller*."

Chapter Eleven

How had she found that out? He'd been careful not to betray himself with any hint of that side of him. She'd been accepting of so much already. "It's an *Other* with the ability to call on the powers of his or her fetch animal. Even to take on some of the characteristics of that animal. But how—"

It was her turn to cut him off. "You attacked the landlord."

The men. Ysbel's ring.

His stomach lurched as he remembered. He'd assumed it was just another dream. His hand found his pocket.

"Are you looking for these?" Ellery handed him the pearl and the ring.

Thanks to Asher, the wolf-head ring was all he had left of his sister. When the time came, revenge would be sweet and very painful. He shoved both deep into his pocket.

"I thought I could pay for a doctor," Ellery said.

"He would have been useless."

"So I was told." She picked at the bedcovers, obviously uneasy. "It seemed like a good idea at the time."

She jerked to her feet, paced restlessly, confusion clouding her face.

"The pearl was yours," he said, hoping to break through the

tense silence. "It was the one I nicked from Mr. Porter. I wonder if he's noticed yet."

She shot him a sharp look. "You're supposed to be indestructible. What happened?"

No more questions about the change? Could he be so lucky? Or had she come so far that nothing ruffled her anymore. Either way, he wouldn't argue.

"I wish I knew," he answered. "The *Keun Marow*'s poison affects *fey* power. Disrupts it. Can even kill if enough of it gets in your system. When I took on your wounds, I took on the poison. I knew that would happen and was prepared. But not for the severity of the collapse. It was like being infected by a hundred such hounds instead of only one."

She cocked her head at a questioning angle. "You've got the reliquary. You don't need me anymore. Why do you care what happens to me?"

"Asher is after you because of me." What a smooth liar he was becoming. With his hand in his pocket, he tumbled the ring between his fingers. Ellery Reskeen would not stand between him and his task. No matter how dear she was or how desirable. He cut her off before she could ask him something else he couldn't answer. "You were either very brave or very foolish to get involved last night."

She offered him a crooked smile. "Probably a bit of both. But I wasn't alone. Evan helped. He brought me the dress, too. You owe him a pound and six shillings for it, by the way. He's told us to keep out of sight while we're here. He isn't sure how long he can guarantee our safety."

"Now that I've revealed myself as *Other*, you mean." It must have been the mother of all cock-ups if Evan had interceded. Despite the reputation of his inn among the *Other*, he didn't like any attention drawn to the fact. His normal clientele weren't so forgiving of strange doings and stranger people. Conor hoped he hadn't bollixed things up for him too badly. He'd accused Ellery of leaving a trail for

Asher and here he'd done everything but paint a bull's-eye on their backs.

"Will it happen again? Your changing like that?"

"No. It's a power, but one I use sparingly. The discipline and magic it requires make it dangerous. Draw on the power too often or too deeply and there's no turning back. The man becomes lost. The beast takes over."

She leaned back against the windowsill, pushed her curls off her face. "It seems everything you do is dangerous."

He gave a short dry laugh. "Now, you're catching on."

She watched him sleep, damning herself for the worst sort of coward. All day they had spent talking. She could have brought up her father a million different ways. But every time, she shied away, and the question remained unasked.

But what a question.

Did you kill my father?

How could anyone drop that into the middle of a conversation nonchalantly?

They'd talked of her father. She'd somehow found herself telling Conor long tales of her childhood. Of the days before her mother died when her father's regiment had been stationed in the Leewards. Of pleading with him to take her along when he was sent home. Of clutching at his legs while his friends laughed or looked away until he'd finally been shamed into relenting. And later as they'd moved back and forth between stations at home and on the continent, she told Conor of how she gave ground as each new mistress entered her father's life, took up the household duties as they moved on.

Security revolved in making herself indispensable, anticipating his needs before he did. Being a doormat when sometimes all she wanted was to throw his haversack back at him and never see another scarlet jacket again.

She liked to think they did well together after a fashion. And if there hadn't been love, there had been respect and affection and laughter. It could have been so much worse.

Conor had listened and told his own stories. Stories of growing up in Cornwall, living in a house full of aunts and uncles and cousins, the comings and goings of a family balanced between the mortal world and the *fey*. He laughed, remembering the pranks he and his cousin, Ruan played on the others. His voice grew proud as he spoke of his gram's untiring work as a healer in the neighborhood, of his father's quiet strength as he tended his estate. The deep love he felt for them all was evident in every word. Ellery couldn't help the envy that gnawed at her. She would have given her life to have such a family—or any family.

She'd asked him only once about Ysbel, the sister he'd lost. His eyes had gone black and empty. The pitiless stare of the *fey*. "My cousin Simon handed her over to Asher. Betrayed her to her death."

But not once had she asked the question that gnawed at her stomach and twisted her insides until she stalked the corners of the room, measuring out the paces hour after hour.

Did you kill my father?

"You don't have to do this, Ellery."

She spun around, her heart leaping in her chest.

Conor was awake and watching her restless fuming.

"Don't startle me like that," she snapped even as a wild fluttering started in her stomach. She couldn't put it off forever. Now was her chance.

He regarded her from eyes mellowed by sleep, yet still she felt like he could pick out every thought in her head. "You don't have to guard me like an invalid—or a madman."

"What are you talking about?"

"I can tell you're uncomfortable."

"I'm not."

He didn't let her finish. "There's a reason mortals know so little of the *fey* realm. It's frightening—unnatural."

"But you're human—strange, to be sure, but not unnatural." She tried laughing off his comment as she started pacing again.

He pushed himself up against the headboard, the quilt falling to his lap.

She swallowed hard at the sight of his chest, at the stippled tattoos that encircled his upper arms, raced across his collarbones, twined over his shoulders. Despite every warning signal, she ached for his touch. For that hungry anticipation she'd experienced when he'd laid his hands on her before. She knew he sensed her scrutiny, but what he thought was hidden in the unfathomable reaches of his eyes.

"There's a new wariness in you," he said. "A tension. Is it because of what I am? Because you saw me shift?"

She tried recreating the shock she'd felt at the changes in him. Tried to work up some horror or revulsion at the marks of the *amhas-draoi* that covered his body. It just wasn't there.

She paused at the hearth. Wanting him and wanting to know the truth warred within her. "It's not that." She ran her fingers across the chimneypiece, fiddled with the candles.

"Then what?" He motioned to the bed. "Come. Sit. I can't concentrate with you fidgeting like that."

She dragged herself over to the bed, sat as close to the edge as she could without making it seem like she was avoiding him. But even there, the heat of his body sent a dizzying wave of need through her. This was ridiculous. She was a grown woman who'd lived cheek by jowl with men all her life. How was it that this man could light fires in her when no man before had ever even caused a spark? It wasn't fair.

He reached out a hand as if he might caress her. Her stomach tightened, waiting for his touch. But before his fingers brushed her face, his hand dropped back to the bed. "Here."

He dug into the pocket of his breeches, came up with the pearl. "I told you before. It's yours. I got it for you."

She took it from him, hating her need, hating her fear. Hating her suspicions. Tears swam in her eyes. She sniffed and gave a shaky laugh. "How did you do it?"

He plucked the pearl from her palm, twisted his wrist in a quick move, bringing his other hand over the top. Flashing her a mischievous smile, he opened his hands. No pearl. "The hand is faster than the eye, and Mr. Porter is none the wiser."

She glanced over at his sword, hanging where she'd left it on the peg by the door. "I thought you might have killed him."

With another quick movement of his wrist, the pearl reappeared. He handed it back to her. "Dealing death is a serious business. I don't kill innocents for sport." His voice hardened. "But I do what I have to do."

"Did you have to kill my father?" There. She said it.

His body grew still, a quick inrush of breath his only visible reaction. She waited, but he didn't answer. He stared out the window, his eyes fixed on a point far distant or deep within. She couldn't tell. The empty silence between them lengthened, stretched until she couldn't stand it. She threw herself to her feet, her nails digging into her palms.

"Conor?"

The gaze he turned on her was as cold and cruel as death. "Yes, Ellery. I had to kill him. There was no other way."

Ellery's pulse skittered in her throat, her blue eyes held the shine of unshed tears.

Conor wanted to wrap his arms around her, hold her while she wept. He fought to hold his hands in his lap. It was time to put the temptation aside once and for all. "He got in the way," he said.

"And so you butchered him. I saw the blood. That wasn't a killing. It was a massacre. You killed them all."

"Think what you like. Asher was denied the reliquary."

"And that was all that mattered to you. Not that my father had a family, people who cared about him."

"According to you, he left behind only a bastard daughter and his latest whore who found a new bed partner within twenty-four hours." His voice was purposefully cold and mocking.

"You filthy prick."

"He broke the seals. If Asher loose is a threat, the Triad reunited would shake the world to its knees."

"I wouldn't know," she countered. "I don't know anything except what you've told me. You could be making this all up. Asher could be a lie, like everything else."

"I never lied to you, Ellery. Not once." He just hadn't told her everything. That was entirely different. That was necessary.

"No. You just neglected to tell me you'd murdered my father and his men in cold blood."

He hated this. Hated the loathing in her eyes, the disgust in her voice. But he wouldn't deny her accusations. Let her think the worst of him. It made what he had to do easier.

"It was a battle," he said. "Casualties happen. Coruna, Talavera, Badajoz. Those men might have died a thousand different places."

"But they didn't, did they? They died at the chapel in San Salas. How can I be sure I'm not next?"

She struck the rawest nerve. He slammed the side of his fist into the wall, the plaster crumbling beneath his temper. "I kill for a purpose."

"Your purpose, Conor. Not mine." She wheeled away from him. Crossed the room. "I'll try my luck on my own. I've survived this long."

He'd succeeded too well. He'd meant to put distance between them. He never intended for her to leave. The woman was a bundle of courage, foolishness, and stubborn independence. It's what he admired about her. And what would get her killed. "Asher will find you. The *Keun Marow* will track you."

She threw his greatcoat over her, buttoned it. "Why? Why bother with me? I no longer own the reliquary."

He swung his legs off the bed. Fought to stand. "He doesn't know that."

"I'll disappear. I can do that easily enough. London. Newcastle. Edinburgh. There are a million places a woman alone can vanish."

Events were spinning out of control. It was time to rein her in. "You haven't any money," he pointed out with smug relish.

She laughed and with a choreographed flick of her wrist revealed the pearl. "Haven't I?" She opened the door. Glancing back, her blue eyes blazed with fury. "*Nos dha*, Mr. Bligh. And may it be a sleep of the damned."

Chapter Twelve

What a fool she'd been. What a complete fool. She'd known. That made it even worse. She'd known since their conversations in the cottage that Conor had played a part in her father's death. The things he'd said. The things he hadn't. But she'd pushed aside the questions, ignored the doubts. She'd wanted to believe in him. And why? Because she was tired of being lonely. Because he'd kissed her. Because every time he looked at her, she felt a strength and a power that had nothing to do with magic.

What a pathetic mess she was.

An icy wind rushed down the street, sending last year's leaves flying. Shutters slammed on their hinges and the branches above her creaked and scraped. She jogged up the street, hugging the shadows. Footsteps echoed behind her. Wishing she still carried Conor's dagger, she backed herself against the closest building as two very human men rounded the corner and disappeared up the street. Letting out the breath she didn't know she'd been holding, she started walking, more quickly now. This track led south, toward the toll road. From there, she could choose any direction, any destination.

As she neared the edge of the village, the houses lay farther apart, separated by copses of scrubby trees and long fields of rocky pasture. She kept to the verge as the road sank between high earth walls topped by bramble hedges. But with each step, the air thickened like smoke. Her lungs burned as she fought to breathe, and she sank to the ground. It's the only thing that saved her.

"Your kinsman's led us a dance." The voice didn't sound human, more like the crackle of crunching leaves, the sough of the wind. "But he's mine. Tonight."

She crushed herself back into the underbrush, but the words floated above. The conversation took place in the copse on the other side of the hedge.

"It's a risk bringing them here," came the reply. "Too many people. Too much at stake should they be seen."

"'Tis not your place to guide my steps. Only to ease my way. Remember that." Ellery flinched at the venom concentrated in that dry, raspy voice.

"I've gotten you this far, haven't I?"

"The bargain's not complete until Bligh is dealt with and the reliquary is mine."

Ice formed around her heart as she gripped the roots of the hedge.

"Conor's no easy mark," the second voice spoke again.

"That's why I have you. You're going to get me Bligh, just as you did his sister."

There was a long silence. The second voice spoke again, the words clipped with emotion. "You didn't have to kill—"

"Enough."

Glancing up through the branches, she choked off a gasp.

The creature speaking seemed human. He wore a frock coat, knee breeches and a starched neckcloth. But his pale skin was pulled mask-like over bones sharp as knives, and his fingers resembled claws as they clutched his cane.

Asher. It had to be.

Could she leave Conor to that?

"What of the girl?" Asher's companion was a tall, rangy man. But she could make out little else. He stood deep in the gloom of the copse, hidden from the moon's faint shine.

Asher on the other hand stood full in the light, giving Ellery plenty of opportunity to watch the dark emotions flit across his evil features. "The soldier's daughter? Her gifts interest me. But her end is certain. She cannot be allowed to live."

Panic choked her, but she struggled to control it. Conor had been telling the truth. She felt the ripple of death that washed off Asher in fetid waves. It soured the air, salted the earth, poisoned all it touched.

She'd run from Conor. And now Conor was her only hope.

Inching on her belly, ignoring the grasping tangle of briars, she climbed down from the hedge. Step by silent step, she crept up the road back toward the village. Every moment, she waited for a shout from behind. A blast of magic. The keening wail of the *Keun Marow*. But Asher and his companion were too deep in conversation to note her passing, and the night kept her secret.

Ellery knew something was wrong. A crowd swelled the doorway of the tavern, spilling into the street. Shouts and angry words carried back to her on an ill breeze. Clouds condensed overhead, smothering the moon, and Ellery shivered, sensing Asher's power in these doings, though she couldn't explain why. Perhaps it was only her imagination run wild. Though by now, the real world was far outstripping anything her imagination could conjure.

Asher's net was closing. He wanted her. Then he wanted her dead. This was all Conor's fault. And Conor was going to fix it. He'd saved her once. He could do it again. She only needed to reach him.

A man's thick voice shouted, "He tried to kill 'em. Run mad, he is."

Another echoed the accusation.

Standing on her toes, she fought to see over the heads of the men. Struggled to catch a glimpse of Conor or hear a snarled threat as he settled them with one arrogant word. Even the reassuring presence of Evan would have calmed her runaway pulse. So far, the men were holding back. But she knew it would take but one wrong word or gesture to turn the rabble into a mob.

Evan had given them two days to be gone from here. Their time was up in more ways than one.

She pushed her way through.

Conor stood on the bottom step, a hand on the banister. Only Ellery seemed to notice it was the one thing keeping him upright. He'd dressed in haste, his shirt untucked and buttoned askew, the mage marks twining across his collarbones vivid in the lamplight. "I've no quarrel with you, Mr. Kay." He raked the gathering with a warning look. "Nor with your friends."

Emboldened by the crowd, Mr. Kay stepped forward. "We're a God-fearing folk. We don't want your devilry in our village."

"Which is why I'm leaving. Let me pass, and I'll cause no trouble."

"It's too late," Ellery called out. Conor's attention shifted to her with what she thought was relief. "The trouble's already here. He's found us."

"Where?"

The men jostled her as she spoke. "South of the village. He's not alone. He travels with a man."

Conor's face remained grave, but his eyes glittered with a new malice. "Not a man, Ellery. A traitor and a coward. My cousin, Simon."

A shiver of drawn steel drew her eye. "No more talking," Mr. Kay said. "I've had all I can take of your kind."

His bravado inspired the men to renew their calls for Conor's blood, pushing forward into the taproom, knocking Ellery aside.

"Look out!" she shouted.

But Conor hadn't needed her warning. His sword appeared before she'd finished speaking, his stance that of a warrior poised for battle. "You'll not win this fight." Conor's voice held the inhuman echo of the *fey*. "It's foolish to try."

As he shifted from foot to foot, light bounced blue and silver from his blade. His gaze became a darkling stare, his eyes gone hard and black as obsidian. Ellery held her breath, knowing that weak as he was, Conor could still end this standoff anytime he chose. One slash of his sword or one spell's summoning would scatter this group in terror. Yet he held back. Waited for Mr. Kay to decide the outcome.

"Conor," she urged. "We have to leave. Now."

"Mr. Kay?" Conor asked, "what say you? Do we finish this?" He strung out each word, enunciating every syllable. Low-voiced. Smooth. His eyes never wavering from the innkeeper. "Call them off," he said. "It's over."

Her breath came in short painful gasps as if a giant hand gripped her throat. Her chest constricted, her lungs unable to expand. "Conor," she whispered, incapable of speaking over the blood roaring in her ears.

Dazed, Mr. Kay lowered his weapon and backed up. The men behind him faltered, confused. Conor remained where he was. Unmoving. Immovable. Sweat damped his shirt, sheened his face. His hands trembled. For all his show of power, the mage sickness still weakened him.

A high keening broke the tense silence, rose and fell as the *Keun Marow* tracked them. Uneasy, the men murmured. Glanced about.

Conor put out a hand. "Come, Ellery."

"I can't."

"Now's not the time to argue over past mistakes."

"No. I mean I can't move. Can't breathe."

Conor gripped her. Embraced her. Held her so that their hearts met and matched. This time she knew what he was doing. This time she made herself ignore the rush of excitement that accompanied his touch. There was nothing of the lover about him. He took her weakness. That was all.

The suffocating tightness eased, and she immediately pushed him away.

A shadow of icy amusement passed across his face. "Better?" he asked.

Determined to keep her distance, she gave a curt nod. "Well enough."

She stumbled toward the door through the men who moved aside as if they walked in a trance. "What did you do to them?"

As he passed, he flashed a sharp glance at Mr. Kay and the others. "The power of the *leveryas*. A touch of it can distract. In its strongest form, it can compel. Control."

Outside, the cries came again. Louder. Closer as the *Keun Marow* encircled the village. Seeking their trail. Ellery's throat began to close again. "We'll never outrun them."

"Not on foot." Conor shoved open the stable door. Led two horses from their stalls. "We'll ride."

"Now we're horse thieves?"

He threw a saddle over the first horse, cinching the girth. "It's steal or die. In my book, that leaves one choice." He paused in the middle of buckling the bridle. "If you insist, I'll send them payment—with interest." He shot her a devil grin.

She knew she was being ridiculous. She'd come to him for rescue, and he was doing his best. And it wasn't as if she hadn't done the same and worse in her day. But her earlier resentment flared, so interwoven with panic and horror, she wasn't sure which emotion held sway. She tried focusing on saddling her frightened horse. The animal sidled and backed, jostling her as she worked.

Every breath burned her lungs. Worked its way up her throat. Asher must be near. She'd never experienced such an overpowering sense of helplessness.

"Mount up." Conor tossed her into the saddle. Strapped his dagger to her waist. His touch was reassuring, his face grim. "Head southwest. Towards Penzance. Make for the village of Polvossa. The house is called Daggerfell. You'll find safety there. Whatever you do, don't stop. Don't look behind you."

His voice sounded muffled as if he spoke to her through a fog.

A man stepped from the shadows. Asher. Tall and thin with a look of madness in his face. In his hand, he held a barbed sword, the jagged-edged sides stained red and black. "Going so soon? And we've only just arrived."

Conor slid in front of her, his own sword drawn.

A buzzing erupted in Ellery's head like the sounding of a thousand bees. Everything around her wavered as if she saw it through water or fire.

Asher's red lips curled back to show jagged teeth. "I see your manners have yet to improve, *amhas-draoi*. You haven't introduced me to your companion." His eyes flicked to her. "Pretty thing, and with so much the look of her father, don't you think?"

Her hand sought out Conor's dagger, her fingers wrapping themselves familiarly around the hilt. For some reason, this seemed to steady her. The buzzing subsided. The figures before her grew solid and real again.

"You'll not have her." Conor's voice held a threatening weight.

Asher reached out. Ran the tip of one claw-like finger down Conor's blade. He never moved. Never flinched. "Won't I? Once I choose to do something, I generally have my way. Ask your sister." His eyes lit with an evil glow. "Oh, that's right. You can't. Well then, ask your cousin instead." He motioned for another to step forward. "I love family reunions."

It was the villain from the woods. Seeing them together, the Bligh resemblance was obvious. He was as tall as Conor and with the same arrogant pose, but this man's face held only traces of Conor's hard beauty.

Conor's whole body seemed to vibrate with rage. This time, the sword wavered. His face became white as chalk. "I should bury this blade in your chest and be done."

"You could try," the man answered, nervously fingering the same wolf-head ring she'd seen on Conor.

"What was your price for handing her over, Simon? What lies did he promise you?"

Though he worked to look unmoved, Simon winced; a shadow passed over him. Then he shrugged. "What does anyone want? Power, of course." He shook his head. "You wouldn't understand. You were always the gifted one. The golden child. Now it's my turn."

"But Ysbel—" Conor's voice broke; his hands shook.

Ellery's grip tightened on the dagger. If Asher caught even a hint of Conor's true condition, it was over. The taunts would end in bloodshed.

"Enough," Asher commanded. "I shall take the girl."

Conor's lips curled in a cruel smile. "You'll not have her."

Asher laughed. "You don't think you'll stop me? You couldn't save your sister. This one will be much the same." He thrust, aiming his barbed sword at Conor's stomach, meeting his blade instead in a shower of sparks.

Her horse shied, Ellery's knees tightened on the saddle as she steadied herself. Adjusted her grip on the knife. Found the best angle. Aimed. Released.

Conor was retreating beneath Asher's attack when her blade found the demon's back. Buried itself hilt-deep into the flesh below his left lung.

A wind whipped around her, a maelstrom that burned and

chilled her both. She threw a hand up to shield her eyes. Then it was silent. And Asher was gone. Simon was a memory.

She and Conor were alone once again in the stable.

She slid off the horse. Her knees shook as she landed. Her whole body shook by the time she'd crossed the room to Conor. "What happened?"

Conor held his side, his breath coming in ragged gasps. He nodded toward the dagger that lay on the stable floor. "Iron. It disrupted Asher's magic."

"Well, that's it then. It wasn't nearly as difficult as you made it seem."

"He's not dead, Ellery. Only interrupted." He struggled up, bit off a curse. "Somehow his wards were breached. Enough to allow you to penetrate with that dagger. He'll need time to recover before he returns." He dabbed a hand at a long bloody weal down his side, hissing in pain. "It's a reprieve, not a victory."

She reached for him. "You need help."

"No," he barked, causing Ellery to flinch. "You still don't understand. He knows about you now. You've got to get out of here."

He caught up her horse's reins, leading him out of the stable. "Remember. South toward Penzance."

She mounted, gathering the horse beneath her. "Aren't you coming with me?"

Conor's head came up, his eyes trained on the darkness beyond the yard. "I'll catch up. We've stopped Asher for now, but his hounds still follow. I need to lead them away. Muddy the trail."

He put out a hand, cupped her cheek. Regret saddened his eyes, and Ellery felt he wanted to tell her something.

Despite her earlier anger, she reached down, caressing the strong line of his jaw. His stubble roughed her fingers, and she thought he moved into her touch. Then the low hungry howl of the *Keun Marow* sounded from the moorlands to the north.

Conor stepped back. Struck her horse hard on the rump. Shouted at her to go.

The horse plunged forward out of the stable yard. She turned its head south, rowling its flank with her heel, leaning into its neck. Against orders, she glanced back. One moment, Conor stood in the road. The next, he vanished.

"You better stay safe, you great lumpen bullock," she whispered.

Chapter Thirteen

Clouds hid the moon, bringing with them a cold, spitting rain. Mud sucked at the tired horse's legs, but Conor held it to the swollen stream bed. He'd not heard or felt the *Keun Marow*'s presence since midnight, but he'd take no chances. Now that Asher knew about Ellery's existence, all he'd worked for up to this moment was thrown into jeopardy. He needed to keep her safe. And out of the way until Beltane. But being weak as a damned kitten wasn't helping.

He steered the horse up out of the water, back towards the road leading south out of Lanivet. If Ellery had followed instructions—not a given, as he was finding out—she'd have passed this way only a short while before him. He'd cut time and miles from his journey by leaving the roads, using remote tracks and paths only the animal instincts of the *Heller* could find in this weather.

The rain increased, a downpour more suited to November than April. Asher may be restrained by the mortal world, but he was not without power. Which brought Conor right back to his greatest problem. What to do with Ellery until Beltane.

The steady plod of hoofbeats carried back to him first. Peering through the gloom, he caught sight of a horse and rider, heads bowed against the storm.

His mount gave a whinny of welcome. The rider whipped her head around, a grim determination in her white face. A dull gleam flashed off the knife she held out in front of her. Then she recognized him.

"I almost buried this in your chest," she commented, sheathing the dagger. She was safe for now, and all her earlier fury had returned.

He pulled his horse alongside. "Would that have been before or after you realized it was me and not Asher?"

She bit her lip and looked away, but Conor noted the tightening of her hands upon the reins and the stiffened square of her shoulders. An angry brittle silence fell over them.

"You should have told me," she said finally, without looking up.

"And when should I have done that?" he asked. "When you were holding a gun to my chest? Or when I was trying to explain the *fey* to you and hope you didn't think I was a madman? Or mayhap when you were lying wounded from a *Keun Marow* attack?"

"Don't be ridiculous," she muttered.

"And what would you have done if I'd told you I killed your father?"

She flinched.

"Look at me, Ellery. How could I explain such a thing to you and make you understand?"

She faced him. "You couldn't then. But now. Perhaps. There is a chance I'll listen."

He had wielded her father's death as a weapon, hoping to hold her at bay. He'd not foreseen her walking out that door, enough hatred in her gaze to punch a hole through him. And that miscalculation had almost unmanned him. The shock of it still stung. He couldn't allow her to run again. She was too important to his mission.

No. That wasn't the real danger.

She was becoming too important to him.

"Very well. But hear me through before you judge."

"Fair enough," she answered.

But would she truly understand? And why did it suddenly matter so much to him that she did?

"To your father, the reliquary was an artifact—a treasure of the *fey* realm to be examined," he explained. "I had to stop the Triad's release. By closing the seals with the blood of the guilty. The trespasser."

"My father."

"Yes. But Asher had already been freed. Not even your father's death could undo that damage. It needed a greater magic than I wield. To effect a true victory, I must draw on the deeper magics of the *fey*. Those that surface only in the thin places and peak at the turning of the seasons."

"Beltane. Lands End," she said.

"Just so. I must bring the reliquary to the stones of Ilcum Bledh by dusk on April's last day. There, at the mouth of the quoit, I can reseal it. I can send Asher back to join his brothers. I can end it," he said, despite knowing now that every moment with her was turning him from his chosen path.

Ellery sat, head bowed, for long minutes after.

Conor waited for her to rant, curse him, or simply ride away. Fog swirled around their feet, drifted up over them until they wandered through a cloud. No sound but their own breathing. The rhythm of the horses as they traveled. When she finally looked at him, not even his keen eyesight could penetrate the unfathomable expression in her eyes. "If it was anyone but you," she said.

"I'm *amhas-draoi*. I do what I must."

"The good little soldier," she mocked, her voice bitter.

"I regret that it's caused you sorrow." He paused. "I know grief, too."

"But do you know where you're going?" She rubbed the back of her hand across her eyes, her cheeks damp with rain or tears. He couldn't tell. His muscles knotted, waiting. "I'm freezing and tired and I have to pee."

"I do." He felt a rush of release, immediately replaced by a strange sense of excitement. It was the last place he wanted to go. He'd avoided it for over a year, but he'd run out of options. "Daggerfell," he answered. "I'm going home."

The wind howled, sending needles of rain against Ellery's skin. It had been like this for hours before Conor turned them off the road and through a bricked gateway. Her whole body ached, and her head was muzzy with exhaustion. A bed was all she wanted. A bed and at least a full day to sleep with no interruptions and no guilt. Heaven.

She had a hazy impression of an imposing approach of terraces and steps, then a house with gables and a tower and rows of windows. Lighted lamps swung in their brackets on either side of the porch and somewhere a gate squeaked. She'd have been impressed if she hadn't been so damn tired.

She slithered from her horse, caught in Conor's arms before she could drop to her knees in the mud.

"We're here. We're safe," he said.

The queasy gut-wrenching panic that had followed her all night slowly dissipated. But without the tension, the exhaustion only rushed in faster to take its place.

"Shall they be glad to see us, do you think?" Ellery squinted up at the house, but the storm whipped the sodden collar of her coat into her face, and rain stung her eyes.

Conor seemed surprised. "They're family, and this is my home. Glad is nothing to do with it."

She shot him a look. "So you don't know either."

A groom appeared out of the darkness, doffed his cap, shouting to be heard over the wind. "Welcome back, Master Conor. Expecting you, we were." His gaze rested on Ellery for a moment. "The girl as well." He nodded as he led the horses away.

"Conor?" she prompted. "What did he mean they were expecting us?"

But Conor had already taken her hand to pull her up into the shelter of the porch.

She shook the water out of her hair, staring up at the carvings above the nail-studded door. The wolf's head symbol of the Blighs surrounded by a crown of leaves. She glanced over at Conor, but he took no notice. He stood stone-faced, rigid as the carving with one hand poised on the door handle.

It moved from under his grasp, thrown open from the other side. "You're late." A lean gentleman with shaggy dark hair and sharp gray eyes ushered them in, glancing out into the wild storm with a troubled look. "We thought you'd be here hours ago. Mishap on the road?"

"Nothing I couldn't handle, Father," Conor replied. "This is Ellery Reskeen." He paused. "A traveling companion."

Conor's father frowned. "We heard about her, too." He sketched her a bow. "Welcome, Miss Reskeen. I'm Mikhal Bligh. This scoundrel's father. Our home is yours," his eyes flashed to Conor, "for as long as you have need of it."

As if suddenly aware of the water streaming off them, he laughed. "You look positively drowned. Here," he took Ellery's greatcoat, "let's get you dry."

"Thank you, sir," she said, reluctantly handing it over. Though soaked through, it had offered some warmth. Without it, the gooseflesh rose on Ellery's chilled skin. She rubbed her arms briskly and tried not to yawn. The flight south through the storm had been nightmarish. Couldn't he just show her a cot in some corner and save his courtesy for tomorrow when her brain might be functioning?

"Conor? Your jacket?" his father offered.

The two men's gazes locked as if each searched the other for something. Golden-yellow met steel gray. Both flint hard.

Both unyielding. Mikhal Bligh looked away first, his lips tight with concern. What did he see in Conor that made him look so solemn? Or was it something he didn't see?

An awkward silence followed. Was Conor going to explain their arrival? Her presence? She squirmed under the disapproving eye of Conor's father. She couldn't stand it. "I don't want you to think . . . I mean, there's nothing improper. That is to say between Conor and myself. I don't want you to get the wrong impression."

Mikhal surprised her by giving a shaky smile as he motioned for her to move out of the hall and into a long parlor. "No? More's the pity. He could use a strong woman to bring him back."

"Father," Conor warned.

But Mikhal only waved him off. "No more to be said on that for now." His gaze speared him. "But I've not finished with you. We will talk—later."

Conor shrugged.

His father crossed to a sideboard. Poured out a brandy for Conor, and glanced her way "Something to warm you, Miss Reskeen? A spiced wine? Claret? A cup of tea?"

Ellery's gaze swept the offerings. Settled on her usual. "Whiskey, please."

Mikhal raised a surprised eyebrow, but nodded and poured her out a bumper, which she downed in one quick gulp. It slid down with a smooth smoky heat before spreading its delicious warmth to every part of her body. Definitely not the hell-broth she was used to. That was like swallowing acid. And about as soothing. This was perfection.

"Where's Mother?" Conor asked.

"In her study as usual," Mikhal answered. "She knew you were coming, but you know her. Probably lost in an archaic translation or some obscure point of reference that can't wait."

"Yes, I'm sure that's it." But he didn't sound as if he believed it.

Their voices faded in and out as Ellery tried to follow the conversation. She was warm. She was relaxed. Couldn't anyone see all she wanted was sleep?

"Con? Is that you? We'd given you up for dead." A young woman hardly older than Ellery ran into the room, her muddy skirts rucked up to reveal riding boots. Her wet hair in a long braid over her shoulder. "Thought Asher was using your bones for toothpicks."

"Your confidence in me is overwhelming." For the first time in days, Conor's face relaxed into a wide easy smile. Made him look almost cheerful.

Mikhal shot her an irritated glance. "Morgan. Your tact certainly hasn't improved during your time with Scathach."

She'd been studying Ellery in open curiosity, but turned to dismiss Conor's father with a laugh. "Did you send me away to become a handmaiden or a shield maiden, Uncle?" She threw her arms around an unsuspecting Conor. "I've been searching every lane leading here since they told us you were on your way. Gram's even had Ruan scouring the neighborhood, and you know how he hates rising before noon when he's ashore."

"I thought you'd be in Skye tormenting your instructors." Conor frowned. "You haven't been kicked out of there, have you?"

Ellery didn't hear the answer, or what excuses he used to explain her presence. The steady stream of banter and welcome dissolved into gibberish, and the overheated room grew stuffy. She was so tired she wanted to cry.

Stepping back from the homecoming, Ellery felt lonelier amid the noise and confusion of these people than in all the days since Molly's death. She had an image of her quiet house tucked among the hills above Carnebwen and longed to be home. Alone. With her old life back.

Her eyes flicked to Conor's pinched, pale face. No, that

wasn't completely true. Not alone. Heat pooled deep in the pit of her stomach.

A voice sounded in her ear. Like water. Or music. "There will be time for such thoughts after a day and a night of sleep and rest. You deserve it."

Ellery spun around, the heat rushing from her stomach to her face.

A tiny woman stood at her elbow, her lined skin parchment thin, her silver hair not tucked beneath a mob cap like other little old ladies, but looped and braided and caught with silver combs. She smiled and patted Ellery's hand, her silver-gray eyes dancing. "*Kerneth*. Child. Wasn't I young once?"

Obviously, Conor wasn't the only one of his family to pick a thought from the air as others picked fruit from a tree. She'd have to learn to guard against such intrusions if she stayed here for long. "It's not like that between us," she explained.

"Isn't it?"

Ellery lost herself in those eyes. Swept up in them as if she witnessed the spinning of the stars, the vastness of the sea.

The old woman's voice deepened, became stronger. "My grandson needs you, make no mistake. Your part in this is not yet over."

Ellery's whole body tensed, and her mouth went dry. She shook her head, trying to focus, but a slash of pain ripped through her skull. She bit off a cry, but the spell was broken. Conor's grandmother was once more a fragile, stoop-shouldered dowager, nothing more than a twinkle in her kind eyes.

She tugged on Ellery's hand as she stepped among them.

The voices subsided. The others fell into line as if a general inspected them.

"Tact is not all that is lacking at Daggerfell these days, Mikhal Bligh," Conor's grandmother said. "Hospitality is also absent. Our guest needs sleep. Morgan and I will show her to her room."

* * *

The corridor was dimly lit. Her room was only slightly brighter with a fire burning low in the grate and a candelabra guttering by her bed. A shelf of books below a window. A vase of narcissus and early spring primroses. A patterned rug on the floor. It wasn't grand or intimidating. It was a comfortable, welcoming room. Snug and settled with age and a friendly charm. Not what she would have expected in the home of Conor Bligh.

A robe and nightgown lay across the bed. A pitcher and basin beside it on a stand. Everything as it should be. Everything as if they'd been expecting her arrival.

"Plenty of time for questions once you have rested. A tussle with Asher is no small matter and to come away unscathed is a victory in itself." Conor's grandmother Lowenna gestured to the bed. "Sleep now, child."

It did look soft. Ellery's whole body ached to fall across it without even undressing. Crawl beneath the quilts and stay there until they forced her out. But whether it was the restorative powers of the whiskey or her own irrepressible spirit, she already felt her mind cranking up. Spinning to understand. Sleep wouldn't come any time soon.

"I hope I haven't put anyone out by appearing out of the blue like this."

Lowenna looked around her as if she'd only now seen the room for the first time. Her eyes went flat and staring. "The house is emptier than it should be. More departures than arrivals these days."

An uncomfortable silence threatened to swallow Ellery. What could she say? She'd seen Simon. The jealousy and fear that prowled beneath his skin. The demon he'd chained himself to with the murder of his own cousin. She wished she were back to being too tired to care. Then suddenly it dawned on her. The simple beauty of the room. The homey feel of it. Oh, God. Her mouth went dry. A tightness ran down her back.

Across her shoulders. "This isn't Ysbel's room," she said. "Please tell me you didn't . . . I can't stay here."

Conor's grandmother laughed, and the panic subsided. "Relax. You aren't trespassing on sacred ground. Or rattling the chains of the dead. Ysbel's room is on this hall, but farther along. And locked."

She must have seen the ghost of a question in Ellery's expression. "Not to keep anyone out or anything in," she continued. "Simply due to a grief too new and a family too burdened with other matters to take the time."

Chapter Fourteen

Conor stretched his legs out in front of him. Another six inches and his feet would be smoldering amid the fire's embers. But still the chills gripped him. Sometimes so hard he clenched his teeth to stop their chattering. He crossed his arms over his chest in a vain attempt to keep warm and tried to concentrate on his father's words. Coming home could never be simple.

Mikhal sipped at his whiskey. "We hadn't much warning you were coming. The message arrived shortly after midnight."

"I'd forgotten how efficient are the ways of the *fey*."

"Yet in this case, helpful. We kept watches posted on the roads. Morgan, Ruan, even Jamys did his share."

"Asher or his hounds would have had them for breakfast."

"Do you think so? I think you overestimate this *fey* demon. Or underestimate your family." His father rose, plucked a rug from the back of a chair. Crossing the room, he dropped it in Conor's lap. "Here. This will help."

Conor thought about pushing it away, but he was too damn cold. He wrapped it over his shoulders, burrowing into the thick, soft wool. The worst eased.

"So where does the girl fit into all this?" his father added,

sitting back down. "You were never one to bring home strays."
His mouth curled into a patient smile.

Here's where it got tricky. What to reveal that didn't tip his
hand. He couldn't expose Ellery's part in the reliquary's discovery. His father wasn't stupid. He'd put it all together and try
to stop the ritual. But Conor had never been one to flaunt his
women in front of his family either. And Ellery deserved more
than to be thought of as his latest mistress.

"A pack of *Keun Marow* on my trail caught her scent instead. They tracked her to her house. Attacked it. I fought them
off, but couldn't leave her there to fend alone in case they returned." He paused, but nothing in his father's expression gave
any indication of his disbelief. He simply sipped at his
whiskey, his gray eyes boring into Conor like two ice shards.
He continued smoothly, "Asher's appearance threw another
spanner in the works. He tried taking Ellery. He wants her.
Like he wanted Ysbel. I won't let it happen a second time."

"So you brought her here for her safety. A valiant idea. I
only hope we don't scare her off in the first twenty-four
hours."

Conor laughed. "She doesn't scare easily." His laughter
turned to a cough that seized his lungs and clutched at his
chest. He gulped his own whiskey. Finished and then wished
he had the energy to get up and pour himself a second.

"You should see Jamys about the mage sickness." As if
reading his thoughts, his father got up and took Conor's
empty glass, refilling it. "He could enhance your healing.
Speed things up." He handed it back.

Conor took it gratefully. "It's better."

Mikhal ran a tired hand through his hair. "You always were
hard-headed. We're not without our gifts. We may not all be
amhas-draoi, but the blood of the *Other* runs in our veins as
surely as it flows in yours."

His father had managed that one smoothly. Turned the conversation right back to where Conor didn't want to take it.

"That's not what I meant. And you know it." He gripped the chair arms—hard. "After Ysbel's death, can you honestly believe this creature isn't as dangerous as I describe him?"

"Never think that, Conor. I know he's capable of inflicting great misery. We live under it every day. But it's you I worry about now. I see a change taking place. It's greatest in your eyes. They see more. Show less. The *fey* in you is taking over."

Conor threw himself to his feet, the rug sliding to the floor. "I'm doing what needs to be done. If that means pushing my powers to their limits, so be it."

He paced, wishing he'd had any other choice but to come here. With Ellery. But his chest ached even now as if he'd been running. The mage sickness knifed through him— seizing joints, cramping muscles, pulling him apart inch by inch. Still, he hated this inactivity—this hiding. At the window, he leaned against the sill, stared out into the rain.

What day was it? Thursday? Friday? He'd lost track. But he had little more than two weeks to heal before Beltane and his final confrontation with Asher. Only a little more than two weeks left with Ellery.

God, was it that long? An eternity. A blink of an eye.

He crushed that thought down deep. He wouldn't think about it. She would be gone. Things would return to normal. Life would move on.

"I'm all right, Father," he said, "It's nothing I can't handle. It's always been a balancing act, hasn't it? The human in us. The *fey*."

His father regarded him with a steady look. "Perhaps. But I sense you've gone beyond. Is it vengeance driving you to trade your humanity for power?"

Conor's mind still burned with Asher's threats; his hands tightened on the sill.

Mikhal's quiet voice pierced the growing rage. "Is it guilt?"

His throat closed around a knot. He gripped the sill. So tightly, splinters of wood pushed beneath his skin. Forced him into the present. He pressed his forehead against the cool of the glass. "I failed her," he said. "She was blameless. But because of me, she suffered."

He spun around. Lines etched his father's face. Sorrow and worry aged this man who'd been more to Conor than any other. He would not fail him a second time. "Asher's days are numbered. I'll make him pay."

Mikhal shook his head. "We'll talk no more about it tonight. But see Jamys, will you?"

"I'm all right," Conor repeated.

"Humor an old man. See your cousin. You'll need all your strength. The *fey* expose every weakness."

"If it'll make you sleep easier."

"You need to protect that woman of yours. She's depending on you."

Conor froze. "I told you. She's not my woman." Did his father know what Ellery's true purpose was in all this? Had he sensed Conor's growing doubts? "She doesn't even like me."

Mikhal chuckled. "Perhaps. But she could be the saving of you, Conor."

Those smoky blue eyes. The luscious weight of her soft against him. The sweet honey of her kiss. His father was right. She could be.

But if he went through with his plans and sacrificed Ellery in her father's place at Beltane, she could be the destruction of Asher.

It was one or the other. And either way, Conor lost.

He stood at the door, a hand on the knob. Ysbel's chambers lay just beyond. Had they packed her things away? Did the rooms lay bare? Or would it look as if she'd simply stepped away for a moment. Hair ribbons tangled on her dressing table, a book open on her bed next to her embroidery basket. A gown hanging over a chair back.

What would he trade to hear her teasing laughter again? Or to see her gentle smile as they sat and talked? How far would he go to exact revenge? He glanced down the corridor. Gram had put Ellery only steps away.

As if scalded, he snatched his hand away. Stalked back the way he'd come. He'd find Jamys.

If only his cousin could heal a conscience.

Ellery came awake to an inky black room, damning whatever woke her. She'd been having a glorious dream. The kind you wish you could summon on demand. Her body still thrummed with the pleasure of Conor's hands on her bare skin, his mouth greedy and demanding against her own.

Steps sounded in the hall outside, and a mumbling that droned on and on, the words too quiet to catch through the closed door. Then both stopped. Her latch rattled.

Asher. Every muscle knotted in panic. Her mind screamed. Conor. Where was Conor? Then she remembered. She was on her own.

She forced herself to breathe, fumbling in the dark for anything to use as a weapon. She'd been lulled by reassurances into giving up Conor's dagger. Now, her hands brushed against and curled around the candlestick by her bed. She wouldn't be completely defenseless.

The latch rattled again. A shaft of gray light appeared as the door cracked open. Ellery grabbed up the candlestick.

In the hall, someone called out. A second voice that shattered the agonizing tension. The door closed with a slam. Footsteps hurried away.

Outside her room, two people stood in conversation. She recognized Morgan's voice. The other was unfamiliar. "Do you think she woke Miss Reskeen?"

"I doubt it. But from now on, you have to give her the draught at bedtime. Her night walking has increased. She's liable to fall down the stairs or walk out a window if we're not careful."

As overwhelming as the wild panic had come, it receded, leaving Ellery empty and more tired than ever. She lay back down, trying to regain the sweet torture of her dream. But the fantasy was lost amid more frightening images.

She did not sleep again.

Chapter Fifteen

Conor stood at the edge of the barrows, a row of humped mounds rising out of the dawn mist like islands. Gray, shrouded branches scraped and shushed in the morning breeze, and behind him water rushed over rocks heading toward the Channel. He took a step back from the reliquary. The dark mage energy it gave off turned his stomach even as it pulled on him, tempting him with the power trapped inside. The remaining brothers fought to get out. Sensed his magic and used it to entice him. He needed to keep it out of harm's way. Out of his way. This was the safest place he could think of. Now if only They would agree.

The lone *fey* stood within the mist, the stern beauty of his face as cold as marble. Only his eyes glowed purple as amethysts. "We shall do this for you. But it cannot stay among us for long. Asher will discover it. And Asher will use it to destroy us. And you."

"Do you think I don't know this?" Conor didn't need a reminder. He needed help. "It's only until Beltane. The power available at the turning of the season and within the quoit's sphere will be enough to send Asher back."

"And the girl. Her blood will assure you of victory over the Triad?"

Maybe it wasn't the reliquary making him sick. "That's the idea."

"Did you sleep well?" Morgan passed Ellery the sausage.

The platter was the third to pass by her. And it didn't constitute half the groaning sideboard. For someone used to buttered toast and weak tea for breakfast, it was a bit overwhelming.

"Yes, I slept fine," she lied, praying the coffee in front of her was strong and hot.

"We were worried. My aunt was restless. When she's in a mood, it's rare anyone sleeps."

"So that was who it was."

"We did disturb you," Morgan said. "Sorry. Aunt Glynnis hasn't been this bad in months."

The coffee slid down Ellery's throat, burning her insides. Clearing her brain. "We had a sergeant who walked in his sleep," she said. "He woke up after taking a wrong turn and climbing in bed with his lieutenant."

Ruan Bligh, Morgan's older brother, laughed as he spread gobs of marmalade on his toast. "Poor bugger."

"It wouldn't have been so bad if the lieutenant hadn't thought it a French attack, panicked and bayoneted him."

Ruan choked on his toast, sputtering and coughing. "He didn't. Bloody hell."

Morgan rolled her eyes. "I apologize for my brother. He's been at sea for eight months, and he wasn't that refined to begin with."

"You're hardly fit to throw stones," he shot back.

"That is more than enough, both of you." Conor's grandmother rapped her knuckles on the table for order.

Ruan flashed Ellery a contrite smile meant to melt her knees.

With his sinfully dark eyes and sleek good looks, it might

have worked. That is if he hadn't had a forkful of eggs half-way to his mouth and a dab of marmalade on one cheek.

"This is why I choose to stay as far away from Daggerfell as possible," he said. "I'd rather be carrying full sail in a hurricane than spend my meals being treated like a two-year-old."

"Then you should act as if you had some sense," Lowenna snapped. "Think with your head and not your—"

"Gram!" Morgan shouted.

Ruan eyed Ellery, gauging her reaction. He'd be disappointed. She'd heard far worse.

Even so, his scrutiny made her very aware of the state of her borrowed gown. She nearly spilled out of the bodice. Morgan was far taller and far skinnier. Ellery was all bosom and hips.

"A feast for a man," one of her father's women had commented once. "Something they can sink themselves into like a meal."

Ellery had been disgusted, even if she had understood. She hadn't been blind to the stares then. She wasn't now. She'd just grown immune to them.

Conor pushed open the door to the dining room. His eyes scanned the group, his gaze centering on her. Her temperature shot up just seeing him. All right, so maybe not immune to every man's attentions. She deliberately looked away.

Another man followed him in. A slighter, blonder version of the others she'd met, she knew him instantly for a Bligh. But his smaller stature did little to lessen the impact of his prowling grace, lean muscled body, and hard angled face. This family didn't turn out anything but man-god material.

Before anything else, he approached Lowenna, dropping a kiss on her cheek. "Good morning, *Dama-wynn*. Sleep well?"

It was the man's voice from the hallway last night.

Lowenna patted his cheek. "Sleep is for the old. I have too much to do."

"You have to rest sometime."

She shooed him toward a seat. "I'll do plenty of resting in the grave. Now, where have you two been? Breakfast's cold."

"I had work," Conor said, pouring himself a cup of coffee.

Ellery watched him from beneath lowered lashes. He caught her staring, and she looked away, frightened of the intensity she encountered in that sun-gold gaze.

"Then Jamys and I rode the boundary lines," he added, dropping his gaze to his eggs. "Checked the ward stones. Strengthened a few. Seemed the energy across the lines was fluctuating. And we need all the protection the wards can provide right now."

The blond held out a hand across the table to Ellery. "We haven't been properly introduced, but I'm Jamys Bligh. Ruan's younger brother. Morgan's older."

His grip was firm, the palm callused. Despite the trappings of wealth, the Blighs worked hard for their money. "Conor's filled me in on the *Keun Marow*'s attack. You two are lucky to be alive."

Conor slammed his fist on the table. "Is anyone listening? Have you noticed the instability of the wards before?"

Morgan finished chewing her bacon. "No. I rode the boundaries yesterday, and the wards were strong."

Jamys picked at his breakfast, concentration furrowing his brow. "There's no explanation for the fluidity in the stones' power. I've never felt such a surge and ebb in the mage energy as I did this morning. At times it was overwhelming. At others a mere fraction of the strength needed."

"Asher?" Ruan asked.

"Perhaps," Conor said, but his eyes sought Ellery out, settled on her with a long curious look.

Her pulse skittered, and a throbbing started deep in her body. God, was she so weak that he had only to look at her to send her temperature rising? He was a killer. He'd killed her father. Killed the men with him. She repeated it to herself over and over. But last night's battle with Asher kept superimposing itself over her anger. He'd saved her. Didn't that count for something?

"I've encountered its like before. On the road," Conor said. "Then again last night."

"Asher's followed you here? To Daggerfell?" Ruan sounded ready for a fight.

The others began to speak. The voices piling on top of one another like dominoes. Layer upon layer of questions and answers until Ellery lost the thread of conversation. Found she didn't care. Conor's stare pinned her like a butterfly under glass. She wanted to squirm. Wanted to look away. Wanted to run from the room.

"No," Conor whispered. Or was it only in her head? "No. I think I've brought this problem with me through the front door."

Ellery leaned over the top board of the loose box, watching the old groom poultice the bay, his hands deftly swathing the horse's ankle in wrap.

"Comfrey's what does it," Jock said, tying off the end and sitting back to admire his handiwork. He lifted a patch over his left eye, wiped his face with a swipe of his sleeve before dropping the patch back into place. "Draws the heat from the bruise, that's what."

The horse swung its neck around, nudged Ellery's hands, snuffling its interest. Searching for treats. She rubbed its nose, blew into its nostrils to show she meant no harm. "I saw locals in Spain use manure. They'd bind the leg with a cloth of sheep or cow dung. Swore it never failed to work."

"Saw that myself a time or two. A foolish bunch of nonsense." Jock snorted his contempt, but eyed her with interest. "What in the world were ye doin' in that devil of a place?"

"My father served."

"Did he now?" was his only comment. Ellery relaxed when

he didn't seek any more information than that. Instead, he stood, patting the horse on its rump. Rummaged in his pocket for a crooked, brown carrot. "I served in the 95th 'til a musket ball blinded me on the left. Not much of a rifleman without two good eyes." He offered her an almost toothless grin.

"Did you grow up here?" she asked.

"With a name like Jock Fraser? Not likely. I'm from up north. Aberdeen. Haven't been back since I was a lad. Arrived here in '09 after Coruna. Capt'n Bligh brought me back here with him."

"Ruan Bligh?"

"Master Ruan? No, you'd not catch him on a battlefield. His heart's with the sea. 'Twas Master Conor invited me to stay."

Ellery's hands clenched the partition. The horse shifted and backed away nervously. "Conor was at Coruna?" She should have known. He'd told her he served.

An odd nervous feeling quivered through her, thinking she had been so close to him once. She squashed it. She didn't want to feel anything for Conor Bligh.

"Aye. Ragged as a beggar like the lot of us. Strolled into the barn where the injured had been billeted. An hour later, he'd done his best for more than half a dozen of the worst there. Me among 'em." Jock shook his head. "Damned if I'd ever seen the like." He took out a handkerchief, wiped his hands and stuffed it back into his apron. "That'll do the old thing," he said of the horse. "I'll check on him in a few hours." He left the box, giving the bay a rub on his muzzle as he passed.

"But what happened then?" Ellery asked.

Jock shrugged. "He left right after. Never said a word. But I knew he'd done somethin' special. My old aunty had told me of eldritch healers who could save with a touch. I found the captain later. Outside a gin shop. He looked bad as I felt. I stuck with him 'til he recovered. Never left his side after that."

"He must be something special to inspire that kind of loyalty."

Jock ambled down the aisle, checking pails for water, mangers for hay. "Aye. He's quiet. And downright scary. That's what throws people off. They don't look past that to see the man inside, that's what." Pausing outside a stall door, he pointed back up the aisle. "Would ye bring me that carry-all there? It's got my brushes in it."

"Jock? Are you in here?" Shadows fell across the stable floor. Startled Ellery into dropping the box.

Conor seemed just as surprised. "I didn't expect to find you here." His words were bitten off and sharp.

At breakfast she'd had the family to act as a buffer. Here, it was only Jock. Her face went hot, but she met him stare for stare. Showed him how little he meant to her. "I came to check on the horses we st—, I mean borrowed from Evan." She snatched up the tote full of brushes, hoping he'd understand she didn't want to talk.

It didn't work. A gleam lit his eyes. "They'll go back this afternoon. With remittance in full." He glanced down at her load. "Is Jock making you help? Or is it your own sense of guilt causing you to worry over the hacks?" He leveled an unsettling stare on her. "I'm sorry, Ellery."

And she knew he wasn't speaking of the stolen horses.

She looked away. Afraid of the regret she saw in his eyes. She didn't want him to get past her defenses. Allow her to dream again. Even if she knew her dream was a fool's wish. Conor was off-limits. End of story.

Jock broke the awkward silence. "The bay's got a bruised heel, Capt'n. He'll take a day or two before he's sound. The chestnut's tired, but she'll do for travel."

"Then we'll send at least word that they're safe. Evan will have to accept that for now. Good enough?" he asked.

Ellery nodded stiffly. "You make me sound like a missish, old do-gooder."

"I'd never accuse of you of being old." He offered her a tired smile, and she remembered how ill he'd been only yesterday. Had it been so soon? Had he recovered so quickly?

Jock entered the stall of a round, dappled gray. He snapped a lead to her halter and brought her out to the ties. "What brings ye out here, Capt'n?"

Conor seemed to come back to his surroundings. "Looking for Mab. Have you seen her? Cook's sent me with some scraps."

Jock chuckled. "More like you've swiped 'em from under her nose. If ye want that old, lazy hound, she's where she always is. Layin' in the sunshine by the tack room door."

Conor started down the aisle, his movements careful, his gait slow. Not quite recovered, then.

"Follow him, miss." Jock motioned her on, a knowing light in his eye. "I'm thinkin' he doesn't scare ye so easy, that's what."

She wanted to stay and help Jock, but it was obvious the old man didn't need her. He'd already turned to the horse, crooning to it as he picked its hooves. She put the tote down beside him and deliberately walked back up the aisle in the opposite direction, away from Conor. A few weeks and she'd be gone. In the meantime, avoid him. Easy enough to do. Right?

Outside, she was greeted by two dogs, one short and terrier-like, its ears perked, its tail snapping like a whip. The other was huge with paws like dinner plates and a coat like sheep's wool. She tried backing away, but they followed, circling her, barking and whining until the giant rug jumped up on her chest for a better look.

"Down, Fang." Conor's order was obeyed instantly. He'd come around the corner of the stable, a third dog at his heels, and now stood watching the tumult, his face shuttered of emotion.

The rug returned the look, growling low in its throat. The

terrier's yapping became frenzied, its back bristling in fear. Conor never blinked as he stared them down. Finally the two dogs scuttled away, yielding to the force of his gaze. Only the third dog remained. Still glued to Conor's leg. Still looking up at him with something close to worship.

"The dogs weren't bothering me."

"No? Then I apologize. Not everyone appreciates Fang's unbridled enthusiasm and warm welcomes."

"He doesn't seem to welcome you."

"No. Dogs don't take to me. All animals, really. They sense the *Heller* in me. Makes them nervous."

"And that one?" she asked, pointing to the dog, now seated patiently at his feet.

"Old Mab? She's the only one who forgives me what I am."

His pointed comment stung. But she couldn't forgive him. Not even if it cost her. The sun chose that moment to dip behind a cloud, and she wrapped her arms around her, suddenly chilled.

He squatted down, scratching the dog's ears while it wiggled and whined its happiness. It pushed a whitened nose into his armpit. "Smell the bones, do you? Hold on." He looked over his shoulder to Ellery. "She's all but blind. But she's still got the best nose in the county."

"Is she yours?"

"Simon's."

Her surprise must have shown.

He stood, shoving the napkin back into his pocket. "We both trusted him once. We were both wrong."

"You saved Jock and the other soldiers."

They watched the messenger heading down the drive toward the gates, carrying a pouch with letters and payment intended for Evan. Conor wasn't surprised at Ellery's comment. He'd felt her curiosity since the stables, and she'd been studying him on the sly for at least an hour. Each time he'd tried catching her at it, her gaze slid away. He'd allowed her the freedom. It wouldn't be the first time someone had stared. And she had more reason than most. She'd seen him at his best and most definitely at his worst. It was really only a wonder she was bothering with him at all.

He knelt to fondle Mab's ears. It gave him distance to think before he spoke. "He told you, did he? He loves that story, though it gets more exciting at every telling. Did I glow in this one? Or save an entire regiment?"

"No. Did you?"

His lips twitched. "No. There were only a few that wouldn't survive. I gave them a chance, that's all." He risked a glance up at her.

She stood awkward and unsure, her head cocked to the side as if considering. "Like you did me when you took my wounds?"

"Aye. It was my fault you were hurt." He looked out over the lawn. Afraid to meet her eyes.

Mab rose and stretched. Conor did the same, though his head spun and spots burst in front of him until the dizziness passed. He healed, but it was damn slow for his liking.

"Does Jock know?"

Ellery's question caught him off-guard. "Know what?" he asked. Harsher than he'd intended.

Her lips thinned, her eyes darkening to slate. "Does Jock know you're an *Other*?"

He sensed the annoyance in her voice. If it kept her at arm's length, he'd live with it. "He has to know by now, though it's never come up. He's been remarkably reluctant to speak to me of what went on that day."

"Is he an *Other*?"

"I don't know." When she looked skeptical, he laughed. "He's never said, though with his way with horseflesh, he could be. Being *Other* doesn't always mean wizardry. It's sometimes so subtle that you don't even know yourself. Like Ruan's weathersense or Jamys's healing or . . ."

He swallowed his words. He couldn't say why, but he'd keep what he knew of Ellery to himself. For now. What was one more secret among so many?

Chapter Sixteen

"Ellery?" Morgan's knock was as brisk as her manner. "I've come with some gowns." She strode into Ellery's chamber dressed in a skirt slit for riding, leather breeches, tall riding boots beneath. A short military-cut jacket fit snugly across shoulders wider than normal for her slender frame. Her fiery copper hair hung gorgeously roped and braided, an odd feminine vanity in someone that seemed immune to all other female conceits. She tossed the clothing across the bed. "Not many, mind you. I'm not a follower of Ackermann's, but they should fit you well enough."

"It's lovely." Ellery held up a gown of soft forest green, trimmed in ermine with a wrap to match, noting the frosty look that passed across Morgan's face like a shadow.

"The others are more day to day. Except for the silk." The frost turned diamond-hard, and her mouth thinned to an angry line.

"They're all perfect." Ellery wondered at Morgan's reaction, but didn't ask. In her life, she'd learned not to bother others with her problems, and they wouldn't bother her. There were too many tragedies around an army fire. It was best not to know.

"I won't be needing them anymore." Grief smoldered in

her sherry-gold eyes for a moment, and then it was gone, leaving Ellery doubting if she'd seen it at all.

"Well, thank you. Again." she stammered, unsure of where to go from here with this conversation.

Instead of taking her leave, Morgan lingered. Not comfortably. She seemed ill at ease as if womanly chats weren't high on her list of pleasantries. Finally, she cleared her throat. "Conor hasn't rested since breakfast. Gram's worried. He's barely healed from the mage sickness."

Ellery's earlier fury returned, burdened now with her guilt at the weakness that set her heart drumming every time the man so much as looked at her. "If he wants to make himself sick, let him. He's a man grown."

Morgan stiffened, her stare intense. Now she was the one who sought answers. "Jamys said he was close to death. I've only seen him worse once. After his struggle with Asher in Spain."

Ellery paused in the act of shaking the wrinkles out of the last of the gowns, tension curling through her. She fought to keep her voice even. "In the chapel of San Salas?"

"Aye," Morgan answered. "He's told you of it?"

"He told me. Enough to know how little he values human life."

Morgan gave her a baffled stare.

Now that she'd begun, she couldn't stop. All the angry confusion she'd held inside tumbled. Her hands fisted in the fabric, and her chest rose and fell with a deep, unsteady breath. "He killed those men. How does that make him any different than Asher?"

"Now wait a moment, he was forced to kill the soldier who opened the reliquary to try to stop the Triad's escape. But Asher murdered the others."

Had she been wrong? Disbelief tremored through her.

"Conor's not a man I'd ever want to cross, but a cold-blooded murderer he's not," Morgan added.

Ellery swallowed, dropping the wrinkled gown from trembling fingers back onto the bed. "Thank you for the clothing."

The questions in Morgan's gaze hammered against Ellery's silence, but she couldn't explain her reaction. Not to Morgan and not to herself. Her feelings were too jumbled. Too raw. If Conor wasn't as black as he'd painted himself, that left her vulnerable to caring about him. Something she wouldn't let herself do. Only disappointment lay in that direction. Men were men. Even the sword-wielding, spell-throwing *Other* kind.

She descended the stairs to dinner, still slightly at sea, still unsure of where she belonged within this household. Not that the Blighs hadn't been welcoming. In fact, she'd been taken aback at how quickly they'd accepted her less-than-proper arrival. In her experience, true kindness was a rarity. Most people expected something in return. She hoped she'd be proven wrong here.

At the bottom of the staircase, she took a deep steadying breath, smoothing her hands down the skirts of her evening gown, one of Morgan's cast-offs. Ellery had been afraid to put it on at first, the maid pouring her into it with much admiring oohs and ahhs and a few grunts as she yanked the stays with determined force. But the effect was worth it. Of smoky blue silk, it moved like water when she walked and its silverwork at the collar and cuff was delicate and intricate as spider webs.

Would Conor notice her? Did she want him to? She hated herself for this see-sawing of emotions. He'd killed her father. She pushed that thought to the fore. Killed him. Killed him. Yes, but he'd saved her. So did the one cancel the other?

"Do you always skulk in corners? Or have we chased you into hiding already?" Ruan stepped out of the shadows dressed elegantly for dinner, a rake's smile giving an edge to his perfect features. "It usually takes a week before the houseguest real-izes he's fallen into complete chaos."

She relaxed. This kind of man she knew how to handle. "It looks as if you're the one skulking in corners."

"Let me escort you." He bent to whisper in her ear. "There's safety in numbers." And just like that, the worldly façade fell away and he was a teasing older brother. "Gram has warned me to be on my best behavior."

"And do you usually follow your grandmother's instruc-tions?"

"Instructions? Threats is how I see them. But I'll say no more. Part of my," he smiled at her, "instructions was to not frighten you with lurid tales of Bligh perfidy. Though if you've spent any amount of time with Conor, you could prob-ably relate a tale or two to me."

He scanned her with a very approving eye.

"It's Morgan's," she announced, suddenly self-conscious at the way her body filled every inch of the gown. Seeing it through Ruan's eyes, she realized it was meant for seductions, not supper. She kicked herself for agreeing to wear it.

His brows rose in surprise. "Morgan's? I don't see that at all. It's like imagining a plow horse dressed for a ball."

"That's horrid."

They walked arm in arm to the dining room. "You don't know my sister. Morgan's been barely tolerated among the women of the neighborhood since she was thirteen and an-nounced men's breeches better suited her."

"Perhaps she found a reason to dress like this. Perhaps someone changed her mind."

At the door, Ruan paused, seeming to consider this before shaking his head. "No, Morgan is 'the club you over the head first, engage in niceties after' sort of woman. No man likes to think his lady might challenge him to a duel as easily as she could embroider a seam."

Ellery had never pictured herself dining in such gentrified

company. Her life in Carnebwen had been simple, not even the fleeting riches of Vittoria enough to buy her way into higher Society. But she found the dynamics not far from the hurly-burly life of an army encampment. People coming in and out. Good-humored ribbing. Food devoured as if diners were unsure whether another meal would be offered. Whether this was normal for all households or held true only at the Blighs didn't matter. It wasn't likely she'd be invited to another such dinner.

Ruan sat opposite, offering a wink of encouragement as course followed course and conversation veered wildly from topic to topic. Only now and then did she find his gaze straying from her face to her cleavage. She'd have been offended if she hadn't known a hundred just like him in the army. Men who treated every female with the same teasing gallantry. Be outrageous enough and they would never take you too seriously. Never get too close.

"There's been another death. A soldier encamped near Portsmouth," Morgan announced. "It's the second one in as many months." This was the first time she'd spoken all night.

"*Keun Marow*?" Conor asked.

He sat as far from Ellery as possible, but every now and then she caught his eyes on her. A questing look in them as if he sought to pierce her thoughts. She wished him luck. Her brain was such a knotted jumble right now, she doubted even a confessed mind-reader like himself could make heads or tails of it. She glanced down the table at him. At least she hoped that was the case. How embarrassing would that be?

Morgan shrugged. "Not that I've heard. Gram, have you heard anything?"

Conor's grandmother looked up. "The *Keun Marow* have gone to ground for now. The true *fey* sense nothing of their presence. And for that, we can take solace. If Asher watches and waits, he does so from a distance. And these soldiers' deaths lie at another's door."

Ruan broke in, turned to Morgan. "Ellery tells me I have you to thank for her stunning display tonight."

The change in conversation was jarring, and Morgan frowned, obviously knowing her brother too well to believe a compliment could be so easy. "What are you getting at, Ruan?"

"Just that you should give in to these lapses of sanity more often. You have exquisite taste when you choose to use it." He sipped his wine. "I hope he was worth it."

If looks could kill, Ruan would have been dead a hundred times over. Morgan's face hardened with rage, unspoken curses boiling in her eyes. She put down her fork and knife with slow precision. Pushed back from the table and stood.

It was obvious Ruan knew he'd stepped in it and had done so completely by accident. His mocking smile had been wiped clean as he sought to backtrack. "Gods, Morgan. I'm sorry." And then his eyes caught hers and held them. And the concern and the love were evident. "He didn't know what he had." And this time the sting of sarcasm was gone. He meant what he said.

Morgan saw it too. She trembled, the emotions flying across her face. But she mastered them, sucking in great lungfuls of air to calm herself. Returning to her seat, she cleared her throat, her tone back to normal. "Unfortunately he did know. He just forgot to mention her to me."

Ellery flopped back onto her bed with a groan of disgust. She was hopeless. Dinner had been tense. The rest of the evening worse with everyone on edge or buried deep in their own problems. Only Lowenna had seemed immune to the charged emotions of the people around her, quietly sewing, her composure almost an insult where Ellery was concerned.

She'd felt Conor's gaze upon her, that dark unfathomable stare that knotted her insides and left her alternately hot and cold. Not an admiring look, despite the dress. This was more

the reaction of a man with a problem he'd rather do without.
So when he'd slid out as the case clock struck nine, she'd been
almost relieved.

Why did he make it so hard? And worse, why did she care?
He certainly hadn't tried to capture her interest, but somehow
it had happened. The quiet confidence. The bullish determination. The reckless courage that pitted him against Asher,
even sick and weak as he was, and the selfless compassion
that allowed him to sneak bones to old dogs or come to the
aid of wounded soldiers at the cost of his own health. She
amended that. It hadn't been just wounded soldiers. He'd
healed her when he could just as easily have let her die. He'd
found the reliquary. Why bother with her?

Only one answer; he wasn't the natural born killer he
seemed.

His brutality. Her loathing. His heroism. Her gratitude.
So intertwined there was no way to untangle them that didn't
leave her more confused. She lurched from the bed. Paced the
room in frustration. This see-sawing was driving her mad.

Her eye fell to Mr. Porter's pearl, now resting safely in a
porcelain dish upon her dressing table, and an idea formed.
Foolhardy. As reckless as anything Conor had done. But she
needed to at least thank him for keeping her alive this far. She
needed to say good night.

Chapter Seventeen

Conor slipped from shadow to shadow through the trees, not even the crack of a twig to mark his passing.

He'd sensed the tremor across the wards hours earlier. Scanned the salon to see if anyone else felt the disturbance in the defensive field. Only Gram met his gaze, her sewing put aside, her chin up as if she listened for a sound that no one else could hear. She nodded once, and he rose. Slid away unnoticed. The hunt was on.

He'd shifted as he sped northward toward the source of the trouble. Brought forth the *Heller*, praying even as he did so that he'd have no cause to fight. He was still weak. Not even Jamys's abilities enough to completely cleanse him of the *Keun Marow's* poison.

Skidding to a halt at the edge of the woods, he already knew what he would find. The death hounds' stench fouled the air. Soured his stomach.

There were three of them hunched above a victim, now little more than mutilated offal. Their mouths dripped blood as they gorged, their nose slits spread wide to absorb the mage energy that curled up from the dead faery like smoke. Bloated with stolen magic, their power would be dizzying.

So much for the praying.

He slid his sword from its scabbard. Tried to circle around behind them, but alerted to his approach, they broke off feeding, peered into the woods with eyes like cinders.

They were well-armed. The largest pulled a wicked-looking scythe from its belt. Another had a short axe strapped across its back. A third held a bloody spiked club in one clawed fist.

Conor broke into the clearing, leaping at the closest of the three with a lunging sword thrust.

The largest hound threw itself sideways as the second advanced swinging his club, hoping to crush Conor's arm or knock away the blade. The third melted away. Lost in the dark.

The two that were left were coordinated and stronger than Conor had anticipated. And he was weaker. He couldn't use magic. That would only strengthen their already overwhelming odds. And without it, he was at a disadvantage that grew every second he lingered. He needed to end this. Quick.

He backed up, parrying the *fey* hunter's deadly club before twisting and ducking to knock aside a scythe thrust from behind aimed at taking his head from his neck. The *Keun Marow*'s blade spun away into the grass.

But Conor's victory was short. The club-wielding hound advanced, every blow tiring Conor's already drained strength. He fended him off, but his arm felt limp and numb from wrist to elbow. Sweat poured down his chest. Stung his eyes. It shouldn't be this hard. It wouldn't be if he weren't still sick.

In a last effort to even the odds, he slid beneath the *Keun Marow*'s guard, bringing his sword up and out, tearing into the creature's chest. Hot blood slicked Conor's sword hand, soaked his torso. The beast screamed, crumpling to the ground.

One down. One to go.

Conor felt the rush of wind behind him as he straightened. Spun to defend himself against the last hound. But this creature was fast. He parried every sword thrust before lunging with his scythe, ripping a gash across Conor's stomach.

Roaring his pain, Conor clutched the wound. Twisted out of reach and slammed his sword home.

It was over. But not without cost.

Winded, his heart thundering, Conor bent head down, hands on knees. Sucking in great lungfuls of air. Spots burst in his eyes. His stomach throbbed. But he couldn't rest. Already he sensed the approach of others.

The ward stone's power ebbed again. He'd strengthened it yesterday and already the warp and weft of the mage energy had unraveled. Enough to embolden the *Keun Marow*. Enough to put everything under Daggerfell's protection at risk. Including Ellery. If Asher penetrated the wards . . . If he got to Ellery . . . Conor would have failed. And there would be no stopping the Triad.

He wouldn't let that happen.

Approaching the ward stone, he laid his hands upon the rock. The buzz and tingle of magic sparked up his arm. Raced through his bloodstream. "*Dor. Ebrenn.*" Each word fell heavy with command. "*Dowr. Tanyow.*" The air around him crackled. "*Menhir. Junya. Gwitha rag Asher.*"

As his voice died into silence, light—red and gold and green—twisted and curled over the rock. Pulsed outward east, west, south where it met and melded with the mage energy from the three other ward stones. A constant current. Safety as long as nothing—and no one—interfered.

"Morgan told me which was your room." Ellery stepped into the bedchamber, shutting the door behind her, leaning against it as if Conor might make a break for it.

He'd been in the act of undressing for bed. His shirt was gone, the tattoos vivid swirls of blue against the muscled bronze of his bare chest. Tired as she was, her heart skipped, settled into an unsteady rhythm.

He glanced at the case clock. One in the morning. "You should be in bed."

"And who are you? My mother?"

His scars from her injuries—she couldn't think of them any other way—were now completely gone, but he carried himself gingerly, wincing as he sat to pull off his boots. "You're tired," he said.

"And so are you, but I don't see you tucked up with a warming pan and a cup of milky tea."

A ghost of a smile touched his face. "Five minutes later and you would have." He pulled off one boot. Dropped it to the floor before straightening.

That's when she saw it. A long, ugly weal across his stomach. A fresh wound. "You're hurt." She rushed forward.

He caught her wrist before she could lay a hand on him. "It's nothing."

"It's not nothing." Now that she was close, she saw the edges had already knit closed, the skin pink but healing. "That's new. Something happened." She met his eyes. "Asher tried again, didn't he?"

Letting go of her wrist, Conor pulled off his other boot and sat back. "The demon's testing our defenses. Looking for weakness. He didn't find it tonight." His gaze remained frustratingly inscrutable.

Conor wasn't going to make this easy. But now that she was here, she felt a fool. She tumbled the stone in her pocket, wishing she'd just gone to bed. But she'd wanted to show him she knew how much she owed him. Prove that he was right to trust her—that she *could* understand if he'd take a chance.

"Did you need anything?" he asked. "I can call you a maid if you like."

She refused to be intimidated by his polite dismissal. She pulled out the pearl, shoved it toward him. "I wanted to give this back to you. It's not mine. And Molly stole it, so it wasn't hers either."

This caught his attention. He stiffened, a guarded look on his face. "I claimed it for you."

"But I don't want it. It's . . ." she looked down at the shimmer of colors. How far could she have gone with this jewel to pay her way? She held it out again. More firmly this time. "It's dirty. Take it."

He palmed the pearl. His eyes sought hers, curiosity and hesitation mingled in their lightning depths. "Why the change of heart?"

"The truth," she answered, softly. "You killed my father. I can't forget that, but I've seen Asher for myself. I see what Father's curiosity wrought. What I don't see is why you let me believe you were responsible for the massacre that followed. It was Asher."

A muscle worked in his jaw. "Who told you?"

"Does it matter? Why did you let me think you'd murdered them all?"

He shrugged. "I had my reasons. It seemed best to let you believe."

"To believe the worst of you?"

He stood up; so close to her she felt his body's warmth, saw his pulse jump at the base of his throat. "Just because I didn't kill those men, doesn't mean I wouldn't have if I had to."

"The good little soldier," she whispered.

"Call me what you wish. I am who I am, Ellery." His voice was low and sensual.

A prickle of anticipation raced across her shoulders, making her shiver. "It's over now. I don't want to think about it anymore."

"And your father's death? My part in it?"

"I know what really happened that day. If you agree, we won't speak of it again."

His stare deepened, lingered. Devoured. She couldn't breathe with the waiting.

"I agree," he said.

The air crackled between them. Lightning flickered along her skin. She could lean up, brush his lips with hers. It wouldn't take much. He was only inches away.

"Did Morgan know what she was tempting when she pointed my room out to you?" he asked, making her wonder if he'd caught her stray thought.

Her lips curved into a sly smile. "I think she meant it as a warning. Don't get mixed up with Conor for your own good."

"Smart woman, my cousin. I eat shy young maidens for breakfast."

"This young maiden can take care of herself." And she could, couldn't she?

She squashed the voice in her head warning her to withdraw while she still could. Things were getting out of hand. She was getting out of hand.

He fingered a strand of her hair, pushed it back behind her ear. The lightning swelled. Became fires lit and running with her blood. "It's not you I worry about, Ellery," he said.

"What do you worry about?" Her voice wavered. Broke.

"Starting something I can't stop—can't control." He grazed her side with his hand, the pressure of his touch catching her breath in her throat.

The bugles blew. Retreat. Retreat. But by then, she'd stopped listening.

She took the final step that brought them together. Reached up to skim a hand over the planes of his torso. Caressed with gentle fingers the line of his latest scar. This time, he didn't stop her. "I've had a lifetime of looking after myself. I've gotten quite good at it."

Out of character, the corner of his mouth quirked in a little-boy smile as he stripped her with his molten-honey gaze. "Until I came along, anyway."

Had she come here wanting this? Knowing what would happen? Her mind screamed at her to get out. Run while she had the chance.

"Conor. Please," she whispered, not knowing whether it was a plea for him to stop or continue.

His kiss, when it came, knocked the air from her lungs. She clung to him. Twined her arms around his neck. Felt his heart beating in rhythm with her own.

His tongue dipped into her mouth. Tempted her with a hint of what lay ahead if she chose to keep on. He fisted his hands in her hair, tilted her head back as his kiss assaulted her senses. Now teasing and sweet, a playful nibble of her bottom lip. Now deep and hot and breath-stealing until she fought against the constraints of clothing. Until only skin-on-skin would satisfy.

She wasn't the only one affected. Conor's breathing came faster, his eyes darkening from bronze to almost black.

Answering to some primitive force of her body, she rocked against Conor's swollen ridge. His whole body tensed before he gasped a half-laugh, half-groan, "Gods, Ellery . . . you'll finish me before we even start."

Her lips curved in a sly smile. "Just by doing this?"

He groaned and caught her before she could do it a third time. "Aye, more's the shame. It's been a long"—raw animal need burned in his gaze—"long time." His hands were inside her robe now, untying the ribbons of her shift. Skimming the curve of her breasts, his light touch only making the aching heat spread faster. "No weapons tonight? Gun? Knife?"

The pleasure swelled. Made her hurt with wanting him. "Too messy." She smiled, running her hands through the un-fashionable crop of his hair. Traced his shoulders, the long, sculpted line of his back. "I'm unarmed."

Her robe was gone. Her shift fell away. She stood naked before him, flushed and shivering with desire.

"So you are." His predatory gaze pinned her in place.

Moved over her with slow, deliberate relish, pausing for a moment when it reached her crotch. His nostrils flared as if he could tell she was wet and ready for him. She trembled under the scrutiny even as a wash of heat swept through her. Centered in her woman's place. She wanted him so bad, she throbbed with it. And he knew it.

So much for playing hard to get.

He lowered his mouth again to hers in another dizzying kiss. He tasted of whiskey, and she drank him in, lost in the freedom of hands and lips and flesh. He backed her against the bed, dropping her onto the quilt, pinning her beneath him as his teeth grazed a line down her neck. He explored her, running his hand down her stomach, over the swell of her hips. Drawing her deep into a whirlpool she couldn't escape. Wouldn't if she could.

He lowered his mouth to her breasts. Slid his tongue over the swollen mounds, taking a nipple between his lips. She jumped under the mind-blowing pleasure-pain sensation that radiated along every nerve. He tongued the hard bud until she moaned. Until she writhed beneath his expert lover's touch. He switched his attentions to the other. But this time she was prepared.

She leaned up in a plea for him to take more into his mouth. He obliged, the slick tease of his tongue combined with the scratch of stubble on her sensitive flesh transforming the earlier fires into a conflagration that consumed her.

Just when she thought she couldn't take any more, his fingers were inside her. She arched her back, gasping against the searing rush. Heard the blood pounding through her as he carried her on a current of desire. "Conor. Please," she moaned, and this time she knew she was begging for more.

She closed her eyes. Conscious thought had left her. She was acting on pure lust. He rolled away, the mattress sagging as he tore off his breeches.

"Look at me, Ellery," he purred.

She obeyed, swallowing hard. He was naked. The satiny gleam of his skin complete from head to toe. And as absolutely perfect as she thought it would be.

He rolled back on top of her, spreading her legs, his cock poised to enter. But he held back, his self-discipline as firm as his manhood.

She couldn't take anymore. Her control snapped. She guided him home, gasping against the burst of pain. His mouth found hers, silencing her cries.

Her inner muscles closed around him. And as he lay there, letting her adjust to his presence, the pain was replaced by a new and different sensation. She shifted, eliciting a hiss of indrawn breath from him.

"*Bleydhes,*" he ground out from a clenched jaw.

She smiled up at him in the darkness. "What does that mean?"

The reaches of his black-gold gaze were impenetrable. Unknowable. "It means she-wolf."

"I can live with that."

She'd barely finished speaking when a knock on Conor's door crashed through the bliss like a dousing of ice water.

Heaven help her. What had she done?

Who the hell was bloody knocking? Conor had never been closer to murder than in that moment.

Ellery broke away. Her eyes were glazed with lust, her lips parted and swollen from his kisses. Her mop of curls lay damp against her brow.

He rolled onto his back, his chest heaving. Still rock-hard and apparently staying that way if Ellery's reaction was anything to go by. "Go away."

Ellery struggled to get out from under him, her eyes wide with panic. "I should never have come here—like this. It was a mistake."

The knock sounded again. "Conor, I need to see you."

He cursed. "Damn it, Jamys. I'm fucking fine. Top of the world. Go. The Bloody Hell. Away."

There was silence on the other side of the door. His cousin's sense of timing may have been horrible, but he wasn't stupid.

Ellery rolled up and off the bed. He threw a hand out to grab her, grimacing for the expected pain to follow. Nothing.

He'd have been grateful to Ellery for taking his mind off the sting of healing if she hadn't replaced it with a mind-seizing, gut-churning passion. That sure as hell wasn't supposed to happen. And she sure as hell wasn't supposed to be here. He'd cocked it up this time.

"You decided to heed Morgan's warning?" he asked, ignoring his remorse, hoping to tease a smile back into eyes clouded with shame.

She fumbled with clumsy fingers at her robe's ties. Flushed. Nervous. "I'm sorry, Conor. I've made everything a mess."

He stood, taking the ribbons from her hopeless fingers. Tied the robe closed with infinite care. Knowing he couldn't console her without making things worse. It was better this way. But it sure as hell didn't feel like it.

"No, you were the smart one here. I shouldn't have let it go so far. But—" He plowed a hand through his hair. Blew out a breath. "If things were different . . ." His words trailed off. There was nothing he could say that would change the future.

"*If wishes were thrushes . . .*" She managed a shaky laugh. "But that's not how real life works, is it? Still friends?" She held out a hand.

His stomach clenched, wanting to be on top of her. In her. Wanting the taste of her on his tongue. He accepted her hand, holding back his desire to throw down. Possess her. Bring her to the point where her commonsense could go to hell, and all that mattered was the mindless explosion of senses. "Still friends," he answered.

She squared her shoulders, chin held high. Her gaze was suspiciously bright, but determined. "Good night, Conor." She crossed to the door. With one hand on the knob, she turned back. "I'll stay until Beltane. But then, I'm gone. For good."

She shut the door behind with a click that echoed loud as a gunshot.

Guilt and frustration tore at him. His bedchamber became a prison, the bed a reminder of what could have been. His throat tightened with a choking rage. He slammed his fist against a wall, the pain nothing compared to the satisfaction of crumbling plaster. He punched it again, startled at the energy surging down his spine, sensing the effortless twisting and shifting of his muscles. The loss of thought beneath the animal's instinct to lash out. The change had never been this easy. A slight draw on his power, and the *Heller* would be realized. The *fey* in him released.

He drew in a shuddering, bitter breath. Let it out slowly through clenched teeth. His father was right. He stood at the edge. And why not take that last step? Bring forth the power he needed to not just imprison Asher but destroy him once and for all.

Being human was highly overrated.

Chapter Eighteen

Ellery stood on the terrace, watching the trees. She wasn't a naturalist by any stretch of the imagination. She'd spent too many nights in the open to appreciate such rustic beauty. But these thick stands of ancient woods seemed different—alive. Shadows dappled the paths she saw stretching away from the manicured park. Shadows that behaved unlike any she'd ever seen. Quick flashes of dark and light that lifted the leaves and sent them scrambling.

She wanted to stroll among those paths. Stretch her legs and ponder her future. Where did she go from here? She should do what she had not had the courage to do at the tavern. Leave and begin a new life somewhere else. The city, perhaps. A place of crowds and noise and anonymity. She'd had a bellyful of the small minds and big mouths of villagers.

But Asher remained an obstacle. She'd seen murder in his eyes, knew now that whether she possessed the reliquary or not, he wanted her. Wanted to see her suffer before he killed her. That certainty held her fast in a web of fear. Tied her to this house and these people until Asher's imprisonment. Tied her to Conor.

Butterflies quivered in her stomach, and a rush of excitement took away her breath. Reactions she didn't want, but couldn't seem to stop. She flushed with the ghost-feel of his hands on her body, the press of his mouth hungry and urgent. Even her dreams were betraying her.

She hadn't asked for this. She'd had her fill of men. Witnessed their careless love, resolving that she'd not fall into the same trap as her mother. She was smarter. Stronger. Too clever than to be seduced by a flashy smile and honeyed words.

But Conor had never once tossed her a charmer's grin, and she doubted whether he would know a honeyed word if the bee stung him between the eyes.

He was a man who carried a beast beneath his skin. She'd seen it for herself. The warping of his body as the change took hold. The ruthless clarity of his gaze. And she knew what he was capable of. Death. Murder. He'd admitted to it all. Her father's staring eyes swam before her. And the bloody carnage in the chapel.

But they were immediately overlapped by other recollections. Conor holding her safe. His battle-scarred hands healing her wounds. Conor laughing at her silly stories. Telling his own. And finally, Conor, sick yet shielding her from Asher with the last of his strength.

She skimmed her hand along the stone baluster, enjoyed the warmth of the sun across her shoulders. Humming sounded from an upper window. A dog answered a shouted call. Laughter floated from the open doors to the library. She imagined herself living here. Among this noisy, comfortable, haphazard household.

No. She would enjoy this brief idyll. And hold tight to her feelings. Keep her heart protected. It was the only way she would be able to walk away from Daggerfell without regrets.

There was that glimmer again. A wisp of something at the edge of her vision. A tinkle of bells. She squinted, trying to make it out. A bird? She didn't think so.

"You're the girl just arrived?"

The hard, brittle voice whipped her around. A woman of middle years stood with one hand upon the open terrace door. She wore a heavy velvet dressing gown, the ribbons yanked ruthlessly closed against the spring afternoon chill. Her hair, a mix of gray and pale blonde, hung loose over shoulders tight with temper.

"I am." Ellery was familiar with the disappointment marking the woman's bony face. Cousin Molly had wrapped herself in that same air of ill-usage and martyrdom. "I'm Ellery Reskeen." She held out a hand in greeting.

The woman slapped it away. Took a step back. Paused. Approached Ellery, almost backing her against the terrace baluster. "These children of the devil. They took my husband. Took my sons. They'll not get me. God will strike them down if they try." She jabbed her finger at Ellery, spittle forming in the corner of her mouth. "He knows them for what they are. Their true selves."

"Do you mean the Blighs?"

"I give you fair warning. As Peter counsels us, *Be vigilant because your adversary the devil, as a roaring lion, walketh about seeking whom he may devour.*"

This was obviously sleep-walking Aunt Glynnis. She looked wide awake now.

And mad as a loon.

No one had mentioned that particular fact to Ellery. And probably for good reason. "Thank you for telling me," she said, keeping her voice as soothing as she could while sidling out of reach. "I'll keep my guard up and pickets posted."

She wasn't quick enough. Glynnis stepped back in her path, a frenzied look in her watery blue eyes. "You think I'm mad. I can tell. But I know what I've seen in this house." She peered around as if expecting eavesdroppers. Leaning closer, she whispered—hissed, really. "And I know what I've heard. Conor means you harm. The animal in him thirsts for blood.

Run. Leave here. Save your soul before it's corrupted by this place. These people."

Ellery swallowed hard. "I appreciate the concern for my welfare." She tried to make her voice casual around the tingle that raced up her spine. Jangled the nerves at the base of her neck. "I can't say I wasn't warned, can I?"

"You're a fool, girl." She looked over Ellery's shoulder. Her eyes narrowed to slits of hate. "It's him."

Conor approached from the side of the house, lashing the bushes with a riding crop. With his arrogant soldier's stride and his shirt sleeves rolled back to reveal the solid corded muscles of his arms, he was every woman's darkest fantasy. He paused when he spotted them, but she knew by the way his gaze sharpened that he had been aware of their conversation. He'd known they were there.

Glynnis's eyes slid between Ellery and Conor. "Is that how it is?" she sneered. "You're double the fool then, girl. He'll take you like the beast he is, and death will be the mercy."

Conor took the terrace steps two at a time. "Gram will be looking for you, Glynnis."

His face was pale, his eyes brooding. He must have heard her. She hadn't tried to hide her venom.

For a split second, Ellery thought the woman would strike him. Instead, she gathered her robe about her as regally as a queen, swung around on her heel, and swept past Conor into the house.

"She doesn't like you much," Ellery said.

"She wouldn't." He rested his elbows on the baluster next to her, his eyes on the trees. She recognized the pose as one of studied patience. But she knew by now it was just a pose. This was a man who waited for nothing. He met life head-on. "I was with Uncle Talan and my cousin Richard the night they disappeared."

"What happened?"

He shrugged, twirling the crop idly between his hands. "I

don't know. We were on the road from Bristol. I went to bed one night. When I woke, they were gone. My aunt thinks I killed them." He met her gaze, his eyes a golden bronze. "She's seen me shift."

"Oh." That could explain Glynnis's fear. But the hate was palpable. And current. She couldn't explain that.

The terrace had lost its magic. Glynnis Bligh and her warnings had soured Ellery on its charms. "Let's walk," she said. At Conor's look of reluctance, she grabbed his hand. "You can show me the scenes of your misspent youth." She expected him to pull away. Reject her invitation with a cool dismissal. And after her visit to his bedchamber, she couldn't blame him.

Instead, he gave her a sidelong smile. "Are you sure you wouldn't rather have Ruan's company?" And the hurdle was crossed. Their footing once again sound.

She sniffed. "I thought you were too busy browbeating your cousins to notice Ruan's attentions."

"You'd have to have been blind not to notice Ruan." They crossed the lawn, headed for the nearest path. "I wouldn't get any ideas. He's been known to flirt with the vicar's grandmother—and she's ninety-five. And bald."

She let go of his hand only long enough to punch him in the arm. "So now I'm right up there with hairless besoms." She tilted her nose in the air. Walked ahead. "I know attraction when I see it, Mr. Bligh. Ruan's charming. And he laughs."

The trees closed around them. The air grew cool, the sun falling in slanted bars through the branches. Conor took her hand back, threading their fingers together, his callused palm firm against hers. "I laugh."

She snatched a look up at him, but his eyes scanned the treetops. The path ahead. The underbrush to either side. Even here, he was on guard. Never letting his body relax into complacency. She glanced back down at their clasped hands. Except for that slip-up.

There were a million reasons why she should let go. Put some distance between them. Turn around and walk back to the house. But not a single one was coming to her. All thought was centered on their linked hands. Giving up, she smiled, letting the delight spread through her. "You're right. My mistake. You're as jolly as they come."

She lost track of time and direction as they walked, Conor pointing out the dovecote, the long low hills at the southern edge of the wood, the private family chapel surrounded by weathered tombs. The woods thickened, became dense, almost impassable in places. The sun barely penetrated the old, gnarled branches. Owls called from overhead. A fox barked. The moist air smelled of rich earth and growing things, but every now and then the breeze bit with a tang of the sea. Ellery felt a pricking between her shoulder blades.

"I feel as if hundreds of eyes watched from the trees," she said.

Conor shot her a sly smile. "Probably because they are. Daggerfell holds more within its boundaries than just what you can see."

"Is that good or bad?"

He shrugged. "We offer what protection we can. They do the same. Gram has most dealings with the *fey* within our borders. But they'll allow themselves to be seen if the need is urgent."

Coming around a bend, the house came back into view. Roughly cut of gray stone with its arched windows and round corner towers, it gave the impression of great strength and age. One flickering light shone in the west tower. Ellery shivered and trained her gaze across the stern façade to the west where the sunset turned the walls to rose and gold. "Does Asher constitute an urgent need?"

"I wish to God I knew, Ellery." His hand dropped to his waist as if seeking the comfort of a sword hilt. He glanced over at her, his jaw set, his stare ominous. "It would make my task a damn sight easier."

"How long have you known Ellery had this power?"

His grandmother's entrance into the library had been silent. But Conor had known she was there. Had felt her watching him. He didn't look up from where he sat hunched over an open leather-bound volume, the vellum pages brown with age and water damage. He'd been here all afternoon, more miserable with every hour. He was almost relieved his grandmother sought him out.

Gram took a chair across from him. Made him face her. "It is Ellery, is it not?"

"Looks that way," he answered. "I've had a suspicion of it since I met her. The effect she had on the *Keun Marow*'s dark energy hardened it. And then last night . . ."

"What about last night?"

He ducked his head. "Nothing. Forget it."

His grandmother allowed him the dodge. Moved on. "And now she affects the house wards in the same way."

He put the page he was holding down. Rubbed his eyes with the heels of his hands. Reading the ancient, faded scratchmarks that passed for writing had given him a headache. "Her mage energy causes other nearby magics to warp and change."

Gram steepled her fingers under her chin. The wolf-head ring of the Blighs gleamed on her hand. They all wore such symbols of their house. But for Lowenna Bligh it was much more. It was a symbol of her eternal love for her husband— his grandfather, Howel. A symbol of what she'd given up for that love. Immortality. A life of the *fey*.

That courage as well as her ageless strength and imperious nature had always intimidated him as a child. It was no different now.

"If simply being near causes such chaos, what happens at

her touch?" she asked finally. "Does she affect your power?" Her pointed look told him exactly what she was thinking.

"How the hell should I know?" He prayed his face didn't give away the lie.

She reached across the table, pulling the book around to her. Opened it. Scanned a page. Settled back with a curve of a smile on her lips. "You've lived side by side for a week. Are you telling me you never touched in all that time?"

His groin tightened, remembering last night. "I was a bit too preoccupied to plan a seduction." Not busy enough. He'd walked right into it, eyes wide open.

Gram studied him, her eyes bright and cold as new-forged steel. Sweat trickled down his neck. His head throbbed. She gave a careful look back at the book. "Not a seduction then. Yet the transference of her wounds to your body almost caused your death."

Conor skimmed a hand through his hair. Eased out the breath he was holding. "How did you know? I never told Jamys how it happened."

"Ellery told me. Your flirt with death I saw for myself when you arrived. Jamys confirmed it."

"Don't tell her."

Gram raised an eyebrow. "You don't want her to know how much you sacrificed for her? How far you went to assure she lived?"

"No." Desperation clawed at him. The beast aching to be set free to fight for what it wanted. But what did it want? The answer grew more elusive with the hours.

Gram's voice tightened. The power behind it was like a palpable force. "How much will you gamble to keep Ellery Reskeen alive until you can spill her blood on the Beltane Sabbath?"

It was like being punched in the ribs. She knew. Of course she knew. He'd been foolish to think he could bring Ellery here and Gram would remain ignorant of his intent. "Don't tell her."

She looked skeptical. "Don't tell her she has only a few weeks left before the man she trusts above all others to keep her safe takes a dagger to her chest?"

"Asher must be stopped."

She leaned forward, bracing her hands on the table. "The witch's eldest spawn is dangerous, but only the Triad together can wield enough power to bring down the walls between the worlds."

"Right. But Asher's army of *Keun Marow* grows stronger every day. Unless Ellery's used to repair the seals, he'll be unstoppable soon. Not even the true *fey* will be able to keep him from finding the reliquary and releasing his brothers. I won't let it get that far. Ellery is the key. She alone can fulfill the *molleth* set upon the trespasser who dares open the casket." He drew in a breath. Spoke in a tone he hoped conveyed the importance of his request. "Keep this to yourself, Gram. The others don't know, and I'd keep it that way if I could."

She sighed, and for the first time, looked her age. "And what are they to make of this young woman you've dragged home with you?"

"They can make whatever they like of her as long as they don't suspect the truth."

"I'll keep my own counsel for now. But only because I sense more to this than what lies before my eyes. There is a difference in you today—and that bodes well." Her back stiffened, her gaze refocused. "If I think it right to do so, I will tell Ellery the truth."

A shadow passed the door. Footsteps sounded, paused. Returned.

She rarely left her rooms so Conor hadn't seen much of Aunt Glynnis. But the ban-sidhe of Daggerfell, as he and his cousins had titled her, was much the same. Time had yet to calm the frenzied, unsettled look in her eyes or the constant wringing of hands chapped and bitten to the quick. She wore a nightgown and robe, but her usual wild tangle of hair had been cleaned and brushed.

"Did you have need of me, Glynnis?" Gram asked.

But Glynnis's attention was centered on Conor. Her fingers curled and straightened before she rubbed them up and down her robe as if trying to clean them.

"Aunt Glynnis." Conor inclined his head in greeting.

It was a mistake. It felt as if his brains had shifted. He rubbed at his temples in a hopeless attempt to ease the pain.

"They told me you'd come home," she whined. "I was worried sick. Just be gone a day or two, you said. Then nothing. They told me you'd died, but I wouldn't believe them. I prayed to the Almighty Father for your return. I knew I was right to do so. I knew he'd answer my call."

Conor understood now, and his heart went out to her. Twenty years had passed, yet she remained frozen in time, waiting for the husband and son who'd disappeared—taken, some said—to return home.

"It's good to see you," he said, letting the fantasy continue. "You're beautiful as I remember."

She blushed, then worry filled her face. Her hands worked her robe faster and faster. "Did you bring Richard with you? Is our little boy here?"

"I'm sorry, Glynnis. He . . . he couldn't come with me."

Her face wrinkled with grief. "Richard away and now his brother Simon's gone as well. Conor's driven him off, Talan. He wants Simon dead. He's touched with the devil's mark. Like so many of this house."

He let the words wash over him, knowing it for the madness it was. He had faded memories of a sweet, shy woman who carried sugared almonds in her pockets for the children and snuck bones for the dogs. But that was a long time ago. Before Talan left her alone among his people. In a world she didn't understand and could never accept.

A young maidservant skidded up breathless to the door. "Mrs. Bligh, mum. There you are." She took Glynnis's arm. "Come along. It's time for your supper."

Glynnis pulled away. "I've prayed for the absolving of your sins. I've begged the Lord to fill you with the Holy Spirit and drive out the evil that you carry. It's not your fault. But you must help him do his work. You must let him heal you. For a future in his kingdom . . ." She grew vague, worried at her skirts as if she were confused.

The maidservant gave them a sympathetic look. Gripped her mistress's arm more firmly. "Come, Mrs. Bligh. Master Jamys will fix you up nice with a tonic for them nerves."

"Talan? Help me get away from them." She held out her arms to him, beseeching him. Conor's gut churned at the desperation in her voice. "Take me with you. I can't stay here any longer. Not among this evil."

"Mrs. Bligh?" the maid whispered.

Glynnis's arms dropped uselessly to her sides. She allowed herself to be led away, keeping her gaze on Conor until the last.

He rubbed a hand down his face. Sat back with a groan. "She's worse."

Gram nodded in agreement. "Yes, and yet she's been more among us these last few weeks than in all the years since Talan and Richard disappeared. She bears watching."

Conor pinched the bridge of his nose. "I'll add it to my lengthy list right after conquering Asher and winning the girl."

"So you do want her." She offered him a satisfied smile.

He blew out a breath. Plowed a hand through his hair. "I don't want her dead. But I see no other way."

She closed the book, tapped the cover thoughtfully. "Still, you search the teachings."

He stretched his neck to work the stiffness out. Pushed back from the table to stand, trying to shake off the gloom

Aunt Glynnis had left behind. "I thought one of the tales
might offer some hope."

"And?"

"I haven't found it yet. But there's an entire library to wade
through. And I've only two weeks to come to a decision." He
scanned the rows of shelves. God. It would take him months—
years—to read through this clutter.

She rose to stand beside him. "You are only one man and
one pair of eyes. It goes against your nature to do so, but ask
for help. There is one who knows this library and its contents
better than she knows her own children."

"Mother."

"She would help you if you asked."

"I doubt it. And I wouldn't blame her."

"Of course not. You are too busy blaming yourself." She
took him by his shoulders. Her head barely came to the middle
of his back, but her grip was strong as steel. She aimed him at
the door. "Go to Niamh. Speak with her. She mourns her
daughter. But she misses her son."

Conor strode toward the library. What he was looking for,
he didn't know. Why he was looking, he refused to examine.
There was only one way to satisfy the curse placed on the reliquary. Ellery's blood. So why waste time searching for another
course?

He threw the library door open, pulling up short at the
sight of his mother seated at a desk, parchments spread out
before her.

She pulled a pair of spectacles from her pocket. A recent
need he didn't remember. Settled them on her nose. "Conor?
Are you quite all right? You look flushed—out of sorts. You're
not still sick, are you?"

"No." He thought about his grandmother's advice. Dismissed it. To let anyone else know Ellery's true purpose was

to court disaster. Any hint of it reaching her ears would send her flying from here. Straight into Asher's waiting arms. He was sure of it. "I . . ." so how to explain his presence here? "I came to see if you wanted to go for a walk. We could take the beach path. Head toward the shore."

She pursed her lips. "I haven't been that way since Ysbel's death. That was always her favorite ramble."

Shit, he'd forgotten. "Well, another way. Toward the dove-cote and the orchards."

"It's kind of you to ask, but I'm in the middle of something. Tracing a passage in the Llanfarnan writings back to its source. I'm hoping I can find something in these entries by Ogham."

"Sounds fascinating."

She gave him an indulgent laugh. "Liar. You never were one for the past. But it's here. All around us." Her eyes glowed with enthusiasm. "And so much of it being lost amid the confusion of the Mortal world. Forgotten. Or discounted as legend. Myth."

How many times had he heard this speech growing up? His mother's passion for her studies at the expense of anything else was a family joke. And yet, her knowledge of the past was as much a power as any he possessed. "You won't lose much by taking an afternoon off. A legend here. A prophecy there."

She glanced at the open door behind him. "Where's that young woman of yours? Wouldn't you rather walk with her?"

"Ellery's with Gram." He offered his arm. "Mother?"

Her gaze dropped to her book, then up to the clock. "Thank you, Conor. But no. I have so much to do before I lose my light. And the weather's a bit unpredictable. I'd hate to get caught in a downpour."

"The weather's perfect."

She took off her spectacles, wiped them with her hand-kerchief. "Is it? Oh, well, you go on. Take Miss Reskeen. She seems very pleasant. Rough around the edges, but that should suit this family." She threw him a fleeting smile. "It takes some spunk to put up with all of you."

Why was he surprised by her refusal? It made sense. "Perhaps another time," he said.

He sketched her a bow, trying to exit with as much grace as he could muster. He couldn't stay. She'd question it. Or worse, she'd not say anything, Her silence, confirmation of her disappointment in him.

Asher stalked his chambers, his slender hands clasped behind him. He'd been so close. Bligh had been on his knees before him and the girl . . Those sweet curves, that lovely unmarked face. Yes, the girl would have pleasured him for many days before she died. And then it had all come crashing down around him.

The dagger had been unexpected, but not in itself alarming. What gave him pause was that the taint of cold iron had penetrated his spells of protection. Disrupted his magic.

And what made him blind with fury was that it had allowed Bligh the time to escape—to cower within the secure walls of his family's estate. Go to ground like the *Other* vermin, he was.

Once his brothers were free and the Triad held dominion, the race of *Other* would be the first to suffer. The abomination of *fey* and Mortal could not be allowed to continue. He would wipe them clean from the earth.

Only Conor Bligh and his woman stood between him and this new age.

But all was not lost. If his spies were right—and he rarely let them live long if they weren't—Daggerfell was compromised.

Safe, no more.

Chapter Nineteen

Conor's eyes snapped open, his mind instantly aware of the breeze through the open window, the cool sheets against his skin, the moonlight throwing shadows across the floor. Everything familiar. Everything that was home.

But his chest pounded, his muscles tensed. Warnings went off in his head. Something was wrong. The land was silent. No scream from the hunting owl or call of the nightjar. No sighing of the trees as the earth cooled.

Instead, the mournful sound of crying met his ears and the rush of running feet beneath his window. He threw himself out of bed. Snatched up his breeches. Instinctively slung his sword across his back.

He'd wondered how long it would take Asher to test Daggerfell's wards once again.

He had his answer.

He reached out, using his powers to search for echoes of the demon's magic, but there was nothing. He'd not come himself, then. He'd sent an assassin to try his luck.

The *Keun Marow* back for another try? No.

The true *fey* within the borders would have cried out at such a disturbance. Shaken the household with their fury and

their fear. But he alone seemed the only one to notice this in-
trusion. The family slept on.

Coming out into the hall, he nearly collided with Aunt
Glynnis. Hysterical, she gripped him, her eyes wild with
malice and horror. "You." A wicked smile twisted her face.
"He's here. He's come home. *Vengeance shall be mine, sayeth
the Lord.* As you took my love away, so shall he take yours."

Simon. Ellery.

He pushed her away and ran for the stairs.

Ellery sighed and rolled over, punching her pillow, adjusting her nightgown. She was too hot. Too cold. Thirsty. Itchy.
The list went on and on, but she wasn't fooling herself. She
knew what it was her body was craving and it wasn't another piece of steak and kidney pie or a cup of warm milk.

How had it happened? How had she not felt the trap closing before it was too late? She'd prided herself on her
strength, her independence. She'd sworn never to be beholden
to a man again. They were takers, all of them. And they offered little in return.

Yet, she stood prepared to throw that aside for the heady
rush she felt whenever Conor was near. For the spiraling heat
that drew her up and up until she thought she might burst for
wanting him.

Somewhere close, a door slammed. The latch rattled. A
sour wind rushed through the room, billowing the curtains.
Glynnis on the prowl again?

Ellery sighed and rolled back over. Stared up at the ceiling.
It was going to be a long night.

Conor pulled up short at the sight of Ruan sprawled on
his side, his hand clamped to his ribs, his face pinched and
white. "He fucking stabbed me."

Conor knelt, pried Ruan's fingers away from the oozing wound. "It's not fatal."

"Small blessings," Ruan grunted from between pressed lips. "Where's Simon now?"

"He's gone toward the back stairs."

Conor straightened, drawing his sword. Testing its grip. "Will you survive until I return?"

"Aye, well enough. Go. Find him. And put a few holes in the blighter for me."

"As good as done." Conor dashed for the stairs.

Simon stood between Ellery and the door. "Asher's anxious to meet you."

Her stomach rolled and her legs wouldn't stop shaking. She tried not to give Simon the satisfaction of knowing how scared she was. "It's an introduction I'd rather pass on if it's all the same to you," she brazened.

"Afraid not, pet. He's asked for you, so he'll have you. That's the deal. And he doesn't take kindly to disappointment."

Remembering the evil glow in the demon's eyes, she could well imagine. But she didn't want to be Asher's latest entertainment. She screwed up her courage. She'd get only one shot at freedom.

He grabbed for her arm, but she twisted out of his grasp, pivoted before he could recover his balance, and lashed out with all her strength.

Her fist landed flush against his cheekbone, the force of her blow numbing her arm. She ignored it in her race for the door.

Simon was two steps ahead of her, his weapon drawn. He herded her back the way she'd come until she stood cornered against the wardrobe. A hint of hesitation crossed his features. Enough to give her hope and the courage to question.

"Why me?" she asked.

"You interest him." He shrugged. "I'm sorry. Circumstances have made us enemies, and I've come too far to turn back now."

"Is that what you told Ysbel?"

The blade froze Ellery where she stood, its edge sharp as ice. She tried backing away, but the wardrobe stopped her. "Don't mention her name in front of me." His voice had gone dangerously quiet. "My devil's bargain is made. And I received everything I wanted from it."

"Conor will kill you," she breathed around the mounting panic.

"He can try." Simon leered toward her, his expression ugly in its victory. Long scratch-marks striped his face, and an angry blotch stained his left cheek. "You're treed, my girl."

She swallowed, the dagger digging into her skin. Her breath caught at the sting of pain that followed. "Perhaps." She found enough courage to smile. "But then, so are you."

She screamed.

Conor set his shoulder to the door, hurling it back against the wall even as he spoke the words that would bind Simon. Hold him fast.

The scene was one of a hard-fought struggle. Discarded bedclothes, an overturned table, a lamp lying amid the shards of a broken pitcher and basin. Ellery was backed into a corner, a scream dying on her lips, a thin beading of blood across her neck where Simon's blade had pierced it.

Simon fought to move, and a puzzled frown crossed his features.

Conor held out a hand. "Ellery. Come away. He can't harm you."

Before she could slip out of his grip, Simon laughed. "Is this the power Asher fears will undo him? Let me show the girl what real power is."

He closed his eyes, began to whisper.

Razor pains sliced through Conor's body, down his legs, out his arms. He jerked back, barely holding onto his sword. Each second brought a new pulse of the knifing agony. Through his gut. Slashing his heart. Tearing at his muscles. As if his body were being scythed from the inside out.

He dropped to his knees, trying not to cry out. He struggled to break the spell's hold, but Simon's curse smothered his attempt as easily as a breeze snuffs out a candle's flame.

Ellery struggled. "Stop it. You're killing him."

Simon slapped her. She staggered then steadied herself, her face cut by Simon's wolf-head ring.

"I should thank you," Simon said. "Cloaking my magic was more difficult than I'd imagined. But no more hiding. No more daggers in the dark."

Lights burst across Conor's vision. His head felt as if a vise were crushing it. Was this inhuman power Simon's reward for turning Ysbel over to Asher?

Just before he lost consciousness, Conor relaxed into the spell, allowing it to wash over him, through him. Then with a discipline honed over years of training, he focused his energy, shut his emotions down to let the *fey* in him take over. The pain subsided. The fear and rage and panic dissipated as the power moved through him.

All his attention on Conor, Simon never saw Ellery's elbow until it rammed into his stomach with a wind-knocking blow.

He doubled over with a shocked whoof of spent breath, his concentration broken.

The curse's final release ripped like a blade through Conor, but he was free of it. He got to his feet. "Get out," he gasped.

Ellery scrambled from behind Simon and dashed out of reach, disappearing out the door.

Thank God, she was safe. Conor saw in his mind's eye the thin red line across her neck, and his renewed rage filled the emptiness. Flowed over.

"Does your taste in murder run only to defenseless women?" he growled. "You should try your new talents on someone your own size."

Simon straightened, his dagger still gripped and drawn. "I did. And I almost succeeded, *amhas-draoi*." He spat the word like an obscenity. The demon magic swirled around him like a protective shield.

Asher's wards were too strong for Conor to defeat Simon that way. And now that Conor was prepared, Simon was equally defenseless. Magic would not win this war between them.

"Fight me on your own. Without Asher's help," Conor challenged. "If you dare."

"I'm no"—Simon lunged with the dagger—"fool."

Conor easily deflected the blow. Stepping into the attack, he tasted victory and vengeance. His sight narrowed to the space between them, the clash of steel.

"Savage." The shrieks behind him stayed his hand. "Killer."

He wheeled on the ball of his foot, his fury coloring everything around him. Only his *Heller* reflexes sent the blade whistling past this new intruder instead of cleaving her in two.

"Satan's child," Glynnis screamed, her face warped with madness. "You'll not kill my son as you killed the others. I'll send you to hell myself before I let it happen."

She held a pistol pointed at his chest.

"Mother," Simon gushed. "Your timing is perfect." He stabbed out and up, aiming for Conor's lungs.

Conor wrenched himself sideways, the dagger burning a path across his side. At the same instant, Glynnis screamed and fired. The bullet's impact slammed him to the floor. Smoke blossomed around him, the report ringing in his ears.

As he fingered the blood welling from his blackened shoulder, the temptation to shift had never been greater. His body tensed, his mind poised to work the magic that brought about the change. He ignored the wound, scrambling to his haunches, prepared to spring.

"Not so fast, Conor." Simon pulled him back from the brink. "One move and Mother joins husband and son in the great beyond." He stood behind Glynnis, pressing her back against him with a firm hand around her waist and the other holding the dagger at her throat.

"You wouldn't."

"Oh?" Simon pushed the blade close. Glynnis whimpered, trying to move away.

"Conor, let them go." Ellery stood in the doorway, her arms crossed protectively over her chest. Behind her, Father and Gram hovered in the corridor.

"He's bluffing."

"Do you think so?" Simon started to slide the blade across Glynnis's throat, a trail of blood springing up behind it.

She screamed.

"Conor." His father's voice held a note of warning. "He'll kill her."

Conor crushed the grip of his sword in his hand. "I'll finish this tonight."

"Let him go, my grandson." This time Gram spoke. "He is not worth the reckoning you will owe for killing your own blood."

Conor lowered his weapon. Blood snaked down his chest, across his abdomen, dripped to the floor. His side ached from the glancing dagger blow. But already his body began renewing itself. He'd live. "Run. Get out."

"No one is to follow us." Simon backed through the doorway, past the others who stepped aside, letting him go.

He pulled his mother with him down the stairs, Glynnis's crying growing fainter before it faded out.

Heavy running footsteps replaced it coming back up the stairs. Morgan rounded the corner, half-dressed in a nightgown, light silken robe, and boots. "He's crossing the lawn, headed toward the gallop. If we hurry, we can cut him off in the wood."

"How is Ruan?" Gram asked as if she hadn't heard. As if she had all the time in the world. She had, once. But now time and the future were unraveling. And Simon was getting away.

Morgan pushed her hair off her face with an impatient gesture. "He's with Jamys cursing a blue streak. He'll recover. But Simon . . ." She pointed to the stairs.

"Follow him," Mikhal answered. "Stay far enough back he doesn't feel cornered, but keep an eye on Glynnis. She doesn't deserve this, no matter what she did in her confusion."

"I'll go," Conor said as Morgan disappeared back down the stairs.

Mikhal cast a glance at Conor's shoulder. His side. "See Jamys about that."

Conor flexed his arm. It hurt, but it mended. The wound to his ribs was already healed. "I'll see to it after we've caught Simon."

Mikhal held him still. "Morgan's abilities outstrip even yours when it comes to tracking. We'll let Simon feel secure enough to release Glynnis first. Give him time to get deeper into the wood. We'll follow once word comes that he's there."

Only respect for his father kept him from charging after them. "Do you think the true *fey* will stop him?" he scoffed. "They let him onto the grounds without a warning. To them, he belongs here. He's a Bligh."

His father's face settled into stern lines, his eyes hard as ice. "Mayhap you're right. After everything is done, Simon *is* still a member of this family."

Conor couldn't believe what he was hearing. Was Father saying that Simon didn't matter? That his crimes didn't matter? Conor wrenched himself free. "I don't care whether he's a Bligh or not. I'm going to rip his goddamned head off when I catch him."

Gram stepped between father and son, her voice like steel.

"His day will come, but not at your hand. You're going to wait here." Her eyes looked past him to where Ellery watched everything through eyes wide and dilated, a trembling lip caught between her teeth as she fought back tears.

Catching the scent of her blood, seeing the jagged line of it staining her throat, Conor's hands shook, and a fist closed around his heart. Too close. He'd cut it too close, and Ellery had almost died.

"She needs you," Gram said.

Conor couldn't look at Ellery again. Not at that long slender column of her neck. Not at the stiffened face that refused to crumple into tears, the chin that remained lifted, defiant. Would her defiance hold when he had to approach her with a dagger and murder in his eyes?

Conor tried moving past Gram. "I can't let him get away."

She stepped back into his path. "Ellery—"

Conor threw up a hand. "Ellery was held at knifepoint by that coward. I want him. Tonight."

He'd stopped her words, but he couldn't stop the thoughts battering his mind. He should have protected her. He should have kept her safe. But safe for what?

The grounds shone silver under the waning moon hanging high in the western sky. Though no breeze moved among them, the trees shivered and whispered. Bells echoed, voices calling across the woods, over the park. Frightened, anxious voices.

Lights danced in the wood, a green faery glow that moved and bobbed from path to path as Glynnis was piskie-led back toward them.

Mikhal put up a hand, holding Conor back when all he wanted was to don the *Heller*'s mantle. Hunt Simon down. Then Asher.

Enough hiding. Conor would take this battle to them.

"He's gone," his father announced. "They've watched him pass the northern boundary markers. He's on horseback. And alone."

"And Aunt Glynnis?"

"She's safe. They're leading her home."

The lights and the bells came nearer before breaking off as Morgan and Glynnis broke from the trees. Glynnis's robe was torn and muddied, her hair a wild mane about her head, but she seemed unhurt.

Morgan supported her as they walked back to the group. "I'll take her in to Gram. Jamys will look her over."

Mikhal agreed.

On their way past, Glynnis caught Conor's eye. Her gaze steadied. "Talan?" she whispered. "Our little boy has become one of them. I've lost him forever to the devil's army." Her gaze shifted to the house. "Christ has forsaken me. And now I'm truly all alone."

Held upright by Morgan, she shuffled by, the weight of her sorrow crushing.

Mikhal started for the path. "I'm going to walk the boundaries. See what I can discover."

"I'm coming, too." Conor re-gripped his sword, the solid weight of the steel unnaturally calming.

A new task taking shape in his mind.

Chapter Twenty

Ellery closed her eyes, leaned back into her pillows and listened to the rain drumming against the house, the steady squeak of Conor's mother's rocking chair. Both sounds calmed her jagged nerves. Eased the lingering feel of Simon's knife at her throat, the sight of Conor helpless on his knees. She couldn't be sure which terrified her more.

Niamh Bligh shifted, began humming softly. Her quiet presence had soothed more than any effusive offers of comfort. Had done so since the men had gone. Since Glynnis's return. Since the house had settled once more into silence.

Opening her eyes, Ellery turned her head to the darkness beyond her window. Was Conor still searching for Simon among those ancient trees? Did Asher stalk Daggerfell's dark woods? Was the safety of this house only a mirage?

She wanted Conor. Here. In front of her. She needed to see him safe and whole. Needed to touch him, feel his reassuring warmth under her hands. Know that he was all right, and that things weren't as black as they appeared.

"Where are you, Conor?" she whispered to the storm.

The rain pounded harder, the wind shaking the casements and howling like an animal begging entrance. Only Niamh's steady rocking kept Ellery from leaping out of bed and hunting him down herself.

A knock broke off Niamh's song, and then the door swung open.

Ellery flashed back to the night they met. Conor stood on the threshold, soaked through, his clothing muddied and stained pink with blood. Fatigue etched lines in his face, but his eyes remained as hot and gold as a summer sun.

She sat up, the quilts bunched between her hands. A wild fluttering began in her chest.

Niamh stopped rocking. "Con," she scolded. "You're drenched. And your arm. You're bleeding."

He stiffened, giving a respectful nod as water sluiced off him, puddling across the floor. "It's fine, Mum. I only came to tell Ellery she's safe." His gaze sought her out. "Simon won't be back. I've done what I can to strengthen and steady the wards. It should be enough if nothing else occurs."

"But being injured so soon after your illness," his mother commented, fixing her spectacles on her nose. "Are you truly all right?"

He swung his arm back and forth, flexing the damaged shoulder. "Nothing a good sleep won't cure. But I wanted Ellery—I wanted to see she was all right." All the while he spoke, his eyes never swayed from her.

"Did you?" Niamh's tone was hopeful. She rose, yawning. "As you see, she's well. But she worries for you." She patted Conor absently on the shoulder. "We all do."

For the first time, he looked directly at his mother. Caught her hand in his. "Thank you. For watching over her."

She smiled. "Me? I merely rocked and listened to the rain. It's comfortable now and then to sit together in silence. It can bring great thoughts." She brushed him with a kiss. "And great serenity. You should try it. You might find comfort in the voices that fill the quiet."

Conor returned the chaste kiss. "I know what those voices say. They seek justice."

Niamh frowned. "They seek peace. Can you give it to them?"

As if refusing to acknowledge his mother's wisdom, Conor focused back on Ellery. "I came as soon as I could."

She put out a hand. Withdrew it. "I needed to see you. To know you were safe."

"I know."

He'd heard her call. And he'd come. The fluttering steadied into a pulse-pounding beat of excitement. "Simon came so close," she said.

"I'd never let him harm you."

And Ellery knew he spoke truth. Conor would die before he let Simon hurt her. The idea that he cared that much what happened to her was dizzying and at the same time sobering. A deep bond lashed them together. Made them solid. Stronger. Yet Asher had used a similar bond against Conor once before. Could their fragile relationship be a weapon in the demon's hands as well? A chill shivered up her back. "I meant you. Simon almost killed you."

He looked surprised, then somber. "I won't let my guard down again."

"Good night, my children." They both looked up at the closing of the door.

"Your mother—"

"Has gone to bed. And so should you. I'll see you in the morning." The weight of his gaze was frightening. "There are things we have to discuss. But not tonight."

"No." She rocked up onto her knees, tossing the quilts aside. Grabbed his arm. "No. Don't leave."

He looked down at the grip she had on his sleeve, his expression unreadable.

She pulled back, confused. "Oh, God. I'm making a mess

of everything again. Go. Go change. You're all wet. And—and dripping."

"You're still frightened from what happened. It's reasonable." His voice held infinite patience as if he spoke to a small child. Was it possible to want to kiss someone and hit them all at the same time?

Tension and fear had held her together this far. The release of both freed her mind and her mouth. She snapped, "You think tonight was any more frightening than anything else that's happened to me since I met you?"

"It was for me." He fell into the chair his mother had just vacated. Ran a hand down his face. "Damn it, Ellery. I was moments from losing you."

Hope burst through her, but she wouldn't let it take hold. Not yet. "And that mattered to you?"

He looked at her like she was insane. "I've brought you into this. I'll see you're protected until it's over."

So much for hope. "That's not what I asked. But it's an answer, isn't it?"

Why wouldn't he say it? Why couldn't he say that he cared for her? That somewhere between her kitchen in Carnebwen and here, things had changed between them.

He stood up and paced to the window. Stared out into the rain.

What did he see in that darkness that lay hidden to her?

"I haven't got the reliquary anymore," she said. "Why does Asher want me?"

Conor spoke without turning around. His voice was dull. Tired. "I don't know. Mayhap Simon thought you knew where it was hidden. Mayhap Asher thought to punish me through hurting you."

She got out of bed. Crossed to his side. "But how would he know that my capture would do that? He's not omniscient. He can't know what I don't know myself."

He whipped around. "What's that supposed to mean?"

It was now or never. She drew in a deep calming breath. "You warned me once you'd keep me safe, but could make no promises."

"That still holds true."

"And if I want you anyway?" Her voice shook more than she would have liked.

"Ellery, I can't. You don't understand."

"But you want me? As a man wants a woman?"

The dark sensual light in his eyes was all the answer she needed.

He wanted her. Desired her. But was that enough? She made up her mind.

For tonight, it would have to be.

She was cut off by the crush of his arm around her waist as he pulled her against him. By the force of his mouth on hers. Immediately, she was soaked by his cold, clinging shirt. Gooseflesh rose on her skin. Rainwater dripped off his hair onto her cheeks, streamed down her face like tears.

An image of her mother flashed before her. The sorrow. The desperation. And in the end, the hopeless resignation. What the hell was she doing? She should tell him to stop. Tell him to leave. But what Ellery whispered was, "You're wet through."

"Aye," he muttered.

Between one breath and the next, his shirt was gone, the carved muscles of his chest dusky in the candle glow. She ached to run her fingers over the swirls of his mage marks, to tease a heat into those eyes born of human desire and not magic.

He glanced down at her damp nightgown. "We can't have you catching cold," he murmured.

With one practiced move, her shift lay on the floor around her ankles. Allowing no time for shyness and none for words, he recaptured her lips in another kiss that erased all her doubts. All her questions.

He glided his hand over her shoulder, around one breast, the checked strength in his callused palm almost unbearable. She shuddered, moving into his touch. Her breathing grew ragged as every stroke only made her more impatient for the next. Oh, yes. This pleasure was worth the regret that would follow tomorrow.

She combed her fingers through his hair, loving his crisp rain-smell, the cool touch of his fingers.

As if in supplication, he fell to his knees, his bowed head resting against the flat of her stomach. ". . . I won't . . . not now . . ." He spoke to himself. No more than a whisper. But the force of his words threatened to break the spell surrounding them.

"Conor?" She hated the need in her voice.

He looked up at her, and any last-minute hesitations that might have been lurking were lost amid the swirl of sin and seduction in his eyes. "You're safe, Ellery." His lazy, sexy smile was equal parts reassurance and enticement.

Then his hands encircled her waist. His teeth grazed the long length of her legs; his breath tickling as he dropped kisses up her inner thighs. Her stomach flip-flopped. Her legs grew weak. Small whimpers escaped her throat with every inch of flesh he tormented with his lips.

She wanted to join him on the floor, but he kept her standing. Pushed her back against the wall.

Then his head was between her legs, his tongue flicking against the soft folds. Tasting the nub that lay hidden there. She jerked back. Choked on a shout that would have left no doubt in anyone's mind what was going on in here.

Her knees turned to jelly. Fisting her hands in the curtains to hold herself up, she melted into him. Into the hot, excruciating feel of him lapping at the most secret center of her. She writhed against him, her pulse quickening as pressure built beneath his hands and his mouth until every stroke of his tongue brought her closer to the edge. As if a bomb had gone off inside her, her inner muscles spasmed. She was wet and swollen and ready, but Conor played her. Probing. Retreating. Knowing just how far to go to keep her suspended in churning, mind-blowing anticipation.

He finally released his death-grip on her waist, allowing her to slide wobbly-kneed to the floor with him.

Boldly taking his face in her hands, she claimed his mouth in a deep, sensual kiss. Savored her essence on his tongue. Rubbed herself against his erection. He was as ready as she was. She leaned into him, whispered into his ear. "Take me."

He threw back his head and laughed. "I plan to. And nothing stops me tonight."

He swept her up in his arms and laid her back on the carpet. No time for the bed. He wanted her now. He wouldn't give her a chance to change her mind. Tonight fealty, responsibility, honor fell away. Only Ellery mattered. Only the pleasure he could give her. The passion she begged for with every caress.

Tomorrow he would gather his burdens back up. Do what he needed to do.

There would be no life with Ellery. But he *would* leave her a life. She would have to settle for that.

Beneath him, her body shuddered with every brush of his fingers. She bit back a moan, her eyes black with desire. The musky, earthy scent she gave off acted on his brain and his body like an aphrodisiac. And watching her watch him only aroused him more, if that were possible.

He skimmed her with his tongue, delighting in the sweet honey of her flesh, the curves and valleys, the growing need that took her over as she panted for more. He wanted to feel her close around him, to join with her and know the crashing ecstasy that would swallow them both.

He sheathed himself inside her, the tightness only making the pleasure more intense. He paused in a bid to relax. He was so close already, the slightest movement might end it before he got started.

"No more waiting," she whispered, grinding herself against him.

He clenched his jaw against the sweet friction. So much for relaxing.

He thrust deep into her. Long, steady strokes that wound him tighter and tighter. She wrapped her legs around his waist, joining the dance as together they found their tempo. Knowing that they'd have only tonight made every sensation sharper, brighter.

He moaned, throwing back his head as each push sent him spinning closer to oblivion.

She bucked and cried out, her release all it took to send him tumbling. His mind fractured, his body burst into fiery pieces. He cried out her name as he held her close against his chest, the beating of her heart in his ear like music.

Magic danced in the air between them, the energy almost visible as it moved back and forth over them, around them. He stretched out his mind, sensing the change in himself, the strengthening of some talents, the weakening of others. All courtesy of Ellery's mysterious ability.

Her eyes were closed, her breathing coming in great sobbing gasps. He pushed a strand of hair from her face, thought about telling her. Not exactly pillow talk. He'd wait. He wanted to linger here, enjoy every delicious second.

If he was right, his seconds might be fast running out.

She lay naked on top of him, his heart only now beginning to slow.

The night had spun out, the two of them spending the hours exploring each other. Tasting. Touching. Whispering words best spoken in darkness.

Guilt should be sucking away at his enjoyment. Pressure

should be making him restless. Distracting him. Instead, the only emotion even touching his drowsy contentment was sorrow. These few hours might be the only time he and Ellery had. He wanted to live them to the hilt.

He clutched her tight, stared into the dark as if the true *fey* might have changed their minds and written his future there.

"Mmmm, it's nice," she murmured, "but I can barely breathe." He released his grip on her. She opened her eyes. "That's a fierce look."

"I'm thinking."

"I can see the wisps of smoke," she teased.

He gave her a weak smile, but his heart wasn't in it.

She rolled off him. Sat up, pulling the blankets around her. "He's out there. Waiting. I can almost feel him. My chest is tight. My skin goes all crawly."

Her sudden departure left him cold. His arms empty. "Ellery, I won't let him harm you." And this time he meant it. No lies.

Even if it cost him his own life, he would confront Asher alone. Without the blood of the trespasser on his blade.

"But what if you can't stop it? Simon has already succeeded once in getting through the wards. How did he manage that if Daggerfell is as protected as you said?"

He sat up beside her. Cupped her face, running a thumb down her cheek. "He took advantage of the one thing I didn't plan for when I brought you here."

"What?"

"You. Your power."

There, he'd said it. Not exactly how he meant to broach this subject, but now was as good a time as any. He didn't know why he'd put off telling her. But watching the consternation and confusion pass across her face gave him a clue. Submerged within a world of *Other* and *fey*, he'd wanted some small corner that magic didn't touch. A place where being an *amhas-draoi* meant nothing. But being a man meant everything.

"I haven't got any power. I'm plain old me. What you see is what you get," she said. "And you've seen rather more than most." She attempted a smile, but it never reached her eyes. Rising, she took a few steps away, resting her cheek against the bedpost, her arms encircling it as if it would hold her upright. "I'm just Ellery Reskeen. Nobody special."

"You are special, Ellery. You're *Other*. You have an ability that moves in ways I've never seen before. It defies everything I know of magic."

Her head came up, interest keening her gaze. He continued, relieved that she didn't persist with her denials, or worse run from his words as if she could outrun what she was. "It's a reactive talent. It works in tandem with the magic around it."

"So I can't turn Asher into a toad or zap him with a bolt of lightning?" A smile hovered at the corner of her mouth.

Conor relaxed the breath he'd been holding. "No. You're more subtle than that. You're like a lightning rod, reshaping the magic of others. Channeling it in ways unlooked for. Strengthening. Weakening. There's no controlling it. It's why Asher wants you. He's never encountered its like either."

She kept silent. Waiting.

"It's why the mage sickness affected me like it did," he continued. "It had passed through your body. Intensified by your magic to unheard-of levels."

Her smile vanished. "You're saying I almost killed you."

"You also saved me. It's probably why your dagger was able to disrupt Asher's wards."

Realization, then horror widened her eyes. "So I allowed Simon to get in. I'm putting everyone in danger just by being here. I should go."

He jumped up, ignoring his nudity as he pulled her close. "No. You're far safer here than on the road. It's just going to take more vigilance." He drew her away to arm's length so he could look her in the face. "It's only for another week."

"But if Asher should try again?" She licked her lips, looked over at the open window as if Asher might leap through it. "If he wants me so badly, won't he try again?"

"I'll be ready. I won't let him take you."

Her eyes snapped back to his face. "And the reliquary? If he comes for that?"

A breeze fluttered the curtains. Moonlight and shadows skipped across the floor. "It's safe enough—for now."

A smile touched her face, lit her jewel-blue eyes. "I guess if I can survive the French, the Austrians, the Spanish, and one randy landlord, I can survive Asher."

He offered her a stony smile. Perhaps she could survive. But could he?

Ellery woke in the half-light before dawn. Conor was gone, not even a whispered goodbye.

Dozy with sleep and sex, she stretched and snuggled deeper into the quilts. Thought back on his confessions last night. Tried to wrap her mind around the thought that she might have a power. Something special that set her apart from everyone. Ellcry Reskeen wasn't just another Army bastard. She was an Army bastard that could shake magic off-balance. Not that it did her or anyone much good. In fact, it seemed downright dangerous. But just knowing about its existence warmed her. Made her feel different. As if she belonged here.

The first birds twittered in the bushes outside, rain dripped through the gutters. But the house was quiet. Everyone still abed. Good. Did they know what had happened in this room last night? Had Niamh foreseen it when she left?

Ellery cringed with humiliation. The whore's daughter fallen into the same disgrace. But this was different. She was no soldier's trull, using her body as the only barter she had.

She'd taken from Conor just as much as he'd taken from her. And though he'd made it clear there was no future for them after Beltane, she could accept that.

If she knew the boundaries, she remained in control. Took what was offered. Enjoyed it for what it was. And when the time came, left him behind without looking back.

She pulled a pillow to her chest, inhaled Conor's scent. A heavy weight settled around her heart.

Who was she fooling?

Chapter Twenty-One

Conor descended the stairs working his shoulder, feeling the satisfying pop and snap of bone and muscle. A wicked smile curled his lips. It was a good stiffness. For once.

Anxious voices rose from the floor below. A woman wept.

Apprehension chilled him. Asher couldn't have found a way through the protections he'd devised. Not so soon. He wanted to run back up the stairs. Check to be sure Ellery was safe.

Jamys entered the hall from the salon. He shouted back into the room, "And keep that girl quiet. Her wailing isn't helping anything." Just then, he spotted Conor. He offered him a grim nod as greeting.

Conor raced down the last few steps. "What is it? Asher?"

Jamys shook his head. "Not this time. It's Aunt Glynnis. One of the men found her early this morning at the wood's edge. Close to the barrows. She's dead."

He stepped back, his gut tightening. "Damn. How?"

Jamys rubbed his bloodshot eyes. "How the hell should I know? There's not a mark on her."

Conor wanted to feel something. Some sense of loss or grief. But all that came to him was a shameful release. Then guilt. "An accident then? She's sleep-walked for years. She almost walked out that upstairs window three years ago. Could this be the same?"

"It's a possibility. Another is suicide. She had enough powders and potions to do herself in ten times over, poor woman."

"Simon's treachery might have been the final blow." Conor thought back to Glynnis's face as she passed him last night. Years of grief had stripped her raw. "I hate to think it. Are you sure there's no way of knowing?"

"None. Perhaps her heart just gave out. Or she saw something in the wood. Maybe—"

Conor's head came up. "You said she was found near the barrows? Then They know what happened to her. They must have seen."

"The *fey*?"

Conor nodded. "It looks like I have more to discuss with them than I thought."

Jamys shot him a look of surprise. "You're planning on summoning the *fey*? Do you think they'll show themselves?"

Conor's voice was firm. "They'd better. I don't have time to play their game. I need answers, and I need them now."

As if she'd been forgotten or—she preferred to imagine— as if she were already a part of this family, Ellery had been left to find her own way through the morning. Glynnis's unexpected death had thrown the household into shock. Servants huddled in knots as if unsure how to proceed. Messengers came and went from the house, riding to Plymouth, Penzance, London to deliver the news. Ellery tried to feel a sorrow. But Glynnis's venomous words haunted her. *He'll take you like the beast he is.*

Conor had taken her. More than once. And Ellery had reveled in the sweet, hot pleasure. So much for her soul.

She ran into Mikhal and Morgan in the great hall, Conor's

father pulling on his gloves. "I'm riding into Penzance. I've got to see to Glynnis's burial."

Seeing Ellery approach, they broke off their conversation to greet her, their smiles strained but welcoming.

"After the threat you suffered last night, I hope this tragedy hasn't unsettled you further. I instructed everyone to let you sleep undisturbed as long as you wished," Mikhal said. "Conor included."

"That was kind of you, but I'm fine. Really." She flushed. Was it her imagination or was her loss of virginity like a brand on her forehead? Neither treated her with any less respect, but she swore she saw a spark of something pass between them. She ignored it. After all, what could she say without sounding a fool—or a slut? "I'm sorry about Glynnis. Is there anything I can do?"

Mikhal shook his head. "All is in hand. It's just a shame that in her view God and *fey* must always be in opposition. The conflict broke her."

Morgan scowled. "She was too weak for such a life. Too weak to understand."

Mikhal turned a wizened eye on Morgan's pronouncement. "Mayhap, but Talan should have known better than to wed her. In his arrogance, he thought he could change her. Make her understand, but he never did. And then he was gone."

Ellery swallowed hard around the knot in her throat. "Someone once told me that it doesn't take belief to make the *fey* world real. It just is. And that some things you simply have to take on faith."

Mikhal's lips curved in the barest hint of satisfaction. "Sounds like my son has been sermonizing at you. He's quite right, you know."

Again Ellery had the sense that Mikhal knew about her and Conor. Knew and, for some reason, approved.

* * *

She found Conor in Glynnis's dressing room rummaging through a dainty white and gold lady's writing desk. No one could have seemed more out of place surrounded by the feminine pale yellow walls, lace curtains, and slender gold-accented furniture. And yet there was something touching about the care he took with each item he uncovered. Letters, diaries, scraps of ribbon, pressed flowers; all the mementos of a life gently laid out piece by piece. Her heart ached with an unexpected jolt at the consideration he took over someone who had hated him. Who had tried to kill him. It was a glimpse into the man beneath the well-armored exterior.

Slump-shouldered over his task, it was easy to see how tired he was. How tension, grief and the effects of injury and illness had worked to wear him down. It was a wonder he'd held together for as long as he had. She wanted to take him in her arms, smooth the frown from his brow. She couldn't destroy Asher, but she could ease Conor's burden for a little while. Long enough to allow him to heal. Strengthen.

He raked a hand through his hair, blew out a breath and pushed back from the desk. "There's nothing here. No note. No journal entry. I've searched this entire room. If it was suicide, she wasn't confessing."

She wasn't surprised he knew she was there. Only that he'd allowed her to witness his weakness. Perhaps last night signaled more than the loss of her sanity. Maybe there was hope for more with him. She'd keep that thought pushed down deep. No sense in getting carried away.

"But Glynnis wouldn't, would she?" Ellery asked. "She'd have known the consequences of taking her own life. No burial in consecrated ground. Eternal damnation. She seemed a very . . . Christian woman."

He snorted his derision. "If you mean fires-of-hell, sins-of-the-flesh Christian. Yes, she was that."

"She suspected there was something between us. She warned me away from you."

"Did she?" His voice was even, noncommittal, but she knew him well enough now to know the effort it took to sustain that control.

She lost her patience. "Your whole family knows, don't they?"

His face went white. "Knows what?"

"Do Society's restrictions end at your family's doorstep?"

"What do you mean?" Confusion replaced the alarm, though Ellery still wondered at his reaction.

"They see nothing wrong with you coming and going from my bedchamber," she said. "Midnight visits. Leaving us alone together. It's unusual to say the least."

He rose and taking her hands in his, led her to the sofa. "Let me tell you a story." He pulled her down beside him, his body dangerously close. "Once upon a time there was a sea captain. His ship foundered just off the Irish coast. He thought he would drown. But he was saved by a *silkie*, a *fey* of the sea whose shape in the water resembles a seal. She brought him to shore, cared for him until he woke. And when he laid eyes on her in her human form, they fell in love." His expression softened as he recounted the love story. His eyes mellowed to a golden-brown, shadows flickering at the edges. "She gave him her sealskin and bid him hide it so that they might wed as man and wife. Ten years and four children later, he offered it back to her, worried she pined for the sea. Do you know what she did? She burned it. Gave up her life as faery and became Mortal."

"Your grandmother and grandfather."

"Just so. My family believes in love, not rules. And they believe when the moment happens, it can't be hindered by the boundaries of Society or even reality. After all, what's one man's reality is another man's fantasy."

"So they throw every woman at your head expecting the lightning to strike?"

He laughed. "No. You're the first."

"Should I be flattered?"

His smile faded. "They hope you'll save me from myself."

She cocked her head, an eyebrow raised. "Do you need saving? You seem to be doing all right without my help."

The shadows that until now had hovered at the edges of his gaze, took over. His expression grew serious. Sorrowful. "I thought so. Now I'm not so sure."

She risked a hand on his arm, enjoying the warmth of his body through the cotton of his sleeve. He caressed her cheek then jerked away, coming to his feet. Her disappointment must have showed on her face. He tucked a curl behind her ear. Gave her an odd little quirky smile. "I'm not sorry about what happened between us, Ellery. Only sorry I can't make it perfect for you. You deserve so much more."

"What if I don't want perfect? What if I just want you?"

"Ouch." He laughed, but this time it was a sad, bitter laugh. "You'll change your mind soon or late. Ask Morgan. Ask Ruan. I'm no knight in shining armor." He cupped her chin. Drew her close. "I'm the wolf howling at your door."

A flood of heat began in her belly. Spread outward in a dizzying throbbing beat. "No need to howl," she said, closing her eyes to let the wash of sensations rush through her. "You have a key."

Despite the spreading shadows of evening, Conor's stride never faltered as he crossed the park. Headed west toward the barrows. He'd played and hunted and worked and explored every inch of Daggerfell's acres. And he knew every tenant, every farmhand, every inhabitant that made his home within its borders.

Except for those who lived beneath the hills. Those he was less sure of. But no less determined to see.

He wasn't sure the true *fey* would show. They were fickle and cunning. If it amused them to help him, they would. But it was by no means a sure thing despite the danger Asher posed to their world as well as his.

He didn't stop at the first barrow, but continued on until he stood surrounded by the mounds, the long grass whispering, bent low across the hills. The magic here sang through him, mingled with his own until the power ran back and forth between him and the ground in a constant exchange. He centered his gaze on the side of the nearest mound and waited.

The idea for this had struck him last night as he lay with Ellery asleep in his arms, the moon silvering her hair, washing her in pale light. Desperation had made it seem possible then. Standing here amid the silence, he wasn't as sure.

Swallows dipped and soared homeward as the day faded into a gray twilight. And still he stood. Quiet. Waiting. His heart and mind sending out an entreaty through the curtain between worlds. His eyes burned with watching, his muscles strained with standing for so long unmoving, but he wouldn't leave. Not until he had the answers he sought.

The last light faded into darkness, and the first star appeared. And just as day slid into night, a voice answered his call. The *fey* would come.

The side of the hill didn't open so much as shimmer like windswept water, the *fey* emerging from the gold and silver ripples. Used to the flash and drama that marked most of their entrances, Conor just rolled his eyes and bit his tongue. He'd give his right arm to witness one of the faery folk walking up, tapping him on the shoulder and introducing himself. It would make life so much easier.

The two males stood to either side of a female who sat astride a milk-white pony. The men were tall and slender, their hair hanging loose about their shoulders, their faces impassive. But the woman, her white-blonde beauty almost painful to look upon, gave him the devilish grin he'd last seen on the Isle of Skye a year ago. Aeval.

"You called us, *amhas-draoi*?" Her voice was barely above a whisper, but echoed in his mind like a shout.

"They sent you to speak with me?" He tried not to let his disappointment color his voice. Aeval's capricious nature and contempt for the Mortal world were well known.

She tossed her head, pouting. "I elected to answer your call, Bligh. You should feel fortunate."

"I'm just surprised. You were with Scathach at the academy when last I saw you."

Aeval's pout turned to a frown, and she shrugged. "Scathach's love of Mortal and *Other* wore thin." Obviously realizing she'd lost her dominance by falling into conversation, she drew herself up and locked him with a freezing stare. Even her voice became cold as a knife blade. "If you seek the reliquary, it is safe. But Asher's army sniffs close. Should the *Keun Marow* find it, their numbers would surely overwhelm the guard we've placed it under. Your time runs short."

"I know. The turning of the season is a week away. And the stones of Ilcum Bledh are close. Asher will have to face me there if he wants to reclaim the casket and free his brothers."

"And if he chooses to stay away?"

"He won't. He knows I have the one who can fulfill the *molleth* set upon the casket. He'll come to stop me."

"Then all is set to our satisfaction. Why bother us until the time?"

He needed to play this just right. He bowed his head as if in supplication. Aeval would like that. She enjoyed subservience in her men and her mortals. When he met her gaze once more, his stare was as hard and as ruthless as hers, and his unyielding stance was that of the most powerful *amhas-draoi*. She would never hear him out any other way.

Her eyes widened, but only for a moment, and then a slow smile tipped her lips. "You seek something else?" Her eyes studied him with new interest, and she shifted on her pony, allowing him a view of the graceful curve of her breasts.

"Answers," he said. "Is there another way to reseal the reliquary? A way that doesn't involve fulfilling the blood curse? The *fey* must know."

"But you have said you have the one who must be sacrificed. Why do you seek another way?"

Conor's heart quickened, his hands clenched into fists at his side. "I would spare an innocent if I could. It's not her crime that she's paying for with her life."

Aeval's reaction was instant. She sat up, her hands gripping the pony's mane so cruelly that it tossed its head. Her eyes snapped with anger. Even the men accompanying her stepped back. "Her?" she said. "That is what this is about? You wish to spare your lover the knife?"

He didn't allow himself a reaction. That's what Aeval wanted. Instead, he took a deep breath. Let it out slowly before he spoke again. "Only a trick of birth sends her down this path. Please. If you know of another way, tell me."

She sneered. "The great Conor Bligh begging? The most powerful *Other* to walk among mortals in ten generations is pleading for his latest bedsport? You demean yourself—and me, *amhas-draoi*. Must I remind you where your loyalties lie? There is no other way. If you are to put an end to Asher's threat, you must sacrifice the woman." She yanked her pony's head around to leave. Her silent companions moved with her. "You're all that stands between Asher and the destruction he plans for Mortal and *fey*. Don't fail us, Bligh."

He clamped his jaw tight, holding back the yell of rage that burned his throat. Never had he fought so hard to remain in control. Never had the burden of his power been so great.

"Wait," he called, almost forgetting the other reason he had for coming here. "Glynnis Bligh, Talan's lady-wife. She was found dead near here this morning. Did you see anything? Did anyone among you?"

Aeval paused. Bending to converse silently with the other two, she twisted in her saddle to look back at him. "Sometimes discovering the truth about the one you love is painful, *amhas-draoi*. And sometimes it kills."

She threw her head back and laughed as the shimmers overtook them and the hill closed, leaving him standing alone among the barrows with only the wind for company.

Chapter Twenty-Two

It was intolerable. All of it. The growing heat. The vile human form he wore. The whining subservience of the few *Keun Marow* he allowed in his exquisite presence. Even the amusing *Other* he'd taken on as a pet was beginning to tire him. The creature's failure to follow through on his boast that he could steal away the soldier's brat had only worsened the situation. Bligh was on his guard. He'd not let a slip like that happen again.

As if cued, Bligh's kinsman flung himself into the room without knocking, a further offense. He'd grown foolish, almost reckless in his insolence. "It's true," he said. "I wouldn't believe it from those monsters watching the house, but I've gone myself. She's dead."

Asher had a momentary stab of excitement before he understood. The old woman. This simpleton's mother. Not Miss Reskeen. "They do not lie," he said, giving him a pointed look. "They know better."

Simon shifted from foot to foot. "You didn't . . . I mean . . . You weren't involved?"

A tight, cruel smile curled Asher's lips. "And if I were? It would only be fitting after the debacle with that Reskeen baggage. She should be here. Now. Mine."

"Conor's strong—stronger than you thought." The man's voice sounded almost proud. Defiant.

A black madness boiled through Asher. "Bligh is nothing. An abomination like all the *Other*. He will die as those *amhas-draoi* before him. Painfully."

Simon drew himself up, his eyes flashing. "The *Other* are more powerful than the true *fey* realize or wish to believe. They may surprise you one day."

"Enough." Asher's frustration and impatience took shape. He lashed out, the dark energy licking through him like venom.

Simon swallowed convulsively before he slumped back in a chair, his face bone-white, the boldness wiped away.

"Do you come to plague me with your ridiculous predictions or have you a reason for disturbing my peace?" Asher asked.

Simon took a shaky breath, subdued and sulky now that he'd been slapped down. "I came to find out if you were the cause of my mother's death. She wasn't a part of this hellish bargain."

Asher spun away to a high-backed chair set near the room's only window. Carved. Quilted in velvet. A fitting piece for a future ruler. He would need to obtain two more just like it. Though, perhaps those could be simpler. Smaller. He was the eldest, after all. The strongest.

Crossing his legs, he picked at the plate of food set out for him. Bit deep into the flesh of a ripe plum. Out of season, but magic had its uses.

His tongue flicked out, caught the last bit of juice sliding down his chin. "A bit late and a bit false to play the loving son, don't you think?"

"I deserve an answer," Simon grumbled.

Asher's eyes snapped to the man's face. Froze him with a stare. "What you deserve is death." He relaxed a fraction. "For your failures as well as your disrespect. But much as I would have enjoyed swinging the scythe, it was not I who ended her life." He drank deep from the claret. "I've not been able to penetrate Daggerfell's defenses since your skirmish. More blame I lay at your door."

"If you'd given me access to the skills I needed . . ."

The wineglass smashed against the far wall, followed by the plate. "You had ample power to complete the task."

Simon flinched at the display of temper, but held his ground. A simpleton, just as Asher had thought. "I was promised," he insisted.

"I was promised Bligh's head on a platter. We have both been disappointed." His glance flicked down to his hand. A fresh wineglass appeared. "Be grateful I overlook it. Once my brothers are released, *fey* and Mortal alike will kneel before me. Or die."

"You've not got the reliquary yet."

"Soon." He gave a barely perceptible shrug. "Bligh has only one chance. And he knows it. If, as you suspect, he's become fond of this woman, he will refuse to use her. He will allow his affection to overrule his sense."

He felt the man's growing dissatisfaction. Dismissed it. Simon Bligh was a tool. He'd offered himself willingly, and he would be grateful for what he was given. He knew what happened to those who openly challenged him. Had burned the carcasses himself.

"You doubt me?" he asked.

Simon pursed his lips. "Conor's as cold as stone and about as emotional. He'll do whatever it takes to succeed. To defeat you."

Asher sniffed, wearied with this conversation. "For all his powers, he is human. He will fall."

Ellery flipped through a fashion magazine she'd found buried beneath a stack of weightier volumes on one of the salon tables. Cousin Molly had subscribed to these types of publications, and Ellery had always laughed at the flimsy silks and transparent muslins, the dainty kid slippers and Chinese parasols, picturing herself in one of those outfits sauntering down Bond Street with a gallant on each arm and another behind carrying her packages.

She looked around her now. Blond, blue-eyed Jamys sat, noodling at the keys of the pianoforte. Quicksilver Ruan dealt and re-dealt a deck of cards, and Conor, whose dark perfection made him seem even more menacing—if that was possible— brooded in a corner by himself.

She had the gallants. And every one better than her wildest imaginings. She only needed the right gown to go with them.

If Molly could see her now.

Across from her, Morgan leaned back and closed her eyes. "I don't think I can take much more of this. I hate just sitting and waiting. Everyone's on edge. And Aunt Glynnis's death has only made everything ten times worse."

Ellery put down her magazine. "Did she hate Conor so much that she could let Simon in? When she knew what he was? What he'd done?"

Morgan's face hardened. "She always blamed Con for Uncle Talan and Richard's disappearance. It didn't matter that Con was barely more than a boy himself when it happened. And when Simon left, she blamed Con for that, too. I don't know how, but in her twisted mind, it all made perfect sense." She dropped her gaze back to her book. Ellery thought their conversation was over, but suddenly Morgan looked up. "Blood's blood. You don't turn on your own. And you don't break ranks." Her gaze and voice were fierce. "Simon destroyed that when he turned Ysbel over to Asher." She threw down her book. "If I ever find him, no bonds of family will stay my hand."

What could Ellery say to that? Compared to Simon's treachery, Molly's paltry insults seemed ridiculous.

She flipped through a few more pages, but now her mind was far from the light summer fashions. From beneath lowered

lashes, she observed the group. Conor sat in a window embra-
sure, his arms wrapped around one bent leg, his eyes trained on
the park beyond. She wished she were bold enough to approach
him. Ask what held him there by himself.

Ruan downed his drink. Dealt out his cards. "Conor," he
called, "Piquet? If we can talk the others into playing we can
try for a rubber of whist."

"Not right now." Conor's gaze swept the room, paused for
a heartbeat on Ellery before moving on. Long enough to
make her stomach flip and a knot rise in her throat. Long
enough to make her wish the floor would swallow her whole.

She went hot with shame at the way one glance made her
stupid for him. Was this normal? Or was this trick of her
body's an inherited weakness? Had her mother felt this same
stomach punch of emotions and sensations that turned Ellery
inside out and hungry for more? And was that hunger what
drove her mother from camp to camp—bed to bed?

A shadow fell across her magazine. She looked up into a
dazzling smile and eyes that gleamed black as sin. "Cards,
Ellery?" Ruan asked.

Morgan sniffed. "Don't humor him. He thinks he's Jack
Sharpe and Don Juan rolled into one." To Ruan, she asked,
"Why aren't you haunting The Cat's Whiskers? Did the tav-
crnkccp throw you out again?"

"If you must know, yes. But in my defense I had no idea
that talented girl was his sister. You're not generally exchang-
ing family history at a time like that, arc you?"

Jamys hit a sour chord. Shook his head. "That's more than
we needed to know."

"She asked."

Morgan rolled her eyes while Ellery looked to Conor,
hoping for rescue. Instead approval—relief, almost—was all
she saw in his gaze. But that didn't make sense. He'd come to
her last night. Staked his claim. Hinted at more.

Had it all been a lie? Just a way to get beneath her skirts?

She flushed. Humiliated at the ease in which she'd surrendered.

"Anyway," Ruan continued, "can't a man spend a pleasant evening in the company of the two loveliest ladies west of the Tamar without being accused of debauchery?"

"In your case, no," Morgan shot back. "Don't you have a ship waiting for you in Plymouth?"

"The *Merrow* is being fitted out with new pumps. And Uncle Mikhal asked that I come home to go over some accounts before I ship out. You're stuck with your big brother, Morgan." He offered her a sugary smile.

She sighed. "Perfect. Bored and annoyed."

"Well, if you don't want my company, mayhap Ellery does." He held out his hand. "A walk, Miss Reskeen? If you like, I can show you the folly my grandfather had built for Gram." His voice lowered. "A lover's tribute."

Conor rose to his feet, his gaze now sharp as a spear point. "You're drunk, Ruan."

Ruan's teasing good humor vanished. "I'm ashore, Conor. And what I do when I'm on dry ground is my business. Not yours."

"Ellery isn't some harbor doxy to be lured into your bed with a sweet word and a walk beneath the stars," Conor said.

Ruan stiffened, his expression lethal. Beneath the charmer lurked a forbidding powerful *Other* in his own right. Ellery hadn't realized he was so—big. "No, she's not," he said slowly. "But perhaps it's you who should remember that, Cousin. Not me."

Ellery's face flamed. She threw herself to her feet, cutting off a strangled sob with the back of her hand.

"Bloody hell, Ruan," Jamys whispered.

She didn't hear anything after that. She stumbled from the salon, humiliation shriveling her insides, tightening her chest until she couldn't catch her breath.

She hated men.

* * *

"Have you ever wanted something you knew you could never have?"

Conor checked himself at the sound of Ellery's voice. Someone was with her. He peered through the crack of the bedchamber door. Gram was there. As usual, she'd sensed she was needed.

He should leave, but curiosity held him silent, waiting for his grandmother's answer.

"For the last ten years," she said.

Ellery hugged a pillow to her chest, her shoulders slumped against the head of her bed.

"Ten years ago, my husband died," Gram explained. "I have never stopped missing him, or wishing he were alive and at my side."

"I'm sorry."

"Don't be, my child. I was aware when he placed his ring on my finger that sorrow would follow in time. But the joy we had while he lived more than offset the pain at his passing. It is better, I think, to experience such love even for a brief time, than pass eternity without."

Ellery didn't look convinced, and Conor couldn't blame her. He'd made a disaster out of this whole thing. "But how do we know the difference?" she asked. "How do we tell what's love and what's only an act to get beneath our skirts?"

"You've seen too much in your short life. It makes you cynical."

Ellery frowned. "It makes me wise."

Gram's soft trill of laughter followed. "Trust to your own instincts. You tread a knife-edge in your attempt to avoid your mother's mistakes. Other than bringing you into this world, your mother's sins—if that is what you wish to label them— are no part of you." She paused. "Don't you agree, Conor?"

Caught, he slid smoothly into the room. "You knew I was there?"

His grandmother held out a hand to him. He took it, stunned at the fragility of her bones. Time passed too quickly. "You have talent," mischief danced in her eyes, "but my experience goes back to the dawn of this age, my grandson."

She stood, patted Ellery on the shoulder. Kissed Conor on the cheek. "And tonight I feel the weight of every century. Good night to both of you."

Her departure left an awkward silence in its wake.

Conor tried filling his memory with images and feelings. The scent of her, the way her dark curls exposed the tender nape of her neck, the flash in her blue eyes when she was angry or determined to have her way, her sharp-tempered sarcasm that she used to hold the world at bay, and the loving, hot-blooded woman beneath the prickles. But Aeval was right. He was *amhas-draoi*. He knew where his allegiance lay. And it wasn't in Ellery's arms.

Finally, she tossed her pillow aside and stood up, her shoulders square, her chin up.

"Listening at keyholes now?" she snapped.

How to answer her that wouldn't get her more upset? "Ruan was out of line. He didn't mean it."

He needed tact, subtlety—and huge doses of exaggeration—if he was going to nudge Ellery toward Ruan. It was the ideal plan. She already liked him. Ruan was smart, funny, respectable—despite appearances otherwise—and altogether too handsome for his own good. Perfect. In all the ways that Conor wasn't. He just wished the damn lunk-head had acted more like a besotted lover and less like an ass. It left it to Conor to talk up Ruan's good points. Win Ellery to his way of thinking.

"I know he didn't mean it," she said, sagging as if all the air had been punched out of her. "He was just trying to liven things up. And it would have worked if we'd been in the mood to be cheered. I guess it's all this waiting for the worst to happen. And then it does. And you know that even worse waits around the corner."

"He's a good man."

She shot him a questioning look. "Who?"

"Ruan. He's not as fly-by-night as he looks. And he likes you. A lot."

Her mouth curved in a sad smile, her eyes searching his. Looking for something he refused to give her. "I like him too, Conor. But what has that to do with anything? I thought you . . . and I . . . was I wrong?"

"I should never have let it go as far as it did. That was my mistake." She wheeled away from him, but he halted her escape with a firm hand on her arm. "There's no future for us, Ellery. I'm not the marrying, settling, dandle-children-on-my-knee kind of person."

"You should have thought of that before you fucked me. Or did you? And you decided to fuck me anyway. I'm no man's whore. Not yours. Not Ruan's."

"I know."

"Do you?" She broke his hold with a quick yank. Paced away. Returned to face him down. "I've scratched and fought and groveled to escape the fate that caught so many of my kind. Orphans. Bastards. With only one way to make ends meet. You saw Mr. Porter. I've fought that kind of prejudice my whole life."

"I'm not the enemy, Ellery."

She looked as if she wanted to hit him. Instead, she placed the palm of her hand flat on his chest. The clean scent of her filled his head, delicious and warm. Her cloudless blue eyes penetrated past every defense he threw up. She knew he wanted her. Knew that but one movement on her part would bring them both tumbling into bed. But she waited for him to make the first move. And that was her mistake.

He gently removed her hand. "I'm sorry. I can't be the man you want."

Without meeting her eyes, he backed up and retreated like the coward he was. It was only when he was at the end of the corridor that he heard her call after him.

"You know, you've never asked me what I want. You might be surprised."

He didn't look back.

Conor worked the sword edge with the whetstone, listening for the sing of rock on steel that told him his angle was constant. He'd come to the stables after leaving Ellery, praying she wouldn't follow. Wishing she had. That had been hours ago, and though the sword had long since been honed to a keen edge, he kept at it.

It was full dark now, his predator's eyesight cutting through the shadows as easily as his newly sharpened blade would cut flesh. He leaned back, wiped his forehead with a sleeve. Stared up at the house.

Lights shone warm across the grass, and the grand strains of Mozart came to him from an open window. Jamys, most likely. Ruan hadn't the patience or Morgan the temperament that allowed for musicality. There was a pause and a few clunky ill-tuned notes followed by Ellery's voice singing a plaintive soldier's song. He pictured her and Jamys seated side by side at the pianoforte. Easy together. Comfortable in each other's company.

Mayhap he'd chosen to push the assets of the wrong cousin. Mayhap Jamys was the better choice for Ellery. His chest knotted with an emotion so close to jealousy it frightened him.

He focused back on the sword, adjusted his grip on the stone. Started again.

He'd been relieved when Ellery's early fury had driven her away from him. Had hoped that this would end it between them, but Simon's attack—coming so close to losing Ellery to Asher's brutality—had knocked him back on his heels. Driven everything but a leaping, blood-pumping need from his mind.

Keep your distance, he'd told himself. Don't get involved.

And then what had he done? He'd given in like some novice. Forgotten every ounce of training in a pair of seductive blue eyes and a body that didn't give a man a chance.

A smile touched his lips. The woman could kiss. He'd give her that much. It had only taken one intoxicating flick of her tongue in his mouth to set him ablaze. But he could have stopped her. Stopped himself.

But he hadn't. And now he faced the problem of what to do about it.

Laughter floated on the wind. And murmured conversation.

Slamming his sword back in its scabbard, he stood to stretch. Wished for the hundredth time it was him in there with Ellery. Wished for the thousandth time he'd never allowed things to get so out of hand. That his course remained set—his goal clear.

He fingered the pommel, his hand closing naturally over the well-worn ridges. As easy as breathing. As easy as sex.

He ran a hand through his hair. Shook his head in disgust. When had duty become a four-letter word?

Chapter Twenty-Three

Ellery leaned over the stall door, feeding the stolen bay gelding pieces of apple. The horse lipped at her fingers, his shaggy head drowsy, his eyes half-closed.

Conor stood watching for a long moment, deciding his next move. His attempt at coupling Ellery and Ruan wasn't working. So if pushing Ellery away wouldn't work, mayhap he needed to have her run of her own free will. She'd lost the natural fear of the prey for the predator. He needed to show her again that not all her wishing could make him the man she thought he was. And that was the point. He wasn't just a man. Something else lurked beneath his skin. Something sinister. Bloodthirsty. Inhuman.

He stepped out of the shadows. "The horses are well enough to travel. Jock leaves for Evan's place first thing in the morning."

She jumped, swung around, her hand to her chest. "You scared the hell out of me."

"It's about time."

She gave the bay one last rub of his nose. "Do you think Evan has smoothed things over by now? We certainly left him with a mess. Those men . . ."

"Were Mortal. What they don't understand, they fear. And

rightly so." He shrugged. "Evan's got the fast-talking tongue of a gypsy. If I know him, he'll have them doubting their own existence before he's done."

She gave an unsteady laugh. Drew close enough for him to reach out. Brush her hair back from her face. Cup the luscious curve of her breasts. He did none of those things.

Instead, it was Ellery who touched him. Placed a hesitant hand on his arm. "Don't."

"Don't what?"

"Don't look that way. Your eyes go bright, but the warmth is gone. It's you—but not you."

He grabbed her. Held her in a vise-like grip until she flinched. "That's just it." His words sharp and violent. "There is no warmth, Ellery. There's nothing. I'm *Other*. I'm *Heller*. And I'm *amhas-draoi*. Any one of those things separately should make you think twice. All three and you should be afraid for your life." He released her. Flung her away so that she stumbled back.

She straightened, rubbing her bruised arms. "Why are you saying these things?"

He advanced on her. Stood so that he loomed dangerously over her. "Because I need you to understand that whatever fantasies you've been spinning about us are way off the mark. There is no us. There never was."

The stricken look in her face would have been heartbreaking. If he'd had a heart. It just made him angrier. More determined to put as much distance as he could between them. For her sake as well as his.

Her eyes flashed. Her chin came up. "I don't believe you."

"And why would I lie?"

"That's a good question. I don't know what your game is."

Ignoring his glowering stance, she stepped closer. The heat off her skin staggered him. And her scent—that musky exotic spice she wore—was intoxicating. She caught his face in her hands. Rose on tiptoe to brush her lips against his. She wove a spell with her body that smashed through his defenses like a battering ram. Molded herself so close he felt the hard pearls of her nipples through the thin cotton of her gown.

Why wasn't she running? Gods, was the woman insane? Didn't she know what he was? Didn't she care? He groaned against the temptation to rub his rock-hard shaft against the *v* between her legs.

"Tell me you don't want me right now," she whispered, her tongue flicking out to taste him.

He closed his eyes. Inhaled a ragged breath. He couldn't push her away. Not when she asked for it with that sultry sex-me voice. When he could smell the wet, hot center of her. That left him only one choice.

He reached within. Unchained the darkest part of him. Let it rise to the surface. Take him over. Howling its release, the beast clawed its way through him. Sank its fangs into his soul. Ate away everything human and left only the cold-blooded *fey* behind.

Muscles hardened. Blood pumped hot and hungry through his veins. His gaze narrowed to a pinprick. Focused on her. He grabbed her off her feet. Held her so that he saw the reflection of his clear gold gaze in her frightened eyes.

Behind him, he heard the horses screaming. Banging against their stalls in mindless panic. They were right to be scared.

"You once said you didn't fear the *Heller* in me," he snarled.

She swallowed. Made no move to escape. "No. I don't."

He dropped her so that her legs buckled. She scrambled back against the stall where the bay plunged and reared.

"Well, you should, Ellery. You should be very afraid."

Ellery picked at the plate in front of her, her appetite not really up to Cook's lavish spread. She ate dinner by herself,

Glynnis's death scattering the family as they prepared for the funeral.

She'd not seen Conor since yesterday and that was from across the hall. He'd shot her a grim focused look, but it was impossible to read the thoughts behind his eyes.

Just as well.

He'd made his intentions very clear—or should she say, lack of intentions. He'd done everything but club her over the head with his indifference. But none of it rang true. She recognized desire. Knew lust. And it was obvious that whatever Conor said, he wanted her. Just not enough. And that was all right. She hadn't expected anything more. She'd dreamed a little. Fantasized even more. But she should have known it would come to nothing in the end. She didn't care what Lowenna said, love was too risky a gamble. The stakes too high.

Jamys came in, breaking off her gloomy introspection. He looked disheveled, a day's growth of beard shadowing his jaw. "I guess I didn't have to worry about getting here before it was gone." He offered her a tired smile. "May I join you?"

"Of course. You look dead on your feet. Haven't you slept at all?"

"It's not been easy reassuring the tenants that Aunt Glynnis's death wasn't the result of *fey* malice. They're a superstitious lot to begin with. And there's enough that goes on around here to keep them that way." He piled his plate with enough food for two men. "That coupled with the inquest in Penzance and coercing a priest to come to Daggerfell to oversee the funeral, and I haven't seen my bed in days." He rubbed his hand over his face. "I think I managed to catch ten minutes standing in a corner. That must count for something." His expression was teasing but warm.

"Here. This should help." Ellery poured him a cup of coffee that he accepted gratefully.

"At least, you seem to have recovered from Simon's attack

with flying colors," he said. "Not many women would handle such an ugly episode so well."

"I'm a tribute to my sex," she said, "And my upbringing. I wasn't raised to scare easily."

"I can only thank the gods that Conor sensed something was wrong," Jamys took a long swallow, "and that Simon's aim has always been bad. I might have lost a brother and a cousin—and you."

The light in his eyes made her wonder if he suspected anything. She kept from having to answer by scooping another forkful of ham into her mouth.

"Asher's influence grows." Jamys clutched his mug with both hands, his jaw firm. Looking decidedly like his deadlier cousin. "We've heard his army of *Keun Marow* have struck twice since your arrival. With each killing, they become stronger. Bolder."

Just thinking of those creatures put her off her food. She dropped her fork to her plate. Swallowed around the knot in her throat. So much for not scaring easily. "Beltane can't come fast enough."

"Beltane?"

"Conor says that's when he'll send Asher back and reseal the reliquary."

Jamys sat back, astonishment wiping out his exhaustion. "He's going to take on Asher? He's crazier than I thought."

Apprehension flickered over her skin. "Why?"

"You saw what Simon almost accomplished the other night. That was just a taste of Asher's power. He's all but indestructible. Mighty even by *fey* standards. That's why they imprisoned him in the first place."

She wished he would stop looking at her as if she were mad. This was Conor's idea, not hers. And until now, she'd thought it made sense. In a magical, nonsensical way. "Conor says the magic found within the thin places will help him."

With all she'd experienced in these last days, her explanation still sounded odd. Like something out of a faery story. But then, she was in a faery story, wasn't she?

Jamys never blinked. "I've been studying the ancient writings. Searching Niamh's archives. The only thing that'll send Asher back is fulfillment of the *molleth*."

"A *molleth*?" Her stomach fluttered. Just the word sounded threatening.

"A curse," he answered. "In this case, the curse placed upon the reliquary when it was created. To reforge the seals, you need the blood sacrifice of the one who violated the casket. Conor's told us the soldier who freed Asher has died."

The fluttering froze to an icy knot. "So the *molleth* can't be fulfilled? There's no way to stop Asher?"

"No. Only the blood of the trespasser or one who carries his blood will work. And Conor's told us the man died without heirs."

The pieces fell together, the picture they created making Ellery sick. She'd been a fool to ever think she had the upper hand with Conor. He'd been using her since the night they met. And in a week, he meant to use her one last time. She was the bait and the trap.

You should be very afraid, he'd warned her. Well, if she hadn't been before, she certainly was now.

Blood roared in her ears. The blood that Conor needed.

She pushed back from the table, ignoring Jamys's look of surprise. She was no lamb to be led to slaughter. She'd leave. Today. And Conor would need to find another way to destroy Asher. Another cat's paw to dupe.

Ellery rolled her borrowed clothes, a knife she'd secreted from the dining room, and a small bit of food she'd been able to sneak out of dinner into a shawl, securing the corners and creating a bundle. Then thought better of it and took the dinner knife back out. She'd keep that close by in case she needed it.

Once clear of Daggerfell, she'd head for London. Or perhaps Bristol. Maybe take ship for America. Brazil. Anywhere Conor Bligh and his damned *fey* madness wasn't. If only she'd kept hold of that blasted pearl, it would have been easy paying her way. But it didn't bear thinking on. She didn't have the pearl.

She cringed, understanding now why Conor had kept his distance. How he must have been laughing at her. The poor besotted twit serving herself up for him on a platter. What other secrets was Conor keeping? Or anyone else for that matter. Did they all know she was doomed to die in a few days' time? Was that the meaning of the looks that passed between the family? Had everyone's kindness been a sham? She gave a thought for poor dead Glynnis and her warnings. Was she the only one telling the truth? And, God forbid, was that why she died?

How far would Conor go to secure his needed sacrifice?

The questions slammed against her mind from all sides until her temples throbbed with them.

Ellery scanned the room one last time. At the fashionable furnishings, the heavy blankets upon her bed, the fire in the grate. She doubted she'd see such luxuries again. With what money remained to her, a garret in some East End tenement was all she'd afford if she were lucky.

A damp chill had stolen in with the setting of the sun, replacing the unseasonable spring weather they'd been enjoying. She pulled Conor's greatcoat out of the back of the clothespress. It was enormous, but it was warm. And she could sell it once the weather changed for good. Serve him right.

Low voices carried from farther up the corridor, but her way was clear, the servants' stair lit only by a thin taper as she slipped down toward the kitchens. Once in the passages beneath the house, she wound her way past storerooms and sculleries to a back door secured by an iron bar. Heavy, but not impossible to lift.

The back kitchen gardens were dark, darker than she'd imagined when she contemplated her flight in her well-lit bedchamber. But it was impossible to go back. She wouldn't remain a guest—or a prisoner—at Daggerfell any longer. Hitching her pack higher on her shoulder, she ignored the fear that sliced through her, warning her she was leaving one threat to face another.

Chapter Twenty-Four

"Conor, you fool. You never told her?"

Gram's look of frustrated disbelief wasn't helping his temper. Or his search. Morgan had gone to Ellery's rooms that night to check on her. Since Simon's attack, Morgan had made a point of stopping in for a few moments to chat. Make sure Ellery was safe.

But tonight her bedchamber had been dark save for a few glowing embers amid the ash in the hearth. Her bed empty. Unslept in. And Ellery was gone.

Morgan had come straight to Conor.

He'd searched the house—twice, his heart racing, a clammy churning in his stomach. Asher. Or Simon. It had to be. Then he'd run across Jamys and Gram. And everything came clear.

"I didn't see a need to tell her," he answered, raking a hand through his hair. "I'd already made up my mind to keep her as far from Ilcum Bledh as possible. What would telling her have done, but frighten her?"

"And your silence was so reassuring," Morgan bit back.

"It's all my fault," Jamys groaned from his seat, his head between his hands.

Gram shook her head, her initial burst of anger settling into resignation. "What's done is beyond our words to mend. She must be found. And quickly."

"I'm such a simpleton." Jamys pressed his thumbs to his closed eyes, his shoulders slumped with fatigue and guilt. "I should have known. And me running on without a thought in my head."

"It's not your fault," Conor argued, "it's mine. And now it's up to me to get her back."

"Go." Gram almost pushed him out the door. "I will see what I can do to aid your search."

"Don't expect much. They weren't helpful when I sought them out."

"I did not give up everything when I wed your grandfather, Conor. There are still those I can call on. Especially once they know for whom you seek."

"I told you, Gram. I'll face Asher on my own. My blade never touches Ellery, do you hear me? She's no part of this fight."

Gram nodded her understanding.

Conor breathed in, centering his mind on the creature inside him. Focusing on the shift. Feeling his body respond. He would need every trait of the *Heller* to track Ellery. Hunt her down before the *Keun Marow* did. Bring her home.

Jamys looked up, his bloodshot eyes glazed with remorse. "So she was right? You really mean to try and defeat Asher on your own?"

Already hovering between man and wolf, Conor's concentration faltered. He swung his smoldering gaze toward his cousin. "Defeat him or die in the attempt." He stalked toward the door, turning back at the last moment. "Unless you've got a better suggestion."

Where had this damn fog come from? Ellery raised her lantern, its meager light doing little more than reflecting off the wall of damp, swirling cloud.

She'd avoided the main carriage drive, hoping to use the track Conor had told her passed through the orchards before coming out at the edge of the village crossroads. But the fog obscured every landmark. She was sure she'd passed that grove of trees once already. And that outcropping of rock looked vaguely familiar. She was going in circles.

She tried searching the skies for some point to guide her, but the moon had yet to rise, and the stars that were visible seemed off-kilter. Not quite where they were supposed to be from one minute to the next.

She swung the lantern to the left. Then to the right, praying she caught sight of something familiar. Something that would lead her to the village and the road away from here.

As if her presence had stirred the woods to life, the dark suddenly seemed alive. Listening. Waiting. Conor had spoken of the *fey* who shared Daggerfell's lands. Would their appearance be help or hindrance? Or was this them at all?

A shape rose up out of the dark like a specter. Dear God. Asher. He'd come back. Or was it Conor seeking her? Either one was a death sentence.

A sob tore up her throat as she spun around, dashing back the way she'd come. Roots and limbs reached for her, wet and slippery leaves set her careening into a stand of holly trees. She ripped herself free, ignoring the stinging pain that followed, dropping the lantern.

She was blind. Out of breath. Her side cramped. She tripped and fell into the base of a fence. Picking herself up, she followed the line, using the posts as guides. Coming to a stile, she scrambled up and over. Then dodged back under the solid wooden stair. There was a space just large enough to fit between the fence and the risers. She crammed herself as far into the hole as she could, clutching her bundle to her chest, using it to muffle the sound of her ragged breathing. They would pass her by. They must.

No leaves rustled. No footsteps sounded. If only her

power was invisibility. That would be a magic worth having right now.

"Ellery." Conor's voice floated out of the fog. Deeper than she remembered. Thick and raspy as if speaking were difficult. "Ellery. It's me. Don't run. I won't hurt you."

Not yet. But give him until Beltane and all bets were off. She wasn't saying anything.

"Ellery. Answer me."

He was right overhead. She tried holding her breath. Closing her eyes as if that would make her disappear.

"I know Jamys told you about the reliquary."

A thump echoed above her head. Then another. Had he settled himself on the stile? She was trapped. She couldn't make a run for it. He'd be on her like a hound on a hare. Like a wolf on a panicked rabbit. And all the knives in the world wouldn't be enough to stop him.

"I won't lie," he continued. "Not now. It's true. That's why I sought you out."

With each word Conor spoke, a warmth seeped deeper through her body. Her limbs felt heavy. Weighted. She tried not to listen to the steady drone of his voice, knowing that he used it to charm her, control her. Like he had those men in the tavern. She shook her head as if she could shake free of him.

"Damn it, Ellery. I have to stop his bid for power. To stop the destruction that will follow if he frees his brothers. The Triad . . ."

He stopped speaking, but his words rolled in her head like endless echoes. Like the sea. She wanted to hear more. Her control faltered. She touched a hand to the bottom of the riser. Only the thickness of one plank kept her from him. From that voice.

"I can't go through with it." His words slammed into her with the force of bullets. "I won't."

The need to reach him rushed out like a receding wave,

leaving her head pounding. His words had no power. Her mind—complete with headache—was her own.

"I'd already decided. That's why I didn't tell you. I'll handle Asher my way."

Even without the hypnotic power of Conor's voice, she wanted to believe him. She wanted him to tell her she was right to trust him. She wanted him.

"If you want to leave, Ellery, I won't stop you. Ruan can take you with him when he returns to Plymouth."

His words were choppy. Bitten off. The voice Conor's, but not. Was it a trick? She couldn't stay under here forever. And Conor wasn't leaving soon by the sounds of him. He had her cornered. And he knew it. Better to face a danger and get it over with for good or bad.

She crawled out of her hiding place, straightening to face her lover or her executioner. The next few moments would tell.

It was Conor. He sat on the stile, his face lost in darkness, but the heat of him palpable.

She wrapped her humiliation and her rage around her like a blanket. She'd not be made a fool of again. "Don't ever try your spells on me. I'm not some simple-minded farmer you can charm into submission."

"No. Not simple-minded. Mule-headed. Blind-lucky, perhaps." He paused. "Shit."

"So I'm the only thing that can send Asher back," she asked, hoping she sounded firm. Brave. "Is that why he wants me dead?"

He took a deep breath before answering. "That's right."

She shuddered, imagining what that moment would have been. Seeing Conor approach. Watching him raise the knife. Her mouth went dry. Still unsure whether to flee, she backed up a step. As if keeping her distance would make it easier. Her eyes adjusting to the dark, Conor's form emerged from the gloom. And she knew exactly why he'd sounded so odd. So unfamiliar.

Stripped bare to the waist, his body's already muscled contours seemed heavier, more powerful. The sculpted bones of his face were longer and thicker, hardening the perfection of his features. The magic of the *Heller* burned flame-bright in his eyes.

Her fingers curled around her knife, even though she wasn't sure she could actually use it. Not on Conor. But if he left her no choice? And even then, would it matter with his body's ability to withstand wounds? She closed her eyes, praying she wouldn't have to find out. "I'll leave. Run to the Continent or maybe even the Americas."

"You won't be safe. The Triad's power isn't bounded by borders or oceans. Once Asher recaptures the reliquary, he'll hunt you down. Destroy you. He'll do anything he must to secure his future."

They had come to the crux of the matter. She opened her eyes. He hadn't moved, but his gaze scalded her with its intensity. Knowing the swooping flips of her stomach weren't all fear, she had to ask the question on the tip of her tongue, no matter the answer. If she wasn't Conor's pawn, anymore, what was she? Really.

"How are you any different from Asher?" she asked.

He rested his elbows on his knees, glanced away into the dark. "I wasn't. Not two years ago at the hillside chapel in Spain. Not two weeks ago when I found you." He paused, the silence weighty with unspoken shame and disappointment on both sides. "You're safe from me, Ellery. I'll not harm you."

She followed the track of his gaze. Even now, the fog thinned, rolled aside by unseen hands. The trees beyond seemed to crouch, waiting for her to answer him. Did she accept Conor's assurances and return to the house? Or did she take him up on his offer of Ruan's protection as far as Plymouth and risk a bid for freedom?

"I'll take you to Gram. You can stay with her until after . . ." He faltered. "I don't know how to convince you."

"When we—I mean that night—after Simon attacked," she asked. "Were you planning to kill me then?"

He stiffened, his body almost rearing off the step.

She jerked away.

He caught himself, settled back. "No," he said, leaving it at that. "Not then." He held out a hand, palm up and open, waiting for her to decide. "Trust me?"

She wavered, wishing with all her heart that she could simply place her hand in his and everything would be perfect. Her faith intact.

Her eyes burned; her face felt tight. She tilted her chin up in defiance of her weakness.

His voice when it came was barely above a whisper. "Ellery?"

One word. Three syllables, but they broke her heart.

"Morgan." Ruan's call shattered the silence like an explosion. "I've found them."

Conor wasn't sure whether to be annoyed or relieved. All he knew was he couldn't take Ellery's devastated look of betrayal much longer. It made him want to scream at her. Shake her until she forgave him. Instead, he sat. Silently. Uncaring. Emotionless.

It didn't hurt so much that way.

He shivered as the magic of the *Heller* drained away, a frozen emptiness replacing the wolf's heat. He was no longer two beings caught within one shell. His mind, his body, and his misery were his alone.

His cousin stepped out of the trees, his lantern throwing darkling shadows over his face. He swung the light from Ellery to Conor, his eyes widening a fraction as he took note of Conor's condition. "You had us worried."

Conor rubbed a hand across the back of his neck. "I've managed to do that a lot lately. I can take care of myself."

"Since when?" Ruan turned to Ellery, spotted the knife she held. "A good thought should you be attacked by a dinner roll." Leave it to Ruan to ignore the situation and go straight for charm. He flashed a smile, but Ellery wasn't biting. Sighing, he tilted his head, studied her. "Are you all right?"

She wasn't, but Conor knew it wasn't his place to say.

She tossed away the knife, pushed her damp hair off her face. "I'm fine, I think."

Ruan glanced around. "I'm surprised we found you. It's dark as a coal scuttle out here. The others are waiting back at the house." His gaze flashed from one to the other. "So we should start back?" He made a move to leave. "Perhaps?" He shrugged. "Anyone coming with the man carrying the lantern, or do you two want to stumble about in the dark?"

"You take Ellery back. I'll be along."

She gnawed her lower lip, mistrust swirling in her blue eyes, her bundle clutched to her chest like a shield. What the hell would he do if she decided to keep running? Pick her up and carry her like a sack over his shoulder? He'd be damned if he'd let her walk out of here alone and defenseless, no matter what he'd promised. She could hate him all she wanted, but he wasn't going to let Asher get to her.

The light from Morgan's lantern splashed yellow light across the grass as she approached through the field. "This is the second time I've had to tramp about in the dark looking for the two of you. It's becoming a bad habit."

She wore baggy breeches tucked into tall boots and one of Jamys's cast-off shirts, her hair pulled back in a knot. Her long, loose, ground-eating strides were more suited to a soldier than a young lady of quality, but Morgan had snapped her fingers at Society a long time ago. "Everyone's worried. I had to threaten Gram to keep her from coming along." She shot a disgusted look in Conor's direction. "Men. Of all the chuckle-headed things to do." To Ellery, she said, "You're safe with him, you know."

Whether it was Morgan's reassuring presence or her words, Ellery relaxed a fraction. Her grip on her bundle loosened, and she no longer looked like she'd bolt if given the chance.

"I don't know what Conor told you, but it's dangerous beyond the protection of Daggerfell. If it's true that you're . . ." she paused, flustered, "if Asher is searching for you, then you're better off here."

"Conor did tell me that—finally," Ellery answered, her voice hard and sharp-edged as glass.

"Well, that's something then." She motioned for Ellery to follow. "Come on. We can commiserate over the stupidity of the male species as we walk." She rolled her eyes. "I could go on all night."

Ellery gave a shuddering breath, misery and anger bright in her dry eyes. "Let's go. I'm tired."

Conor relaxed the breath he'd been holding. Ellery was furious, but she wasn't foolish.

The women moved off, Morgan's lantern lighting the way.

Ruan hesitated. "Conor? Are you coming?"

"Go. I've things to do."

Ruan shook his head. "She'll get over it in time. You know women. Emotional. High strung."

"Right."

"You just wait. A week or two, and this will all blow over."

"It's best this way. She's better off. I'm better off." When Ruan acted unsure whether to leave, Conor threw him a hellfire grin. "But it was damn good while it lasted."

Ruan answered with a shaky laugh, but the sober light in his dark eyes told Conor his cousin knew what he was trying to do. He nodded. "Come when you're ready."

Left alone, the night was his.

He looked up at the moon, bloody and orange as it rose through the branches.

Funny, but he'd wanted all along to keep his distance from Ellery. Had held the crush of feelings locked inside. Had fought the need to touch her, hold her, stamp her as his own. Tonight, he'd finally gotten his wish. She despised him and—what twisted the blade deeper still—she feared him.

There was no future with her. Even when she lay in the crook of his arm, the curve of her cheek soft against his skin, her breath warm and even as she slept, he'd known there was nowhere to go from there. He'd shed that part of him when he'd taken up the life of the *amhas-draoi*.

He loved the thrill and the rush of excitement that came with every use of his power. He scorned anyone who suggested another way. Mocked anyone who told him he might find equal pleasure in a family, a home.

If he survived the coming days, he'd go on alone. And if he didn't?

He slipped off the stile. Melted into the trees, leaving the question hanging on a breeze.

He'd have his answer either way in a week.

The house stood glowing and warm, the lighted, comfortable rooms shooting a new pain into Ellery's heart. This was a home. This was a family. It was everything she'd always wanted. Everything she'd never had. Seeing the concern and love that passed between the Blighs ripped open a longing she'd thought she'd put behind her when she'd left the army's tail and stitched together a life of her own here in England.

Only in these last few days had she begun to imagine a life like this. Starting a family of her own. Starting a life with someone who loved her, not because she could darn a sock or cook a meal, not falsely out of penury and need. But because he loved what and who she was. Because he could dream and hope and imagine a life, too.

By the time she'd returned with Morgan and Ruan, she'd been convinced the others had truly not known what Conor had planned. Either that or the entire family should have gone on the stage. She'd stood by as Jamys had apologized and Mikhal had explained. She'd not resisted when Niamh and Lowenna had hustled her into a hot bath and a linen night-gown. She'd even nodded as they comforted and sympa-thized, and accepted their tea with steady hands. But the words passed through her, barely registering above the din of her own screaming thoughts. Only the worry and fear in their eyes cracked the wall of numb she'd built around herself to keep the hurt at bay.

Conor's mother left after a time, perhaps sensing that all Ellery wanted was to be alone for a long fit of weeping and self-pity. But his grandmother wasn't so perceptive. Or per-haps she didn't care.

She sat at the edge of Ellery's bed, her gaze as impenetra-ble as the fog had been. "What Conor did was done out of fear, not malice."

Ellery drew her knees up, wrapped her arms around them as she looked to the window. "Fear that I would run, you mean."

"No," Lowenna snapped. "Fear of falling in love with you."

There was that word again. How could Lowenna equate Conor's actions with anything close to love? Deception. Be-trayal. These were better suited. She blinked to hold back tears desperate to flow. "He sought me out, lied to me. All for one purpose." Swiping a hand across her face, she forced the pain back below the surface. "He would have killed me," she murmured.

Lowenna gave a slow nod of her head. "As he was, he might well have done so and excused it as necessary." She smoothed a hand over the blankets. Caught Ellery's wrist, making her meet her gaze. Silver gray and stern as winter, it was impossible to look away. "All that has changed since his return home. Being *Other* is a treacherous road, and few know the temptations of the *fey* as well as I. Conor was gifted at birth with great abilities and promise, but only one person truly held his heart. Ysbel's murder unlocked his viciousness and a ruthless power. It forced him to acknowledge the ease with which he could become Asher's equal in both magic—and cruelty. He struggles still." The brilliance of Lowenna's eyes, the gravity of her words pierced Ellery to her core, that small part of her that yearned for Conor even when the rest of her wanted him drawn and quartered.

"What has that to do with me?" she grudged.

Conor's grandmother offered her a warm smile and a motherly pat on the cheek. "You can do what all of us here cannot. You can keep Conor from following that path into a darkness that will consume him in the end." Her wrinkled cheeks dimpled. "You must hold his heart now, dear."

Chapter Twenty-Five

Glynnis's funeral lasted only the time it took to place her in the family crypt, an aged priest performing the ceremony in a high, wheezy voice that set Ellery's teeth on edge. Low clouds threatened rain, and a damp, foul wind blew steadily from the south, hissing through the loose stones of the tomb, whipping the priest's black cassock into bat's wings. Next to her, Morgan straightened her hat, muttering something under her breath about spriggan mischief.

Ellery stood between Morgan and Lowenna, hands locked together in prayer and her gaze centered on the patch of grass at her feet. Not due to any spiritual reverence. She'd decided long ago that if God did exist, he spent little time worried over the problems of men. But because that way, she didn't have to look in Conor's direction or acknowledge his existence. It was petty, but she couldn't trust herself. She was still mad as hell.

Back at the house, Ellery started up the stairs, hoping to hide in her room for the rest of the day. Perhaps for the rest of the week. Until she could leave here and never look back. But Morgan stopped her, challenged her.

"I thought you braver than that." She stood hands on hips,

her face grave. "Hiding from Con isn't going to solve anything between you."

"No, but at least I don't have to fight my urge to rip him to shreds." Ellery sighed, shoulders slumped. "It's better if I just stay out of the way. I'll be gone soon, and your family can forget I even exist."

Morgan frowned.

"You don't understand," Ellery added, then choked off the rest of her words. She sounded whiny, and she hated whiny. That was Conor's fault too. She'd never been whiny before he came along. Or needy. Or weepy. Or dizzy with a joy that skimmed under her skin and flashed through her insides until she buzzed with it.

She scowled. That kind of thinking got her nowhere.

Morgan followed Ellery up the stairs. "I understand plenty. But if you're half the fighter I think you are, you won't let Con chase you away." She took her by the wrist. "What he did was wrong. Gods, that's not saying the half of it. And I'm not making excuses. But if you'd seen him in the weeks after Ysbel's death. If you'd watched the changes wrought in him by her murder." Ellery remained stone-faced. "I'm not telling you to forgive him, but sometimes . . ." She shrugged.

"I turned the other cheek once, and got slapped again for my trouble."

Morgan laughed. "Come down. It won't be as bad as you think. He's under siege by Mrs. Bushy and her daughters. She's a friend of Gram's and out to snare husbands for her four girls. The hunter's become the prey."

Conor did look caught—and miserable. He stood, drink in hand, a head taller than any other man there. He scanned the room for rescue, his eyes alighting on her, a haunted need in them that twisted at her resistance. Frightened at her reaction, she ignored his silent plea and looked away.

She couldn't have made it through the next hour without Morgan's help. She took charge, introducing Ellery to the handful of guests who'd come out of obligation or curiosity, explaining her presence at Daggerfell, easing Ellery's way through the longest day of her life.

She knew Conor watched. The weight of his stare pressed upon her, keeping her edgy and tense, sending her pulse racketing out of control, her throat dry. It was anger. Nothing more. Her first instincts had been right. He was trouble. And his trouble had turned her upside down and inside out. She hated him. But she loathed herself for wanting more. For wanting him—still.

Tight, uncomfortable silences punctuated the hush-voiced conversations. Glynnis haunted them all, and her death, though ruled accidental, remained a mystery. Only the determined Mrs. Bushy seemed oblivious as she moved her girls from Conor to Ruan to Jamys, extolling their virtues in a loud unruly voice as if she hawked vegetables at market.

Glancing around, Ellery's heart jumped. Conor bore down on her, his gaze ominous and single-minded. Did she stay and confront him? The coward in her screamed panic, and Ellery excused herself in a rush of apology as she fled toward the hall. She couldn't speak with him. Not now. Not when she didn't know what words might flow, what emotions would rise to the surface first. Retreat. Regroup. Then attack.

Stupidly not watching her steps, she careened into a gentleman just outside the salon doors.

He steadied her, his hand like a vise. "Pardon me, miss. No fire, I hope." One hand gripped her, a muff cap tucked beneath his other arm.

"None, thank you," she answered. Her eyes swam with frustrated tears, but she had the hazy impression of a swordbelt crossing a silver braided chest, white facings, silver buttons. If only he'd let her go before Conor cornered her. "Excuse me. Please."

She drew away, staring up into a square-jawed face, glacial blue eyes, and hair guinea-gold, knotted into a tight soldier's queue. Not the heart-stopping magnificence of the Bligh men, but a ruggedness that made you look twice. Or three times. Too bad, she was in no mood for handsome men. She offered him a defiant flip of her chin and an arrogant glare that brought a thin smile to his lips. "A whole family of hellcats," he murmured under his breath.

The servant accompanying the officer beckoned him forward. He nodded her a dismissive salute, his attention already centered on the room's occupants.

"Colonel Sinclair of His Majesty's 14th Light Dragoons, sir," the servant announced. "Come for a word with you."

Curious, Ellery put off her flight. Conor wouldn't dare come after her now. Not with this newcomer appearing, all business by his demeanor and his grim face. She watched from the hall as the colonel surveyed the room. She knew that pose. An officer getting his first glimpse into enemy territory. Reconnoitering his position.

But it was Morgan's reaction that surprised her the most. Her eyes flashed to the man's face, her smile dying. He nodded in her direction, but instead of returning the civility, she spun on her heel and walked away. Interesting.

Mikhal showed the man back out into the hall. Ellery drew close into the shadows, interest overcoming good manners. What did this colonel have to do with the Blighs?

"Can I help you? As you can see we're taken up with family today."

"I'm well aware, Mr. Bligh, and I hate to bother you at such a time, but it's about your sister-in-law's death that I'm inquiring."

Mikhal raised an eyebrow. "You've caught my attention."

"I'm conducting a military investigation. Five soldiers have died under similar circumstances to Mrs. Bligh's. Unmarked. In the open. Most near hills or mounds," he reddened, looking decidedly uncomfortable, "or close by ancient standing stones. It sounds ridiculous but I thought if I could speak with you—"

"Come with me, Colonel, into my study." He gestured toward Conor and his nephews to join them, but Morgan was there first, her expression thunderous. "You're not welcome here."

"Morgan," warned her uncle.

"You don't understand." And Ellery froze at her words coming from Morgan's mouth. Thought she understood when she heard the venom in them. The hurt and betrayal. "He's only here to cause us grief. He excels at it."

Colonel Sinclair's face was as remote as hers. "Miss Bligh. I hope your trip south was uneventful."

But Morgan had already stalked off, her strides only slightly hindered by the rare gown she'd donned for the funeral.

"My study, Colonel? And you can explain yourself to us all." The four of them disappeared behind closed doors.

"There's a story there, I'm thinking." Lowenna's voice whipped Ellery around. Conor's grandmother stood beside her in the corner, her flashing gray eyes locked on the study door.

"Do you think he's what brought Morgan home?" Ellery asked.

Conor's grandmother sighed. "Morgan is a confusion of wants and needs even she doesn't fully understand. But her mother is gone. It is up to me to untangle what I can, and comfort what I cannot."

She started to follow Morgan's route toward the back of the house, turning back once. Her lined cheeks were pale, her lips pursed. "I'll say this and no more. Each hour you spend in anger is an hour lost forever. Don't wait too long." Age settled into her eyes like fog shrouding the brightness of the sun. "We walk a razor's edge. There is great magic to be had within the quoit's boundaries and at the turn of the season." She stood stoop-shouldered as if the merest breeze might topple her. "It may be enough to do what needs doing." But even her shrouded gaze held the power to scorch. "Then again, Ellery Reskeen. It may not. And regret is a cold and cheerless lover."

Conor found Morgan in the greenhouse, hidden between cold frames and a wall of tropical palms. The last place anyone would look for her, so the first place he'd searched. Her hair hung loose around her shoulders, hiding her face, but the way she was shredding a leaf between her fingers gave him a good indication of her emotions.

"He's gone. Doesn't look like he'll be back."

She flicked her hair back, her expression a slash of white-hot fury. "No doubt riding home to his wife." The leaf fell in a million tiny pieces at her feet. "If we're lucky, he'll fall off, break his fat head, and we'll be good and rid of him."

"Is that how it is? I had a notion when the temperature dropped to freezing at your first glimpse of each other."

"It's no way." She broke off a palm frond as if snapping a neck. "Forget trying to comfort me. Gram's already come and gone. It was a shock, I'll admit, but I'm over it."

"I can tell."

She blasted him with her gaze.

"You don't scare me. I know that look. And just so you know, you've got nothing on Ellery."

He plucked his own leaf. Twirled it between his fingers.

She sniffed. "Speaking of whom, instead of pestering me, why aren't you trying to patch things up with her?"

Served him right. He let the leaf flutter to the floor. He'd known it was a bad idea following her. But between Ruan, Jamys, and himself, he'd drawn the short straw. He blew out a breath. Who the hell's idea was it to draw straws anyway? "You can't throw me off the scent by changing the subject. I came out here to talk about Sinclair."

Morgan shrugged. "He's military. Proper blue blood. Said he

loved me. Forgot to mention he was already married. The end."
She slid him a glance. "So why aren't you trying to mend things
with Ellery?"

"You're not going to forget it, are you?"

She shook her head. "No, so you may as well answer me."

He plowed a hand through his hair. "It's not exactly easy to
explain away murder. And Ellery isn't amenable to sitting still
long enough for me to explain anything."

"Those sound like excuses. She's heartsick. Wants to plant
you a facer, but she'd come round if you gave her the chance."

"I'm not going to give her that chance. Not the chance to
forgive me and not the chance to get hurt all over again when
things go sour."

"You don't know—"

"You know as well as I do the odds of my coming back
alive from Ilcum Bledh. I barely survived the last battle with
Asher. Ellery's anger means she won't be hurt when . . ."

"That's the craziest thing I've ever heard. She's upset—
bloody hell, who wouldn't be—but that doesn't mean she
doesn't care. Or that she won't be torn apart with grief if you
don't come back down that hill when it's all said and done."
She looked away. And back again, her gaze somber. "She
won't be the only one, Con."

Conor slammed his hand against the wall, cutting off her argument. Turning it back to the reason he'd sought her out. Unwilling to think beyond tonight. Or to add the burden of his family's
guilt on top of everything else. "Sinclair and you. It's over?"

Morgan subsided, sullen and annoyed. "It is."

"Good. Then I can reassure your brothers you're not about
to do something stupid. As for Ellery and me? Leave it alone."

"Conor?"

The look he settled on her spoke volumes, he hoped. He
wasn't up to much more. "Leave it. Alone."

* * *

Conor lay on his bed, hands behind his head, staring up into the dark. He'd yet to undress or even shed his boots. He hoped for the silence to enfold him, to have the brooding sweep of his thoughts drag him under where loneliness and grief couldn't touch him.

He closed his eyes. No use. Sleep wouldn't come. Every muscle jumped with an edgy anticipation, and his mind ricocheted from thought to thought, leaving him scattered. Powerless. Not a state he was used to or handled well.

He'd tried drowning his confusion in drink.

No luck.

An asset in a fight, his body's extraordinary healing made getting plastered impossible. And his words with Morgan had only pushed him further into this net of warring emotions.

Responsibility. Revenge. Honor. Love.

Twice, he'd almost gone to Ellery. But it would have embarrassed them both and done nothing to solve the greatest obstacle. Asher.

His mind spun out, searching for a way to defeat the renegade *fey*. One that wouldn't spell his own death. Was there a way? Had he missed something?

He thought of the *amhas-draoi*, but that brought him nowhere. Knowing he had the sacrifice and refused to use her would not put him in the brotherhood's good graces. Actually, he wasn't sure what they would do if they found out. Would they help him, or would Scathach and the rest of them force him to follow through with Ellery's murder?

His stomach muscles clenched just thinking about it. His shoulders, back, and neck tight as wire.

No. He'd not summon them. He'd keep his decision quiet. Ellery's identity a secret.

He'd face Asher alone.

How had it gotten so complicated?

But he knew already. He carried the answer with him always.

He dug in his pocket, drew Ysbel's ring out and rolled it between his fingers. Such a tiny trinket, but it chained him to a path with the strength of irons. Marched him toward a showdown with Asher that he'd undertake even if an escape could be found tomorrow.

He'd meet the demon at the ancient stones of Ilcum Bledh. Face the creature who'd stripped away the most important person from his life. Used her and made her suffer. And with her murder had crushed a connection that had held him solid in a world he felt less and less comfortable in.

He pinned his gaze on the blackest corner of his ceiling, but his mind remained trained inward—on the days after Ysbel's death. He'd wanted to give the *Heller* within him full rein, ride the night on a rush of destruction and death. Send anyone to hell who stood in his way. He'd nursed that hate, fanning it to life any time he faltered or thought to turn away from what he'd become—more animal than man.

Until the village tucked between the moors and the sea.

Until the night he'd returned from the dead to a young woman's challenge.

A knock dragged him back to the present. Followed almost immediately by Morgan's head peering around his door. "We need to talk. Can we come in?" She'd brought reinforcements.

"Bit late to ask," he answered, fisting his hand over the ring.

Morgan ignored his sarcasm as she beckoned Ruan and Jamys in behind her. All three looked at once both sheepish and unflinching as they took up positions around his room.

He sat up, knowing what was coming. Dreading it, anyway.

Ruan and Jamys settled near the door as if expecting him to make a dash for it.

If he thought he could make it, he might try. He was too keyed up, too pulled taut to sit quiet through their browbeating.

Morgan was the spokesman. She went right for the throat. "You're not going alone."

"Say that again?"

"You're not facing Asher alone. It's foolish and makes no sense."

"What's foolish is thinking your presence would help. You don't know what you're getting into."

"Don't sell us short, Con. We're not unschooled dolts. I've been with Scathach for five years. Ruan and Jamys," she motioned to her brothers, "are skilled if not trained. We can do this."

"I won't allow it."

Ruan straightened, shrugged matter-of-factly. "Short of tying us up, you can't stop us from being there when it happens."

"And what makes you think I won't?" Conor swung out of bed. Rubbed an impatient hand across his jaw. "Hell, you're barely out of the sick room. And that was Simon, for God's sake."

Ruan touched his side. "That was a coward's blow, and you know it. I owe that bastard one."

"But it's not Simon alone. What will you do against Asher? You've got more sense than this, Ruan." His gaze sought out Jamys. "Are you in on this lunacy? All three of you would be sport for Asher. For his packs of *Keun Marow*. He's already killed four *amhas-draoi*." His gaze swung between the three of them. "He's already killed Ysbel."

Jamys stepped forward. "We're a family, Conor. That means we hold together. Fight one Bligh, you fight us all."

"It also means I don't let you get yourselves killed." He speared Morgan with a glance. "You talked them round to this foolishness."

Morgan went stiff. "I told them what I knew about Asher and what I knew about you. They made the decision."

"Is that right?"

Ruan cocked his head, tried for a smile. "Four are stronger than one, Conor. Don't turn your back on our help without some thought." His gaze turned somber and cold as blue ice. "Remember. We loved her, too."

Like a fist to the chest, the words knocked him back. They understood how close he'd come to letting the beast in him rule. And they had given him time to make his choice without interference. His time was up. "It's not your fight," he said.

But he knew now the words were pointless. They stood firm.

Ruan clapped him on the shoulder. "It is now."

Chapter Twenty-Six

Conor found his mother just where he expected to; buried deep among a stack of ancient texts, the pages crumbling, the leather bindings cracked or looking as if mice had gotten to them.

Morning sun streamed through the tall windows overlooking the rose gardens. The sky was a breath-stealing blue, the trees a spring collage of pink and white and green. But the view was lost on Niamh. Her eyes were trained on the words in front of her. Her mind locked on unraveling the mysteries within the writing. It had always been that way.

She broke off reading at his approach, giving him a pointed look over the top of her spectacles. "It's taken you long enough to come to me. But better late than never." She motioned for him to take a seat.

He must have shown his surprise as he fell into a chair across from her.

"Call it a mother's gift." She smiled. "And your grandmother's nosiness. She told me what you were trying to find. And why." She leaned forward, put out a hand. "Is there really no other way?" Just before she touched him, she withdrew, clearing her throat. "I'm sorry." She took off her glasses, wiped them with a corner of her skirt. "You're a grown man now, aren't you? Well past a mother's worry." She disguised her obvious discomfort with a dismissive laugh as she settled the spectacles back on her nose.

But it only illustrated how deep their estrangement was. How much separated them. Even now.

"I anticipated your coming—eventually," she said, her tone clipped and business-like. "I've been looking through the Book of Cenn Cruaich. The writer delved extensively into the witch, Carman's attempted overthrow of the *fey* world."

"Have you found anything to help me?"

"No. But did you know the sorceress, Bechuille, who imprisoned the Triad originally spent the last years of her life on the Isle of Man?"

"I'll be sure to tell Asher when I see him," he mumbled.

She raised her head. "What's that?"

He straightened. "I said that's fascinating information," he said, speaking louder.

She shook her head, laughing, "Liar," as she pushed a pile of parchment toward him. "Here. Begin with these. They're earlier translations of poems discovered in the library at Clonkellin. Dense reading, but you never know what you'll find if you suffer through."

The pages were damp. Mildew furred the corners and darker blotches of who knew what stuck parts of them together like glue. And the smell was incredible. Decay mixed with old shoes and urine.

Where had his mother dug these stories up? Or was this her way of getting him to leave? Give him the filthiest manuscripts in the archives. See how fast he runs.

Determined to both find the key to Asher's imprisonment as well as show his mother she wouldn't scare him away so easily, he pulled off the top piece of vellum, smoothed it out in front of him. Bent his head to the task.

He never looked up, though he felt her eyes on him from time to time. He knew what he'd see within them if he did.

Always close, he'd felt the distance when he'd come home right after Ysbel's death. The grief in his mother's face and the chill in her gaze when it rested on him had been as painful as any wound. To avoid it, he'd simply stayed away. He didn't have to face the guilt that chewed at him. The disillusionment in his parents' faces.

He'd let them down. Ysbel's death was his fault.

The clock ticked away the hours. He read page after page. Gaping holes in the shelves where volumes had been now littered the tabletops, the floor. Neither had spoken. But with every minute gone and every entry read, his body wound tighter. His muscles twitched with impatience. His head throbbed with tension.

It was as if Ysbel's ghost sat at the table between them. Giving him a not so gentle elbow in the ribs. Screaming in his ear. Forcing him to confront his mother.

The words started in his chest, clawed their way up his throat. "To answer your question," he blurted out, "no. Unless I find something here," he gestured at the mess piled around them, "there is no other way. And of course it's your business." Once he'd begun, it came easier. "I've probably never needed a mother's worry more than I do now."

"Conor," she whispered, her voice shaky with emotion. "My son. We'll find a way. We must."

She sounded so sure in his success he didn't have the courage to contradict her. She'd lost one child to Asher. If she needed this belief to hold the fear at bay, so be it.

He began reading where he'd left off. But the air in the room was different. The mood broken by their confidences. The silence between them now brought comfort. Reassurance.

This time it was his mother who spoke. "I know everyone says I'm lost in a world of books. That I don't know what goes on around me half the time." She paused as if he might argue. When he didn't, she cleared her throat. Started again. "But I know what you think. What you've thought since word came of your sister's killing." Her voice was hesitant. "None of it was your fault."

He wouldn't look up. Wouldn't search out the truth in her eyes to find nothing but empty platitudes. That would hurt worse than the chilly indifference. He kept his eyes on the page.

"I mourned her, Con. I hated Asher for sending me such pain. Hated Simon for his greed. Hated Glynnis for her weakness." Her voice calmed. Steadied. "But I never hated you. Never blamed you."

His eyes swept up to meet hers. A soft honey brown that belied the steel behind them. He read real sorrow. Old griefs. New strengths. But no reproach. Her words spoke the truth. "You're all I have. The only child left to me. And I will protect you as fiercely as a she-wolf." This time when she leaned forward, she touched him. Ran her hand down his face. Patted his shoulder. "I only wish you'd come home earlier to hear me say it. It might have spared you a year's worth of regrets."

The urge he'd felt pushing him toward this showdown eased. Almost as if Ysbel were sitting back, arms crossed, congratulating herself on a job well done. His gaze flicked to the empty chair. He gave it a lopsided watery smile before turning back to his mother. "As you said yourself—better late than never."

Ellery rambled the orchards, Mab sniffing ahead of her, tail waving like a flag as she searched the brush for game.

She'd used the dog as an excuse to wander out here. Poor thing needed a run, she'd told the skeptical grooms as she'd urged the dog away from its dinner. What she really wanted was to get away from the apologetic glances and sheepish, awkward conversations that had marked her days since Conor's confession. They probably wished she'd disappear and let them get back to their normal well-ordered life. Or throw herself on Conor's dagger and end Asher once and for all. Not bloody likely. She was no hero. She liked living, thank you very much.

Wind lifted the ribbons on her bonnet and chased her skirts around her ankles. A questing, churlish breeze that seemed to be seeking. Probing. For information. For weakness.

She clutched her pelisse tight as the gusts licked over her before moving on. The sun shone no less brightly, but a shadow darkened the sky, made real the ominous threat hanging over them all.

The jingle of harness pulled her heart into her throat. Had this ill breeze brought Simon with it? Was this her fault? A result of this crazy power Conor swore she had?

She backed off the path, hoping stealth would allow her to get far enough away before she made a dash for the house. But Mab ran ahead, the old dog barking with joyful abandon. So much for stealth.

"Miss Reskeen, isn't it?" A man stepped from the trees, leading a leggy, gray gelding. In a stylish coat of bottle-green and buff breeches tucked into mirror-clean boots, she almost hadn't recognized the officer from Glynnis's funeral. The man Morgan was trying desperately to forget.

Mab trotted beside him, her tongue lolling in a big doggie grin, her tail drumming against his leg. Some guard dog she turned out to be.

She called Mab to her side, donning her best lady-of-the-manor reserve. "How do you know me, sir? We've never been properly introduced."

His smile turned a handsome face into something dangerously appealing. A fact of which he seemed all too aware. "No, we haven't. But Mr. Bligh mentioned you when I was here last. A close family friend, I believe?"

Family friend, indeed. That was putting more than a touch of rouge on the pig. She offered him a chilly smile. "You've been mentioned as well. Though the terms were far less complimentary. Rogue. Scoundrel. Libertine. Need I go on?"

His smile vanished, his gaze going stone-hard. "At least she's mentioned me. That's something, isn't it?" The horse tossed its head, pawed impatiently at the ground as if sensing its rider's flicker of anger, and Mab's gaze moved between the colonel and Ellery as if unsure who to favor. Then, tail straight, ears pricked, she turned and, barking, ran up the track. Around a bend.

"Go home to your wife, Colonel Sinclair. You're not welcome at Daggerfell. Surely you see that."

"Can you take a message to Morgan for me?" Before she could refuse, he continued. "Tell her I'm sorry she found out the way she did. Tell her I can explain."

"I've listened to the explanations of men all my life. Excuses is more like it. If you were worth having, you'd tell her yourself, or better still, leave her alone. You've hurt her enough."

He stiffened, his back parade ground straight, his chin set. "Thank you, Miss Reskeen for your help."

"I'm not trying to help you, Colonel Sinclair. I'm thinking only of Morgan." She crossed her arms. "Good day," she said, hoping he'd take the hint.

Tipping his hat, he swung into the saddle, pulled his horse's head around to follow Mab back through the trees and onto the track that led toward the village.

Ellery watched him leave. Good riddance. He looked like the worst sort of officer. Proud. Impatient. Full of his own self-worth.

She called for Mab, but the dog wouldn't come. Following the sound of frenzied barking, Ellery rounded the trees. As she got closer, the yips and yowls grew shriller. More frantic. A snaky feeling made Ellery swallow hard. She started to run. Oh God, if something happened . . .

At the far side of the trees, she slid to a stop. Sinclair had dismounted and tied off his horse. Beyond him, Mab still growled and snarled, her back bristling with viciousness.

Ellery risked a look over his shoulder. Wished she hadn't. Her heart slammed against her ribs. Her breaths came short and quick as fear ricocheted through her like bullets.

A corpse dangled by its neck from a low bough across the path. Dressed in black, a dagger had been thrust hilt-deep into its chest.

The colonel approached it, nudged it with one hand so that it twisted back and forth, its head lolling at a grotesque angle.

"Is it . . ." Her words wouldn't come.

"A dummy." He reached up. Yanked the body to the ground. "Dressed to look human."

She shoved it with the toe of her boot. Flipped it onto its back so that its eerie painted stare grinned up at her. "No," she whispered through chattering teeth. "Dressed to look like Conor."

Conor stood at the door, a hand on the knob. Ysbel's chambers lay just beyond. This time there was no hesitation. He slid the bolt back, flung the door open. Stepped inside as if he'd been gone only hours and she'd be here waiting for him.

Golden afternoon light from the diamond-paned windows splashed across the coverlet, climbed the sage-green walls, caught and clung to the dust that hung on the air. Her things still littered the mantel, the tabletops. Her bookshelves. But they'd been straightened and tidied. A sure sign that Ysbel no longer occupied the room. She'd been a complete mess.

He sank onto the bed, ran his hand over the patterned quilt, tried to capture a hint of her scent. But there was nothing here. Her shade might linger, but Ysbel was gone. And not even Asher's destruction would bring her back to him. He pulled the ring from his pocket, rolled it between his thumb and finger, watched the light flash over the gold. Fisting his hand over it, he dropped his head. His eyes burned as he shook with dry, wracking sobs. "I'm so sorry, Ysa. It's my fault. All of it."

The answering warmth that flowed over him and around him soothed the tightness in his chest. Across his shoulders. But it was the subtle aroma of hedge rose and lavender that eased the bruising in his heart. It wreathed him like a cloud, and he knew she was there. And she forgave him.

Chapter Twenty-Seven

Ellery wandered the upper gallery, pausing now and then to glance up at a portrait of a long-dead Bligh. Rain drummed on the eaves overhead, streamed down the long windows along the north wall.

It was the eyes, she decided. In every instance, there was a quality about the eyes that marked them out as different, not quite human. She couldn't put her finger on what it was. The shrewd, piercing stare, the almond, upturned slant, or the ethereal light of their gaze that burned from the canvases as if the subjects might step from their backgrounds and speak.

Feeling a chilly draft from an open doorway, she glanced over her shoulder. Conor strode toward her, purpose in his step, decision in the set of his jaw. He was perfection and then some. The powerful muscled body, the sculpted arrogance of his face, and the eyes that glowed burnished bronze. Like the eyes in the paintings. The eyes of the *fey*.

How could a man so vital just stop being? But she knew. She'd seen it too often in the hours and days after battle when men she'd spoken with, laughed with, ridden beside suddenly weren't there. Erased.

She swallowed around the hard lump in her throat. Tried not to remember the horrible, spine-chilling dummy in the woods. The effigy of Conor. Asher's warning to them all that he waited and watched. That safety was a thing of the past.

Thank God, Sinclair had been there. She'd been a gibbering idiot until he'd shaken her back to sanity. He'd demanded an explanation, but what could she say that didn't make her sound as insane as she seemed? And so she fobbed him off with lame explanations until he'd given up and brought her home, handing her off to Lówenna with a grim face and a searching stare. Thank God it hadn't been Morgan to meet them in the stable yard. That would have really fired up an already charged atmosphere.

Now as Conor approached, she took hold of herself. It wasn't murder she saw in his flint-hard gaze. But something equally significant.

"I need to speak with you." If he felt any lingering sense of guilt over his treachery, she couldn't tell. He was as cocky as he'd ever been.

"And if I don't want to speak with you?"

"Then you'll listen." He grabbed her by the arm, glaring down at her.

"Or what? You'll fry me with a look? Cleave me in two?" Her rage and fear exploded through her with the power of a gun shot. She tore away from him. "Drag me to the quoit and slam a dagger through my heart?" She couldn't stop the words now. They came fast and furious and without thought. "You had your chance to talk, Conor. You had days to tell me what was going on. And you chose to lie. Lie and . . . worse . . . you pretended you cared. That we . . ." She choked back a sob. Refused to give him the satisfaction. Crossing her arms, she centered all her loathing in one level stare. "I don't care how much magic you can wield. Where it counts, you're all man. You'll say anything—do anything to get what you want."

His jaw jumped. "I had an obligation. My mission was to stop Asher. It still is."

"Then complete your mission, and leave me the hell

alone." She wrapped herself in cold dignity. It was all she had left.

"Not like this. You're not running from this conversation— or from me." The unbending will behind his words stopped her. "Do you know what I've been doing all day?" he asked. "I've been with Father, his lawyer, and the local bishop."

He paused, but she kept silent. Where was he going with this?

"Marriage, Ellery," he continued. "I want to marry you."

He slid his wolf-head ring off his finger. Took up her left hand and slipped the gold ring over her knuckle. "It's too big. But it'll do for now."

She should be trembling with joy. Giddy with a wild delight. And if it had happened days ago, she would have been. But not now. Not when the truth of Conor's deception still battered her. She fingered the ring. Watched the flicker of light play over its snarling face. "Why?"

"What do you mean why?" He stiffened as if confused at such a reaction. "My family will make sure you're protected. Taken care of."

"And how do we get past the fact that I'm still damn mad at you? Not exactly the best way to begin a life together."

"Let's face facts, Ellery. There won't be a life together. Even if I manage to find a way to defeat Asher, I won't be coming back."

She clenched her teeth against the pain of those words, but that was all. Her throat ached with the effort of holding back. "You don't know that."

His voice and gaze were solemn. "Yes. I do. So what do you say? Can you ignore the fact you want to kill me long enough to become my wife?"

"It's a generous offer."

His mouth twisted in a grim smile. "Don't show so much enthusiasm."

A home. A family. She was pragmatic. And he was right.

She had nowhere to go. Her house was in Mr. Porter's hands. And no doubt he'd sold off anything of value that she'd abandoned. The funds left to her were meager, and she had few skills and no references that would allow her to get a job of any respectability.

As things stood now, marriage to Conor was her best—and mayhap her only—option.

"Very well, Conor," she said finally, "I'll marry you."

"What the hell happened?"

Conor burst into the room, worry and fear sharpening his words.

Ellery's heart kicked into her throat at the thunderous boom of his voice, but Jamys and Gram remained unmoved as they bent over Morgan. Stitched up the ugly gash on her upper arm.

"It's all right, Conor," Jamys explained without looking up. "She's not got your gift for healing, but she'll recover. We're lucky it was a dagger strike and not a clawing or we'd have the worry of mage sickness on top of everything else."

"How did it happen?"

Lowenna stretched and stood, wiping her hands on a towel. "She and I were returning from the village. The *Keun Marow* attacked at the bridge. Just at the western edge of the park."

Conor slammed his fist into his hand. "I've told you to stay within Daggerfell's boundaries. It's not safe. Especially at night. And after Ellery found that . . . well it's not safe."

"I was summoned to attend a birth. Mrs. Nevis is before her time. And very young."

"I don't care if the whole bloody village is in labor. You should have told them you couldn't go."

It was like a bolt of lightning had struck. The moment of horrifying silence that followed fell brittle as glass. "I will not turn away someone who needs me." Lowenna concentrated such a freezing glare at Conor that Ellery hissed, her temples instantly throbbing, and Morgan and Jamys exchanged frightened glances as if their grandmother had sprung horns—or wings. A forbidding glimpse of the true *fey* hidden within the shell of the tiny healer woman.

Conor met her icy gaze with his own scalding anger. "Then you should have sent for me."

"I took Morgan."

"And she was a great help," he sneered.

Morgan's head shot up. "Don't patronize me, Con. I'm more than able to handle one death hound. It was a lucky hit."

He ran a hand through his close-cropped hair. Stalked the chamber with long, angry strides. "And if there had been more than one? Or it had been Asher himself?"

"Well, it wasn't. I'm capable of taking care of myself."

"I can see how capable."

"Fuck you."

"Enough," Jamys shouted, the display of rare temper shutting them up instantly. "Conor, out. Morgan is fine. Gram's fine." He leveled a long, thoughtful look at Ellery. Offered a strange, quirky smile. "Can you get him out of here?"

"Me?"

Was he insane? The last thing she wanted—or needed was to be alone with six and a half feet of muscle-bound, fuming *Other*. Especially one she'd been crazy enough to become engaged to. One she hated. One she was trying desperately not to fall for.

And wasn't that final proof she'd lost her mind?

Conor had confessed to wanting to kill her. And still she couldn't shake the memory of the soul-shattering kisses they'd shared. The sense of being completely safe in his arms. She was absolutely the most hopeless woman she'd ever known.

She realized they were all staring at her. "Oh, all right." She grabbed Conor's arm. Tugged him toward the door. "Come with me. A drink will calm you down." She risked a flash up at his grim face. "And it won't do me any harm either."

He allowed himself to be led down the stairs, back toward the main part of the house. He kept silent, but beneath her fingers, she felt his tension. The slow-fading anger.

Once in the library, she poured him a whiskey. One for herself. He slugged it down and poured himself another. It seemed to steady him.

"What were you doing there?" he asked, still gruff, but definitely thawing.

"I was with Jamys when they got back. I thought I might help."

"Now you and Jamys . . ." he muttered. Poured a third tumblerful. Downed it like it was water.

She thought about following his lead and having another whiskey. Decided against it. Her head still pounded, and she needed all her wits for this strange inner tug of war. "Your frothing at the mouth wasn't helping anyone," she ventured.

"And what would you know about it?" he snapped back.

"I know that yelling at Morgan gets you nowhere."

"She's a fool."

"She's an *amhas-draoi*. The same as you. Give her some credit. She got your grandmother home in one piece. If it makes you feel better, ride the boundaries again."

"And what good will that do? They need constant monitoring. The magic across the stones is fluctuating so wildly, there's no way to know when or if the mage energy will wane. Or where."

She tried to pretend it was the whiskey that churned her stomach. Made her queasy and sick. But she knew it wasn't.

It was guilt. Plain and simple.

She was the cause of this trouble. She was the reason no one was safe.

She sank into a chair. Closed her eyes while rubbing her temples.

Could this nightmare get any worse?

"It's not your fault, Ellery."

She opened her eyes to find Conor kneeling in front of her, his hands braced on either chair arm, his gorgeous face inches from her own.

Oh, yes, it could get so much worse.

"You read my thoughts," she stammered, trying to focus anywhere but on the burnished bronze of his eyes. The hard line of his jaw. The sensual curve of his lips. Where was her loathing? Her fury? It was as if they'd packed up and moved out, leaving her adrift and empty. Completely confused.

"They're not hard to read when they're screaming in my head." His lips twitched. How could such a little thing like a smile knot her insides and send heat rushing through her? It wasn't fair. She didn't want to feel anything—and certainly not lust. "I don't ever want you to think this is your fault," he said. "I brought you to Daggerfell because it was the safest place I could think of. It still is."

"But I'm the one causing all the problems. Asher's after me. And this ridiculous power you say I have is just making it harder. I'm putting everyone at risk."

"It's only until Beltane. A few more days."

"A lot can happen in a few days."

He blinked as if coming up for air. Or back to his senses. Rising, he couldn't put enough distance between them. Once again, stone-faced, the mask of the warrior firmly in place. He shuddered. "A lot already has."

The voice sounded in Ellery's head first. Like an echo of a drumbeat. Soft but insistent.

She pushed it away, not ready to swim up and out of sleep, but the voice would not be denied, and soon she could no longer ignore its relentless drone. She stretched. Opened her eyes. Choked off a scream.

Asher stood before her.

Throwing herself back against the headboard, she fumbled for the dagger beneath her pillow, its resting place since Simon's attack. Barely a breath separated her seizing the handle and letting it fly toward the pale figure. But this time there was no blast of fire and brimstone as he disappeared. This time the blade passed through him, lodging with a *thwang* in the wall behind. Only a ripple of shadow across his body. Or was it a body at all? He glowed with a pale green light that lit the room.

Her gaze narrowed. The door. The paintings on the wall, the furniture. All of it was visible behind him. As if he weren't really there. As if she imagined him. But his laugh as he flickered in and out of sight was all too real.

Amusement gleaming in his eyes, he spread his hands. "I'll not hurt you. Couldn't if I tried. I'm not really here. Not in the flesh."

"I'll scream."

"I doubt it. You'd have done it by now. And what would that accomplish? I've already told you I'm not here to harm you."

Ellery wasn't convinced. She sidled toward the edge of the bed, praying she could get as far as the door. Even translucent, the demon's inhuman stare sent tremors of panic sliding down every nerve.

He caught her in his gaze, freezing her to the floor. "If you don't want your man to suffer, stay. Hear me out."

Oh God. Conor. A hard, cold knot settled in the pit of her stomach. She dropped back onto the bed, swallowing hard. Trying to slow her breathing. She dipped a head toward him. "But tell me how?" she asked, surprised at the calmness in her voice.

"Bligh's wards are strong. But there are chinks in every knight's armor."

This was her fault—this effect her strange power had on magic. If Morgan's injury was a warning—here was the ultimate proof. Asher in her bedchamber—or at least Asher's ghost. Just as frightening, if you asked her.

"I only want to talk to you," he continued. "'Tis all I've ever wanted."

She crossed her arms, her courage returning as the truth of Asher's words sunk in. He couldn't harm her. He wasn't here. "Is that why your pack of devils attacked me? Why you sent a hired assassin after me?"

He offered her an apologetic shrug. "The *Keun Marow* are crude and difficult to restrain. They were instructed to retrieve the reliquary. Nothing more. Bligh's presence there provoked them into overstepping their instructions. You can be assured they were firmly chastised." His whiplash smile never reached his eyes.

"And Simon?"

"A headstrong young man. I'm afraid, hatred of his cousin overruled his good sense."

His image quivered, faded to almost nothing before returning stronger, more substantial. Was this her magic at work again? She tried not to show her alarm. If talking to him meant there was a chance—no matter how slim—that Conor's showdown with him could be averted, she'd risk it.

"What do you want then? Get on with it," she said.

His body bent to a sitting position. Though no chair was visible, his talon-like fingers curled around invisible armrests. Wherever he was, he was settling in. "The reliquary. I want the reliquary."

She'd no idea where the reliquary was. She hadn't seen it since their arrival at Daggerfell. She wasn't about to tell Asher that. Instead she asked, "Why?"

"I'll assume Bligh's told you the story of the Jevan Triad. My brothers and myself."

"Enough to know I don't want you anywhere near that box."

He frowned. "Bligh doesn't know it all. No one does

anymore. It was too long ago. And those that did pass on the tales were tainted by the *fey*'s telling of things."

"They must have had good reasons for locking you three away."

He nodded in agreement. "Of course, but they never understood. They were small minds who couldn't see past their own fears and insecurities. They still like their walls. Like to hide in the shadows and let the superstitious mortals chase them into the corners of the world."

None of this had anything to do with Conor that she could see. And if the *fey* wanted to keep to their world, let them. She grew impatient. "You told me this was about Conor."

He spread his hands in supplication. "It has everything to do with Bligh. With all the race of *Other*. You saw the way those villagers attacked him once they marked him as different. You see the way all the Blighs hide their abilities behind the drab little life of farmers. Sailors. Never allowing their powers to be known. The talents that mark them as special. Superior."

"And why do you care?"

He looked shocked she'd asked. "I care as I care how all *fey* are treated. I care because if I don't, nothing will change, and the *fey* will remain pushed to the fringes forever."

"So how can you change that?"

"By bringing the worlds together. Uniting the races so that we might all share the light. The Triad as a force could bring down the walls. The *fey* would no longer hide. The mortals would no longer persecute."

His eyes blazed. His voice took on the ring of a sermon. The injustice. The discrimination. Twisted sense from a warped mind.

She'd not listen anymore. What if someone caught her in conversation with the demon *fey*? They might think she was in league with him. "Conor's not dense. If he fights to keep you away from the reliquary, it's for a good reason."

"He's infected with the same prejudices that hold all the *fey* in shackles of their own making. He would rather rot in secret than take a chance on what could be his if he just stretched out his hand and took it."

She got to her feet. "You're insane."

He rose as well, putting a hand out as if he could hold her. "Wait."

A sudden thought occurred to her. "And what about Ysbel? That was no accident."

His expression grew guarded. Cool where before the passion for his cause had ignited a fire in his eyes. "Bligh's cousin's jealousies run deep, as I told you."

She started to walk around him. Through him would be just too odd. "Go back to whatever hell you're haunting. I'm through."

Her hand was on the door when the snaky voice shuddered through her. "You care for Bligh, don't you?"

Her pulse thundered. Her hand shook. That was the real question, wasn't it?

"What would you do to ensure he doesn't come back to you in pieces? Or worse?" His slithery words congealed her blood. Curled around her heart until it shriveled into a tight little ball. "Conor Bligh has the mark of greatness on him. It needs only a world that can appreciate his kind of magnificence. I could give him that world. I could raise him up to greater heights than he could ever realize as one of Scathach's soldier boys." His voice dropped to a hissed whisper. "Or I could tear him down so that nothing remains of the *amhas-draoi* but a putrid carcass."

"If you admire him so much, why kill him?"

"He is with me or he is against me. To realize my dream of a united world, *fey* and Mortal, I would sacrifice even such a treasure as Bligh, though it would break my heart to do it. " His tone softened. "If you care for him at all, you can save him."

"What do you want?"

"The reliquary. Bring it to me before Beltane and all is forgotten. You and Bligh can live out your lives in peace. And perhaps even find a place within my new order for yourselves. A place of power. Of distinction."

She focused on Conor's wolf-head ring. Locked her eyes on it as she fought to breathe. "And if I can't get it?"

"If he meets me at Ilcum Bledh, I will kill him slow and feed his body to my *Keun Marow*. Your choice." He paused. "Sleep on it."

She knew without turning around that he'd gone. The unearthly green light vanished, throwing the room back into darkness. Inhaling a shuddery breath, she released the knob. Looked around. There was nothing to show her she hadn't been dreaming. But she knew.

Just as she knew with a certainty that Conor had been right. He wasn't coming back.

She sank to her knees, clutching her stomach. Asher's power was too great. She'd be a bride for a day. A widow forever.

Hot tears tracked her face, and finally she wept.

Chapter Twenty-Eight

Conor strained to peer through the morning fog that drifted over the sea like smoke, picking out the sails of a distant ship hull down on the horizon. Waves creamed onto the beach, the outgoing tide exposing tiny brown shore crabs and shoals of fry in rocky pools. He inhaled deeply, letting the freshening breeze off the Channel clear his mind of the muddle left after hours of reading. Refusing to remain closeted with the dry words of the long-dead another moment, he'd left the library at dawn. He didn't want his last days spent bent over a book. Instead, he walked the boundaries, inspecting each ward stone in its setting. Reinforced them. Reassured himself.

To the west, he'd stalked the lonely hills and fields. To the north, he'd tramped the glades beneath Daggerfell's towering ashes and oaks. Made his way east to the shore and stood watch as ships headed up the Channel toward Falmouth. Southampton. London.

He'd imagined going to Ellery, arousing her with a sensuous caress, sheathing himself in her moist heat as he kissed her awake. Bringing her to climax even as her dreams faded into day. He rubbed a tired hand down his face. That was the last thing he should do. He'd almost killed himself staying away from her last night. He couldn't falter now. Not when he was so close.

He'd found the passages he'd sought, though they only confirmed what he suspected. There was another way. One that didn't call for fulfillment of the curse. But it was only slightly less final than death.

Could he do it? Could he give himself up to the emptiness, the soul-draining change that would enable him to put an end to Asher once and for all? There would be no turning back once he drew on the ancient *Fomorii* power. Let the Ancient Ones dominate him. Transform him.

He sighed. It didn't matter. He would do what he must. But he would make certain Ellery never saw him that way. Would remember him as the man he was and not the being he would become.

He'd tried making it right. If Beltane spelled the end, she wouldn't suffer for his recklessness. He'd leave her his family. His home. And if the gods granted them a child from their one night together, then his son or daughter would bear the protection of his name. Of his honor. It was the best he could salvage from that disaster.

He straightened, stretched. Now that his mind was made up, the ache across his shoulders faded. A calm settled over him.

He picked at the lichen on the rock where he sat, watching the gulls croak and shriek as they swooped to the tide pools to feed. He tossed a pebble, scattering them up the beach. All but one who watched him with a cocked head and a clever gleam in his eye. "Go on," he said, flicking another stone toward the gull.

A subtle, spicy aroma reached his nose at the same time a slide of scree sounded from the dunes above. He turned just as Ellery reached the beach. "He thinks you'll feed him."

"To what?" he answered more sharply than he intended, but the sight of her so soon after his lusty imaginings had caught him off guard. The breeze sent another wave of her lush fragrance toward him, and his groin tightened.

"I didn't find you in the library." She joined him, her hands bunched in her apron pockets, her expression serious. "I thought you might be here."

"I'm done. I'll learn no more of use."

She glanced up at him with eyes dull and glassy, then down at her feet. Then scanned the sea as if salvation lay just out of reach.

He touched her mind, hoping to catch a hint of her thoughts, but nothing stood out sharp enough from the whirl of emotions for him to catch hold of. That she was upset, nervous and afraid was clear. Why—beyond the obvious—remained a mystery. But at least she was talking to him again.

"Walk with me." He pushed off the rock. Straightened. "I've one more stone to check at the southern edge of the property."

She fell in beside him, years on the march giving her a long stride that easily matched his own. That thought reassured him. She was a product of the Army. Used to loss. The uncertainty of battle. Death. That's what he tried telling himself, even if he didn't wholly believe it.

As they walked, she kept her eyes focused on the track. Jaw set. Chin up. Whatever gnawed at her, she was fighting back. Holding her own.

He decided to break the silence. She hadn't hunted him down without a purpose. Maybe she just needed some nudging to open up. "You needed to speak with me? What is it? Not getting cold feet, are you?" He offered her a game smile.

She returned it with a tepid curve of her lips, but her gaze now was razor-edged and battle-ready. Whatever inner war she'd been waging, she'd won. Hands down. "Put off this battle with Asher. At least until you've spent more time researching the archives. There has to be a less costly way to end this."

This was an order. Plain and simple. And despite what Ellery thought, he'd never been good at taking orders. He bristled. "No." Stepping up his pace, he left her behind.

"But why not?" She jogged to catch up. "You can't just dismiss me with a no and think I'll let it go."

"We've gone over this a thousand times, Ellery. I've explained it to you. Asher cannot be allowed to continue unchecked." He plucked a broken branch from the ground, swung it at the trees as he walked. "He must be dealt with. Otherwise, he's always a threat. And the Triad's return will hang over both mortal and *fey* like Damocles' sword."

"I'm not saying ignore his threat. But you have the reliquary. You've said you wait for the turn of the seasons. But the seasons turn every three months. Midsummer. Autumn. The winter solstice." Her breath grew heavy as she held to his speed. "You can delay, and perhaps you and your mother will have found the answers by then."

"It must end now. I can't—" They broke from the trees out into a wide rocky field. The sun had pierced the haze of morning, and he paused, squinting against the blaze of light that met him.

Ellery took that moment to grab him by the arm. Spin him around to face her. She shot a glance at his pocket, knowing what lay there. "Can't or won't?"

"Ysbel has naught to do with why I face Asher."

"She has everything to do with it." She stopped. Took a deep breath and reined herself in. When she spoke again, her voice was calm. Deliberate. "We have the reliquary. We can use it. A tool to force Asher to our terms."

An image of the jeweled casket entered his mind. The evil power that lay within it. The insidious mage energy that pulsed around it, through it. Tempting him. Luring him into believing that it was all true. The Jevan Triad would bring peace and light to the two worlds. Not the tragic suffering he'd been taught. That swirl of darkness was the reason he'd placed it with the *fey* for its protection. They could withstand the reliquary's influence. They knew the promises were false. They remembered what had happened last time.

"No, Ellery. We do this my way. There are things you can't understand. To let Asher near the reliquary would be disaster."

"But hear me out." She struggled to argue.

"Enough," he said, his own mounting fury combined with the influence of the *leveryas* startling her to a standstill. "I know what I'm doing." He gave her a pointed look. "Don't make me regret my choice."

She dropped his arm, stepping back as if he'd slapped her. Her face went pale, her mouth pinched and white. "You arrogant, hard-headed, shatter-brained . . ." She stamped her foot, her hands curling into fists he wasn't sure whether she was preparing to use.

He took his own step back.

He'd gone too far, but she'd pushed him—goaded him beyond sense. He'd meet the devil and be done. Break him as he'd broken others. Send him to hell even if he had to follow him down to the deepest fires to do it. He put out a conciliatory hand. "I didn't mean it. Not the way it sounded."

She threw it off, her eyes freezing him with blue ice. "Mayhap not, but if you keep to this path, you'll be dead by Monday and your regrets won't matter, will they?"

Ellery stood outside Conor's bedchamber, scanning the hall up and down. No one. She almost wished someone would stop her. Call out. Question her right to be there. Though no doubt at this point, her entrance into Conor's room merited little comment. That thought alone made her grimace. Marriage prettied up their relationship, but it didn't change it. Conor had only asked her out of duty. A sense of misguided responsibility. And she had accepted out of . . . well, she wouldn't look too closely at her reasons.

She rubbed her damp hands down her skirt, took a deep breath, and entered.

Conor's ambiguity aside, she knew where her heart lay. In pieces around her with Asher's threats dealing the hammer blows. She'd lain awake all night, running the conversation with the dark *fey* over and over in her mind. But nothing changed. In the end, Conor died.

Despite his infuriating high-handedness, she would not let that happen.

She started in the obvious places. Under the bed. In a trunk that sat beneath the window. At the back of the clothespress. Nothing.

My family thinks you'll save me from myself. Conor had told her that just days ago. Well, she would. She'd save him from the grand and senseless gesture of meeting Asher in battle. Sacrificing himself in a futile bid to stop the demon. She'd formed a plan.

Not a perfect plan by any stretch, but it would have to do. She didn't have time for perfect. And that was the point, wasn't it? They needed time. Time to search the archives. Time to convince the true *fey* to help. Time for Conor to come up with some way to end Asher's threat without killing himself.

The reliquary could give them that time if they used it to their advantage. They had what Asher wanted. Would do anything to get hold of. So, exploit it. There was nothing that said Conor had to make his stand on the first of May. It was only his determination for final revenge that held him to the spring festival. So she'd force the issue. She'd take the reliquary for herself. Tell Conor what she'd done after. She couldn't risk the chance he'd hide the reliquary even more completely. And she'd found it was always better to ask forgiveness than permission.

She wasn't foolish enough to believe Asher had meant any of the promises he'd made. But he was clever. He'd bargain if she could get him to believe she might actually give it up to him.

She straightened, hands on hips, gazing around the room, trying to imagine she was Conor. Where would he hide such a treasure? Where would he feel was secure enough to protect it from Asher, Simon, or anyone else bent on discovering it? Inspired, she began along the walls by the hearth, feeling for invisible seams, hidden catches. The going was slow. Desperation chewed at her, making her breath come quicker, her hands fumble. Lunch would be over soon. Should Conor discover her like this, the sparks that had flown this morning would be nothing compared to the all-out conflagration that would come. The chiming of the mantel clock sent her heart skipping into her throat.

She sat up. Shook off her fright. He was *Other*. Perhaps he'd transformed the reliquary into something else, hidden it in plain view as—she scanned the room—the clock. A table . . .

Ruan.

She swallowed, her eyes locked on the man standing arms crossed, feet apart, watching her with open curiosity.

"Mice?" The twinkle in his eye didn't completely negate the suspicious narrowed gaze focused on her.

She cleared her throat. "I lost something. I thought it might be here."

This time there was no mistaking his amusement. He covered his bark of laughter behind a spate of coughing. "Down there, was it?"

She cringed, realizing the smarmier meaning behind her words. Leave it to Ruan to leap to that conclusion. "Men." She shot him a look of disgust.

"You said it. Not me. If you're looking for Conor, he's having lunch with Aunt Niamh and Gram." His expression grew considering. "Or maybe you knew that. Which is why you're here," he arched a curious brow, "looking for something."

She rose, shaking out her rumpled skirts. Did she dare ask Ruan? Of all the Blighs, he seemed the least affected by the magical trappings. Completely—she thought back to his earlier comments with distaste—predictably normal among a family of super-normal. Would he understand her better than Conor because of it, and should she risk finding out?

She chose to be reckless. Her head came up, her shoulders back. "I need the reliquary." She spoke with what she hoped was firm resolve. "Do you know where it is?"

She could swear the room dropped to freezing as soon as she opened her mouth.

Ruan speared her with a gaze cold as steel, his body pulled taut as a cocked bow. "Why?"

So much for a sympathetic ear.

"To save Conor."

His expression remained as opaque and inscrutable as ever. "Go on."

"Asher wants it. If he thinks we might give it up, we can buy space to seek another way. A way that doesn't risk Conor's death."

He rubbed a thoughtful hand over his chin. "Conor would never agree."

"I know." She prowled the room, exasperation and worry making her restless and impatient. "He's already told me so."

Ruan just watched. Silent. Studying.

Finally, she stopped at the mantel, took up a bone figurine of a leopard or a tiger, the carving crude and unschooled, yet still carrying a rough beauty. She fingered the warm, smooth face of the snarling animal. "He wants this battle with Asher. I doubt he'd choose a different path, even if one were found. Vengeance overpowers all else, even . . ." Her shoulders slumped.

"It's difficult to stray from a course you've charted. Especially when you've followed it for as long as Conor has."

She glanced over. To the door. Back again. Surely Conor

was finished eating by now. He'd be here any moment. She had to get Ruan to agree or get out. She fiddled with the figurine, impatient. Nervous. "So you see why I have to do this my way." Her eyes strayed back to the door. "Please, Ruan. Help me."

"I understand your dilemma. But I don't countenance deceit. You should be honest with him "

"Are you going to tell him?"

"No, but only because there's no reason to. The reliquary isn't here. Conor's taken it to the barrows. He's given it to the *fey* for safekeeping."

"Then it's safe. Asher can't get it."

Wild hope boiled through her until Ruan's grim face dashed her down again.

"If Asher defeats us, nothing is safe. The *Keun Marow* feed off the magic of *fey* and *Other*. Conor's death alone would give them a strength unseen by any in our time."

She held out a hand. "Stop!" She didn't want the words spoken. To give her deepest fears voice was to give them control.

Conor dead. Conor as feast for those horrible, nightmarish creatures. She covered her face. Let the anguish come. Burn through her. Pass on, leaving an echo of grief she'd loose when she must. But not before she had to. Now was the time for action.

She straightened to face Ruan. "Surely, you can't want Conor to face Asher any more than I do. Please. We have to find a better way."

She met his eyes and saw his thought pass like a shadow over his features. She was the way. That's what he was thinking. Her death at the quoit was the one way this could all be avoided. And yet Conor had refused. She would live on, and Conor would die to make it so.

But if he died without defeating the demon, would she have gained anything but hours—days at the most?

Her hands curled to fists. Impotent rage churned her insides. She wanted to scream.

The reliquary was the key to everything. Only how to use it to gain the greatest advantage?

A snap and a sudden sting across her palm caused her to open her fist. The bone figure lay in pieces, its head crushed from its body, pearls of blood lining her hand.

"I'm sorry," she said, knowing he would understand.

Ruan flushed, his jaw clenched, frustration darkening his eyes to slate. "So am I."

Chapter Twenty-Nine

Ellery did what she always did when in doubt; she worked. Lowenna had seen this need to keep hands and mind busy and offered space in her own sprouting herb garden.

"I've warned away the gardeners. You shouldn't be interrupted. I tend this plot myself."

When Ellery drew in a sharp, heady breath, Conor's grandmother smiled. "Tending the earth will bring you solace. It always has for me." She glanced up at the house, still caught in long, morning shadows. "Conor wrestles with himself. He longs for a life he sees slipping away. You can bring him back. You can hold him among us."

"But for what? If Asher wins, there's no life for anyone." Ellery pushed her hair off her face with the back of one gloved hand. "And Conor's made it clear he doesn't want anything to do with me. I think you've overestimated my appeal. Or Conor's interest."

Lowenna offered a serene smile before departing. "Perhaps," was all she said.

Gardening wasn't one of Ellery's strengths. Left alone, she dug into the earth with more enthusiasm than skill. But the solitude and the heat on her back, the spring birdsong and the gritty dirt between her fingers did more for her spinning, twisted thoughts than all the words of comfort that came before.

The sun moved higher before being swallowed by fast-moving clouds that flattened out across the sky, dull as gun-metal, their edges licked black. They crowded in, turning a bright morning into an oppressive, humid afternoon.

She stabbed at the soil, plunging her spade into the soft loam with wicked relish. It was Conor. Cousin Molly. Her father. It was everyone who'd ever underestimated her. Under-valued her. Used her for their own purposes and called it love.

She missed lunch. Hunger gnawed, but she'd prepared. Un-wrapping a napkin, she laid out her cheese, her bread, two brown, wrinkled apples, leftovers from the fall. She reached an arm above her head, working the knots out. It felt good to be sore. It had been too long since the exertion of physical labor. A lifetime since she tended her own home, her own garden.

Meals. Mending. She couldn't say she liked the chores, but they gave a sense of satisfaction she'd never realized she missed. It also made her bloody tired. A bonus. It meant she wouldn't brood over might-have-beens and what-ifs. Wouldn't dream of kisses that burned away the world around her, leav-ing her body a white-hot shell of searing heat. Wouldn't yearn for a love that wasn't meant to be.

Rain speckled the walk. Her apron. She raised her face to it, letting the cool drops splash over her cheeks, ease the flush of her thoughts. She shook the crumbs out, stuffed the napkin into a pocket and tossed the apple cores beneath a bush. The drizzle became steadier. The sky darker.

She'd worked most of the anger and resentment out of her system. And managed to clear a good portion of Lowenna's garden for planting. But she wasn't ready to go in. Wasn't ready to face the compassion mingled with disappointment. She was too new at navigating the crosscurrents of familial feelings. Self-conscious. Awkward. And they were Conor's family, after all. Not hers. No matter how hard they tried to include her. Make her feel as if she belonged.

Ignoring the rain, she walked away from the house. Away from the terraced gardens and then the manicured lawn. Past the rows of tall slender poplars, the heavier stands of ash and elm. Over the footbridge and beyond the ivory columned folly, abandoned slick and dripping until summer.

This track ran uphill. She'd purposefully avoided the low-lying, wooded paths Conor had led her through. This track was different. Nothing sheltered the meandering curves, only scrubby brush that huddled against the stone walls as if for protection against the wind. It blew steadily, driving the rain into her face. Taking her breath away with it when it pushed on.

Sky and ground mingled, making the top of the hill indistinguishable until she crested the rise, surprised by the suddenness of her ascent. Behind her, the roof of the house poked above the crown of trees. Before her, the track dipped steeply down. Ending at a long wide stretch of beach. The Channel beyond. All of it gray. Misted with rain. Except for the man who stood alone with his back to the water, one hand resting on a boulder, jutting from the sand. A sharp, black shape amid a swirl of fog and foam and wave.

She felt the tensing of his body from here, the way his head came up, his gaze diamond-hard and focused on her. He never moved. Never shifted from his lonely spot until even the gulls settled back among the rock-strewn beach.

She'd turn away. Pretend she hadn't seen him.

Childish? Yes. Cowardly? Most definitely.

Still, he waited. Rain sliced across the long, elegant bones of his face, over his chest. Puddled under his boots.

What the hell. She flung up her arms in exasperation and walked down the hill to him.

* * *

Conor leaned against the rocks, arms crossed, watching the fog rolling toward shore. Trying not to watch Ellery. Gods, she was beautiful. And more amazing to him was that she knew it and didn't care. Took it for granted.

Not in a bad way. Not in a way that made her vain or conceited. But just as if it wasn't anything to be especially proud of. A trick of birth that she could have done without and been just as satisfied.

She stood at the water's edge, tossing stones into the surf. The rain had passed, leaving her damp hair in ringlets, her gown clinging to every amazing curve. "The month is almost over," she said. "Only a few days left." She skipped a pebble twice across the wave tops before it sank.

"I know." He tried to keep the worry from his voice. The expression on her face when she turned around showed him how badly he'd failed. "I'd hoped you wouldn't notice."

She grimaced, flinging the last of the stones into the sea. Wiped her hands on her apron. "Small chance of that." Leaving the water, she joined him at the edge of the dunes. Plucked a stalk of tufted grass. Eyes downcast.

The light dimmed as the sun sank behind the clouds. It was late. They should head home. Out of the rain. But neither one made a move in that direction. Too much remained unsaid. The peace too fragile.

She hugged her arms to her body as if she were cold. "I keep thinking about how far I've come. Everything seems like a dream. A nightmare at times." She paused. "I haven't forgotten, you know." Her words were barely more than a whisper. "I keep trying to reason myself back into hating you. Into running as far and as fast as I can."

This was where he should tell her she was right to run. To get out. Or risk being hurt worse. But the words wouldn't come.

Her face glowed like a flame, her eyes bright and blue and clear as the sky. "But I can't make myself hate you," she said.

"This—what I'm doing—it's lunacy. I know it. I'm in love with someone who's admitted to wanting to kill me."

Love? She loved him? A flash of heat scorched through the frozen center of his heart; the part of him that had died with Ysbel blazed back to life. Grew. Expanded until his chest ached with a new and dreadful pain.

She couldn't love him. Shouldn't love him. But she did. And it was so tempting to simply yield. Forget years of training and give in to this new and terrifying reality.

She stood, waiting for him to answer. Waiting for him to say something. But words weren't enough. And he was too afraid to wrap her in his arms, taste the sweet release of kissing her, the press of her body against his. Once released, his need would take over. He'd probably panic her all over again.

Instead, he kept the excitement locked within. Gave her no reason to regret her confession. "It was never a question of wanting to kill you. And once I knew you, knew what you could be to me, the sacrifice became impossible."

He plowed his hands through his hair to keep them busy. And off her. She had no idea what she was doing to his resolve just by standing there.

So close. So Ellery.

He closed his eyes. Breathed deep. Maybe that would calm his runaway reaction. "Say you believe me. Right after you tell me you love me again."

"I believe you. Now. And I love you." Her voice, low and smooth, wrapped around him. Poured through him.

His pulse galloped as every nerve in his body screamed at him to grab her, hold her, never let her go until he'd devoured every inch of her. Showed her with action what he couldn't put into speech.

Duty and loyalty and service seemed to melt in the sweet honey of her words. Could it really be that simple? Could she really know him for what he was and still want him? The realization of her words pushed every other thought out of his mind.

He opened his eyes, and she was there. Inches away, her gaze wary and nervous, her skin flushed. Fear seemed to shadow her still. Fear of him. Of them. It was enough to stop him cold. Make him take a step back to keep the space he needed to maintain control.

"Why?" He sounded like he'd been running. Hoped she didn't see his own emotion, so close to the surface, it radiated along his skin like lightning. "What changed?"

She frowned, her face serious, her bright eyes darkening to slate. "I thought of Glynnis. And Talan. She never understood. Never wanted to. And then it was over. He was gone, and she never got the chance to try." She looked away, out across the water to where the fog melted into the waves. "I don't want to end like her. Alone. Bitter." When she swung back, there was desire in her gaze and defiant bravado. As if she faced down an enemy. "Wondering what my life would have been like had I seen past my anger."

But even now she could end bitter and alone. He didn't know what to say. How to answer her.

She broke the silence first. "I won't ask if you have to do this."

"There's nothing for us if I don't."

"Scant more if you do," she said firmly.

She left him, walked with long, purpose-filled strides away up the beach until Conor thought she might just keep going. The past few minutes, a guilt-ridden hallucination. But then she whipped around, headed back. Gone was the hesitant vulnerability. In its place was the Ellery of past battles. Determined. Focused. Scary as hell when she got that certain light in her eye.

"Is that the only reason you face him? Or is it something more? Something personal." Her eyes flicked down to his pocket. Back to his face. She didn't wait for his answer. "Is there really no other way?"

"I've searched the records—the teachings—for any scrap. I even questioned the *fey* themselves."

Her doubt was slight, but he caught it in the widening of her eyes. The way she stood. Since meeting him, she'd seen things she would have scoffed away as fantasy only weeks earlier. But a part of her obviously still found it impossible. Fought her new reality. "They won't help?" she said, finally.

"They reminded me I already had the one thing that could send Asher back."

"Me."

"Exactly."

She let out her breath in a whoosh of air. "In sparing my life, you risk your own."

"It's the only way."

She fisted her hands, brought them up as if she wanted to strike out, a savage helplessness glazing her features. "Why?" she shouted. But her words weren't meant for him. She hurled them at the sky. The sea. The ones he knew were listening unseen. "Why does it have to be this way? Why can't you fight your own battles? Leave us out of it."

No answer. He didn't expect one. But this time he ignored his better judgment and took her into his arms. Stroked her hair. Let her cry for the injustice.

And not once did she pull away. Not once was she afraid of him.

Chapter Thirty

Ellery had gone looking for Conor three times today. And been turned away again and again. He was riding the boundaries with Jamys. Conferring with Ruan and Morgan. With his mother and not to be disturbed.

Now another day was gone. That left two until Beltane. And she'd seen him for a total of half an hour over breakfast with the entire clan in attendance. Not exactly a place for sharing confidences—or kisses—and she wanted both. Dinner wouldn't be any better. The whole family would be there. Laughing, chatting, pretending everything was all right.

It was going to be hell.

She climbed the stairs on her way to dress for dinner. Her chamber was bathed in a somber evening light, the drapes not yet drawn, the fire not yet lit. Her window stood open to a cool, mellow breeze. A small victory after hours of argument with maids who refused to believe an open window wouldn't lead straight to lung rot. She'd told Conor once she appreciated walls, but parts of her still needed a rush of wind and open space. A wing chair was drawn up close to the casement, its back to her. A crawly feeling snaked up her spine, and she shivered, pulling her shawl close around her.

Someone was there.

She froze, ready to turn and run. Then the figure stirred, grunted, and let out a growly half-snore. Ellery's shoulders relaxed, her stomach unknotted. She approached the chair, bending over a napping Conor, his elbow on the chair's arm, his head resting on his hand.

She touched his shoulder. Whispered his name.

His reaction was instant and dramatic.

"*Andraste magla. Gwydion kompella. Bligh fetha!*" His eyes flew open, sleep still clouding their depths. Grabbing her wrist, he pulled her roughly against him. One arm shot up and around her neck, choking her. Her shawl slid to the floor.

She had a moment's flash of terror before he came fully awake.

He gasped, cursed, his movements now just as violent. He released her, flinging himself out of the chair. Putting the space of the room between them. His chest heaved. His hands shook. Horror filled his face.

"Gods forgive me." He dragged in a deep, ragged breath. Let it out. "I haven't slept in days. You startled me." He rubbed his hands down the sides of his breeches. "Damn it. I swear, Ellery. On my life, I didn't know it was you."

Her initial shock had ended before it blossomed into full-bore panic. But Conor's apologies continued. "If I . . . I didn't hurt you. Tell me I didn't hurt you."

"You didn't hurt me. Really." She stepped toward him, but he stiffened. Backed up.

This was ridiculous. They could circle each other all night.

She crossed the room, grabbing him before he could dodge away again. "For pity's sake, Conor. I'm fine."

He shuddered, his shoulders slumped, his head lowered in defeat. "Do you see now why I need to face him?"

She frowned. Where was this going?

He straightened, his expression grim. "Even if Asher no longer sought you. Even if he released all claim on the reliquary. Hell, if he planned henceforth on a peaceful life of growing potatoes, I'd still meet him on the Beltane Sabbath. We've no life until he's gone."

She glanced down at his hands. The long, wide fingers, the callused palms. The strength in them. The violence.

"You'll always wonder," he said. "In the most secret corners of your heart, you'll always question whether I could kill you if left with no other choice."

"No." She covered her ears. She didn't want to hear this.

"That's why I'll climb to the quoit and draw on the power there to destroy him once and for all." He pulled her hands away. Made her listen. "If I don't, the questions will gnaw bit by bit. And rip us apart in the end."

Hot tears gathered at the corners of her eyes. But her body seemed lighter, a weight she hadn't understood suddenly lifted from her shoulders. She offered him a brave smile. "I may not like it, but I understand a warrior's sense of responsibility."

He gathered her against him as if she were fine crystal. "And as you've pointed out to me before, I'm a good little soldier."

She sniffled into his shirt. "A few days from now, you'd better be the best."

Amusement filled his tawny eyes. The hard, empty ruthlessness replaced with a new calm. It sent her bruised heart flip-flopping. Emotions slammed her from all sides. And then he kissed her. Just a gentle brushing of his lips across hers. A quick taste when she wanted to feast.

She moved into his embrace.

His hesitation was barely noticeable. A tensing of his shoulders, a hitch in his breathing, but it was enough. This unease between them had to end. And it was up to her.

She caught his head, brought it down to take his mouth in a confident kiss of persuasion.

He held back, dropping his arms stiffly to his side, somehow afraid to enjoy what she offered.

Desire raged through her, so forceful there was no time for tenderness or even words. What should have taken months and weeks had been distilled down to a few days. And the breath-taking, runaway emotions of love, passion, exasperation, and affection reduced to their basic elements. Come together at this heady moment. "Don't you dare hold back. Not now," she said.

His gaze was flat. Unconvinced. "Mayhap it's best if—"

Putting a finger to his lips, she whispered, "Don't say it. Don't say anything." She backed him toward the bed, tripping him down onto it. Straddling him so that her skirts rode up around her thighs. She wouldn't give him a choice.

Conor groaned as she popped the buttons on his breeches, as she hiked her gown further up to her waist. He opened his mouth to speak, but the glare she gave him stopped his words. Made his lips curve in a surrender smile.

Her kiss melted into his kiss, and then he was the one taking from her, his tongue, his teeth, his hands, his reluctance replaced by an impatience that startled her with its ferocity.

A quick shift, a slide of his fingers and hot liquid pleasure filled her. It was raw and wild and frenzied. She threw her head back, grinding against him, anything to extend the pulsing agony of his touch. Then his fingers were gone, and she moaned with the ache of his leaving.

But not for long.

He wrenched her gown aside with a ping of lost buttons, and her shift fluttered after. Flipping her onto her stomach, he licked down her spine, over the swell of her buttocks, between her thighs.

She squirmed beneath the onslaught of hands and mouth, wanting more yet not wanting what he was doing to end, but he held her firm, wouldn't allow her to escape.

This wasn't the gentle lovemaking of their first joining. This was a demand for surrender. Nothing less would satisfy him. Cupping his hand between her legs, he let her feel the hard ridge of his erection nestled at her rear. Rubbed against her in a provocative invitation to things forbidden.

She closed her eyes, arching her back to let him know she was more than willing.

He leaned forward, the pressure of his cock awakening wicked fantasies. Reaching up, he kneaded her breast through the fabric of her gown.

She groaned, the sinful crush of his hot, sweaty skin, his short, rapid breaths creating an exquisite torture that swept through her, pooling in her center.

He dragged her onto her hands and knees, his fingers deep inside her, his body covering her own. She threw her head back, her breaths coming in sharp, rapid bursts. Broke her own rule by speaking. "Take me. Now." Her voice was husky with anticipation.

His dirty-sexy laugh sizzled along every raw nerve.

Then he was guiding himself into her from behind. Holding her firmly back against him. Her arms gave out as he plunged into her again and again. Filling every inch, her muscles contracting tight around him. The violent domination heightened every sensation. Exposed every sinful secret. She fisted the bedcovers, stifling her sounds of pleasure in the thick quilts. Just as she teetered on the edge, the sharp kicks of delicious heat twisting through her, Conor pulled out. Rolled her over.

Poised above her, he paused to let her gaze rake his body. Come to rest at his groin. It was obvious he wasn't finished with her. Just seeing his erect shaft made her heart slam the blood through her body in eager expectation. He was dazzling, with the lithe suppleness and chained strength of the hunter in every sliding muscle. And she was easy prey. His eyes glowed pale yellow, his gaze unfocused with a brutal hunger that excited her. She throbbed with unfulfilled need. So close and yet . . .

He held her captive, refusing to release her hands, ignoring her low whimpers of wanting as he moved over her, nipping, sucking, lapping the curves and corners of her body until every sense was alive, every inch of her skin aroused to his touch. She closed her eyes, but lights danced in front of her, burst around her.

When he finally parted her legs and drove into her again, she closed around him, rose up to meet him. He thrust over and over, forcing her to his rhythm as the sweet flood of heat between her legs swelled and moved out along her nerves until she was consumed by it. Until she shattered into a million pieces.

Aftershocks spiraled through her, blind tremors of ecstasy that faded to be replaced by another and another as she fell.

His body flexed against hers. The muscles in his neck stood out, his arms hardened around her. He shuddered, groaned, and laid his head on her shoulder. They remained that way for long moments as their breathing slowed, their pulses quieted. A breeze from the open window pebbled her damp flesh, but she was too tired to move.

Conor never spoke, and though he shifted his weight off of her, he kept his face averted, his thoughts shielded.

From far-off, a dinner gong sounded.

She sank further into the bed. Closed her eyes.

Like she thought, this was going to be hell.

Conor sat motionless, his gaze trained on the glowing embers of a dying fire, an untouched tumbler of whisky at his elbow. The heavy shadows of the study wrapped round him like a winding sheet, but he made no move to toss on another log or light a candle. He enjoyed the dark. Found comfort in it.

The door opened behind him, throwing a slice of dim, flickery light across his shoulder. "Wedding jitters?" His father's arrival banished the ghosts, ripped through Conor's shrouded thoughts with the perceptive edge of familiarity.

Conor thought of Ellery, upstairs asleep. An ache started low in his chest, burned up his throat, clamped his skull in a vise-like grip. Why now? Why had he found this precious gift now, only to have it snatched away? He focused back on the fire. Asking these same questions over and over for hours had gotten him nowhere. Call it fate. Irony. Cosmic humor.

"She'll make a good Bligh, Conor," his father said. "Strong. Clever. And with a sense of humor if I'm not mistaken."

"She hasn't had much chance to use it these last days."

Mikhal honored Conor's need for darkness. Snuffing out his candle, he eased himself into a chair. Sighed. "No. Joy has been lacking, but we'll make up for it. Tomorrow, no glum faces. It's a celebration." He locked Conor in a steady penetrating stare, his tone serious. "Your mother tells me what you plan."

Conor stiffened. "I told her not to speak of it to anyone."

"I'm not anyone. I'm her husband. And you are my son. She shouldn't have to bear this knowledge alone."

"It's the only chance I have to meet and match Asher." Conor braced for an argument that didn't come.

"Have you told Ellery what you've decided?" His father's shrewd gaze was relentless.

Conor's breath came quicker. The tightness in his chest spread to his whole body. "Ellery will mourn me as dead and move on. You must never tell her otherwise. It would bind her when freedom would serve her better."

"She doesn't strike me as the kind you need to shelter from the facts."

His hands gripped the arms of his chair. "Promise me, Father," he leaned forward, the words coming in almost a hiss of breath, "promise me she shall never know. I don't want her to wait for a husband," he paused, "or fear a beast."

As if he'd used up all his energy in that one long stare-down, his father sagged back against the cushions. Looked to the fire. "I'll say nothing."

First Ysbel. Soon it would be him. His parents would lose both children in a span of years. And both deaths could be laid at his feet. They may not blame him for Ysbel's murder, but that didn't mean he'd absolved himself. His mother had been pale but calm as he'd explained his plans. His father, too, seemed drained of any emotion. As if they'd passed the point where heartache and sorrow could touch them. It was a relief, even if it was surprising.

"You see why I must do this?"

His father's gaze flicked up, the fire mirrored in his solemn eyes. "We knew when you joined the ranks of *amhas-draoi* that your life was no longer ours. We did our grieving then. Your mother and I trust your judgment in matters of magic and war." He gave a tired smile. "It is only in matters of the heart we feel you may need some guidance."

The silence between them was grave, but peaceful. There was no more to be said. His father knew how Conor felt. And though he'd lost faith in the last year, Conor had always known the steadfastness of his father's love.

So when Mikhal spoke, it startled Conor back from his thoughts. "Do you wish for a child between you?"

He took a moment to shake off the fog of waking dreams. "In my head, I pray that she remains barren. A new man may think twice before saddling himself with a dead man's whelp."

"And your heart?"

"That's easy. I want her to have a child so in years to come when memory has faded the sharp edges of her anguish, she might remember me."

"She'll do that regardless."

Conor thought of the time he'd wasted holding himself back from her. Of the sorrow and grief she'd experience in the days ahead. Of everything he'd put her through from the moment he'd burst into her life, soaked and half-dead.

A log collapsed, sending up a shower of sparks. "Perhaps," he replied. "Perhaps not. And which would be better, I cannot say."

Chapter Thirty-One

Morgan knelt behind Ellery, fussing with the hem of her makeshift wedding gown. The style was old-fashioned and they'd hidden the expanded side seams with a drape of creamy lace, but still the borrowed pearl-gray silk gown hugged every curve of Ellery's body until she could barely breathe. If she inhaled too deeply, surely her breasts would spill out of the tightly laced bodice. And if she didn't, she was liable to faint before it was all over. But none of it mattered. She was marrying Conor this morning.

Excitement sang through her, and even the worry and fright that haunted her steps couldn't completely quench the happiness that lit up her insides like a flame.

Morgan grasped Ellery's shoulder. A confident soldier's grip swathed in the gauziest of sea-foam green silk. "I'll not let it end like this. Uncle Mikhal and Gram may have warned away the others from Ilcum Bledh, but I'm not so easily swayed."

Conor's father poked his head around the door before Ellery could answer. "They're ready."

And then it was time.

Mikhal Bligh had offered to give her away. And Ellery had been honored. Now, dashing in a coat of royal blue that fit snug across his broad shoulders, he was almost as breathtakingly handsome as Conor. Years had added a patina of wisdom and gravity in the small lines around his storm-cloud eyes, but he carried himself as proud and erect as a man half his age. He smiled, tucking her hand beneath his arm. "You're lovely."

She glanced up at him. "Be prepared to catch me is all I have to say."

"Nerves?"

"Stays."

He chuckled as he led her into the drawing room.

A week ago, the scene of a funeral, now the walls were festooned with garlands of flowers. Seasons held no sway over the conjured bouquets of primrose, narcissus, peonies, and enormous pink and white cabbage roses. Gold and orange chrysanthemums and purple Michaelmas daisies combined with summer's scarlet columbine and spring's lacy, delicate blue violets. Entwined among the blossoms hung ribbons of gold strung with tiny silver bells that swayed in the breeze from the open windows, making a sound like rushing water or windswept treetops.

She looked to Lowenna who winked and motioned toward the far end of the room where a man in a plain frock coat stood waiting, a visible line of disapproval between his bushy, gray brows.

The vicar did this? Ellery's eyes widened in disbelief.

Conor's grandmother wrinkled her nose, pointed behind the cover of her open fan.

Conor stepped up beside the vicar, a dark angel in unrelieved black, magic palpable in his every movement, from the straightening of his cuffs to the adjusting of his cravat. His lean face was carved into sober lines until he spotted her. Then his eyes lit with a fire that singed her to her toes and set her heart fluttering like a captured bird. Conor had done this? For her?

Lowenna nodded, smiling.

Conor came forward to meet them, his fingers closing firmly around hers. She smiled. "He looks none too happy," she whispered beneath her breath at the vicar's continued scowl.

"He's here as a favor for Father," Conor murmured as they walked back together. "We're not exactly doing it properly."

"If he only knew the half of it," she replied.

The vicar cleared his throat and began, and with each word spoken the ill feelings and exasperation she'd carried through the last day drained away. She loved Conor. She buttressed her mind against anything beyond that clear thought.

Then it was Conor's turn, his vows deep and resonant, his gaze never straying from her face as if he were memorizing her.

The bright, fluttery feeling came back. She tried a deep breath to calm herself, but her stays crushed her ribs. She gasped, coughed, fought the suffocating pressure of her gown with quick rapid pants. Prayed she didn't fall on her face.

"Miss Reskeen?" The vicar's worried voice startled her.

"Ellery?" Conor asked. "The vows?"

She repeated the words. To love. Honor. Cherish. All things she could do easily. To obey. She stumbled over the final vow, thinking over the night to come.

She looked back at the family ranged behind them in a half circle. Lowenna, ethereal in white and silver. Mikhal hand in hand with Niamh. Solid, dependable Ruan and sweet-tempered Jamys. Morgan, a shuttered expression in her eyes as she looked from Ellery to the windows and back. All of them had taken her in, welcomed her, accepted her even when they knew her life meant Conor's death. They had become the family she had searched a lifetime to find.

"Until death do you part," the vicar coached. "Should I repeat it?"

Duty burned clear in her mind. "No. Not at all." Clearing

her throat, she fixed Conor with a steady look, the worry melting away with her decision. "Until death do us part."

"Come with me," Conor whispered. "I want to show you something."

They snuck away from the others, still finishing up the wedding breakfast, soothing the ruffled feathers of the vicar with extra helpings of sausage and egg and a fresh pot of tea. Meeting Ruan's wicked smile and knowing nod, Ellery's cheeks went hot, and she hurried to catch up to Conor.

As they neared her bedchamber, her heart pounded, and a tingly ache began deep in her center. But no, they passed her room without a pause, coming to a stop in front of the mysterious and off-limits door to Ysbel's apartments.

She pulled away. "We can't go in there."

He grabbed back her hand. "No. It's all right. I've been in already. She won't mind."

Was this the same man who'd refused to even mention his sister? Who'd locked his heart away after her death? She offered him a raised eyebrow, but curiosity kept her mouth shut. She'd wondered every time she passed this way what lay inside. What Ysbel had really been like. Now was her chance to find out.

He opened the door, ushering her ahead of him.

The room was a soft wash of greens; walls, curtains, bedcovers. A thick white carpet lay on the floor. Framed watercolor landscapes created an elegant yet welcoming impression. Ellery recognized the long stretch of dunes by the sea. The bare-limbed orchards in winter covered with snow. The folly almost engulfed in purple wisteria. All bearing the signature YB. This was Ysbel's artistry.

Conor stood by the bed, studying a miniature, his face bent in concentration. He nodded down at the portrait. "She wasn't a beauty. Too tall. Too thin. But she glowed like a torch. Turned every head when she passed."

She resembled Jamys more than Conor. Blonde hair loose across her shoulders. A long, angular face with a hint of stubbornness in the chin. A wide, straight mouth. But her eyes were the same tawny gold as Conor's. The same animal intensity. They held her. Caught her in their clever gaze.

"Was she . . . ?" But she didn't finish her sentence.

He replaced the miniature on the desk, but kept his gaze on it. "She had power, but no formal training. Nothing beyond the household magic we all learned and the small bits I passed on to her in my times at home. More because I liked showing off for her than because she wanted to know."

Blinking, his focus snapped to her. He gathered her hands in his. "It'll be over soon. I give my word."

"I don't want your word. And I don't want to talk about it." Now that she'd made up her mind, she just wanted to forget— at least for today.

A stabbing cold plunged through her. Sharp as a knife blade.

Pulling away, she dropped to the bed. Clouds gathered over the sun, sending long, grasping shadows crawling over the floor. She curled her legs beneath her, wrapped her arms around her body as if that would banish the sudden chill.

Small hope of that. This frozen feeling went straight through her.

Conor broke the silence. "Asher thought I had the reliquary." He sat down beside her, leaning forward, elbows on his knees, hands clasped together. "He bargained for it then, too. If I turned it over to him, he'd let my sister go unharmed."

Ellery felt the chained emotion behind his words. If he'd made a semblance of peace with his role in Ysbel's death, it was still fresh. A healing just begun.

The angles of his face hardened as he stared unseeing into the past. "I like to think that Simon betrayed Ysbel to Asher thinking I'd hand the reliquary over with no difficulty. He'd be rewarded for his part. Asher would get what he wanted, and Ysbel would be free."

"But you didn't have it."

"No. Asher didn't believe me at first. Then he sought to punish me anyway. He sent me her ring as proof. As warning."

She fingered her own wedding ring. A simple gold band. There'd been no time for the artistry of the wolf's head. It didn't matter. And yet—it did. "But you have the reliquary now."

He faced her, danger in his gaze. "Know this, Ellery. I wouldn't have given it to him even to save Ysbel. She would have been safe, but for how long? It's a treasure too deadly to toy with."

"He'll kill you," she whispered. *Unless I can stop it*, was her unspoken thought.

He offered her a gallow's smile. Hitched his shoulder in a shrug. "Perhaps."

Reaching over, he twined his fingers with hers. With his other hand, he cupped her cheek. The hard, shriveled knot in her stomach relaxed under the familiar calluses of sword hilt and pistol grip roughening his palm. She let out a shaky breath.

"I've had a reason to fight since the battle at San Salas," he murmured, his voice smoky and smooth. "But more important to me now, I've found a reason to live."

". . . riding St. George!"

The hour was late before Conor closed the bedchamber door, shutting out Ruan's last ribald comment. His cousin had done his best to keep the atmosphere light, only crossing the line into bad taste when absolutely necessary. Needless to say, as the hours wore on the reception had become increasingly bawdy.

"Did he say what I think he said?" Ellery asked.

Conor's face went hot. "You weren't supposed to hear that."

"Then he shouldn't shout it as if he were barking orders from the quarterdeck."

Conor shrugged. "Seaman's good lungs."

"Seaman's filthy mind."

He laughed. "True enough."

Ellery sat on the bed, dressed in a confection of sheerest muslin, her hair still damp from a bath. A robe that did more to entice than disguise fell open, giving a perfect view of her round, shapely breasts and the long, graceful column of her throat. He saw himself sliding his tongue down that curve of dusky skin. Inhaling the scents in her hair, her flesh. He crossed the room with deliberate indolence. It gave him time. "It's done."

She raised an eyebrow. "That sounds ominous. Do you mean the wedding?"

"There was a moment when I thought you might run screaming in the other direction."

She smoothed a hand down the turned back sheets, her eyes downcast, her thoughts veiled. "Was there?" She fumbled with the quilt edge. Ran her finger over the stitched embroidery. Avoiding his gaze.

"I'm glad you gave up your ridiculous schemes. Ruan told me he talked you out of them." He sat on the edge of the bed next to her. Pulled off his boots. "Just like a woman to meddle where she doesn't belong."

Her eyes swept up, her hand suddenly quiet. The silence stretched between them, uncomfortable and tense. Then just as quickly, the moment passed. She leaned in. So near he watched a trail of water slide down her temple and over her cheek to pool at the corner of her lips, pouty and begging to be kissed.

"What are you waiting for?" she whispered in the most sex-me tone he'd ever heard as she reached for the waist of his breeches to pull him closer. "We've only hours," she murmured. "Don't waste them." Her eyes went hot and dark.

What the hell was she up to? This was every trick of the courtesan that Ellery had ever learned on display tonight. And according to her, she'd learned from some of the best. Her fingers brushed over his groin.

At her first skimming touch, he'd gone hard as a rock, every cell in his body alive and standing at attention. But this new, hornier version of Ellery spelled danger. He'd be wise to heed the warnings. Except he couldn't breathe much less think as she pulled his shirt tails out. Unbuttoned him like she was unwrapping a box of chocolate.

He cleared his throat, trying to gain time to assess this new and interesting situation. His discarded shirt fell to the floor. "Ruan didn't really mean that last bit. It was merely a suggestion." He backed away, but she followed, rolling up onto her knees on the bed. Slipping the robe from her shoulders, pulling the nightgown over her head in a swift, practiced move. And then she was naked, her skin blushed with firelight and invitation.

Suddenly her smile vanished. Her voice went chillingly soft. "Come on then, it's what you want, isn't it? A stupid slag who'll ask no questions and never disagree." She splayed a hand across his chest, traced the dark swirls of his mage marks, teasing him with the velvet of her touch. A cat with her claws sheathed—for the moment. "I can be that woman. I've known her kind intimately."

Why hadn't he kept his mouth shut? He should have known Ellery wouldn't give way without a fight. Had she ever? He shook his head. "It won't work. Playing cat and mouse with Asher and the reliquary is begging for worse trouble. You'll end like your father. And I won't see that happen."

She snatched her hand away, sank back onto the bed, her face white as chalk except for two bright spots high on her cheeks. "You son of a bitch. Don't you throw my father's death at me. You killed him. Not Asher."

Tonight wasn't supposed to unravel this way. He shouldn't have questioned his earlier good fortune. That would teach him. He took a deep breath. Let it out slowly. "Yes. I did. But death at my hands was easy compared to what Asher would have done to him. What Asher would do to you if you tried your tricks on him."

"If you'd only hear me out—"

He stood up. "No more."

Ellery threw herself off the bed, coming toe to toe with him, trembling, her jaw hard, her hands locked into fists. "You arrogant . . . If it's not your way . . ."

He tried to stay focused on her eyes. Ignore her closeness. The scent of her. The pulse skipping at the base of her throat. He forced his arms to remain at his sides. "It's late. Should I just go?"

Without answering, she reared back. Came at him swinging, landing a punch flush on his exposed chest. "Idiot! I hate you. Hate you, do you hear me?" She aimed again, but this time he dodged. Grabbed her and pulled her close in a bear hug. "Let me go." She thrashed in his arms. "Damn it, Conor. Let go."

"I won't be killed on my wedding night." He amended that thought even as she elbowed him in the stomach. "At least not by my wife."

She was out of control. The eruption of her rage spent with teeth, nails, elbows, knees—any part of her body she could free long enough to use as a weapon. He held tight, never allowing her to get too close. Doing only what it took to keep out of harm's way without actually hurting her. Finally, he pushed her back onto the bed, falling on top of her, using his weight to hold her down. By now, he was fully and painfully aroused.

"Get off of me," she fumed, her chest heaving. "I can't breathe."

"Are you finished?"

"Not even close." She wrapped a leg around him, tried to leverage her freedom. Sought to dig her nails into his wrist. He shifted, holding her down. Bent his head to steal a kiss. To taste the delicious heat of her anger.

She bucked in an effort to dislodge him, even as her lips moved against his. And then she flicked her tongue out, ran it over the curve of his mouth. Lifted her head off the pillow to take him more deeply, in a hungry, devouring kiss that turned him inside out.

He broke away only long enough to take her captured arms, place them over her head.

She glared up at him. Not all her anger spent, then. But the battle had definitely changed. Entangled with desire and desperation. He couldn't see a loser in a fight like this. He offered her a wicked smile. "I seem to remember being in a similar position once before."

"Apparently you haven't learned much." She wasn't going to give in gracefully. He'd have to coax her into surrender. The rush of pounding heat centered in his crotch, the luscious curve of her breasts crushed skin on skin against him made him more than happy to oblige.

"Let me show you how much I've learned," he said, lowering his mouth back to hers.

Even as she returned his kiss, she struggled, thrusting up with her hips to dislodge him. The movement sent a spasm through his system. He returned the favor, rubbing against her, letting her feel his erection.

"I hate you," she said, but the fight was gone from her voice. "You're arrogant, conceited, big-headed . . . I could go on and on."

"So could I," he murmured as he trailed kisses down her throat, nibbled the slender sweep of her collarbone, the soft flesh of her breasts.

She shivered, arching up to meet him. "I hate you so

much." She writhed beneath him as he drew out the seduction. Took his time. Each caress, each suggestive brush of his lips and hands meant to torture. "Oh God, Conor. I hate you," she moaned as he took a nipple into his mouth. Tongued it until it went pebble-hard.

He broke off. "I know you do," he said, his control dangerously close to slipping with every sinuous rock of her body. "I hate you too."

Ellery grit her teeth against the exquisite mastery of Conor's touch. Even so, a throaty purr escaped her lips. Made her cringe with humiliation. How could she be so easy? How could he make her so both so mad and so hot that she wanted to scream? She fought to free her hands, but his grip was too strong. He clamped down on her wrists until she gave up in frustration. Taking her in his mouth, he sent her senses spinning, sweet jolts shooting straight to her center with every lave of his tongue.

He raised his head, his breathing raspy, his voice reckless. "If I let go, you'll not harm me." A statement, but one of trust—not control.

She shook her head, too impassioned to speak.

He released her, but only to unfasten his breeches.

Now was her chance. She could make him pay for his arrogance. Make him suffer for the pride that wouldn't let her in even when all she wanted was to help.

Instead, she fumbled with the buttons, pushing his breeches down over his hips. Anything to have him back. On top of her. In her. Their joining a bulwark against the crouching fear that threatened.

She clung to him as he plunged deep, sent the black emptiness howling inside her to another place. His arms braced on either side of her head, he thrust again. Hard. Fast. As if he could outrun his own uncertainties by taking and possessing her with a raw, animal hunger. Arousal surged along her every limb, sparked down every nerve until she burned with

it, until she lay poised at the edge of oblivion with nowhere
to go but down.

She grabbed his shoulders and with a shift of her weight,
flipped him onto his back. Let her gaze steal over his impos-
sibly perfect body.

He reached up, caressed her cheek. A look of such infinite
tenderness and regret on his face, she wanted to weep. Instead, she leaned over him. Kissed his forehead. The end of
his nose. His lips. With delicious turnabout, she took his
nipple into her mouth. He gasped, almost coming off the bed,
his whole body radiating excitement.

Her hands and then her mouth skimmed his shoulders. His
chest. His washboard abdomen. Following the arcing path of
his tattoos, she tasted the salty-sweet musk of his body. Filled
her nostrils with the scents of sweat and sex and skin that kept
her wet and throbbing with need.

His cock stood erect, heavy and gleaming and moist with
her essence. She stroked the length of it. Glided her fingers
across the tip. Loving the tremors that passed through Conor
at her touch.

Glorying in this strange new strength she'd discovered, she
bent to take him in her mouth. Reveling in the slick softness
of his member on her lips, she slid her tongue over it. Felt him
jump under the tantalizing assault.

Cursing, Conor caught her arms in a steel grip. Dragged
her up and off of him. "Not that way," he ground out between
clenched teeth, "I want to be inside you."

She smiled as she straddled him. Lowered herself onto him
with a long, shuddering moan. His hands encircled her hips as
she rocked forward, slowing them down. Drawing them into
a long, wicked dance. Raising herself up, she took him again
into her. Slowly. Inch by inch. Watching his face. Watching his
hunter's eyes glaze with a hunger only she could satisfy. This
was power. Wanton, erotic, sinful—and oh so glorious.

For a split second, her mother's life gleamed clear in front of her. The squalor and the insecurity she had suffered for these moments of perfect strength. In the end, they had killed her.

Conor gasped, his muscles taut, his chest glowing pale as marble in the light from the banked fire. Ellery leaned forward, twining her fingers around his neck even as she exploded, the pleasure washing over her body in a wave of lush heat. She held on to Conor as each successive wave pulled her back into herself. Back into reality.

She lay her head on his chest, listening to his heartbeat, tasting the damp of his skin.

A perfect moment.

She shivered. It would kill her, too.

Chapter Thirty-Two

Asher scanned the skies. Whispered dark words into the wind. And nature bent to his command. The sun, orange as flame, sank into a white-capped sea. Clouds stretched black fingers over the stars. Obliterated the moon. Tonight was his. And all the mornings after. Only Bligh kept him from the reliquary and his brothers. And the *amhas-draoi* would die before the sun rose again.

He summoned the *glamorie* one last time. Donned the ridiculous raiment of man. Slid a finger down the long, barbed sword, licking the blood that welled from the cut. He was ready.

"You may join me after sundown," he said to the *Keun Marow* waiting on him, the most recent leader of his army. "By then, the need for subterfuge will be at an end."

The creature's eyes narrowed to slits as it shouldered its own crude weapon. "We will wait until we know the way is clear. He's bested you more than once."

Asher's frayed patience snapped. He rounded on the *fey* hunter, murder in his voice. "You speak to me as if we were equals. Partners. You forget your place. Yours is not to question, but to do as you're told."

The *Keun Marow* cringed, its nostrils flared in panic, its gray skin blanched white.

Much better. There would be no wavering now. Dissent would not be allowed.

But the creature's stupidity was unequaled. It shuffled forward, hunched in surrender, squinting up at him out of one bold eye. "He might still use the girl."

Asher smiled as he motioned to Bligh's kinsman, standing sullenly in the corner. "I don't think so. Do you, Simon? Go ahead. Tell them what you told me earlier today."

The man took a few grudging steps into the room, his arms folded across his chest.

His grim countenance and sour disposition grew worse by the day. It was good that Asher no longer needed him. He'd not regret killing him when the time came. When the purging of *Other* began.

"Speak of what you've learned," Asher barked.

The man straightened, defiance further marring his unpleasant features.

Oh, yes. His days left were few.

"Conor married the woman yesterday."

Asher laughed. "Took her to wife. Can you fathom it? He'll not wed her one day and sacrifice her the next. Not even Bligh's as treacherous as that."

Simon scowled. "I tell you there's got to be a mistake. Conor's hard as stone. Not even Ysbel kept him from his mission. He let her die as easily as snapping his fingers."

Asher crossed the room. "But she was a sister, after all. Not his slag." He licked his lips as he gripped Simon's shoulder. "Too bad I had to kill her. She was delicious in bed once tamed to the whip."

The man's body grew tense as a drawn bow. A muscle jumped in his clenched jaw. But he remained silent.

Asher smirked. It was just too easy. So much guilt. So much hate. It ate the man like a cancer from within. Asher felt it and fed on it. Death when it came might almost be thought a release.

"As I said, victory is assured. Meet me at Ilcum Bledh by midnight. All of you."

The creature nodded, but Asher felt its continued skepticism. He would deal with it tomorrow. Place a new leader in charge. One of these ragged monsters was as good as another. Still, perhaps if he offered it an incentive. "Don't forget. I'll have a feast ready and waiting." He gave Simon a shuttered glance. Hardly any mage energy that hadn't been begged, borrowed or stolen from others, but now was as good as later. The *Keun Marow* weren't picky. Two would serve as well as one. "Simon, you come with me. I want you to watch Bligh's destruction. A new age built upon his bleached bones."

He nodded tightly. "Very well."

Asher leaned in close, tilted the man's head back with one crooked finger. Looked him in the eye. "Perhaps I'll let you deal the death blow. Would you like that?"

Simon's answering stare was long and cool. "Yes," he said finally. "I'd like that very much."

Afternoon was fading into evening as Ellery strode across the field toward the barrows, anger and love, disappointment and resignation all simmering just below the surface of her skin. Tightening her chest. Pricking her eyes.

He'd never even said good-bye.

As if he'd said it all last night. Or as if last night hadn't mattered.

Well, damn it, it had meant something to her. It had cemented her decision. She would go to Ilcum Bledh. She would fulfill the *molleth*. For Conor. For all the Blighs. In return for a happiness she never expected and would have denied existed until now. Because as she'd come to find, even this brief taste of love had been better than an eternity without.

She hadn't been the only one to notice Conor's sudden absence. She'd stumbled upon a confrontation between Mikhal and Morgan.

"You'll stay here, and that's an order."

"I won't let Con face Asher alone." Ruan and Jamys stood at either side of their sister as if guarding against her escape.

Sorrow passed across Mikhal's face like a shadow. "Alone is best, Morgan. Conor wants none to witness what he must do. Call it a final wish."

Ellery grimaced. Not if she could help it, it wouldn't be.

They never noticed her, but still she had backed away without making a sound. At least this way they might not realize her own departure until it was too late.

Bats swung low across the trees, and the air smelled sweet with lilac and the first wild cherries. She wrinkled her nose against the faint tang of woodsmoke. The Bel-fires already? Dusk would mark the beginning of Beltane. Sundown to sundown. Tonight the countryside would celebrate the turning of the season with giant bonfires.

Morgan had talked of the wild revelries in the hills and the deep, creek-fed valleys where drinking and dancing would strengthen into something more with the passing hours as couples honored the new spring in their own way. For most, the day's origins lay obscured in myth and legend. But for the race of *Other*, it was a sacred time of great power and deep magic when the walls between *fey* and Mortal were thinnest.

Conor was counting on it.

As was she.

She'd once asked Conor if the *fey* considered Asher enough of a threat to act. He hadn't answered her. But Ruan had, even if he hadn't recognized it. The *fey* held the reliquary. The *fey* must understand the danger. Certainly, they would do what needed to be done to end the threat. Use her to repair the seals and send Asher back.

The mounds rose unnaturally in a low, flat field surrounded by thick woods. Like waves, they rippled and curled, their tops awash in the last bright gleam of westering sun. She shivered as heat danced over her skin, across her face. Settled around her shoulders like a comforting arm. Or a coercing one. Suddenly, the heat became a flame that licked at her insides. Buried itself within her like a blade. She clamped her mouth shut on a cry of both pain and fear. She'd come here for one purpose. She wouldn't back down now.

The sun flashed and was gone, leaving a sky murky and starless. The air thickened. Became heavy. And she knew that somewhere close by, Conor was already at war.

"You." The voice came from behind her, the word hurled like a curse.

Ellery swung around to face a woman whose perfect features were twisted into a mask of outrage and disbelief. Her hair and skin shimmered like pearl, but her eyes glowed white-hot. Furious. "Where is he? Where is Bligh?"

"He's not coming."

The woman eyed her with distaste. "He chooses now of all times to grow a conscience." She turned to address a tall, elegant man, his beauty hard as crystal. Ellery hadn't seen him at first, her attention taken completely with the ice goddess. "I should have known he'd fail us," the woman spat.

"He's weak, Aeval," the man said. He looked down his nose at Ellery. "Too much of the human runs in his veins."

"Conor thinks he can destroy Asher," Ellery explained, "not just imprison him. He wants to end the threat forever."

Aeval stopped her furious pacing to level a scathing look at Ellery. "You're frightened. I feel your terror."

Ellery lifted her chin, faced the *fey* as if she stood at the cannon's mouth. "Not of you."

Aeval smiled, the chilly smile of a snake. "No? Do you know

who I am? In between his whispered words of passionate non-sense, has Bligh told you anything of us? Of me?"

"No."

That seemed to make her even more furious, but it was quickly mastered, and her expression was once again regal, solemn as dead kings. "Bligh is no match for Asher," Aeval said. "He goes to his doom. And all for the tupping of a common strumpet."

"Not so common," Ellery shot back, tired of being every-one's favorite target. "In this, I'm more powerful than you or Conor or any of the *fey*. I can rid you of Asher. My blood alone can reseal the reliquary."

Aeval raised her brows, eying Ellery in a new light. "So it can." She tilted her head, considering. "You have more courage than I'd have thought."

"I'm doing what I have to." It grew harder to breathe, the longer she remained. She inhaled, but her lungs felt squashy, useless. Was this Asher's power growing? Or did all the true *fey* affect her this way? An idle question in another few mo-ments. "You do have the reliquary, don't you?"

"For now, we guard it," the man answered.

"Will you take me to Ilcum Bledh?" Ellery swallowed around the choking dread. "Will you use me to save Conor?"

The man hesitated, but Aeval grabbed her by the arm. "I will. Come."

With a rush of wind, the world fell away. A brilliant glare dazzled Ellery's eyes, an iridescent shine of colors that washed over her, through her, merged with her hair, her body, swam with her blood. Aeval's hand was the only thing she felt, the only sound a chiming of faery bells. Bright and sweet at first, they sharpened, intensified into something louder, more sinister. The harsh, discordant cries of battle. And then the river of light was gone. And she stood on a barren hill with the ancient, weathered stones of Ilcum Bledh before her.

And within the doorway of the leaning tomb's mouth, dwarfed by the giant stones, two dark figures struggled.

She was in time.

Conor reeled back, striking his head on the sharp-edged stone of the quoit, lights exploding in his eyes. He shook it off, dazed, but knowing that even a moment's lapse would bring Asher down on him.

The demon shifted from foot to foot, still inexplicably wearing the *glamorie* of a London man about town, though he'd discarded his walking stick for a barbed sword. "It's over, *amhas-draoi*. Admit it," he hissed.

"Not bloody likely."

Swiping the blood from his eyes, Conor pushed off the standing stone, but he'd taken only a few steps before Asher's spell engulfed him. Bones grated together then snapped, tendons tore. His chest felt crushed within a giant fist. He dropped to his knees, gasping. His body's healing ability kept the wounds non-fatal for now, but each new break, each ruptured artery weakened him. It was a slow death Asher wanted. Agonizing. Tortured. The air darkened, became like fog. Then smoke. It stung his eyes and burned his throat. Just inhaling and exhaling wearied him.

Asher's shadow fell over him. "You're a coward, Bligh. I told your kinsman you'd never go through with the sacrifice. That your honor would keep you from using the girl."

Conor's gaze flashed to Simon. His cousin stood just on the far side of the heel stone. For a split second, their eyes locked, but there was no spark of affinity. Nothing in Simon's expressionless stare to give Conor any hope of help from that quarter. His fingers dug into the soil, slick with his own blood. Blood dripped from his mouth, the razored flesh of his arms. It welled within gashes intersecting his mage marks like gruesome tattoos.

"I warned her. Did she tell you?" Asher mocked.

Conor's head snapped up.

"I told her how it would all end, but she wouldn't believe me." His lips pulled back from his red gums, revealing jagged, yellow fangs. Bending close, he whispered in Conor's ear. "She won't mourn you long, Bligh. She'll be too busy screaming."

Conor roared his fury, flinging dirt into Asher's eyes as he lurched to his knees.

Asher stumbled away, clawing at his face as he tried to clear his vision, but it gave Conor the opening he needed to slide under the demon's guard, coming up behind him.

He struck with his own power, knowing he had one chance to bring this to a close before his wounds killed him. He'd run out of choices.

Ellery couldn't take her eyes off the battle. She started forward, but Aeval's hand on her shoulder held her back.

"You can't stop it. Not that way."

Ellery pointed, her breath coming in quick, shocked gasps. "He's killing Conor." Her voice cracked in anguish. The squashy-lung feeling was back, but added to it was a new dizziness. The world tilted and spun, her stomach in her throat.

"It's almost time."

The *fey* from the barrows was back. In his hands, he held the reliquary. Was this the same jeweled box hidden in Molly's wardrobe? It looked the same, but this one pulsed with a dark energy, throbbed with expectation. She'd almost call it excitement.

"We must hurry. Already the brothers sense Asher's victory. They try and sway us with their black speech. Bring us under their influence."

"Look." This time it was Aeval who pointed up the hill.

Ellery followed the track of her gaze. And bit back an oath.

Conor concentrated on the quoit, on the ley lines that spread away from Ilcum Bledh like spokes on a wheel before they joined the great web running beneath the earth. Reaching out, he tapped the energy there, felt the ancient power rush into him, filling him, infusing him with a strength that was his and yet more. He drew on it, honing it to a spear-point. Emotions fell away with the hopelessness and the desperation. All was light spreading in a wide, horizonless plain and a deep pounding rhythm that matched his heart beat for beat. He sensed his ties to the Mortal world loosening as the magic took over. As he became part of the web, a living conduit for another's power. A voice sounded in his head, high, low, a fusion of *Fomorii* consciousness, a cacophony of words in a language long dead, but droning like the hum of bees around his skull. He let it speak, let it act through him as it sensed his change and realized the battle had now truly been joined.

Chapter Thirty-Three

"What's happening to Conor? What's going on?" Ellery demanded, squinting through the deepening gloom.

Aeval bit out an order, quick and sharp. "Go, Maban. Tell the rest. They must feel it already. I'll see to the reliquary." Her eyes snapped to Ellery. "And the girl."

The man vanished, leaving Aeval and Ellery alone at the bottom of the hill, half-hidden from view by the crowd of trees that surrounded the ledged slopes of Ilcum Bledh like supplicants. "Come," Aeval said. "Bligh draws the magic into himself. We must hurry before he goes too far to return."

A crackling like air before a lightning strike sounded. Ellery staggered beneath the percussion. "What do you mean gone too far?"

Something was wrong. Something had changed on the hilltop.

She knew war. Been close enough to battle to know the smell of it, the metallic taste of steel and gunpowder, the blood that shook your veins until you thought your heart would burst. And she thought she'd known Conor, thought she'd seen enough to understand his brutal, warrior skills paired with the unimaginable *Heller*'s shift. But this was different. Conor's self-command was no less, that precision of movement that spoke of a natural ability perfected by strict training. But the struggle had slowed, spun out as if the air and time around them had been pulled in all directions like taffy.

She grabbed Aeval's shoulder, spun her around. *fey* or no *fey*, she wanted answers. "What in God's name is happening?"

"Conor has dropped his inner walls to draw the deepest power of the *fey* in. His magic and ours together can destroy Asher."

Her gaze leapt to the hill. Watching as Conor dodged between the stones of the quoit, on the attack. His blade flashed in the new-risen moon.

"So this is a good thing?" she demanded, pulling her attention back to the faery.

A flicker of something close to grief passed over Aeval's face. "It is . . ."

"But?"

Aeval's reply was interrupted. The hilltop had taken on a gauzy, misted veil of light. It radiated from the drunken, yawning stones of the tomb, poured up into the sky. The ground shook, and sounds like a chorus of thousands moaned around them. The hair on Ellery's arms stood up. A sucking wind coiled around her as the light that had shot into the air now spilled down the hill like a running wave, leaping, curling. It would be at their feet in seconds.

Aeval had to shout to be heard. "To gain this power, Bligh must break the ties that hold him within the Mortal world. In all ways, he becomes *fey*."

The silver-edged light flowed over them, coming up as far as their knees before spreading out in a shimmering pool. Aeval seemed infused with color, her hair and skin now aglow with the strange flickering ghost-shine.

"Like you?" Ellery's own voice came out high and tight with strain.

Aeval shook her head. "No. The magic he calls forth is

even more powerful and ancient than mine. He may bend it to his will for the space of time needed to defeat Asher, but it will consume him in the end."

The breath-stealing crush had kept Ellery to short quick pants, almost bringing her to her knees. "He'll die?" she gasped.

Again Aeval shook her head. "It's not death that awaits him. He will be a living vessel, housing the magic of the *Fomorii*, a race of gods and beings older than the *fey*. We cannot let a possessor of such strength have the freedom to walk among us. He will be . . . guarded."

Ellery snatched a glance at the reliquary, now glowing with the same pale, luminous green that had rimed Asher in her bedchamber. "Imprisoned, you mean." She squared her shoulders. "I won't let you shut him away like a criminal. That's worse than death."

Aeval's eyes narrowed, but this time she nodded. "Then we must offer the blood." Drawing forth a curved, bone-handled dagger, she gestured toward the quoit. There was no malice in her gaze, only an infinite weight of years.

Could she really do it? Now that the time had come, her body felt leaden, her blood roared in her ears. She'd seen the men of the forlorn hope; those soldiers first up the wall, first into the breach. Courageous. Foolhardy. A little mad. She was all of those things.

Head high, Ellery started up the hill.

Conor shed Asher's attack with an ease he'd not expected. Even the roar of voices in his head had dimmed to a tolerable clamor, so that if he chose, he could ignore the relentless chant that stripped him layer by layer of the humanity left to him. He lashed out, pushing past Asher's wards, connecting with a slide of steel that ripped a wound in the demon's side.

"Where are your lackeys now, demon?" he sneered. "Deserted you? Like rats from a sinking ship."

Asher retreated, his face caught in lines of confusion. Beyond, Simon watched. But he remained fixed as stone, neither moving to aid Asher or hinder Conor. His turn would come. If the *Fomorii* allowed, Conor would use his last freedom to send Simon to the devil. The blood-right was his no matter the connection between them.

A movement below caught his attention. Trespassers on the hill. Were these the *Keun Marow*? Had he spoken too soon? Barely drawing on his new strengths, he reached out. Touched the minds of those approaching. What struck him stunned the breath from his body. Aeval. Ellery. The reliquary. All three in this place meant only one thing; his sacrifice would be for nothing if he didn't act to stop her. Aeval must not be allowed to top the rise.

Ellery followed the path up the steep, rocky slope, each step increasing the numbness that began at her fingers and toes before tracking up her limbs toward her heart. A dull echo sounded in her ears, reminding her of the roll of the sea back in her cottage in Carnebwen.

"Go!" Conor's voice sounded in her head like a blast. He broke free of Asher to stride toward her. "Fool! Leave now!"

He was no more than twenty yards away. And now the change in him was clear. The thick-boned musculature, broadened shoulders, and corded arms of the *Heller*. His eyes gleaming wolf-gold and ruthless in his tight-jawed face. Bile rose in her throat at the vision of his scarred and bleeding body, wounds that for any normal human would have long ago meant death.

She stumbled to her knees, scraping her hands on the scree, tearing a hole in her gown. Dead leaves whirled up from the ground, rattling in a cold draft of wind that rushed overhead. Behind her, Aeval screamed.

Ellery rolled onto her back, her arms instinctively covering her head as she stared up into a vacant space that until a moment before had contained the faery. Aeval was gone, but the reliquary lay abandoned on its side, the scarred, jeweled face of it staring back at her. The earlier feeling she'd gotten from the casket had grown. Now just glancing at it made her recoil. The brothers grew impatient.

She scrambled to her feet, but the numbness made her awkward. She fell again.

The trees at the bottom of the hill bent their branches in an answering whirlwind. Fought the gathering clouds, allowing the moon to slide free. Dust kicked up by the gusts choked her. Stung her eyes. Scoured her face and arms. Aeval appeared again. The mask of elegance replaced with a fierce, defiant glare. "She will fulfill the *molleth*. It is so written."

Ellery ducked her head, crawled toward the shelter of a rocky outcropping scrubbed with bushes.

Conor paused only paces away. "Get her out of here, Aeval. This is naught to do with her." Even his voice had changed. Deeper. Colder. As if it came from far away or was overlaid by another's tongue.

Acval raised her knife. "She desired it. She came to me. I do only as she asks, but even were she unwilling, I would choose her death over yours."

"It's not your place to decide," he answered.

"What you attempt will serve only to deny the *Other* their greatest hero in an age. She's insignificant. A small price to pay."

Aeval flicked out her fingers as if she tossed him something. Mist seeped from the ground. Gray and shadowy, it clung to the earth, spread to shroud the rippling, silver light. Wrapped itself around the reliquary, dulling the sense of wild exhilaration it gave off. She turned to where Ellery knelt, beckoning her forward.

Ellery crouched, suddenly afraid to climb from her refuge. To face these twin visions of hell.

"It's madness, Conor," Aeval shouted.

"How dare you argue with me?" he roared.

It didn't seem as if Conor had done anything, but suddenly Aeval shuddered, her eyes rolling back into her head before she blinked out of sight.

There came a beat of giant wings overhead. "Like plucking sweets from a child," hissed a strangled voice from behind.

Ellery screamed as a talon raked her shoulder, another clutching her around the ribs. Then the ground dropped away. She twisted far enough to come face to chest with the leathery, black skin of a beast out of a nightmare. Looking down, she saw the hill receding.

"Asher!" Conor shouted and hurled something at them.

It spun end over end, moonlight skimming the red glittering edge, flashing on the basket hilt of Conor's sword just before it struck.

Ellery screamed again.

The sword struck true, piercing the outspread demon's left wing. It fluttered uselessly as Asher plunged earthward in a lurching descent that carried him back toward the quoit.

Conor met him, retrieved sword in hand, the power of the Old Ones surging through him like a tidal wave. His gaze flashed to where Ellery lay, clutching her arm. An angry graze bruised her cheek. She met his look, and he flinched at the terror in her dark eyes. Scared of him, was she? To hell with her. He'd warned her. Told her how it would be. He'd no time to be gentle now.

Asher stood crookedly, propped against the tallest of the standing stones. Shed finally of his human form, his bat-like wings swept the ground. He nudged Ellery with a rough kick to the side.

She whimpered, trying to back into a shallow of rock at the tomb's base.

"Is this who you die for, *amhas-draoi*?" He struck Ellery again.

A black rage clawed Conor's heart. "No. She is who you die for." He pushed with mind and spell, unleashing his new-found strengths.

The magic knocked Asher back. Sent him stumbling beneath the tomb's overhanging capstone, the force powdering Ellery with crumbling earth and rock.

Why didn't she move? Get out of the bloody way? Why did he care? That part of him faded as other parts took on new life. The woman was no longer his concern. Woman? He meant Ellery. Surely he meant Ellery. She was . . . The voice in his head drowned out the thought, propelled him forward.

He advanced, not allowing Asher to use the shadows and corners of Ilcum Bledh as sanctuary. The great standing stones seemed to hum with a voice of their own. A heavy groaning as if angered at being disturbed. As Conor ducked under an eroding corner of the lintel stone, Asher struck with his wicked blade. The steel bit into his shoulder, the barbs tearing more flesh as Asher yanked it free. Conor fell to his knees with a cry of shock, only barely parrying another blow that would have severed head from shoulders. He rolled away, coming up onto his haunches, his own sword out to defend against the physical attack.

Asher merely smiled, releasing his black sorcery into the space between them. He'd no need for sword when magic did just as well.

Wounds reopened, blood again flowed, but Conor's transformation held the worst of the pain at bay. Not even Asher's tortures could seep through the *Fomorii* consciousness taking him over.

He fought back, but exhaustion and injury took its toll. No amount of wizardry could stem the blood loss or halt the sizzling lance of dark energy burning through him. Asher would win. He raised his head, met the startled, frightened eyes of the woman. Such anguish amid such fear. Did she sorrow for his loss, or was it the greater defeat? He liked to think it was grief for him. She looked a comely thing.

"Conor," she whispered, reaching out a hand.

He blinked. Was that his name? The voice denied it. But the voice had lied once already. It had told him he would win. That Asher would fall. He shook his head, trying to remember, but so much was already lost. He'd hold tight to the name. Conor. Conor. That would be the last to go.

Asher reached down, lifted the woman by the collar of her gown, wrapped his arm around her neck, pulling her close. His tongue flicked out as he licked her cheek. She shuddered, but Asher grabbed her hair. Yanked it, forcing her head back, lowering his mouth on hers in a grotesque parody of a kiss, his eyes focused not on the woman, but on Conor. Watching him for a reaction.

She struggled, but Asher tightened his hold around her neck, subduing her.

"I shall break her as I broke your sister," he taunted. "Ysbel took two weeks to die, the flesh finally melting from her bones. This one looks stronger. Perhaps three?"

"You'll speak of her no more! Do you hear?" Broken words shouted from somewhere behind them. A man tumbling out of the darkness, bringing a knife down in an arcing slash of silver above Asher. And the simultaneous shriek of demon and man.

The momentary break in concentration was enough.

Conor lashed out with the last of his strength.

Asher met him head-on, the very air screaming with the force of their magics.

The woman between them bore the brunt as dark and bright mingled within her, warping and altering as it twisted through her, silvering her with light, her skin on fire with a blue-white glow.

The stones' hum became a roar.

The woman stiffened. In a dramatic burst of shadow and sun, the magic exploded out of her. Into the air. Into the ground. Infinitely more powerful. Infinitely more deadly.

Asher dropped her, his body bearing the mark where she'd touched him like a flaming white brand.

Aftershocks spun out of her as pulses of warped magic. An unnatural twisting of good and evil. They shuddered the hilltop. Shook the combatants to their knees. Cracked the tomb.

The giant stones, old as time, heavy with anger, rumbled and collapsed around them.

Conor flung up an arm to shield himself. But the woman. Ellery. Lurching forward, he threw himself across her just as the great lintel stone crushed them all.

Chapter Thirty-Four

Did she live? She must. The pain was too much for the afterlife—or so she sincerely hoped. Like a fuse that's burnt to the touch-hole, there was naught to her but cold ash. She'd done her part. She'd set the world alight. Cast back the shadow that threatened it. Now all she wanted was to rest. To sleep.

A voice called her, but it was no voice she recognized, and so she ignored it. Let the dark close in around her. Let the soothing hand of death ease her hurts. Carry her away.

"Back up, Morgan. You're trodding on my feet."

"If you'd stop hovering like a biddy hen, perhaps he could work."

"Stop arguing, both of you. Conor's not helped by it, and it's already given me a headache. Sift through and look for Simon. He's probably over there." The yellow-haired man pointed to a place amid the debris where one side of the quoit had been torn from the ground as if by a giant hand.

The five huge stones that had made up Ilcum Bledh lay scattered like children's blocks along with chunks of torn earth, smaller boulders, and ragged splinters of rock. The two that accompanied the healer—a dark-haired man and a female dressed strangely in men's breeches and shirt—began digging through the crush.

Conor had no time for their squabbles. He had pulled the woman from the wreck of the tomb, her cap of dark brown hair crusted to her face, her body limp and broken. Her left hand lay across her chest, a ring glinting on her finger. So she was married. Somewhere a husband still lived, ignorant of his loss.

Well, she had saved him. He would do what he could to return the favor.

"Conor?" The yellow-haired man turned to him. Conor sensed his worry. His hesitation. The man's glance fell on his bloodstained body. "Do you have the strength left?"

Conor nodded.

"It's beyond my skills, and Gram's too far away. Can you do anything?"

"I can." He carried her out of the rubble. Laid her gently among the meadow grass and wild heath that blew in the salty air. It ruffled her hair, a strand blowing across her lips. A memory snagged in the tangled folds of his mind. The woman laughing, surrounded by grass like this, her jewel-blue eyes alight with desire. He shook his head, and the vision ran like rain meeting the sea.

"What's her name?" he asked

The man seemed startled. "But, Conor . . ." He bit off whatever he planned to say, "Never mind. It's Ellery. Her name is Ellery."

A nightingale called in the woods below the hill. Dawn was only an hour or two away.

"Ellery, can you hear me?" Conor put his hands on her. Focused. The pain became his. Carried him away.

Smoke and the thunder of cannon. So loud it shook the bones of the earth. Was this Talavera? Burgos? Where was her father? She'd last seen him near the picket line, shouting at her to gather the horses. Douse the fire. They were overrun. The French coming over the bridge. Through the woods. No time for reinforcements. Just run. Fast as her legs could carry her. Follow the men. Don't let them out of her sight. But they pulled farther and farther ahead. Disappeared into the fog and the trees. Left her behind. Left her alone.

Hot air seared her lungs. She fought to breathe. Hands steadied her as a flask was held to her lips. She spluttered against the burning liquid.

"Careful, Ruan. She's waking."

A voice cracked her skull like an egg. She moaned. What had been in there? Pure blue ruin, by the way her eyes felt as if they'd been sucked from her sockets. The rest of her left for the crows. She moaned and pushed it away.

"Bloody hell, I think he's done it," the voice said again.

"Done what?" she croaked, struggling to sit up. To open her eyes that seemed glued shut by a film of mud and dust and filth. The confining hands fell away.

She looked around. Not the Peninsula. This was England. Cornwall. Ilcum Bledh.

Jamys knelt beside her, an arm still propping her up, the vicious flask in his hand. Ruan watched, relief and worry mingled in his quick, appraising eyes. He glanced to where Morgan stood, stern and unforgiving, staring down the hill. Recent memories washed past the older. Now she remembered. The reliquary. Asher—she ignored the sick churning in her stomach—Conor.

She grabbed Jamys's coat, her fingers trembling. "Where is he?" She swallowed. "Tell me he lives."

"It was he saved you. I've never seen the like." Awe colored his voice, and he shook his head in disbelief. "You were all but dead, and Conor brought you back."

He looked up, past Morgan to where someone else stood. Alone. Head down. And she realized that not all the stomach heaving, whirling-head queasiness was due to her injuries.

Conor reeked of *fey* magic, raw and unrefined and instantly recognizable now that she knew how it affected her.

"It's too late," Jamys said. "He doesn't know any of us. Barely knows his own name."

She rose with Ruan's help to her feet. "He'll know me."

"Don't be so sure," he answered. She shot him a look, but he put up a hand. "I'm only warning you. He's not . . . he's not Conor anymore. He's someone—something else."

She shook off his arm, took two staggering steps before she regained her equilibrium. Walked gingerly down the slope to where Conor stood.

Approaching him, she slowed. Suddenly unsure of herself. Afraid that Ruan was right. That this wasn't Conor. He still carried himself with the sinewy self-control of the *Heller*, and his torn shirt exposed the cold marble of his skin, his mage marks lit with an unearthly silver glow. This was the Conor Bligh who had killed her father. Uncaring. Callous. Single-minded. How much had he lost while she lay unconscious? And what could she do to draw him back?

"They tell me . . ." Her voice came out shaky, and she cleared her throat. "They tell me you saved my life."

He swung around, and Ellery reeled back, his empty, flaming gaze like a slap in the face.

"I did what was necessary." His voice was as hollow of warmth as his eyes.

She squared her shoulders. "That's not true. If you'd done what you ought to from the start, I'd be dead, Asher would be imprisoned, and you'd . . . you'd be Conor."

A flicker of emotion passed over his face. Then his gaze shifted to the reliquary. Ellery hadn't noticed it at first. But it lay where she'd last seen it, discarded in the grass. Only now the restless buzz of impatience had ceased. The brothers were quiet. It was just a box.

"The demon *fey* was reckless. That was his downfall," Conor explained.

Ellery rubbed her arms up and down, not all of her goose-bumps coming from the chilly spring dawn.

"We'd have done things differently. Not so hard, really, when you think about it. And instead of a creature with a heart of brimstone and death, you could have a sorcerer with the power of the ancients guiding his steps." His smile was as mocking and cruel as Asher's had been.

It tore at her heart. "You don't mean that, Conor. You fought so that no one would hold dominion over the worlds, *Faery* or human."

He frowned. "That's a name I remember from somewhere." A shift, barely noticeable, but it had been there. And for a moment the *fey* had given way to the man. There was hope then.

Ellery recalled Lowenna's words. With Ysbel's death had come a viciousness and a temptation to use his gifts to hurt as he had been hurt. But he'd pulled back from that road. She'd pulled him back. Somehow. Could she do it again? "You're Conor Bligh," she stated firmly.

His eyes went dark, his voice harsh and stiff as if speech was unnatural. "No longer. He traded that life for another. He has passed beyond names."

A spark of anger fanned to life. She'd gone through too much to be thwarted by some primeval *fey* with delusions of grandeur. "Look, you. I want my husband back. His vows to me come first. And I expect him to live up to them. Better. Worse. Sickness. Health. Does any of that sound familiar?"

He didn't answer. Instead, his gaze returned to the reli-quary. He squatted, putting out a tentative hand as if he meant to lift the lid. "It could be ours," he purred. "They would serve us."

She lurched to push him away. "Are you mad?" Knocked him back into the grass before sliding between him and the casket. "Damn you, Conor. We just rid ourselves of one mon-ster. Are you trying to start this horrible mess all over again?"

He raked her with a gaze that could strip paint. "Do you dare touch us?"

"Damn right I dare."

Anger didn't begin to cover the burn that lit her like a torch. She'd been to hell and back. She ached head to toe from a hundred different hurts. She'd lost her father, her sister-in-law, and now her husband to Asher's ambition. This ended here.

She dropped down beside him. Ignored the almost incapacitating wretchedness that came with being so close to such concentrated *fey* magic. Ignored his hard, stony gaze and rigid muscles. Took his face in her hands. And kissed him.

She was so close every freckle across her nose stood clear. The flecks of steel in her blue eyes. The scent of her skin. Her mouth moved slowly over his in a queer tangle of lips and tongues and teeth. Her breath sweet and soft in his lungs. Images flashed into focus. The woman, drenched and shivering in a long, baggy coat, yet still offering him a brave smile. And in his arms, a lithe strength hidden beneath the generous curves. Feelings slashed through his armored heart. Concern. Gratitude. Pride.

He gripped her shoulders, started to push her away.

She clung like a burr, refusing to release him, her hands upon his chest, her body uncomfortably close. More images. Her hand in his surrounded by smiling people. Weeping for him on a rock-strewn beach. More feelings. Desire. Affection. Need. Love.

He threw her off. Broke away, breathing hard.

"That wasn't the response I got on our wedding night," she quipped.

She was too pale. And she shivered. He felt her trembling, though they barely touched. Was she ill? Was she wounded? He put out a hand, wanting to brush her cheek, bring some warmth to that ghostly white skin. But a voice stopped him. Bound him to a chilly indifference.

"You're Conor Bligh," she repeated, force behind her words. "My husband. And if you think I'm going to let you go now, you're mistaken. I love you, you great lumpen bullock."

"Love is a weakness," the voice said, though it came from his lips. Did he really think that? He couldn't recall, but it didn't sound right. The voice fought him. Warned him. So much could be his if he only accepted them. Became them.

"Bullshit." Her slap snapped him from his whirling thoughts.

He frowned, though laughter boiled up through him. Leave it to her to resort to violence to make her point. The voice faltered, began again, but now Conor knew its game. Could fight back. Pressure built inside him as if too many shared too small a space. Pain returned. And the familiar itchy tingle of healing. Both he'd lost when the *Fomorii* took hold.

"Love is a strength," she urged. Her eyes shone with tears. "Look around you. You have cousins who risked their lives to get here to help. You have parents. A grandmother. An uncle. You have a family who love you. That makes you stronger than any moldy, ancient power ever could."

Breath squeezed out of his lungs. Tremors shook him.

"And you love me. You wouldn't have saved me if you didn't." The tears that had gathered now slid down her face, merging with the dirt. Curving into the corners of her mouth. "You wouldn't have brought me back. The *Fomorii* wouldn't care." Her words broke to a whisper. "Conor would."

The voice splintered into hundreds of voices. Thousands. All howling in anger, then understanding before melting back into the ground, spreading out to be lost among all the magics running beneath the earth. No longer focused into a conscious being. No longer him.

Without the will of the ancients, the injuries he'd suffered—his by right as well as those taken from the woman—

exploded through his body like shrapnel. He doubled over, his lungs filling, his body a splintered mess.

Crying out, she grabbed him. Screamed for help.

He reached up, his fingertips grazing her shoulder. As she dropped her eyes to his, he smiled. "Ellery."

Then the black pulled him under.

Chapter Thirty-Five

Ellery had never felt more useless in her life. Useless and in the way. Jamys and Ruan between them had carried Conor's limp body back to Daggerfell. Morgan had led her as if she were made of spun glass and too fragile to walk on her own. She'd tried shaking her off once, but the young *amhas-draoi* in training was as pig-headed as her cousin and refused to relinquish her death grip.

"You've been almost killed at least half a dozen times since sundown," she scolded. "You'll let me help you, or I'll heave you over my shoulder."

This was no bluff. Ellery knew Morgan had the power in her slender frame to do just as she threatened, and so she submitted, gritting her teeth, and praying to any god listening to keep Conor alive until they could get him home.

Gram and the Blighs had met them at the door, and from then on it was a blur of snapped orders, closed doors, whispers, tears, questions, and the fog of unreality overlaying all.

She'd fought off the concerned offers of assistance to get as far as Conor's bedchamber—what did she care about baths and clean clothes at a time like this—but once there she'd been halted by Conor's father who paced restlessly up and down outside the door. "Heavens, child. Hasn't anyone seen to you?" His voice was somber, his eyes shaded with exhaustion.

She glanced sheepishly down at her ruined gown, her grime-encrusted hands. "Morgan tried."

A glimmer of amusement broke through the worry. "If you can wrestle with the will of Morgan and come out on top, you're stronger than any among us."

"Please, sir. Please let me go to him," she pleaded. She needed to see Conor. Touch him. Know that he still breathed. That she hadn't killed him by bringing him back. Had she been wrong to do so? Should she have just let him go? Let the *Fomorii* have him? Each question only brought more pain with it. And more doubt. And more questions. A death spiral.

A scream ripped the air, slamming her heart into her throat. The chamber door buckled, light flaring beneath the jamb, through the keyhole. White. Scorching.

She pushed past Mikhal, but he was quick, grabbing her arms. Holding her back. "*Omdhiserri,*" he coaxed. "Calm yourself, child. *Omdhiserri.* It's for his own good." He gentled her like a new-broke colt though she resisted, weeping and struggling. "Trust to Lowenna and Jamys. They fight Annwn for Conor's soul no less fiercely than you did on Ilcum Bledh. They will bring him back—again."

She collapsed on his chest, sobs tearing her in two. Her nose running, her throat sore from the wrenching grief that only now found its outlet.

Mikhal held her, smoothed her hair, and let her snivel all over his shirtfront. "It will come right in the end," he murmured. "Shhh, my daughter. You'll see."

The comforting words of a father. The strength of a family that loved her. What she'd told Conor was right. Love was a strength. Family was a strength. And she had found both.

It would come right in the end. She believed that now.

The door opened. Lowenna's silver-gray gaze glowed like

moonlight, her smile wide. "He lives. And he remembers. It is truly over."

The room was just as it had been, though it was full night, and only a candle cut the darkness. He'd walked here under his own power, an accomplishment of sorts after weeks of lying flat on his back. But even now, echoes of a pain too impossible to describe set his teeth on edge and sent spots dancing in front of his eyes. He ignored it. He'd not be coddled any longer. One more solicitous glance, and he wouldn't be blamed for any violence that followed.

A drifting curtain sent him to the window. The lawn was a blanket of shadows. Trees, shrubbery, pathways, all shades of black and gray and silver. Just beyond the hill, a corner of the folly roof speared the night, picked out in brilliant white by a disc of a moon.

A familiar warmth settled across his shoulders. Comforting words whispered in his ear.

He spun to catch her before she disappeared, but the room was empty. Just the feeling of Ysbel stayed. Laughed at his fear.

He pulled the ring from his pocket. "I've kept it. Never let it out of my sight—" Amended his words. "Well, except once or twice. And if you knew Ellery, you'd understand what I was up against."

He sensed that Ysbel listened and was highly amused. "What do you think of her?" He smiled as words took shape in his mind. Highly expressive words with a few idiots thrown in for emphasis. "You're right. I should have told her a long time ago." There was another long pause when he felt the soft-spoken iron will that had marked his sister in life, felt it telling him what he must do. And because Ysbel asked it of him, and because he knew—as usual—she was right, he would.

* * *

He stood at the water's edge, skimming pebbles across the wave tops. The bandage wound tight across his ribs hampered his distance, but his aim remained true. He picked another from the rocky strand, flipped it in his palm before letting it fly out across the water. One. Two. Three. Four. Five. Before it sank.

"Not bad," came a voice as familiar to him as his own. Ellery rounded the point, wind whipping her skirts, her dark hair blowing free of its bonnet. "But I've been practicing while you've been laid up."

"Then you should be the world's best stone-skipper. You've had plenty of time to train."

She wrinkled her nose at him, her spray of freckles hidden in her sun-browned face. "You don't sound convinced."

He bent to gather a handful. "Let's say, I'm skeptical." Dropping half in her open palm, he stood back. "Challengers first."

She stepped up to the edge of the waves, her light summer gown a tease of veiled curves and exposed flesh. His whole body throbbed with suppressed desire. It had been much, much too long.

"Ready?" she asked over her shoulder, shocking him back from the imagined indecent scene tightening his groin.

He cleared his throat, changed position. "Proceed."

Whipping her arm out, the pebble shot out across the water. Bounced five times then sank.

"Damn," she muttered.

He smiled at the easy profanity. So Ellery.

Mother had told him of at least two proper matrons who'd been scandalized already by Ellery's lack of airs. But one had been Mrs. Bushy who'd lost a potential husband for her daughters so she didn't really count.

She stalked back up the shingle, her hem soaked and dripping. "Your turn, but I get another chance. The wind was wrong. And the stone was too light. And I slipped during my release."

He laughed. "Excuses. Excuses."

Taking his place at the water's edge, he planted his feet in the prints left by her shoes. "No advantage. I'll toss from the same spot."

June storm clouds gathered to the southwest. His gaze was drawn to their soft, feathered underbellies. To the misty rain already falling out across the water. And he knew now was the time.

He dropped the pebbles. Dug into his pocket. Pulled out Ysbel's ring.

"What have you got there?" Ellery shouted.

He held it up, rolling it between thumb and forefinger, his eye moving steadily between the rain showers, the ring, and the sea.

"Conor." She started toward him, the gravel crunching loud beneath her feet. His focus never wavered. "What are you doing?"

Her steps came faster as his arm drew back. She was almost running by the time he flung the ring out over the waves. Grabbed him before it had even hit the water.

"What the hell are you doing? That was Ysbel's."

He tore his gaze from the spot where the ring had disappeared. Settled it on Ellery. "She doesn't need it anymore." He took a deep breath. For the first time since Ysbel's death, it felt easy. Sweet. Without shame or guilt to sour every lungful of air. "I don't need it anymore."

Ellery remained staring at him as if he'd lost his mind. He offered her a lopsided smile. "She asked me to let her go. Told me I had too much to live for to stay tied to a ghost."

Twisting his wrist in a clever move, he put his hand to her ear. Brought it back down with another wolf-head ring rolled between his fingers.

She shook her head. "You didn't throw it."

He moved the ring so the sapphire eyes gleamed bright in the fading sun. "I'd not lie to you."

She gave a quick, stunned gasp.

Just the reaction he was hoping for. He took her hand. "Ysbel's ring is gone. Like its wearer, to a better place, I hope." He slid Ellery's gold band from its place on her finger, replaced it with the symbol of her new life, his new hope. "This ring is yours by right."

She twisted it on her finger. "Why?"

He stepped back. "Why?"

A strange, waiting expression settled over her features. And, understanding, he suddenly laughed.

Ignoring the restrictive stretch of bandage, he grabbed Ellery round the waist and swung her up into his arms. Her mouth was cool and soft and moved under his with delicious invitation. He lowered his lips to her neck where her pulse beat bird-like while her breathing quickened. They were alone. It wouldn't take anything to have her beneath him. Calling his name. A name he kept only by her courage. By her love.

Breaking away, he looked down into her dark, fathomless eyes. Drowned in them. As he hoped to do for years to come. "You want me to say it? Because I'm in love with you, you precious little fool. I'm in love with you." He lifted his head to the sky. "I'm in love with Ellery," he shouted. "Do you all hear?"

Her smile was as wicked as her thoughts. "Now, it's truly over."

Discover the Romances of
Hannah Howell

Nail-Biting Romantic Suspense
from Your Favorite Authors